New Dawn Fades

KEVIN RATTAN

DEDICATION

For Elise, of course.
And for Gary, because he wanted to read it again

CONTENTS

A glossary is available at the end of the book.

For an illustrated glossary, image gallery, and more, visit: **https://newdawnfades.web.app**

ACKNOWLEDGMENTS

As ever, I'd like to thank Graeme Hurry for his help as a beta-reader, and Matt Smith of shimuzu.co.uk for another fine cover. And always and every time, my wonderful wife, Elise, for her expert editing.

DRAMATIS PERSONAE:

NOYIM:

Beth
Justice of the Family Court

Daniel
Innkeeper; member of the League of Free Noyim

David
Traditionalist contact of Ruth's ('David' may be a pseudonym)

Ethan
Team Leader in the Auxiliary Court; Beth's assistant

Eve
Daughter of Samuel; member of the League of Free Noyim

Ezra
A corrupt representative in the Noyan Assembly

John & Joshua
New Beginning settlers; old friends of Samuel and members of the League of Free Noyim

Jude
A member of Ethan's team in the Auxiliary Court

Mary
Second in command of Michael's gang

Michael
Ostensible restaurateur, actually a major bi-tech dealer and gangster

Miriam
Daughter of Beth's cousin, Simon; a Marshtop settler

Nathan
Young rival of Samuel for leadership of New Beginning and the League of Free Noyim; lover of Samuel's daughter

Ruth
Beth's friend, a representative in the Noyan Assembly

Samuel
Founder of the traditionalist settlement New Beginning, and leader of The League of Free Noyim

Simon
Beth's cousin, a Marshtop settler

Zachary
A member of Michael's gang

COMMONWEALTHERS:

Beynan Hotep
Scion of the politically powerful Massowic family/clan
Dil Mahtal
Journalist and gossip columnist
Hatcher
Junior Bi-technician
Fange and Amaya Gwahnal
Rich and powerful bi-tech manufacturers on Noyan
Hozefa, Commissioner
Head of the Office of Regulation on Noyan
Jodan Hyrom
Regulator, hails from Caliban, a small colonial planet
Mino Cherayn
Minor embassy official
Mitchesons, The
Business rivals of the Gwahnals
Mito
Senior Bi-technician and aphrobug addict
Naja Habada & Miri
Undercover operatives posing as Noyim
Nicholas Maitland
Undersecretary at the Commonwealth embassy
Sanja Gwahnal (deceased)
Son and heir of Fange and Amaya Gwahnal

GALLASKIANS:

Hartan
Moyem Jimawn's liegeman and valet
Moyem Jimawn
*'Cultural Attaché' at the Gallaskian Mission and Hetman
in the imperial navy*
The Imperial Nuncio
The equivalent of an ambassador at the Gallaskian Mission

CHAPTER 1

"The Noyim are a race of perverts, corrupt of body and of mind. You should be happy there."

Thus did Grandfather Massowic send me forth to live amongst barbarians. I felt more than a little aggrieved – the girl had been of age, after all, and hardly an innocent – but I soon came to accept the truth of my grandfather's words: the Noyim were indeed perverse, and I was, for a time, very happy amongst them.

– From: My Time on Noyan, Memories of a Youthful Exile, *The Rt. Hon. Beynan Hotep na Massowic*

Bey yawned, opened his eyes – and instantly regretted it. Bright, white Noyan daylight seared straight through his eyeballs to the back of his aching head. His eyes snapped shut, but the damage was already done. Dazzling red-gold afterimages danced in his vision, keeping time with the painful aftershocks rattling around his skull.

How much had he drunk last night?

Too much, evidently, given the state of his head – and the fact he'd forgotten to tell the house to opaque the windows last night. That only happened when he was seriously drunk.

"House: cut the light, for fuck's sake."

He waited a moment, then risked a one-eyed squint. And relaxed; the room was in total darkness. Sensing the

1

change, the bedsheet made a determined effort to snuggle closer. He shoved it away.

"House: lower the opacity. Slowly... Stop! Take it up a bit. A little bit more... Stop. Perfect."

The stupid sheet was already nuzzling him again, trying to reclaim its place. He kicked it aside, sat up, and rubbed the grit from his eyes. The bedroom was a mess. His favorite chair was lying on its side, legs kicking feebly. It must have spent the entire night trying to right itself. The fresco on the far wall – a ridiculous extravagance, and still not fully grown-in after two whole months – was badly bruised. He vaguely remembered falling against it last night. How long before the bruising grew out? A week? A month? He hoped it wasn't permanently damaged. The damn thing cost a fortune.

And as for his clothes... His trousers were draped over the struggling chair. His shirt was dangling from the 3-V stalk, high up where wall curved into ceiling. He watched, baffled, as the shirt cycled from white to bright yellow, and back again. At what point in the evening had he decided that was a good idea? And why was his left shoe all on its own in the middle of the floor? Where was the right? What he wouldn't give for a cleanerbug nest...

And that, right there, had to be the most depressing fucking thought ever...

Never, before he came to this backwards shithole of a planet, had it ever occurred to him that he'd end up pining for cleanerbugs. They were just something you took for granted. Like running water. Or a house that didn't have to be told every simple fucking thing like remembering to opaque the windows for you when you were too drunk to do it for yourself.

But not on Noyan. The only thing you could take for granted here was disappointment.

Fuck, but his head hurt. And his belly. Had it ever been this sour before? Or this gassy? He belched, loudly – and the contents of his stomach made a sudden, irresistible rush for his throat.

He bolted for the bathroom, hand clamped to his mouth. And made it just in time to drop to his knees and vomit copiously into the bowl.

Fuck Sanja Gwahnal! Why hadn't the little bastard shown up at the Mitchesons' gala dinner last night? He was supposed to be there. But no, he'd left Bey to deal with a whole room full of tedious provincials all on his own. No wonder he'd ended up so horribly drunk. And no wonder he was kneeling here now, watching the toilet slowly ingest his vomit.

It was beyond disgusting. The ghastly stuff should have disappeared the moment it touched the surface. Not on Noyan. The sooner this place was brought into the Commonwealth, the better.

Finally – when there couldn't, surely, be anything left inside him – he wobbled to his feet and headed for the sink. Rinsing helped remove some of the foul taste; slipping in the gum-guard and letting it feed did the rest. Teeth nice and clean, it was time for the rest of him to catch up. He wouldn't rush the house through its cleaning cycle today. He needed every bit of pampering he could get. He'd even let it do the full dry cycle for once.

Ten minutes later, he emerged fully restored and ready to face the world... Except for the hangover, which, if anything, was getting worse. He needed serious liquid right now.

He grabbed his trousers, pulled them to his hips and left them to finish sorting themselves out while he retrieved his shirt. And tried to work out what the fuck he'd been thinking with the white-yellow cycle. Then it made sense, but not in a good way. A stream of yellow liquid – not beer, by the look of it, but something that *used* to be beer before someone drank it – was curving down from the left shoulder and slowly, frothily, filling the shirt from the bottom upwards. Then, when the whole thing was urine-colored, it turned back to white, and the process started again.

Well, that was embarrassing. But at least it meant the shirt wasn't damaged. He'd half wondered if the strain of processing his sweat had given the poor thing alcohol poisoning. That would have been such a waste. His clothes were about the only Homeworld luxury he'd been allowed to bring with him. There was nothing of remotely the same quality anywhere on Noyan. And even if, by some miracle, he managed to find a black market dealer who could replace them, the cost would be far beyond his sadly reduced allowance.

He pulled the shirt on, and hurriedly reset it with a swipe of his hand. It returned to its usual pristine white, with the small, tasteful simulacrum of the family crest once again fluttering over his heart. Time to head downstairs.

First stop was the refrigerator, in search of something to soak up yesterday's excess. Sadly, it contained nothing but moldy cheese and a bottle of native ale. Neither appealed. He wasn't ready for alcohol yet, and the cheese should have been disposed of days ago. The lying bastard of a dealer promised him the fridge was self-cleaning, but the damn thing had been fully grown for months now, and still hadn't integrated with the house's waste-disposal systems.

It was a lesson: don't deal with cut-price dealers. Michael might charge more, but his stuff always worked.

A couple of mouthfuls of water from the kitchen fountain helped a little, but he needed to eat, and soon. And that meant going out. Either that, or settle for house-pap like a damn pauper. And no way was he doing that. He'd never live it down if anyone found out.

He headed back upstairs and played a frustrating game of hunt-the-shoe. It wasn't like there were a lot of places for it to hide. His bedroom was tiny compared to back home. So where was the damn thing? Downstairs? Or worse, had he lost it at the gala dinner? He hoped not. If he'd been drunk enough to leave a shoe behind, there was no telling what else he might have done.

He gave up, righted the hapless chair… and found the missing shoe squashed beneath it. It wriggled onto his foot, and he was good to go. He turned to head back downstairs, and the house chimed for his attention.

"Yes? What is it?"

"You have a visitor, sir. Regulator Jodan Hyrom wishes to speak with you."

"Without an appointment? Tell him to go fu—" Bey bit back the rest of the sentence. This wasn't Homeworld. Regulators didn't need appointments, not even to see a member of the Massowic family. The house was going to let him in whatever Bey said. In fact, it probably already had. And that really wasn't good. The last thing he needed was a regulator poking around his place in search of illicit bi-tech.

"House: you're nothing but a useless vegetable. What are you? Oh, never mind. Tell him I'll receive him in the living room."

But the regulator wasn't waiting for him in the nice, safe, contraband-free living room. He was in the kitchen – home of appliances, and a prime location for an officious busybody on the lookout for black market bi-tech. Which no doubt explained why he was taking such an unhealthy interest in the not-yet-fully-integrated refrigerator. The door was wide open, and all Bey could see of the regulator was his broad orange-uniformed back.

"Can I help you, officer?"

The regulator closed the door and turned around. "Yes. You can tell me where you purchased this refrigerator."

Bey took an involuntary step backwards. Not only was the man's expression as hostile as his tone, his skin was disturbingly pink. Not the more common white-pink, like Sanja and his parents, but practically fuchsia. Bey had never seen anything like it. But whatever freakish-pink-people planet the man came from, there was no excuse for such rudeness. Even on Noyan, regulators usually treated their victims with due deference. Especially when those victims were Homeworlders, and on a first name basis with Ambassador Ashef.

"I beg your pardon?"

The regulator's scowl deepened. He moved closer, intruding on Bey's personal space. Bey retreated, acutely aware of the animal warmth of the man, his sheer physical presence. He wasn't especially tall, but he was deeply intimidating. Whatever colonial hellhole he came from, it hadn't just left him with weirdly pink skin, but also a nose flattened by violence, and a face scarred with the pockmarks of some hideous childhood disease.

"The refrigerator, Massowic." The regulator jerked a thumb over his shoulder. "Where'd you get it?"

What was this? Possession of an unlicensed refrigerator was hardly a serious crime. Certainly nothing worthy of this level of hostility; especially not directed at someone with his background and family connections. The man had to know he was risking his career, treating a Massowic like this. It made no sense.

Unless he was acting under orders.

Oh shit. What the hell had he done at the gala dinner? Everyone who mattered was there. And he'd been so very drunk... He'd acted up, no question. But how badly? Enough to offend someone senior? Someone who wasn't impressed by Bey's connections? Someone like Ambassador Ashef himself.

Oh God, he hoped it wasn't Ashef. If Ashef was on his case, he was fucked.

He didn't have any choice. He'd have to play the Massowic card, and pray Ashef wasn't behind this nasty little visit.

"I really have no idea, officer. I can't say household furniture has ever been a particular priority of mine."

"Is that so? Well, maybe those priorities could do with a little readjusting."

The regulator came even closer. His eyes were cold and

full of menace. Bey took another step backwards. He hadn't faced physical intimidation like this since he was in his teens. It was too much. His head ached, his sour stomach was gurgling, and this crazed colonial was so close Bey could smell him.

He fled to the living room. The regulator came with him. "Breaching the embargo's a serious offence, Massowic. And that particular piece of 'household furniture' isn't on any approved list I've ever seen."

"Really, officer? I wouldn't know. Everything on this planet is so backwards. It's hard to keep track of what's allowed and what's not." This was ridiculous. If he went much further, he'd be through the front door and out on the street. "But tell me, officer, um… I don't think I got your name?"

"Hyrom. Regulator Hyrom. Just like it says on the badge." The man tapped the patch on his chest; his name, picture and credentials conveniently doubled in size.

"Well, Regulator Hyrom, I can't help but feel we've got off on the wrong foot. Why don't you sit down and tell me what brings you here this morning. Surely it can't be a burning desire to inspect my refrigerator? It doesn't even work properly. And if it should happen to breach the embargo, that's only – at worst – a minor technical infringement…"

"'A minor technical infringement'?" The regulator seemed to savor the words. "And it doesn't even work properly… Well, of course. That makes all the difference. That changes everything. Perhaps you'd like me to help you fix it?"

Bey stopped. He'd reached the front door and had no choice but to make a stand. "No, I'd like you to focus on your real job: catching smugglers. Not harassing Commonwealth citizens in their own homes. What are you going to charge me with? Possession of a dangerous fridge?"

And the regulator finally smiled. He even backed off a

little to give Bey some room. It didn't help. There was a nasty, triumphant edge to the man's smile. And his eyes were as cold as ever.

"Dangerous? Funny you should say that. Why do you think it's 'dangerous', exactly?"

"It was sarcasm, Regulator Hyrom. Or don't they have that where you come from? Now, can we please get this over with? I'd like to get on with the rest of my day. Just tell me why you're here."

"Why I'm here? I'm here because that contraband bi-tech you were talking about – the stuff I shouldn't be bothering people like you about... Well, last night, some of it killed your friend Sanja Gwahnal. So, you and me, we're going on a ride out to his place. And on the way, you can tell me all about why you think your fridge is dangerous. And whether that has anything to do with young Master Gwahnal's death. House: open the door."

Sanja, dead? This couldn't be happening. It was a dream, an alcohol-induced nightmare. Sanja couldn't be dead.

But Regulator Hyrom's official car was real enough. Its carapace glistened with the orange and white livery of the Office of Regulation, and it opened at Hyrom's command. Bey climbed inside, and no sooner had the regulator joined him than the carapace closed and cool air flooded in to displace the heat. The change was welcome, but like the smooth acceleration and perfect one-way transparency of the windows, it was also a reminder that the embassy wasn't subject to the same restrictions as mere citizens.

Hyrom glared at him from the seat opposite. "How old are you, Massowic?"

"Twenty-four. Why?"

"And how old was your friend Sanja?"

"Nineteen."

"A child."

"Not on Noy–"

"A child. And you're an adult. Not just an adult. A

Homeworlder. From an important family. Sanja follow you around like a puppy, did he? Some kind of role model you were. What did you teach him? Possession of unlicensed bi-tech is only a... what was it, 'a minor technical infringement'?"

And – finally – Bey understood. No wonder the man was so hostile. He had everything backwards. He thought Bey was to blame for corrupting the boy. But it hadn't been like that. Not at all.

Sanja had saved him. Bey had been lost, wrenched away from all the comforts of home and cast out of decent society. And then he'd met Sanja. The boy had been sharp, street-smart, and astonishingly independent – nothing like the stereotype of a naïve youngster from a backwater world. He'd shown Bey that what Noyan lacked in comforts, it made up for in forbidden pleasures. Sanja introduced him to meat from real animals, and native girls who were so much less inhibited than their Commonwealth peers, and always keen to earn extra money. And he knew where to get the best illegal bi-tech. No way would Sanja have been killed by dodgy buds. He knew bi-tech. He was a Gwahnal, for fuck's sake. His parents were the largest bi-tech manufacturers on this entire shithole of a planet...

It was a trick! This whole thing was a trick. Sanja wasn't dead. Hyrom was just trying to rattle him, get him to confess to buying off the black market.

But why? Was he jealous of Homeworlders? Did he think convicting a Massowic would be some kind of feather in his cap? Or was this a message from someone higher up? Maybe he really had pissed off the wrong person last night.

Whatever the reason, he was done playing along. He turned his head to stare pointedly at the passing scenery. Not that there was much to look at now they'd left the suburbs for the city. On their left were row after row of ugly native buildings, all yellow stone and brutal right-angles. On their right was the Spate, the river that gave the city its name. And up ahead, the old stone bridge that had once been the only way to cross to the other side. The car bypassed it, which was a relief, and carried on paralleling the river until they joined the main east-west roadroot.

City gave way to suburb, and suburb to dry brown countryside barely distinguishable from the desert beyond. The regulator was taking this very seriously, for a bluff; they even turned off the roadroot system at the right junction for the Gwahnal estate. He could see the lakeside greenery up ahead. Were they going to veer away at the last minute? But no; the car carried on straight through the open gates and onto the winding roadroot drive.

This was too real. The Gwahnals weren't the kind of people you approached uninspected and unimpeded, even in an official vehicle. Not unless something very bad had happened.

And then he saw it, nestling amidst the lush vegetation beside the lake: the ruins of Sanja's house. Yesterday it had been an elegant spiral tower, tall, green and graceful; a testament to what could be achieved even with the antiquated bi-tech allowed under the embargo. Today it was… different. The delicate tower had crumpled in on itself, like a wax candle placed too close to a roaring fire. Its skin, once a living masterpiece of polished jade, was now a diseased husk, mottled with grey and disfigured by yellow pustules the size of dinner plates. Teams of bi-technicians were crawling over the dying building like flies on rotting fruit.

Houses shouldn't die like this. They were supposed to seize up over decades, slowly transforming into arthritic wooden shells; dignified memorials to their former living selves.

They shouldn't rot.

And they shouldn't kill their masters.

But this one had. Sanja really was dead. Bey couldn't deny it anymore, not faced with this abomination.

Regulator Hyrom had been telling the truth. Somewhere inside that monstrosity were the remains of the only real friend he had on this entire planet.

He peered across the lake at the emerald domes of the Gwahnal mansion. Were Fange and Amaya looking out at the ruins of their son's house? Did they blame themselves for granting him so much independence? How could they not?

The car parked itself among a group of official vehicles close to the tower. The carapace lifted, letting in a rush of hot, humid air, ripe with the stench of decay. Bey hurriedly leaned out to spit the taste from his mouth, only to find himself being unceremoniously dragged out of the vehicle and towards the rotting building.

"Come on, Massowic. Let's take a look at your handiwork, and see what comes of buying black market bi-tech."

Bey shuddered. Against all expectations, the house was still alive. The flesh around the front door was puckered, quivering, as the house resisted the door-muscle's straining efforts to close. He'd never seen, or heard of, anything like it.

"I see it," he said, "But I don't know what it's got to do with me."

"You don't? What if I tell you that I've got men going over your place right now? That they're looking for every last bit of unlicensed bi-tech you've got? And if you and Sanja shared a dealer, well then, your 'minor technical transgression' might just end up as an accessory to manslaughter charge. Your name's not going to save you this time, Massowic. Earlier today I had to tell the Gwahnals their only son and heir was dead. Dead because he used black market bi-tech. Dead because his grown-up friend encouraged him to flout the rules. Dead because of you."

The man's face was just inches away, glaring, hostile. And horribly, horribly confident. But manslaughter? No way. Everyone used unlicensed bi-tech. Yes, it was illegal. Yes, if you were caught, you had to pay a fine. But no way could they push it as manslaughter. Grandfather wouldn't let it happen.

But grandfather Massowic was a long way away. And the Gwahnals were close by. And rich. And powerful. And if Hyrom convinced them... If they thought Bey was to blame for their son's death...

A group of bi-technicians were huddled nearby, arguing intensely. One of them looked up, saw Hyrom and nodded respectfully. "Sir, the pace of decay is escalating. We don't have much time left."

The regulator's grip relaxed a little. "Do we still need breathing kit?"

"No, sir. The cleared areas are all safe now."

"And the rest of the team's inside?"

"No, sir, I–"

"What about the guard detail? Where are they?"

"Sorry, sir." The bi-technician swallowed nervously. "I thought you knew. The commissioner called. Last night's roadroot attack did even more damage than we thought. It's been escalated to–"

"Damage? You serious?" Bey must have misheard. Damage to the roadroot system? Was that even possible? The damn things were practically indestructible.

"Shut up, Massowic. What did the commissioner say, Mito?"

The bi-technician's eyes flicked to Bey, and straight back to Hyrom. "Just that the attack's now Priority One. They want all hands on deck to stop the fungus spreading past the new growth. The commissioner's reassigned all our guards and half the tech team."

"Of course he has... So, how stable is the house?"

"It's not. We're down to just over ten minutes per treatment."

"That's it, then. We can't risk any more decay. Not till we're done. Secure it."

The bi-technician nodded, and hurried over to a nearby vehicle. He returned moments later with what looked like an outsized pinecone, but had to be a factory-sealed hive. He placed it against the straining door muscle, twist-released the cone, and held it to the wall. Hundreds of tiny insects poured out onto the ravaged surface. For a few frenzied seconds they seemed to be scattering randomly. Then, quite suddenly, they were still – a long, branching line of insects mapping out one of the house's major arteries.

The bi-technician turned to face them. "All done, sir. Two minutes for the catalyst to do its work and you're good to go. Five minutes, and it'll be rock solid."

But Hyrom wasn't willing to wait even two minutes. He dragged Bey through the door and into a familiar world turned strange and nightmarish. This couldn't be Sanja's entrance hall. Where were the beautiful inlays in the walls, the delicate traceries of miniature glowbulbs? Everything had turned black, and the few glowbulbs that remained had faded to a sickly gleam, illuminating nothing.

Worse: the stench was unbelievable. The sickly-sweet smell of decay filled his nose and throat and made his eyes water. He stumbled against the nearest wall, encountered slime, and recoiled. He tried to flee, desperate to push past Hyrom and escape the appalling stench, the darkness, the stickiness underfoot. But the regulator dragged him deeper inside.

The central atrium was unrecognizable. The skylights had clouded over, shrouding everything in artificial twilight. The only light came from a constellation of temporary glowbulbs set up haphazardly in the middle of the open area. They revealed how completely the space had been transformed. The mosaic floor was deep black. The great spiral of the staircase winding around the atrium walls had buckled with the building. It gave the room a twisted, narrow aspect, where all had been light and airy. How had this happened in one night? This kind of decay should have taken years, decades of willful neglect.

Hyrom finally let go of his arm, but only to shove him towards the staircase. Bey gazed warily at the twisted stairs, reluctant to climb them. But a glance at the regulator's face was enough to convince him to proceed. He tested the first step. It seemed solid enough, and he carried on upwards, carefully staying close to the wall. The catalyst had solidified the rotting stairs, but each step was at a different angle, and the further out from the wall, the more pronounced the slope.

The landing was even darker than the entrance hall. The only light here was cold, white, institutional. It spilled from an open door further down the hall: the door to Sanja's bedroom.

He would have stopped, then, if Hyrom let him. But the regulator once again grabbed his arm and dragged him onwards and into the room.

Sanja was lying naked on his sleeping pad, staring unblinking at an emergency glowbulb suspended from the ceiling. His body, like that of his house, was twisted out of shape. He'd died gasping for breath, struggling, in pain.

Bey felt nothing. It was too unreal. This strange, rigid pretend-Sanja couldn't be his friend. Sanja would never just lie there like that. It couldn't be him.

A tear rolled slowly down his cheek. He wiped it away, baffled. How could he be crying, when he was numb inside? He turned from the body.

"Why did you bring me here, Hyrom?"

"I told you. To see your handiwork."

"I didn't do this."

"Yes, you did. You – and whoever sold him the junk that killed this place. And I'm going to make you pay for it. I'm going to ruin you. There's only one thing that can save you. I want the name of Sanja's dealer."

CHAPTER 2

Remember, the Nullists who founded Noyan never intended their colony to have a future. We, and our way of life, are an accident of history. Those who remained true to Nullism – inevitably – died out. Those who were less committed chose to beget a new generation, to create life, conscious life, without knowing – because they could not know – whether that consciousness would have wanted to exist. And in order to restore the balance, to make amends for doing what no true Nullist could ever do, they created Choosing.

Choosing is the child's opportunity to pass judgement on their parents – to thank them for the gift of life, or to protest against having been born.

– From: Collected Speeches, *Justice Jeremiah of Deep Mine*

"Ruth – wait. I need to catch my breath."

It wasn't true. What Beth really needed was a moment to summon her courage. But Ruth wasn't interested in waiting; she disappeared into the off-comer building. Beth had one last glimpse of her pony-tail, and she was gone

Beth stopped at the entrance. The militia were still scuffling with a few of the off-comer technicians behind her; maybe she should stay outside and supervise… Except Ruth would know she was just making excuses. And laugh at her.

Besides, what was the point of coming here, if she

wasn't going to go inside? Her mistake had been letting Ruth talk her into this little adventure in the first place. It was too late to back out now.

She stepped over the threshold. And recoiled. It wasn't like entering a building; it was like being swallowed by some monstrous animal. There was no grand entrance, just a dark tube-like corridor whose slimy walls were ribbed like the gullet of some huge predator.

How did anyone, even an off-comer, live in a place like this? She didn't belong anywhere near this monstrosity. She belonged back in the Family Court, with four solid stone walls around her.

And the smell! The thick, rotten-egg foulness was so strong she could taste it. Any other time, she'd have turned around and gone straight back outside; but Ruth would never let her hear the end of it if she did. It wasn't worth it. She pressed on.

There was a large open space at the end of the corridor. It was less dark here. The off-comers had set up a handful of green-tinged phosphorescent lights. They illuminated much of the ground floor, but threw the rest into deeper shadow. Ruth was down on one knee, inspecting the sagging remains of a spiral staircase circling the walls. She broke into a huge smile at Beth's approach.

"This place, Beth. It's amazing. I've never seen anything like it. I'm so glad you made me come."

"Me? Make you? You're the one who–"

"This is going to be huge. They never told us a house could rot like this! I'm going to skewer them in the Assembly. I can push for a Committee of Inquiry on the back of this."

"Good. I'm glad you think all this…" Beth waved a hand to indicate the horror of their surroundings. "Was worth it. But why do I have to be here?"

Ruth stood up, trouser knees freshly stained with green slime. "You know why. I never could have got in the door without you. The Family Court has the right to investigate.

I don't."

"Fine. I got you in. But I don't see why you still need me."

"Because it's not a Family Court investigation otherwise. Come on, Beth, you can't tell me you're not even a tiny bit curious about what caused all this." She nodded at the distorted stairway. Beth determinedly avoided looking.

"Not in the least."

"Well, if you're really set on being a stick in the mud… The next step has to be at least a token investigation, and then we can open this place to the press. We've got a real opportunity here. Let's show the public what the Commonwealth doesn't want them to see."

"Pity we can't get them to smell it, too." Beth finally broke into a smile of her own. "A few pictures in the Gazette are all very well, but one whiff of this place and they wouldn't be able to give off-comer houses away…"

"Don't kid yourself, Beth. Bi-tech houses are the future."

"The future? This doesn't look like any kind of future to me."

"It's hardly typical, though, is it? Bi-tech housing is cheaper and safer, despite what you see here. We just need to control it ourselves, not let off-comers tell us what—"

"Okay, okay." Beth raised her hands in surrender. It was an old argument, and they weren't going to resolve it today. "I get it. You love off-comer technology. So, make yourself useful and find out what happened to this monstrosity. I'll check out the scene of the crime. We might as well do some actual investigating while we're here. You never know. If we're lucky, they'll have messed with the crime scene, and I'll get to charge them with obstruction…"

Now it was Ruth's turn to grin. Her heart was in the right place, despite her bizarre love of off-comer technology.

"So – where do I look for the body?"

"In his bedroom, I expect. Supposedly, he died in his sleep. The whole house was full of poison gas before the regulators ventilated it."

"Upstairs, then?" Beth eyed the sagging staircase dubiously.

"Yes, Beth. They usually have their bedrooms upstairs, just like real people. They're not that different from us, you know. Well, except bi-tech beds are part of the floor, and they call them 'pads', but apart from that..."

"Thank you. But I don't need the details. Just a pair of climbing boots."

Ruth followed her gaze to the buckled staircase. "Do you want me to come with you? I could help with the trickier parts..."

"Or bring the whole lot crashing down. No, you just focus on your nasty off-comer tech. I'll manage."

At least, she hoped so. She could send for a ladder... but that would only encourage Ruth to treat her even more like a fragile old fossil, and she was *scraped* if she was going to let that happen.

The climb wasn't as bad as she'd feared. The steps might look rotten, but they were solid underfoot. And they were reasonably level, at least close to the wall. The one truly daunting section was at the very top, where the steps had sloughed away from the landing, leaving an uncomfortably large gap.

Ten years ago, she would have stepped across and thought nothing of it. But ten years was the difference between middle-aged, and just aged. Too many years of sitting on her backside through endless Choosing ceremonies had taken their toll on her back.

It wasn't really the width of the gap that was the problem. She simply couldn't lift her leg that high, not anymore. Maybe she should swallow her pride and ask Ruth for help. Except, that would take time, and suddenly, against all expectation, she had a reason to hurry. There were voices, off-comer voices, coming from further along the landing; and light, pouring from an open doorway.

She prodded the landing floor. It felt slick, sweaty. Skin-like. She snatched her hand back, said a silent apology to her skirt, turned around, and sat down on the landing. A quick shuffle backwards, and she was able to swing her legs up and clamber to her knees. It was neither a fast nor a dignified way to climb the final step – but it got her where she needed to be.

One last heave, and she was on her feet. Her back gave a warning twinge, but nothing worse than getting out of bed in the morning. And the voices were clearer now. She headed down the landing, and through the open doorway.

And blinked, dazzled by the bright light hanging from the ceiling. Two men were standing on the far side of the room. One was young and frightened; the other older, pink-skinned, and angry. A third figure on the floor wasn't moving – the body. She filed it away for later consideration.

The off-comers registered her arrival. The older one scowled at her. "What are you doing here? We didn't send for a cleaner. Tell them to keep everybody out until I say otherwise."

"And you are?"

"I told you to leave!"

"Yes," said Beth, stepping further into the room. "I heard you. And I asked who you are."

The man's eyes bulged. A vein pulsed in his neck. "My name is Regulator Jodan Hyrom, and you are intru–"

"Thank you, Regulator Hyrom. I'm Justice Beth of the Family Court. And I'd like you to explain why you're interfering with the scene of a crime."

The off-comer blinked. When he spoke, his voice was tight with controlled anger. "I'm doing nothing of the kind. The Office of Regulation is the competent authority here, not the Family Court."

There were so many responses she could make. She

could explain Custom to this off-comer fool. She could call on Ruth for help; Ruth loved to talk, like all representatives. But Beth was tired. And the direct route was so much simpler.

She reached into her jacket pocket, took out her standard-issue revolver and pointed it directly at the man's head.

"I disagree," she said.

The off-comer stared at her, seemingly too astonished to be afraid. "Do you seriously think that you can frighten me with that?"

Beth cocked the hammer. The click was satisfyingly loud. The off-comer's gaze shifted from her eyes to the gun, and back again.

"Very well," he said. "But my departure is made under protest and in no way constitutes recognition of Family Court jurisdiction. I have authority here under the grant of extraterritoriality. I expect at some point in the future to charge *you* with obstruction of *my* investigation."

He took hold of the younger man's arm and made to leave. Beth shook her head. "No. You leave. He stays."

"He's in my custody!"

"Was, not is. You – what's your name?"

"Beynan Hotep."

"Well, Beynan Hotep," – Interesting, where had she heard that name before? – "I'm placing you in the custody of the Family Court, pursuant to my investigation into the death of Sanja Gwahnal."

"You can't do this!" The regulator's eyes were bulging; a deep red flush spreading through his peculiar pink skin.

"I already have. Now, hadn't you better go and inform your embassy? I'm sure they'll want to know the Family Court has taken over the investigation."

And there it was: the off-comer was finally afraid. He glared at her, let go of his companion, and stalked out of the room. Beth resisted the urge to blow a raspberry after him, and carefully released the cocked hammer instead.

She didn't like guns; never would have drawn it in the first place, if she hadn't seen the body. But the body changed everything. Because the moment she saw it, she knew: Sanja Gwahnal had been murdered.

"You," she said, to the remaining off-comer. "Stand over there, and keep out of my way."

She waited to be sure the young man obeyed. Then she went to examine the body. It was lying on a sleeping pad, frozen forever in a final convulsion: back arched, legs bent, hands clawed. The face was a contorted mask, lips peeled back in a grotesque parody of a smile.

He'd died in pain, unable to breath. And yet he was still in bed. He'd lain there, choking, and hadn't even tried to get to the window or the door and find clean air?

She didn't believe it.

There were small, blue bruises on his upper arms. Fingermarks, maybe, where the killer – or, more likely, killers – held him down while he choked to death. But they'd been careless. No one choked like that without attempting to save themselves. They should have moved the body, placed it by the door. With luck, they'd have made other mistakes, and she'd catch them, and Judge them.

The victim's face was both familiar and unfamiliar. She'd seen it before in countless black and white photographs in the Gazette. But those pictures had been happy, relaxed – and they hadn't conveyed the freakishness of the off-comer's red hair, blue eyes and pale white skin. How to understand someone so alien? She knew so much and so little about him. He was rich. Famous. Nineteen. No longer a child, but still some months short of Choosing...

Now there was a thought. It was the oldest motive on Noyan. But no – the Gwahnals were off-comers, and off-comers didn't hold Choosing ceremonies. And with no ceremony, they'd have no reason to fear the Choice of Death.

So, the body itself told her little; only the fact of murder. What about the room? This was the victim's most private space. What did it tell her about him?

All four walls were covered with fine, velvety hair; red-brown, mottled with dark grey patches. Were those original? A symptom of disease? What about the bald patch on the outer wall? Illness? Or a window? It was hard to imagine that it had ever been transparent.

At least the niches in the walls made sense. They housed a collection of Noyan pottery – and a single, small globeflower. She took a closer look. The thing was no more than six inches across, its tiny petals exquisitely arranged to reproduce continents and oceans in beautiful and exact miniature. Globeflowers were inoffensive as off-comer tech went; there was even a certain charm in the way the petals opened and closed to mimic the ever-moving line between night and day. But this globeflower had died with the house that fed it. Its geography was lost in eternal twilight, continents and seas distinguished only by shades of grey. She made a mental note to have it photographed; no doubt someone could tell her which planet it counterfeited.

So: a pottery collection; a globeflower; a sleeping pad. Nothing else. Was this an aesthete's room? Was the real Sanja very different from his public image? Or was she misreading a place she wasn't equipped to understand? Were there hidden comforts all around, ready to spring from wall and floor at a word of command? Was such a thing even possible? Ruth would know.

It was no use. She was lost. This was Sanja's home, full of the symbols of his inner life – but those symbols were strange to her. Even familiar items – the Noyan pottery, the sparse furnishing of the room – might mean something very different to an off-comer like Sanja Gwahnal.

Everything about this house was alien. And dead. Did Sanja's house tell the same story as it had when it was alive? She had no way of knowing. How, then, to make sense of Sanja Gwahnal's life? And if she couldn't do that, how to make sense of his death?

Perhaps she should hand this one back to the regulators after all. They understood off-comers in a way she never would.

But they hadn't realized this was murder. And she'd seen that at first glance...

There was a change in the light. Hotep was moving, retreating in the face of a commotion approaching from the corridor. She turned to face the doorway. A group of uniformed off-comers surged into the room. They fanned out protectively, making way for a tall, hawk-faced man with pink-brown skin and graying black hair. More uniformed personnel followed, among them Regulator Hyrom. An unhappy group of militia brought up the rear; Ruth at their head, protesting furiously. "Undersecretary Maitland! This is totally unacceptable! I insist you wait outside until the Justice is ready to see you."

The man's gaze flicked to Beynan Hotep – who shrank away – and then back to Beth. "You're Beth the Justice?"

"I am, and who–?"

"Please explain why you threatened this regulator and obstructed him in the performance of his lawful duties."

"Ruth, who is this clown?"

"His name's Nicholas Maitland. He's undersecretary at the Commonwealth Embassy. And he's ignored repeated instructions not to interfere with your investigation."

Maitland waved a dismissive hand. "Instructions that have no legal force, as you well know, Representative. We're not interfering with the Justice's investigation – she's interfering with ours. So, I ask again, Justice, how do you justify preventing Regulator Hyrom from carrying out his lawful duties?"

Beth put her head on one side. She itched to deal with this arrogant off-comer the same way she dealt with the regulator – at the point of a gun. But the uniformed men surrounding him had a professional air. Would she even succeed in drawing her revolver? Worse – if she did, would Maitland leave, or would he call her bluff? Things might get very complicated very quickly if she had to shoot him. Maitland was clearly important. Her off-comer prisoner hadn't so much as glanced at anyone else since the Undersecretary entered the room.

"I don't need to justify it," she said. "Regulator Hyrom was attempting to usurp the prerogatives of the Family Court. He committed two prima facie breaches of Custom, first in failing to inform the court of a suspicious death, and then in disturbing the scene of a crime. Be grateful I don't intend to Judge him."

Hyrom took a furious step forward. Maitland raised a warning finger – a tiny gesture, but sufficient to stop the regulator in his tracks. "Judge him? I think you overreach yourself, Justice Beth. This is an internal Commonwealth matter, and as such, entirely outside the jurisdiction of the Family Court."

"On the contrary, Undersecretary – all murder comes under the Family Court."

"That may be so, Justice. But this is not a case of murder."

"That remains to be proven."

"Madam, you are being deliberately obstructionist. I shall have no choice but to lodge a formal complaint with the Assembly. The more you delay us, the harder it becomes to discover why this house died. You're putting further lives at risk."

"I'm doing nothing of–"

"Nonsense, Undersecretary." Ruth pushed herself between Beth and the arrogant off-comer. "I'm sure the Justice has no objection to your bi-technicians carrying out their own investigation. Provided they don't interfere with her work. And that she receives a full copy of their findings."

"Out of the question! Don't be absurd, Representative."

Beth put a restraining hand on Ruth's elbow, and

answered for herself. "In which case, you'll be the one putting lives at risk, Undersecretary. Now, if you wish to claim jurisdiction, you can petition the proper authorities. In the meantime, please withdraw and allow me to carry out my duties. There's been a death here, probably a murder. The victim was approaching his twentieth birthday. It's not unknown, even among us, for parents to murder their children for fear of the Choice of Death."

And finally, Maitland's composure slipped. He stepped forward, nostrils flaring, eyes shining with anger. "This is absurd! There was never any question of a Choosing ceremony! The boy was a Commonwealther. The Gwahnals are a respectable family!"

Beth tried to respond, but Ruth got there first. "Undersecretary Maitland, are you suggesting Commonwealth citizens are exempt from Custom?"

Maitland retreated a step. All emotion emptied from his face. "Of course not, dear lady. You misunderstand me. I meant that no Commonwealth child would ever wish to invoke the Choice of Death. Our children are taught to revere their parents."

"How very convenient for their teachers," said Beth. "But this young man grew up on Noyan. Perhaps, unlike you, he understood that he had a perfect right to avail himself of Choosing. And perhaps his parents had reason to be afraid. There's only one way to find out — by investigating. This is unquestionably a matter for the Family Court."

"I disagree. I shall be launching an immediate protest with the Assembly — and expressing the Commonwealth's strong objections to political interference in our investigation."

"If you're referring to me," said Ruth, "I am here solely in my private capacity as a duly levied member of the militia. Justice Beth thought my knowledge of bi-tech might be of service to the community."

"In which case, Representative, I'm sure you'll be

pleased to learn that I've decided to agree to your request for a simultaneous investigation by the Office of Regulation."

"With a full report on their findings to be provided to the Family Court?"

"Subject only to the usual restrictions."

Ruth gave Beth a barely perceptible nod: it was the best they would get. Beth shrugged her acceptance.

"So, my dear Representative..." Maitland gestured grandly towards the door. "Your services will no longer be required. Perhaps I can give you a lift back to the Assembly?"

"I'll make my own way, thank you, Undersecretary. Please don't wait around on my account..."

Maitland departed, uniformed guards folding in around him. Regulator Hyrom trailed miserably along behind. Ruth waited for them to clear the room before turning to face her. "He's right, Beth. I have to go. The longer I'm here, the messier the politics becomes."

Hotep was still present, watching and listening. Beth signaled the militia to take him onto the landing. "That's why I need you, Ruth. Politics is your area, not mine."

Ruth shook her head. "Sorry, but I can't help here. Only in the Assembly. If I'm right, this place busts the embargo wide open. Someone's been smuggling bi-tech that's so far in advance of anything I've ever seen that... that... I can't even... Just trust me – this stuff shouldn't be here."

"I thought you were all in favor of smuggled off-comer tech?"

"I am. That's why I can't be here. Too many blurry lines. You have to be free to investigate without politics complicating everything. There are things that just don't make any sense..." She beckoned to a militia man standing by the door.

"Timothy – the papers. Here, check these out. How come, if our friend Sanja was such a big fan of fancy contraband bi-tech, he was also hiding these in his house?"

Beth took the papers and flipped through them. They were an eclectic mix: pamphlets, leaflets, manifestos; even some serious publications she had on her own shelves at the Family Court. But they all had one thing in common. Sanja Gwahnal, the spoiled scion of a rich off-comer family, had an entirely unexpected interest in Noyan traditionalism.

"It fits," she said, slowly. "He collected our pottery, too. It fits. And at the same time – it doesn't fit at all."

CHAPTER 3

Consider Nephrate: a world where primitive industries polluted the land and poisoned the sea, where nation warred with nation for control of ever scarcer resources, where countless millions were born into poverty and squalor. Consider Homeworld, its nearest neighbor: blessed with peace and plenty. Can we blame them for trying to help? How could they possibly know that their wondrous biological technology would reduce a whole planet to barbarism?

- *From:* The Regulator's Handbook, *preface to the fifth edition.*

"One last thing, Regulator Hyrom. Why did you let the Justice take control of the house?"

Maitland was peering at him from a seat in the back of his official vehicle. The undersecretary seemed outwardly calm, nonchalant even, but Jodan knew that he'd been judged, and found wanting.

"She had a gun, Undersecretary. I had no choice."

"That's not strictly true, though, is it?"

"Sir?"

"You could have let her shoot you."

Maitland's smile was wintery. Then it was gone, hidden by the descending carapace. The car accelerated away. Jodan turned and trudged back towards the house.

A crowd of natives were milling around, ant-like, in

front of the door. They were all the same: brown clothing, brown hair, brown skin. So alien, and yet so utterly familiar. He'd grown up around people just like these: small-minded peasants, smugly sure that theirs was the only way to live. The likes of Maitland would never understand them: you had to be born a peasant, and refuse to stay one.

He used his elbows to clear a path to the house. Mito was in the atrium, inspecting the buckled staircase. Hatcher was alongside him, watching and learning, a sentinel bug suckered to his forehead to provide more light.

Short, seedy Mito and tall, gawky Hatcher: that was an unfortunate pairing. Mito was the very last role model the boy needed. There had to be another bi-technician he could pair Hatcher with. He'd have to take a look at the roster when he got back to the office.

Assuming he was still in charge at that point.

"Mito. Hatcher. Anything to report?"

Hatcher whirled around. Jodan's eyes clamped shut, but not quickly enough to stop himself from being dazzled. He sighed, and blinked away multi-colored blotches while the shame-faced boy mumbled an apology and tapped the bug to a lower setting.

"Nothing we didn't already suspect, sir." Mito turned to face him. "It looks like an invasive DNA sequence reconfigured the homeostatic systems, undermined the structural integrity of the walls and clogged the air conditioning. But there's no way of telling if the agent was a natural mutation, or something spliced in. Not unless we find the bud."

There was a bead of sweat on the bi-technician's upper lip. It quivered as he spoke, but somehow didn't fall. Jodan scowled. That sweat wasn't a sign of hard work, not with Mito. The man was a degenerate, flaunting his arousal. And his Homeworld privilege. Any other aphrobug addict would have been thrown out of the service long since, not promoted to Senior Bi-technician.

"So, get a move on. Don't tell me you can't spot a freshly spliced bud when you see one. This house was perfectly healthy yesterday."

"Sorry, sir. We've tried." The damn sweat-bead stayed in place no matter how hard Mito shook his head. "There's nothing less than a week old in the whole place. And no way was something this virulent lying dormant that long."

"Which only means you didn't find it yet. So, take another look. We need that bud."

"Yes, sir." But Mito didn't move. His gaze flickered towards Hatcher, surreptitious, conspiratorial. Yes, he definitely needed to separate these two.

"Uh, sir...?" Hatcher was nervous, diffident. "Wouldn't it help if we had a few more men on the job? I mean, if..." The boy sensed Jodan's disapproval. He swallowed, looked to Mito for support, received none, but plunged on anyway. "It's just... Wouldn't we be better concentrating our resources here? We could pull the team off Hotep's house, and—"

"And then what, Hatcher? Say we find the bud. It can't tell us who Sanja's dealer was. Hotep can, but he won't. Not unless we have leverage. Something to convince him to do the right thing. Like proof he's been using black market bi-tech. Hotep's not a side show. He's our best chance of catching the people who did this. The team stays where it is."

"Yes, sir."

That was Hatcher quelled. What about Mito? *One. Two. Thre—*

"Hotep's got powerful friends, sir. Are you sure it's worth the risk?"

Jodan laughed. He couldn't help himself. Mito's teeth-sucking faux-concern was just too much.

"What's the matter, Mito? Worried about my career? I think it's a bit late for that, don't you? No. You let me worry about Hotep and his powerful *Homeworld* friends. You worry about finding that bud. Hatcher – come with me. And bring your tool bag."

He led the boy to the back of the house. "Hatcher, you're a good kid. You could go a long way. But you have to learn not to let the likes of Mito use you to do their dirty work."

"But sir, I didn't—"

"Did you ever stop to ask yourself why, if he wanted the team pulled back from Hotep's house, he wasn't willing to suggest it himself?"

"I don't know what you mean, sir."

"No, of course you don't. But next time someone pushes you to speak on their behalf – ask yourself why they won't speak up for themselves."

"Yes, sir."

"Okay, we'll say no more about it. I'm not angry with you. I just don't want you picking up bad habits. You know Mito's an aphrobug addict?"

"Yes, sir."

"Have you ever noticed he doesn't have any tracks behind his ears? Where do you suppose he keeps his bug?"

The boy stared at him, baffled. Then came dawning comprehension, and finally disgust. "Sir, you don't mean…"

"Best not to think about it, eh, lad?"

There. If that didn't make the boy think twice about emulating Mito, nothing would.

"Now, let's get to work. Three months ago, I put in a request for permission to spot-test Master Gwahnal's new racer. Unfortunately, some of those 'powerful friends' Mito was talking about made sure it was turned down. So, we're going to do it now. Better late than never, eh? Where's the garage?"

"It's down a corridor by the—"

"Just take me there, lad. If we can prove the racer killed the house, it'll be that much harder for them to stick us with the blame for this mess. It's not our fault if they won't let us do our job, is it? Come on, waiting around here isn't going to get us anywhere…"

The door to the garage was at the end of a heavily decayed corridor. The house was pitch-black here. He borrowed a spare sentinel bug from the boy and suckered it to his forehead, then rapped on the door with his knuckles. The muscle was clenched tight, puckering the wall, but it was every bit as solid as the rest of the house. He stepped aside.

"Okay, Hatcher. You'd best cut through it."

"Yes, sir."

The boy retrieved a mid-sized claw from his bag. It bit deep into the frozen wall – and released a cloud of foul-smelling yellow gas all over Hatcher. Jodan grabbed him and pulled him to safety. They retreated down the corridor, the boy doubled over, coughing.

"Are you all right, son?"

Hatcher nodded, eyes watering. He was blushing, obviously more embarrassed than hurt. Jodan told him to wait, then took a deep breath and headed back to retrieve the tool bag. It was mercifully well equipped – shiny new tools for a shiny new owner – and had a full set of air sponges.

"Here, put this on. Remember not to breathe through your mouth."

He touched a second sponge to his upper lip, and did his best to hide his discomfort as it squirmed into his nose. He never could get used to the sensation, no matter how often he wore the things. It was just too intimate.

He signaled Hatcher to get back to work. The boy did so, cutting a wide arc around the door and releasing yet more of the yellow gas. Then he peeled back the newly cut wall. Jodan nodded his thanks, and squeezed through the fresh opening.

The sentinel bug revealed shiny, sagging walls with exposed, rotting tubing – and what he was looking for: Sanja Gwahnal's racer, on the far side of the room. The once-sleek vehicle was almost unrecognizable. The chassis had slumped down onto what must originally have been wheels, before they buckled and sloughed off their rotting tires. The carapace was wrinkled and distorted, as if it had aged decades in a single night. The car was in worse condition even than the house. Perhaps it really was the source of infection.

"Well, Hatcher, what do you think?"

The boy scrambled through the opening. "I think it's a good job these things are filtering out the smell, sir."

Jodan laughed. And turned away, coughing. Laughing while wearing an air sponge was never wise. And sneezing had to be avoided at all costs. He waited for his breathing to steady, and then headed for the racer. Part of the carapace had sheared away entirely, revealing the remains of the fur seats inside. They were melting now, but had obviously been perfectly legal. As for the controls, they were far more primitive even than the regulations required.

"Looks like he could steer it himself, sir," said Hatcher, peering over his shoulder. "Didn't know they still made those. Do you think he actually raced it?"

"Who against? Natives? What'd be the point? Still, we'd best check out the performance parameters, see if they were legal. Let's have a look at the engine, shall we?"

Hatcher retrieved a smaller claw from his bag, and carefully exposed the engine. Or what was left of it. The bones of the axle and main structure were intact, but most of the muscles and soft tissues had withered away. Jodan prodded experimentally at a flaccid grey tube that must once have been a mighty bicep. It gave way spongily at his touch. He pointed at a nest of tendons lying slumped and detached below the steering column. "See that, Hatcher? This thing's been dead a while. That takes eight hours, minimum."

He straightened up. He'd seen enough. This engine hadn't broken any rules. It wasn't the source of infection. More likely it picked it up when... Yes. There it was, just a few feet away: the house-pap nipple. And it was oozing dark green ichor. "Look over there, lad. The vehicle didn't poison the house. The house poisoned the vehicle. Time to move on."

They left the garage and drifted from room to room, following in the footsteps of other, more thorough, searchers. Every appliance had been checked, tagged and ruled out. It seemed Mito was right; there was plenty of contraband here, but none of it was new enough to be the vector of infection.

He glanced at Hatcher. The boy was wasting time fiddling with a 3-V on the far wall. A pricy model, no doubt – all delicate stalk and elegantly rounded projector – but nothing fancy enough to warrant special attention.

"What are you doing, boy?"

"Sir? I'm just looking at—"

"Well stop it. It's been tagged. Leave it alone."

"Sorry, sir. It's just… It's not fully grown yet. Can't be more than ten days old. But I can't see where it was grafted."

Jodan went to take a closer look. It was true: there wasn't any obvious sign of grafting. But it was hard to tell, with the wall surface so badly deteriorated. So, no visible scarring, but if he felt around the base…. Still nothing. No nodules, no telltale hidden scarring. It was as if the wall had simply extruded the device…

The world receded. He was alone in a silent universe, staring at the evidence of catastrophe: a wilting bud growing from a dead wall.

He swallowed. Or tried to. His throat was suddenly so very dry.

And then the world was back. And with it, a sense of overwhelming urgency. He snapped orders at Hatcher, sending him scurrying after Mito. Then he went in search of the house brain.

He found it in the basement; a large – disturbingly, frighteningly large – nodule growing on the main house root. It had the usual hard wooden shell, but that hadn't protected it. Brains like this had a weak spot: a membrane across which genetic codes could pass. And there it was, or used to be: a gaping hole near the bottom, with foul black liquid oozing out. That was where the poison had entered the system.

Not that it mattered, now. Nothing mattered, beside the awful fact that this brain was here. On Noyan. In a private house.

Footsteps were approaching. Mito, with Hatcher in tow. Jodan didn't even glance at them. "Tell me, *Senior Bi-technician* Mito," he said. "Why wasn't this found earlier?"

"I... I don't know, sir. It never occurred to... We... We didn't know..."

"You knew he had illegal bi-tech."

"Of course. But we never thought–"

"Clearly. I want this thing analyzed. Immediately. If it's what I think it is, this is the worst – the very worst – breach of the embargo since Neph.... No. Not 'since' anything. There's nothing to compare it with. This could be worse than Nephrate."

Worse than Nephrate. The very idea was a kind of heresy. But it was the truth. Embargoed worlds worked on mass-production: one bud, one item – and built-in obsolescence to keep the cycle moving. This brain would blow the local bi-tech industry apart. Why buy a bud, when all you needed was a trace of its DNA, and the house could grow the thing wherever you wanted. As often as you wanted.

"...not that bad, sir."

"What?"

Mito was talking. And sweating. And not, this time, with lust.

"I said it's not as bad as it seems, sir. It's not like he was just anyone. He was a Gwahnal. Just because he had something like this, doesn't mean anyone else–"

"Can you prove that? Can you guarantee it's a one-off?

That nobody else has one of these?"

"Well, no. Of course not. But—"

"No. You can't. Because if we had guarantees like that, the embargo would only apply to natives, not citizens. There's a reason we don't allow replication-capable brains on a planet like this. Noyan isn't even a Protectorate yet. The natives can't just skip mass-production and go straight to the licensing model. If something like this gets out, it'll destroy the economy. We'll lose any influence we have, any hope of ever civilizing them. The Family Court will just go on killing innocents forever. And if, God forbid, the Gallaskians manage to get their hands on one, the whole strategic balance between us and the Autarchy becomes an issue. This puts the whole Commonwealth in danger."

Mito wasn't arguing. He'd shrunk back, wilting before Jodan's glare. Hatcher barely seemed to be listening. He was staring intently at the house brain.

"Sir," he said. "I don't think that's a standard Mercator. It looks like an F series, but it's too big. I think it's a custom job. It looks like… It looks like the bloody thing was made here, sir."

Jodan blinked. He turned to stare at the boy. Then he did the only thing he could.

"Mito. Get me a secure line to the embassy. Right now!"

CHAPTER 4

Famous for his love of modernity, Michael the Restaurateur nonetheless chose to refurbish an existing stone building rather than have a new one grown to his specifications. He is on record describing this as an aesthetic decision, claiming that a bi-tech building would be out of place in the Old Quarter. But at least one mischievous commentator has suggested that the decision reflects Michael's age more than his aesthetic judgment. Perhaps, despite his known zeal for new technology, Michael still shares his generation's lingering prejudice against living structures...

— From: Feature article, *The Noyan Gazette*

Michael glared at the wall. The hidden door was just so insultingly obvious. Not even the dimmest, most clueless regulator could possibly miss it. The brickwork was shoddy. The plaster glaringly fresh.

He growled, deep in his throat. The nearest workers edged away. And stopped, held back by Zachary. And Zachary's gun.

Michael pointed at the woman with the trowel. "You. Do it again."

She made another attempt to blend new plaster into old. And only made it worse. He grabbed the trowel from her shaking hand, shoved her roughly aside, and skimmed it expertly across the brickwork.

"The regulators aren't stupid," he said. "If they can see a difference, they'll know something's there. You have to make it seamless."

He smeared the plaster lightly, softening the edges and blending new into old. Then he stepped back and peered intently at the wall. The outline was less stark than it had been, but the vaulted doorway still stood out as a lighter patch against the dull grey background of the basement wall.

"It needs dusting." He pointed at the worst sections. "There. There. And there. See to it, Zach."

"Yes, Michael." Zachary ducked his head nervously, as frightened as the rest of them. Good.

"I'll be back in an hour. If I can tell where the new plaster starts, I'll have the brickwork torn down and rebuilt – with every one of you *parents* on the other side."

He thrust the trowel back into the woman's trembling hands, and stalked off down the corridor. In truth, the wall wasn't too bad. Give it another few hours for the fresh mortar to dry, and the regulators would walk right past these vaults and never know they were there.

Arrogance – that was the off-comers' problem. They were so confident in the superiority of their wonderful biological technology, it never occurred to them to learn how the Noyim did things. Traditional stone buildings were a mystery to them. Off-comer buildings had roots, not foundations. Did the regulators realize how deep you had to dig to support a building this size? Did they even know these basement levels existed? They knew all about the upper floors – the restaurant, the brothel, the gambling den. But no regulator got to see the hidden, windowless basements where other, less acceptable, activities could be pursued. And no off-comer ever saw his bi-tech stores. He patted the wall and walked on.

A drawing room waited incongruously at the end of the corridor; chairs, mirrors, even a potted plant. Elevators were another thing easily hidden from unsuspecting regulators. The attendant was a young boy, new to the staff. He fumbled nervously with the elevator's single, well-hidden button. He was right to be frightened. They all were, today.

The elevator rattled upwards. Bare plaster walls slid slowly by, with no exits to any other levels until it reached the third floor, and slowed to a stop. Here, plaster gave way to wallpaper and a wooden door: the drawing room once again had its missing fourth wall. The attendant hurried to open the door, and stepped aside.

Michael stalked down the hall to the second elevator. This one was used by the public, and was entirely conventional. The attendant closed the inner lattice door, and took him straight up to his penthouse. Mary was waiting in the foyer. He led her into his office.

"Well?" he said.

"Just what you thought. Little Joel was dealing on the side."

"He admitted it?"

"Eventually." She handed him a small green bud. It wasn't much to look at. The stem was wilting, but the outer shell was still waxy and tough. It probably had another couple of days before it stopped being graftable.

"3-V?"

"Refrigerator."

"Right."

He crushed the bud into a pulpy mess, then dropped it back onto her waiting palm. It didn't matter what the bud would grow into. Just that it was his, and had been stolen.

"He had help?"

"He did."

"Who?"

Mary licked her lips. She wasn't meeting his gaze…

"Well?"

"It was Bala."

"Huh. Never would have guessed that. Were they screwing?"

"Used to."

"Right."

Bala. That was bad. If off-comer technicians started thinking they could go into business for themselves...

It was early yet, but he needed a drink. There was a half-empty bottle of Gallaskian brandy in the liquor cabinet. He poured a large measure into a tumbler.

Mary was still in the doorway, carefully packing the ruined bud into a small paper bag; making sure no incriminating leaves or fragments of stem were left behind for the regulators to find. She was thorough – a professional in a world full of amateurs. He liked that about her. That, and her capacity for violence.

"So, Bala. Do they have their own manufacturing set up? She could do it, if she wanted to."

Mary slipped the paper bag into a jacket pocket. "Nothing so fancy. They were just selling our rejects. That's what Joel said, anyway."

"You didn't believe him?"

"No, I believed him all right. Otherwise, we'd still be talking. It's just – he was very keen to spread the blame around, once he started talking. I don't think Bala was really in on it. Just helping out an old boyfriend with some of our rejects."

"No. She was in on it. Kill her."

"But she's a Commonwealther. Won't the Gwahn–?" She registered the look on his face, and stopped. "Right. Consider it done."

He took a long swig of the brandy. You had to hand it to the Autarchy. They might not trade much with outsiders, but what they did trade was quality.

"These rejects," he said. "Were they seconds, or total write offs?"

"A mix. Maybe two out of three would have grown true. Some were pretty bad."

"Bad enough to kill a house?"

"Not in a million years. Besides, he never would've

dared sell to Sanja. The kid would have gone straight to you. Or his parents."

Michael went over to the large picture window and stared out at the city below. "Yeah. So, big surprise. It wasn't an accident. Someone killed Sanja. Deliberately. And the way they did it, using bi-tech, that's not random. This is a set up. Someone wants the regulators coming after me – get the off-comers to do their dirty work for them. Then, when I'm out of the picture, they move right in and take over my business. And I know just which scraper it's got to be."

Mary said nothing. He turned to look at her. Waiting. Making her ask.

"Who?"

"Mordecai. Has to be. Last I heard, the Auxiliary Court was sniffing around his rackets. Sooner or later the Family Court's going to take an interest. The way he sees it, he's got to move up to survive. I make ten times what he does, more even, and ninety percent of what I do doesn't even breach Custom. Drugs, whores, bi-tech. That's the way to go. All big earners, and not a thing to do with the Family Court. Count on it. Mordecai wants in. He's the one."

Mary fingered her long nose thoughtfully. "So, what do we do? Go to war?"

"No. Mordecai wants the bi-tech market? Fine – it's all his. He's got the regulators all stirred up. Let him take the heat. We suspend all business, as of right now. Wait it out. Keep our heads down until this blows over. We'll be fine. There's nothing to link us to Sanja. Well, nothing except..."

"Beynan Hotep," said Mary, completing his thought.

CHAPTER 5

The Noyim are not after all so very different from us. Even the Family Court, that most alien of institutions, spends much of its time doing wholly laudable work hunting down genuine criminals. I hope and believe that the pessimists are wrong, and Noyan will soon be as much an integral part of our Commonwealth family as Homeworld itself.

– From: My Time on Noyan, Memories of a Youthful Exile, *The Rt. Hon. Beynan Hotep na Massowic*

"I keep telling you, Justice. I've no idea where Sanja got his bi-tech."

Bey smiled. She could believe him, or not. It was up to her. He couldn't care less. She should have interviewed him hours ago, if she wanted answers. He'd been scared then. And tired. And hungover. And so, so thirsty. He'd have told her anything for a glass of water. Not now, after he'd eaten and drunk his full. The Gwahnals' mansion was an excellent host; the food and drink here as good as anywhere on Noyan. And it was a fine judge of etiquette. This was the perfect room to offer the Justice for the interview. He was a highborn Homeworlder, so couldn't be placed too low; she was a monster from the Family Court, and couldn't be placed too high... So here they were, in one of the Gwahnals' more informal reception rooms. It was the perfect compromise: elegant but not overly luxurious, with walls of polished, living wood and furniture that almost looked hand-made; the kind of place Fange could meet with important native business contacts.

"That isn't what Regulator Hyrom seems to think."

"I can't help what Hyrom thinks."

Fuck her. No way was he helping the Family Court. Not even a Justice who looked like a little old granny. *Especially* not a Justice who looked like a little old granny. How did she even fucking live with herself, doing that job?

And why had she pushed that chair away? Why reach for it, and then shove it back when it waddled over to help?

"You were his best friend, and he never told you who his dealer was?"

"No. Never mentioned him."

"But you know it was a man?"

Shit. She might be old, but she was sharp. She'd picked up on that slip way too quickly. He couldn't afford another. Michael wasn't the forgiving kind.

"It was an assumption."

"An assumption. I see. And I suppose you can't tell me where to look for 'him' either?"

Bey spread his hands helplessly. "I'm sorry. That was Sanja's department. Like I said, I never met him. Or her. I'd love to help, but..."

She must know he was lying – but what could she do? She couldn't prove anything... Unlike Hyrom: who must have all the proof he could possibly want by now. But only for possession. Not manslaughter. That was a bluff. He saw that now. But it was still the worst fucking luck. Everybody used black market bi-tech. Why did he have to be the one whose friend died?

"In that case, there's no point in detaining you any further. Come on. I'll drop you off on the way back to the court."

"You mean... That's it?"

He wasn't sure whether to be relieved, or angry. She'd kept him waiting around for hours, and then that was it? Ten minutes of pointless questioning and a lift back to the city?

"That's it, Hotep – unless you've suddenly remembered something you need to tell me?"

"No. Sorry."

"This way, then."

He'd never dreamed he'd end up accepting a lift from a Justice, but the alternative was handing himself over to the regulators. Or worse, an awkward encounter with Sanja's grieving parents.

Two burly natives were waiting in the corridor. They'd spent the last few hours preventing him from leaving the room. Now they stepped aside, and followed meekly along as the Justice led the way outside – to her waiting automobile.

An automobile. He should have realized.

Of course she wouldn't have a nice, safe, modern vehicle. She had to have a fucking native automobile – a primitive, brass-trimmed, wooden-wheeled black box, with only a windshield and a cloth canopy to protect its occupants from the elements. Worse, the windshield was made of glass, ready to shatter into a thousand deadly shards at the smallest impact. The thing was a fucking death-trap. And she was cheerfully climbing into a seat behind a large wheel that looked like something out of an ancient sailing ship.

"In you get, Hotep."

He glanced around for a face-saving way to refuse. But what else could he do? Go back inside and ask Fange and Amaya for help. That didn't appeal at all. And how bad could it be, really? The natives drove these things all the time.

He walked around the automobile and climbed into the other seat. It made no effort to accommodate him. Nor did the vehicle seem to be in any hurry to depart. What was it waiting for? Another passenger? No: there were only two seats. What, then?

Ah. It couldn't leave. One of the burly natives was standing in the way. They wouldn't be going anywhere until he stepped aside. But he wasn't leaving. He was bending down and energetically turning some kind of handle.

Then, suddenly, there was a cough, a loud bang, and the whole automobile shook. A cloud of smoke rose in front. Bey sat bolt upright, ready to fling himself to safety... and slowly settled back into his seat. Clearly, this was expected. The man stepped unhurriedly out of the way... and stowed a bent metal rod right under Bey's seat without so much as a by-your-leave. Next thing, the vehicle lurched forwards, and they were on their way.

The automobile soon began to pick up speed. He could feel it, viscerally, in the wind whipping around him. The windshield might as well not have been there; not when there was no door, and nothing between him and the open air. He glanced to the side and saw the unforgiving roadside spinning by horribly quickly, far too close for comfort. A fall would be fatal. Even leaning out too far could lead to serious injury.

The natives were crazy, risking their necks like this. He needed out, right now. He'd ask the Gwahnals for a car. He'd walk back through the fucking desert. Anything, rather than stay in this death trap. He opened his mouth to tell her to stop, but the Justice spoke first.

"Oh – something I forgot to ask you. You made a scene last night, at the big gala dinner?"

"Wh...What?"

She turned to him, smiling, oblivious to the danger. She couldn't seriously expect to have a conversation when they might be killed at any moment?

"You walked out, in the middle of the dinner?"

"I did? Yes. Yes, I did."

He'd seen the whole mortifying scene play out on the

3-V in the reception room. Dil Mahtal ran it at the end of his show, a little light relief at the end of a grim news segment. Knowing Dil, he'd probably put Bey up to the stupid stunt in the first place. And suggested the urine shirt, too. There was no way to know. Most of last night was a complete blank.

"May I ask why?"

"Why what?"

"Why you walked out?"

The automobile was veering towards the verge. Had it lost all sense of direction? He braced for disaster, whimpering, but the Justice turned the wheel, and the automobile lurched sickeningly back into its lane. He stared at her, wilting. Was she steering it, moment to moment? How absolutely fucking terrifying.

"Oh. Right. Yes. Uh… I'm not sure. It was something to do with the Mitchesons seating the Gwahnals on a side table."

"There was something inappropriate about that?"

How fast was this automobile going? It couldn't be quicker than a bi-tech vehicle. It just seemed like it, with the wind whistling by where the door should be. Bey's legs were cramping from bracing himself.

"It was a deliberate insult. They should have been at the head table. I was probably trying to teach the Mitchesons a lesson."

"You must be very close to the Gwahnals."

"What? No. Not really."

"So why did you care?"

"I didn't. I don't. The Mitchesons versus the Gwahnals is a tedious local business rivalry. But I was very drunk and bored out of my mind. I wouldn't have gone, if I'd known Sanja wasn't going to be there. I was probably just looking for a way to get out of there, and thought it'd be funny to make a scene. Like I said, I was dru–"

His mouth snapped shut, jarred by a brutal transition from the Gwahnals' roadroot driveway to the native road beyond. The automobile made no effort to adjust for the rougher surface. The ride, already uncomfortable, became unbearable; every jolt and bump was transmitted instantly to his spine. And yet the Justice was talking again, seemingly inured to the discomfort.

"So, on the night Sanja died, you made a very public scene, for reasons you struggle to explain, but which just happens to provide you with a rock-solid alibi for his murder? And I'm supposed to believe that's a coincidence?"

And, finally, Bey understood. This lift hadn't been about helping him at all. It was a way to terrify him into confessing. Hyrom had tried the same thing. But where he'd used bluff and physical intimidation, she was using this nightmare of a drive.

At least Hyrom wanted him to confess to something he'd actually done. He *was* guilty of using contraband bi-tech. But this mad bitch wanted him to confess to killing Sanja. He set his jaw and stared straight ahead. She could terrify him all she fucking liked, it wouldn't do her any good. He was done cooperating.

"The Mitchesons have the contract for the roadroot system, don't they?"

The Justice's question was such a non sequitur, he couldn't help responding. "What? I think so. I don't really–"

"So, any attack on the roadroot system is an attack on the Mitchesons?"

"I suppose so. I hadn't really thought about–"

"And the attackers used some kind of fungus?"

"According to the news, yes." The 3-V pictures had been unbelievable. Mile after mile of half-grown, supposedly indestructible roadroots simply rotting away overnight.

"Does that make sense to you?"

"What?"

"Traditionalists. Where would they get a fungus that

could do something like that?"

She was right. It didn't make sense. But that bothered him less than the fact the automobile had just driven straight over a pothole with a bone-jarring crunch.

"Well, now that you mention—"

"And here's the thing I can't help noticing. On the very night the Mitchesons' roadroots were attacked using sophisticated off-comer technology, who should fail to show up at their gala dinner but Sanja Gwahnal: the son and heir of the Mitchesons' biggest rivals. And one of the few people who'd have access to the kind of technology used in the attack."

"No way. If you think Sanja—"

"And then later that same night, Sanja Gwahnal was killed by person or persons unknown. Again using sophisticated off-comer technology."

He glanced at her. She was hunched over, arms spread wide on the wheel, attention focused on the road ahead. And what she was saying was insane. But oddly compelling. Except for one thing...

"You think Sanja was involved in the roadroots attack? That's insane. He was just a kid."

"I'm merely pointing out that there were two attacks using advanced off-comer technology on the very same night. One against the Mitchesons. The other, the Gwahnals."

He shook his head. "Except there weren't. The roadroots were attacked. Sanja wasn't. He just used some bad bi-tech, and it killed his house, and him. It sucks, but it was an accident. It's only a coincidence it happened the same night."

"It might be a coincidence, but it definitely wasn't an accident. You saw the body. Why was he still in bed when he died? He was choking. Why wasn't he trying to get to the door, or a window? And there were bruises, on his arms. Someone held him down."

And just like that, he was back in the room, looking at

Sanja's body. His stomach lurched. He wanted to throw up. But the Justice was right. No way should Sanja still have been lying in bed like that, all twisted and gasping for air. He'd have tried to get out, to get to clean air. You wouldn't have any choice. Your body wouldn't let you just lie there.

All of a sudden, he didn't feel like throwing up at all. He felt like crying. "But… who'd do that? He was just a boy."

"Hardly. He was nineteen."

"Right. But for us, you're not an adult until you turn twenty-one."

"So why wasn't he still living with his parents? If he was still a child, why did he have his own house? Is that normal?"

"Well, no, but–"

"No. In fact it's very unusual, isn't it? Even Noyim don't normally leave home that young. Why did the Gwahnals give him so much freedom?"

"I don't know."

It was bizarre, now that he thought about it. He'd just accepted it as the way things were, here on Noyan, where childhood was short, and natives were adults at sixteen. But the Gwahnals weren't the type to go native. They were much too dull and respectable for that. It didn't make sense.

"You can't even guess?"

"No. Only, like I… Justice – the road!"

The automobile was veering back towards the verge. Why wasn't she looking ahead? Was she insane? The automobile was clearly too stupid to manage itself.

"Only what?" she asked, turning the wheel. The automobile corrected itself. He sagged gratefully back down in his seat.

"Only nothing. He was very mature for his age, that's all."

"Interesting. Do you know what the Gwahnals said,

when I asked them about it? They said they spoiled him. That he was their son and heir, and they could 'refuse him nothing'. Was that your experience?"

"Well, they always seemed to give him everything he wanted, so yeah. Pretty much."

"Yes. And over the years, I've found that spoiled children are the most likely to make the Choice of Death. Sanja was almost the age. Do you think the Gwahnals had reason to be afraid?"

He turned to look at her. It was easy to forget this little old woman held the vilest office on Noyan.

"Do you have any idea how insane that sounds?"

The automobile screeched to a sudden stop. Bey careered head-first towards the windshield and certain death. He flung up his arms to protect himself, but too late. He was going to smash into the glass. He couldn't save himself...

Then he hit. There was no smashing of glass, no jagged edges tearing open his face, no sudden pain-filled death. Just a small bump. He glanced back at the Justice, embarrassed. She was glaring at him.

"Do you know why the Family Court is responsible for investigating suspicious deaths?"

"No, I can't say I do."

"Because long before the first off-comer ever set foot on Noyan, there were parents who killed their children for fear of the Choice of Death. So, no, I don't think it sounds crazy, at all."

The automobile made no move to set off again. It just sat there, huffing and shaking. Ahead of them was the on-ramp for the main east-west roadroot. It stretched to left and right as far as the eye could see: flat, green and perfectly straight. There was no traffic visible in either direction.

"What are we waiting for?"

"I'm trying to think of a better way back to the city."

"Better than a roadroot?"

The woman scowled and moved her feet. The automobile coughed, and moved forwards. It juddered briefly when it left the native road, and then the journey became much smoother. Bey relaxed infinitesimally. But he still kept his legs braced, in case the crazy old lady brought the automobile to another sudden stop.

"You really think it's impossible an off-comer parent might fear the Choice of Death?"

"Yes! Of course it is. Look... Just because we live here, doesn't mean we're going to... I mean, if you found yourself living with cannibals, how long would it take for you to start killing people for food? How long before you thought it was okay to kill and eat your own family? That's about how long it's going to take for Commonwealthers to go along with Choosing."

"So, there's no way Sanja had any interest in participating in a Choosing ceremony?"

"None whatsoever."

"In that case, why was he hoarding literature advocating for it in the strongest possible terms?"

"What? Sanja? You've got to be kidding."

"On the contrary, he had an extensive collection of traditionalist literature. I can see that disturbs you. I imagine the Gwahnals would have found it even more disturbing. What do you think they might have done, if they knew?"

"They wouldn't have killed him, if that's what you're thinking. Worst case, they'd have sent him off planet to get his head straight. But it'd never happen. You're wrong. No way was Sanja interested in anything traditional, Noyan or otherwise. You've seen his house. He was all about new things, not old. He wanted this planet to become civili... to change... as much as everyone else does."

"Not everyone," said the Justice, dryly. "But I find it interesting that you, his friend, knew nothing of his interests. Perhaps he thought he had good reason to keep them secret. Tell me, what did you do last night, after you walked out of the Mitchesons' party?"

It was another sudden change of topic. This time, it didn't throw him quite as much. He was getting used to her tricks.

"I have no idea. Next thing I remember is waking up with a hangover."

"So, you might have gone to Sanja Gwahnal's house?"

"I might have, but I didn't, or Hyrom would have been all over it. He'll have talked to the Gwahnals' gatehouse. It would have told him if I was there. You can ask it yourself if you don't believe me."

He glanced at the woman, and saw her wince. Why? Of course! She was a fanatic. She hated bi-tech. Why was he surprised? She was a Justice of the Family Court. It went with the territory. And it explained why she wanted to paint Sanja, of all people, as some kind of martyr for her sick cause. She had to be worried that everything she believed in – Choosing, the Family Court, all of it – was doomed. Sooner or later, Noyan was going to join the Commonwealth, and when it did, that'd be the end of the whole evil system. The Family Court wasn't the future – Regulator Hyrom was.

Oh shit. Regulator Hyrom.

He couldn't go back home. The place would be crawling with bi-technicians. He had to persuade her to drop him off somewhere else, somewhere safe. He put on a friendly smile and turned to face her.

"Uh, Justice, I was wondering..."

CHAPTER 6

Michael's Place is rapidly becoming the place to see, and be seen. Serving a mixture of solid Noyan fare and familiar Commonwealth delicacies, the restaurant boasts a wine collection that the Ambassador himself would envy, and stocks a small selection of Gallaskian brandies. Already a well-established hot spot for the richer and trendier Noyim, its reputation among the smart young Commonwealth set can only grow...

— From: Feature article, *The Noyan Newsletter [a Commonwealth Information Services publication]*

Michael hung back and let Zachary exit the elevator first. It wasn't like Mary to summon him. She knew better. What was so important that he had to come down, instead of her coming up?

Maybe he was just paranoid. But if old Benny had been a bit more paranoid, he'd still be in charge, and Michael wouldn't have stepped into his very dead shoes.

He counted to three, then followed. There was no ambush, no welcoming committee, no hail of bullets. Mary and Zachary were at the far end of the lobby, peering through the heavy maroon curtains into the restaurant beyond. He went to join them.

Mary leaned in close, keeping her voice low. "Cherayn's here. Says the embassy thinks it was murder. They're not

53

blaming us at all. They're fingering traditionalists. Saying it was a terrorist attack."

"You serious?"

"He swears to it. Says they're linking Sanja's death with the roadroot attack."

"I don't buy it. Neither one. Where would trads get that kind of knowhow?"

"You think he's lying?"

"Has to be. Or someone's lying to him, and he's too dumb to realize it. No way are the regulators falling for that line. Not for a minute."

"But if they do…"

"Then we're scraped. If they're not hunting dealers, Mordecai's no use as bait. And the longer we stay out of the market, the more he takes over."

Mary scratched the side of her long nose. "Maybe we should open up again? Start selling?"

It was tempting, but… "No. I don't believe it. It's a game. They're trying to get us to break cover. I need to talk to Hotep, find out what he's told them. Any sign of him?"

"Not a one. Want me to put more people on it?"

"Anyone we can spare. See to it. I'll go talk to Cherayn. See if I can work out if he's lying, or just dumb."

He pushed through the curtain into the somber, candle-lit darkness of the restaurant. The maître de bowed and stepped aside; waiters moved unobtrusively into protective positions. Michael ignored them, and the urge to hurry straight to the booths at the back, where Cherayn would be enjoying a more private dining experience. But Michael couldn't just walk straight through the restaurant – not hospitable Michael, the charming host. He worked the tables, greeting regulars with friendly familiarity, asking newcomers if they were enjoying their meals. He talked briefly to a smugly wealthy gem trader, and wondered what she'd think if she knew how much firepower was trained on her right at that moment. And, finally, he slipped into the off-comer's booth and sat down across from him.

"Enjoying your meal?"

"Huh?"

Cherayn's strange blue eyes were as jarring as ever. Michael forced himself to smile. He spent a lot of time around off-comers. He could cope with disturbing skin colors, huge noses, thin lips. But blue eyes... They just weren't human.

"I said, are you enjoying your meal?"

"What? Yes. Very much, thank you."

Michael's smile widened. He couldn't help himself. He just had to play with the freak-eyed mother.

"Chef will be glad to hear it. He had the pig specially fattened. It could barely walk by the time we slaughtered it. You should have seen it waddle. The fat really adds flavor, doesn't it?"

Cherayn turned pale. He swallowed, hard, and when he finally spoke, his voice was so faint Michael had to strain to hear him. "It's... very nice, thank you. Would you care to join me?"

Michael managed not to laugh. The last thing Cherayn wanted was company to witness his shame. Cherayn was here to eat real meat; the kind that came from dead animals. He didn't want lean, healthy bi-tech slices, cut without cruelty from a sausage of unfeeling muscle. He wanted bones and blood and fat and gristle; the very things that disgusted his fellow off-comers; proof that the flesh he was eating had once been a living, breathing, thinking, feeling animal. The horror was part of the appeal. And Cherayn, vicious perverted Mino Cherayn, couldn't get enough of it. And that made him useful.

"Sorry, Mino. I don't feel much like eating. I'm too upset. You know, Sanja Gwahnal was in here only a couple of days ago. I was talking to him like I'm talking to you now. Terrible thing, a young man dying like that."

"Terrible. A horrible way to go. Everyone's scared silly about it. We never thought we'd see these kinds of sophisticated attacks on Noyan."

"I thought it was an accident? Something about black market bi-tech poisoning his house?"

Cherayn stopped sawing at the slab of meat on his plate. He leaned conspiratorially across the table. "No – word is, that was Undersecretary Maitland playing games. He wanted an excuse to crack down on smugglers, but got outmaneuvered by the Family Court and ended up hip-deep in guano. Rumor is, the office knew it was terrorists all along, and Ambassador Ashef's hopping mad they didn't just come clean from the start. Reckons we could have pushed the Assembly into applying for Protectorate status off the back of it."

"No! Really?" There was a quarter-full bottle of wine on the table. Michael reached for it and topped up Cherayn's glass.

"Really…" Cherayn stopped, suddenly wary. "All this is just between you and me, of course."

"Of course. But I don't buy it, Mino. I don't think anyone poisoned the house. I think it just died. I've never trusted bi-tech houses." A meaningful glance at his stone walls prompted an indulgent smirk from the off-comer. "Come on, Mino. This is all about protecting the bi-tech market. The embassy doesn't want Noyim having doubts about bi-tech, so they make up this story about terrorists to keep everyone quiet. Got to keep people buying all that lovely bi-tech."

Cherayn took a sip of wine and shook his head. "I see how it could look that way. But this isn't just the official line. It was on the grapevine for hours before they came out and admitted it. They're serious about this. There's a lot going on behind the scenes. There are rumors it was Moyem Jimawn who tipped off the press about the boy's death."

"Who?"

"Moyem Jimawn. Officially he's the Autarchy's 'Cultural Attaché'. Unofficially, well… Some of the circles he mixes in don't seem like they'd have a vast interest in Gallaskian culture. He and Sanja Gwahnal were friends, apparently. That's not something the undersecretary's happy about."

The undersecretary wasn't happy? Scrape the undersecretary. Sanja – friends with a Gallaskian agent? And this was the first he'd heard about it. What were the Gwahnals playing at? What else didn't he know?

Maybe it was time he had a good long talk with Fange and Amaya. The kind of talk where people understood how bad an idea it was to lie to him.

Cherayn was shrinking away from him, gulping nervously at his wine. Stupid, stupid, stupid: he was letting his anger show. He made an effort to smile. "You like that wine? Here. Have another bottle. On the house."

He lifted a finger to summon a waiter. And saw Mary, signaling to him from the curtains. He waited just long enough to see Cherayn receive his complimentary wine, then headed for the exit.

The news was excellent. Matthew and Hannah had picked up Hotep. Finally, something was going his way.

"Good. Go and take charge. Matthew's the kind of idiot who'd bring him in the front door. Or deliver him in pieces. I want Hotep scared, not hurt. Understood?"

"Understood."

He headed back up to his office. He'd made some changes since that morning, and not for the better. Heavy blast curtains lined the windows, replacing his prized city view with a wall of blank grey. He resented the necessity. The curtains were a sign of weakness. And maybe not a necessity, after all. Not if Cherayn was right, and the off-comers were fingering traditionalists for Sanja's death…

He glanced at the other intrusion on his space: a bank of 3-Vs linked to tiny cameras roosting discretely throughout the building. He stood in front of them, watching the projections and waiting for Mary's return.

Matthew and Hannah appeared first; scouting out the kitchens. Mary and Hotep followed, his left bicep firmly in her grip. There was a brief delay while they waited for the lobby to clear, and then she was steering him towards the elevator, leaving Matthew and Hannah below.

Hotep had been useful, once. He'd provided excellent cover for meetings with Sanja, and could always be relied upon to be too drunk, or too stupid, to understand what was going on around him. But he wasn't useful now. He was a problem.

But not for much longer.

Michael pulled his revolver from its shoulder holster. It wasn't the most expensive model on the market, or the highest caliber, but it was factory-made, reliable, and easily cocked for rapid shooting. He'd choose speed and reliability over stopping power any day. And swap all three for a bi-tech weapon in a heartbeat. He didn't buy the Gwahnals' story about 'non replicable' DNA. That was just a blind, a way of keeping the upstart Noya in his place; one he'd deal with, in time. In the meantime, he'd show this off-comer he was still someone to be feared, even without modern weapons. He checked the gun and holstered it. Careful preparation never hurt anyone. At least, not the one who prepared.

The elevator arrived. Mary hustled Hotep through the foyer, and into his office. The off-comer seemed to be having difficulty walking. Was he drunk? Or just terrified? Either way, it was time for the oldest trick in the book.

"Beynan? Are you all right? Mary! What have you done to him? Beynan's a friend! You'd better not have hurt him."

Mary instantly released the off-comer's arm and started babbling an apology. "Sorry, boss. I thought you—"

"I don't pay you to think. Get out!"

"Of course. Sorry Boss. Sorry Hotep... I mean, Beynan. Sorry."

She retreated, wisely keeping the smirk off her face

until she was safely out of Hotep's eyeline. Michael patted the off-comer's arm reassuringly. "I'm so sorry, Beynan. I said I wanted to see you. I had no idea Mary would be so... overzealous. Here, let me get you a drink."

He settled Hotep into a nearby sofa, and poured two generous measures of brandy. The off-comer cowered away, his hands shaking so badly he almost spilled his drink on his fancy shirt. What was he, a child? Maybe it was true, what they said: no one ever really grew up until they'd made the Choice of Life, or the Choice of Death.

Not that he'd waited that long. He'd grown up the day he killed his pimp.

"To Sanja!" he said. Hotep nodded and gulped at the brandy. Michael sat down beside him. "It's a sad day for us both, losing a friend. And you know what hurts the most? They're blaming me! They're saying my bi-tech killed him!"

Hotep choked on the brandy, eyes watering. "What? Who's saying that?"

"The regulators. The Family Court, too, maybe."

"I didn't tell them anything, Michael. I swear."

"So why are they blaming me?"

"They're not. They don't know anything about you. They don't know where Sanja got his bi-tech! I didn't tell them anything."

Hotep had brown eyes, like a normal person. That was good. Michael could look into them, and read the truth. He put an arm around the off-comer's shoulders.

"Of course you didn't. You were a good friend to Sanja, and you're a good friend to me. And it wasn't my bi-tech that killed him, you know. I've never sold bad product, and never will. But I did supply Sanja sometimes, and malicious people could misunderstand that. I need to be sure. I'm not going to hurt you Beynan, whatever happens. But I have to know – did you tell the regulators about me?"

Hotep's eyes were wide. He was shivering under Michael's encircling arm. When he spoke, he was all but babbling. "No. Not a word. Nothing. The Family Court grabbed me before I could say anyth–"

Hotep's mouth snapped shut. Michael smiled. "Before you could say anything about *what*? What were you going to tell them, before the Justice showed up?"

"Nothing. I promise. I wouldn't... I'll tell them the same as her. I don't know anything about Sanja's dealer. That Sanja used to get everything for both of us. I won't tell them anything."

Michael took his arm from around the off-comer's shoulders. Poor rich idiot. If he'd already talked, he'd be safe. Michael wouldn't have dared touch him, for fear of regulators watching his every move. But the fool had kept quiet. And one little bullet would make sure he stayed that way forever. He shifted slightly, giving himself easier access to his gun. And stopped, distracted by a disturbance on the security wall: an argument, in the lobby. Someone was facing off with the bouncers. That was rare. Most people knew better.

And then, incredibly, his people were backing off – one of them nursing an arm that flapped uselessly at the elbow. Mary came into view, heading furiously towards the scene. And stopped. And stepped aside to let the attacker through.

What the scrape? The attacker was a small middle-aged woman. She was pushing past his people, making for the elevator. Who the...?

The Justice of the Family Court. Who else? No wonder everyone backed off.

He surged to his feet, grabbed a handful of Hotep's hair, and dragged the squealing off-comer to the security wall. "Do you know who that is?"

"It's... It's Justice Beth of...of the..."

"Of the Family Court, Hotep. The Family Court. So, you didn't tell anyone anything...? You stupid *mother*."

He threw Hotep back onto the sofa. One way or another, he was going to kill this scraper. But he wouldn't use his gun. Too quick. He was going to spend a long, long time doing it.

But not today. Not with a Justice of the Family Court headed his way.

The intercom buzzed. He hurried to his desk and jammed the button down. Mary's voice came through. "Boss? We have a situa—"

"Tell those idiots to back off!" he bellowed into the microphone, hoping the Justice would hear him through the speaker. "They're molesting a Justice of the Family Court! Tell them to leave her alone. The Family Court is always welcome here."

Hotep was sobbing. The urge to vent his rage on the off-comer was almost overwhelming. But he couldn't. Not until the Justice was gone. He watched her move from lobby to elevator. The moment the doors closed, she slumped against the wall, hands gripping the small of her back. So, she'd hurt herself in the scuffle. And she didn't know he was watching. Best to keep it that way.

"Security wall: off." The projections winked out of existence, leaving an unprepossessing array of dull green spheres. He hurried to the foyer and waited for the elevator doors to open.

"Justice, what an unexpected pleasure..."

She stalked past him without so much as acknowledging his presence, and without any sign of the weakness she'd shown in the elevator. And if she was surprised to find the off-comer in his office, she gave no sign of it. Interesting.

"Hotep? Are you all right?"

The off-comer nodded, but said nothing. Speech was clearly beyond him. That, at least, was a mercy.

"He's fine, Justice. He's just had a bad day. So have I. We've both lost a good friend."

"Really?" She turned to face him. "Sanja Gwahnal was a friend of yours?"

"Yes. And a good one, too."

"And Hotep? Would you describe him as a friend?"

"Of course."

"So – two friends of yours. One's dead, and the other's in a state of considerable distress. Your friendship doesn't appear to be very good for people, does it?"

"I don't know, Justice. There's worse people he could be friends with." He glanced past her, and caught the frightened off-comer's eye. "Regulators and such like."

The Justice put her head on one side. "Was that a threat?"

"Not at all, Justice. I'm just looking out for Bey. As a friend."

"Do you always kidnap your friends? Look at him – he's terrified."

"I don't know what you're talking about, Justice. No one's been kidnapped – have they, Bey?"

The off-comer shook his head. He was staring at Michael like a rat mesmerized by a snake.

"See, Justice. I was just concerned for him. I wanted to be sure he was safe."

"I take it you don't think I intend to harm him? No? Very good. In that case, he's coming with me."

"Of course, Justice."

He shook with the effort of reining himself in. But what choice did he have? He couldn't take on the Family Court. All Noyan would unite against him. He wouldn't stand a chance...

And yet, and yet... The world was changing. The Family Court didn't have quite the power it once had. It was part of the past. He was part of the future. If he could take them on, and win... If he could prove he had that kind of power... The very idea brought pleasure so intense it was almost physical. Michael grew suddenly calm. It was liberating, the knowledge that if it came to it, he could always kill her.

"Tell me," he said, as she helped Hotep to his feet. "I'm hearing all sorts of rumors. How did Sanja die? Was it really an accident?"

"No, I don't think so. Someone killed him."

"Any idea who?"

The Justice draped Hotep's unresisting arm around her shoulders. "There are a number of possibilities. But he was approaching the age of Choosing..."

"You think his parents did it?"

"It's a possibility that has to be investigated."

"Of course, Justice. If there's any way I can help...?"

"I don't think so. Unless you happen to know who killed him?"

"Me, Justice? Of course not. I can't imagine anyone wanting to kill Sanja. He was such a nice young man. A bit wild, but sound underneath. I think you must be wrong. I think it'll turn out to have been nothing more than a terrible accident, in the end."

The Justice nodded. She took a tentative step forward, stopped to resettle Hotep's weight across her shoulders, and then headed for the elevator. Michael waited for the doors to close. Then he told the 3-Vs to resume projecting. The Justice was once again slumped against the elevator wall, but continuing to support Hotep, even so. And the moment the elevator reached the ground floor she forced herself upright and banished all trace of pain from her face. He watched, fascinated, as she made her way through the lobby and out of the building. Then he put in a call to the Gwahnals.

CHAPTER 7

By its very nature, Choosing cannot be unjust. If, after due consideration, a full-grown child wishes their parents dead, then surely those parents deserve to die – if only for raising such an ungrateful child. And if a child wishes their parents to live, regardless of how cruel or neglectful they might have seemed to others, who has the right to gainsay the child? In Choosing, justice is a tautological necessity.
— From: Reflections, *Justice Daniel of Sweetwater*

The lobby carpet stretched ahead of her like an endless patterned desert. She longed to drop Hotep, but she couldn't afford to show weakness here, with Michael's heavies watching. Among them was a man nursing his right arm, and a grudge. She struggled on towards the door. She didn't have the energy for a rematch, and there would be no advantage of surprise second time around.

The door was stiffer than she remembered. She used Hotep as a battering ram to force it open. Her car was parked haphazardly a few feet from the entrance, and already colonized by a gaggle of street urchins. One daring brat was even sitting at the wheel, pretending to steer. She shouted at them to go away. They looked up, saw her encumbered with Hotep, and jeered. That was it. She shrugged the off-comer's arm from her shoulders, leaving him to stand on his own two feet.

Or not.

He landed on his knees, squealing. Served him right. He should have been supporting her, not the other way around.

The urchins stared open-mouthed. Then they scattered.

Such disrespect for a Justice of the Family Court would be unthinkable in a settlement – but then, settlers were still alive to community and tradition. City-dwellers were different. And Spate's Old Quarter was the worst of all. Here, outcasts were openly tolerated, and backstreet scrapers murdered children before they were even born, turning Choosing on its head and utterly disavowing the debt parent owed to child. When she thought of what her own mother had gone through, her refusal even to consider ending a life she hadn't chosen to create…

Screeching tires grabbed her attention. A large truck was skidding to a halt behind her car; six officers piling out of the back. The Auxiliary Court had come, belatedly, to her rescue, Ethan at their head. He hurried over, deep concern on his annoyingly handsome young face. "Are you all right, Justice?"

He placed a tender hand on her arm. She shook it off.

"You're late," she snapped, and pointed at two of the largest auxiliaries. "You and you: take this off-comer idiot home. The rest of you head back to the court. The excitement's over. Ethan, grab the cranking handle, you're coming with me. As for you, Hotep – stay at home, and keep out of trouble."

Her car was three steps away; she made it in six, and hauled herself painfully into the driver's seat. She'd done something to her back in the scuffle, and it refused to cooperate.

Ethan was ready with the cranking handle. She waited for the engine to cough into life, and then set off towards him. He jumped out of the way, grinning. She scowled, braked to let him climb into the passenger seat, then pulled away from the curb.

The street was cobbled; a traditional touch she would normally welcome. But right now, every jolt and rattle transferred itself instantly to her spine. How typical of the Old Quarter. Nothing here could be trusted. Everything looked just the way it should: cobbled streets, good solid stone buildings, all with flat roofs so people could sleep out in the heat of summer. But the people themselves were the least traditional anywhere on Noyan.

"I have to hand it to you, Justice." Ethan was leaning back comfortably, hands behind his head. "I wouldn't have gone in there on my own."

"I didn't have any choice. Not after you let them snatch Hotep off the street."

Ethan's smile wavered. He sat up. "We couldn't help it, Justice. If we'd tailed him any closer, we'd have been spotted."

A shameless old man was crossing the road ahead, blue outcast tattoo clearly visible on his forehead. She stamped hard on the accelerator and sent him scurrying back to the curb.

"Maybe. But that doesn't alter the fact you let them grab him."

"I'm sorry, Justice. We should've been ready. At the very least, I should have had a team on standby in the Old Quarter. It was always likely to be Michael."

"Why?"

"Lots of reasons. He's the biggest dealer. And he has the best product. Off-comers know the difference – and Sanja Gwahnal could afford to pay for quality."

A van pulled out in front of them. She worked the clutch and moved down a gear. "Good. I'll need to know everything we have on him. Who's running the investigation?"

"Investigation, Justice? There isn't one. Bi-tech smuggling isn't a breach of Custom."

"And that's all he does? With those kind of heavies

working for him? People who're willing to snatch an off-comer off the street? You're telling me he's a legitimate businessman, but you still want a whole truckload of backup before you'll go in there?"

"Well, no. But—"

"No. So why's no one investigating him?"

Ethan had the grace to look embarrassed. "He's got powerful backers, Justice. Lots of people use his bi-tech. Not just off-comers. Representatives, even. Michael isn't just any dealer. He's *the* dealer."

"Are you saying the Auxiliary Court is afraid to investigate?"

"It's not that. We try, but someone higher up the chain always says no. We need evidence to justify opening an investigation, and we can't get evidence because they won't let us investigate. So, we're blocked."

"Not anymore," she said. "This is now a Family Court matter. I don't need anyone's approval. And I'm telling you to investigate."

Ethan peered at her intently, and then nodded. "If that's what you want, Justice. But be careful. There are powerful people out there who aren't going to like it. And there's Michael himself. I'm not sure even being a Justice will protect you, if you get too close."

Beth smiled. She was back in a world she understood. "In which case he'll come to the attention of the Family Court, and learn some institutions on Noyan are still capable of discharging their responsibilities. But I don't think it'll come to that. Michael's not stupid."

"I hope you're right, Justice. I really do."

"I want him investigated, Ethan. I want to know everything there is to know. I want it done thoroughly, but discreetly. Understood?"

Ethan nodded. Beth smiled. She much preferred this version of him, silent and subdued, over his usual self-confident self.

They were approaching Government Center. The roads

were wider here, the buildings grander. Grandest of all were the Assembly and the Family Court, facing each other across the broad plaza of Main Square. This was where she would normally stop. But not today. She couldn't face the many broad, shallow steps leading to the court's imposing front entrance. Her back would never survive the ascent. She pressed on instead, driving into the maze of streets that led to the Auxiliary Court.

She pulled over and she swung her legs out, ready to climb down. And stopped dead, as a spike of pain lanced up her back. Ethan offered assistance. She refused it. Tried again. And reluctantly accepted his help. She couldn't risk spending the next few days lying flat on her back in bed.

She let him help her inside, then sent him back to the car for her satchel, while she called the elevator. He was back before it even arrived, and together they headed for the second floor. Then they split up; him to organize his team; her to find an office to requisition. There was plenty of space in the central, open area, but there was also a 3-V that stayed permanently on, polluting the air with off-comer propaganda under the guise of news. She preferred either a good old-fashioned wireless, or silence. She could have made them turn it off, but this was the auxiliaries' territory and she knew better than to interfere.

She found a suitable room by the back wall, and settled down behind its solid wooden desk. An office junior appeared with a hot sweet cup of casab tea. She took it gratefully, and sent him on his way with a message for Justice Jacob. There were two new outcasts in the cells at the Family Court, hold-overs from yesterday's Choosing ceremony; degenerates who'd refused the Choice of Death. They needed processing. She would have preferred to supervise the tattooing and sterilization herself, but Jacob was more than competent. And she had more pressing concerns.

The satchel was full of Sanja Gwahnal's inexplicable pamphlets. She emptied them onto the table. There were dozens of them, ranging from glossy full-color publications through to simple monochrome leaflets. Some were virulently opposed to the off-comers' biological technology. Others were straight-forwardly nativist, demanding the expulsion of all off-comers and making no distinction between Gallaskians and Commonwealthers. And then there were two short academic works on Choosing, both of which graced her chambers at the Family Court.

So, what was Sanja Gwahnal doing with this material? Was he secretly attracted to the Noyan way of life? And, if so, did his parents know?

She'd learned nothing from interviewing them. She should have made them come to her, not ventured into their territory. They'd been waiting for her in the innermost dome of their complex, a vast space filled with alien vegetation. It was like stepping into another world – a humid jungle planet, overgrown with not-quite-trees and almost-bushes, and buzzing with the sound of unfamiliar insects. Logic told her there couldn't be anything dangerous; not in the Gwahnals' private sanctuary. But logic hadn't prevented her from breaking out in a cold sweat, or wanting to flee when something multi-colored broke the surface of the central pond and stared at her with clusters of disturbingly intelligent eyes.

The Gwahnals were every bit as alien as their surroundings. They shared the same freakish red hair and disturbing blue-green eyes; more like twins than a married couple. If it weren't for Amaya's longer hair, and Fange's hint of stubble, she wouldn't have been able to tell them apart. There must be a world full of such bizarre people, somewhere out there. She wondered what it was called, and whether she'd ever heard of it. Probably not. She'd never had a great interest in off-comers.

The interview was a waste of time. The Gwahnals used their grief – real or feigned – to deflect her questions. They denied any knowledge of Sanja's interest in Noyan traditionalism; seemed genuinely horrified by the idea that he might have wanted to exercise the Choice of Death. In the end she'd cut it short, and gone in search of Hotep.

That interview had been far more productive. She'd felt so much more comfortable in her own car; and the off-comer's obvious panic left him little room for dissimulation. Like the Gwahnals, he'd been viscerally hostile to the idea that Sanja might have wanted his own Choosing ceremony. But unlike them, he didn't have an obvious motive to feign disgust. Did all off-comers share this loathing of Choosing? If so, why did they come here, and live among people they so despised? And why had Sanja collected the traditionalist materials currently spread out across her desk?

She sorted them into piles: pro-Custom tracts in one pile; anti-bi-tech in another; anti-off-comer chauvinism into a third. There seemed no particular pattern. The pro-Custom pile was taller, but only because one volume of collected speeches was particularly large: there were far fewer items in that group.

She went through them again, re-ordering them from moderate to extreme. A pattern began to emerge. There were many more leaflets advocating violence than peaceful resistance. And, interestingly, although they used different names, colors and sizes of paper, the printing on each was remarkably similar. And the font was always the same…

"Justice! You've got see this."

Ethan was in the doorway, beckoning. She was tempted to stay put, just to spite him, but curiosity got the better of her. She followed him out into the open office. Everyone was gathered around the 3-V, watching an off-comer news report. She was mentally preparing Ethan's dressing-down when she registered what the presenter was saying. The off-comers were no longer pretending Sanja Gwahnal's death was an accident. They'd switched to claiming it as another 'terrorist attack' – supposedly by the same group that attacked the roadroot system: the 'League of Free Noyim'.

The group's name was eerily familiar. It adorned several of the most extreme pamphlets currently sitting on her desk.

CHAPTER 8

So much for the 'indestructible' roadroots. So much for the endless claims of 'superior' off-comer technology. Can you imagine a sturdy Noyan road being destroyed by a fungus? Of course not!

The Movement for Tradition and Continuity extends fraternal greetings and heartfelt thanks to the League of Free Noyim. Thank you, brothers and sisters, for exposing our enemies' true weakness...

— From: A Welcome Blow for Freedom, *The Movement for Tradition and Continuity*

Samuel pushed his way to the front of the jostling crowd. Bridgeway's stand was always the most popular on market-day. It stood out amongst its staid neighbors, a riot of color demanding attention. Rows of tall, pink sugar-cones drew the adults; bowls of brightly-colored candies attracted children like magnets. He dropped his last few pamphlets onto the counter and ordered a cooling lemon sherbet; perfect antidote to the heat of the day. The stall holder served him politely, but never quite took his eyes off the many small hands closing in on candy-bowls and boiled-sweet pyramids. Samuel took a long swig of the cold, sweet sherbet and swirled it around his mouth, clearing away the dust of the market-place.

He closed his eyes, enjoying the first unequivocally good moment of a ruinously bad day, losing himself in the sensation of coolness, the delightful combination of sweet and sour. He took another swig, savored it briefly, and glanced around at the stall-holder, waiting patiently for payment, and the wide-eyed children gazing hungrily at the longed-for candies. He smiled, and paid for both the sherbet and a large handful of the brightest candies. He scattered the candies across the counter and watched, amused, as children descended on them like locusts. In moments the counter was bare and the children were disappearing with their prizes; all save the smallest boy who, left empty-handed, began to cry.

"Here, Matty." Samuel flicked him a half-penny. "Buy yourself something."

The boy grinned, tears instantly forgotten, and installed himself at the counter, ready to haggle. Samuel laughed and went back to drinking his sherbet. Moments like this were so few these days. Few and brief.

The sherbet finally reduced to nothing more than a lingering aftertaste, he set down the cup, retrieved the last of the fatuous pamphlets, and gave up his place at the counter. He walked along the stalls, glad-handing customers and stall-holders alike, passing out pamphlets as he went. Everywhere he looked he saw smiling, happy faces. No one was reluctant to take a pamphlet; not today. Everyone wanted to read his absurd paean of praise to the League's successful attack on the roadroot system.

Didn't they understand? Sanja's death had rendered the whole operation meaningless. The idiots were celebrating a victory, when they should be mourning a defeat.

The crowd parted, a sudden brief eddy opening to reveal John – loyal, earnest John – making a bee-line for him across the square. And he had Joshua in tow.

He couldn't face them, not now. He ducked behind the nearest stall, hurried past two specializing in spice and fragrant oils, and joined a crowd gathered at a booth selling skewers of grilled meat. He lost himself gratefully amongst them, glad of the market-day hustle and bustle.

New Beginning was not normally a place where anyone could lose himself, least of all Samuel.

He moved on without making a purchase, weaving between stalls until he happened upon a group of brewers from Sweetwater. They seized on him, peppering him with questions on the likely size and quality of the upcoming casab harvest. He had no choice but to stay and talk a while, assuring them it would be a vintage year with fruits plentiful and plump. Then he hurried over to the makeshift pens where the hill farmers kept their desiccated livestock. He spent a little time there before pretending an interest in an itinerant trader's cart. It was weighed down with clothing and fancy goods, and provided a useful cover to put more distance between himself and his well-meaning friends.

Everywhere he went, he dispensed pamphlets and fake good cheer. There were familiar faces throughout the crowd: some were mere fellow-travelers, supportive of the movement but unwilling to get their hands dirty; others were active League members – small-holders who provided safe-houses, tinkers who gathered information, even a few who were happy to participate in front-line action. For these especially, Samuel was ready with a smile and a friendly word. It was not in his interests to spoil their misguided celebrations.

Eventually, he reached a point where he could take no more: no more people, no more smiles, no more hand-shakes. He slipped away from the square and headed for the cooler air by the oasis. Noisy children were playing happily in the water, including many who'd benefited from his largesse at the Bridgeway stall. What a perfect day for them: no school, no work in the fields – just the excitement of market day, scrounged treats, and play. He sat down beneath the shelter of a broad-leaved casab tree and wished he could share their happiness. But he couldn't. Somewhere along the line he'd lost the knack of sharing happiness with anyone but Judith. And then, when

Judith…

A naked child dived, shrieking, into the water. He was glad of the distraction. There was nothing to be gained from thinking about Judith. Better to face up to the question that had been haunting his day.

Who killed Sanja?

The embassy? They were the obvious suspects. But if they'd decided to take out Sanja, why was Samuel still alive? Why were the Gwahnals? It didn't make sense. And the off-comers were many things, but they weren't irrational.

The Mitchesons?

No. Not them. If they knew anything, they'd have gone running to the embassy, telling tales. And they'd have done it *before* their precious roadroots were destroyed.

But who else? Could a League member have discovered the true–

"Sam?"

He twitched guiltily. John and Joshua, so long avoided, were standing over him. And there was no place to hide, no crowd to lose himself within. Even the children had moved on.

"You startled me. I was miles away."

"Sorry." Joshua ducked his head, deepening his perpetual stoop. Was he worried about hitting his head on a casab branch? Hardly. He wasn't *that* tall.

"Sorry, Sam," John echoed, a half-beat behind. As ever. They were old men, both of them. When had that happened? Samuel forced a smile.

"No. It's fine. What can I do for you?"

Joshua shuffled his big feet. "Leah and me, we wanted to ask… We'll understand if you say no. What with Sanja, and… And then there's Nathan all fired up… But we were wondering… We wanted to ask a favor…"

"Ask away."

"Right. Well. It's Rebecca, Sam. Her Choosing comes up two weeks' tomorrow. We wondered if you'd speak for us. It would mean a lot, to all of us."

Rebecca's Choosing? They still thought that mattered? What was wrong with them? Sanja was dead. Didn't they understand what that meant?

But no, of course they didn't. He'd worked long and hard to make sure none of them understood. So, here they were: nervous, excited, hopeful, looking to the future.

Idiots.

And he was an idiot too. Because despite everything, he was moved. He stood up and gripped Joshua's arm. "I'd be delighted. But are you sure? Wouldn't you rather have a properly trained Advocate?"

"We're sure."

"Justice Joanna won't like it. You know she wants us using full-time officials."

"That's why we're not having her officiate. We don't need more outsiders poking their..." Joshua glanced around, suddenly wary. "Anyway, we're getting Abraham from Overwater. Daniel's putting him up at the inn for the night."

Samuel nodded understanding, and approval. It was a sad necessity, but the Family Court had to be kept at arm's length. Their cause might be the same; but their methods were very different. No Justice could ever be seen to condone direct action, however justified.

"So, Rebecca's coming up to her Choosing, is she? Hard to credit. How old was she when you moved here?"

"I'm not right sure... It was the year after the big drought. That must be fifteen, sixteen years ago now? She would have been turning three. Four maybe? Yes. That's right, she'd just turned four."

"Four? Where does the time go?"

"Scraped if I know." John laughed and shook his head. "Another year or so, and we'll be holding ceremonies for children who were born right here..."

Samuel stared at him, eyes cold, voice wooden. "We've already had one."

"Scrape, Sam. I'm sorry. I wasn't thinking. I didn't mean—"

"No. Of course you didn't. I understand. I wish I could forget Eve's ceremony, too."

John's mouth was flapping uselessly. Joshua stepped into the breach, all earnest intensity. "But you shouldn't, Sam. You should celebrate it. What Judith... When she did what she did, afterwards... That doesn't alter the fact that Eve made the Choice of Life. You should..."

Samuel tuned him out, letting the words float past him, unheard and unacknowledged. No one had the right to tell him how he should feel. Better if he had no daughter. Better if she'd never been born. Better if she'd been scraped.

If he didn't have a daughter, he'd still have a wife.

"It wasn't your fault, Sam." John had found his voice again, and was using it to spout nonsense.

Not his fault? Of course it was his fault. He should have known. He should have been there. She never would have done it, if he'd been there.

How could he have missed it? How could he have failed to realize what Eve's Choice of Life meant for Judith? She'd always regretted her Choice of Death. How could he not have seen what it would do to her, when her own daughter made the Choice of Life?

He forced a smile. "Come on," he said. "It's market day. Let's go and have a drink."

He had no interest in sharing his innermost hurt with these people. All he wanted was to go away and leave them far behind.

The market square was much quieter now. Some of the traders had already left; others were packing up. Only the food stalls were still doing a roaring trade – food stalls, and the inn, which was full to overflowing. Drinkers had spilled out into the square, unable to find a place inside. That wouldn't be a problem for Samuel. There was always a place for him, if he wanted it. He steeled himself to endure yet more friendly faces, but was spared the effort when a breathless youngster intercepted him at the door. He was needed in the Assembly Hall; the wireless had fresh news about Sanja Gwahnal.

The Hall always seemed so much bigger when it was empty: even more so like this, with Nathan and his cronies huddled together around a wireless on the far side of the circle. Nathan had claimed the inner tier for himself. His young followers occupied the bench behind and above. Except for Eve. She was with Nathan; only the polished wooden wireless came between them.

Samuel strode across the empty space, glad for once to have Joshua and John dogging his heels. No one else here would be on his side.

He nodded a greeting to Nathan. It went unacknowledged. The wireless filled the silence with a recitation of headlines, a news program repeating the highlights and signing off. It confirmed the breathless boy's report: the Commonwealth embassy had finally conceded the obvious truth: Sanja had been murdered.

And they were blaming the League.

So, either they knew nothing – or far, far too much.

The broadcast ended. Nathan raised a lazy finger, signaling Eve to turn off the wireless. Silence fell. Samuel filled it. "Well? What did I miss?"

Nathan's pose of laziness gave way to outrage. "That wasn't enough for you? You want more?"

"I'd like to know if–"

"You want an excuse for doing nothing. As usual. And there isn't one. Not this time."

"Is that what you think we did last night? Nothing?"

"Destroying a few roadroots? Big deal."

"It was a big deal. And you seemed happy enough at the time. What's up? Embarrassed you managed to get yourself lost on the way back?"

"No. I'm not embarrassed. I'm furious. Sanja's dead. They killed him. And we're doing nothing! That's not how it's supposed to work. They kill one of ours, we should kill ten of theirs."

Eve was blushing. Was she angry, too? Or upset by the open confrontation.

"Ten? Why not twenty?"

"Why not? You need to call an Assembly. Right now. It's time to go to war. No more pinprick attacks. No more sabotage. War."

Nathan's cronies were stamping their feet. No surprise there. But they wouldn't be the only ones listening to Nathan this time. Call an Assembly? No way. Not until he was certain of winning the vote.

"War with whom, Nathan? Sanja's killers? We don't even know who they are."

"It doesn't matter! The off-comers are going to come for us, next. We have to strike first."

"And let them dictate our timing? No. We move when we're ready, and not a moment sooner."

"We are ready. The people support us. They just need us to lead the way. Once we start fighting, they'll rise up and we'll–"

"They might. They might not. We don't know. Not for sure. But I'll tell you what we do know. We know we didn't kill Sanja. And everyone else is going to realize that, and soon. And what are the off-comers going to do then? There goes their excuse for coming after us. And along with it, any credibility they have left. They'd love us to go to war. They want an excuse to crush us."

"So that's your answer? Sit back and do nothing? Let them pick us off one by one? What's wrong, Samuel? Going soft in your old age?"

"Not soft. Just older, and wiser. Come on, John, Joshua. We're done here."

Angry cat-calls followed them out. That was okay. Angry opponents were stupid opponents. What bothered him was John tugging at his sleeve the moment they were outside.

"He's right, Sam."

"About what? Going to war?"

"About calling an Assembly."

Joshua was nodding agreement. He longed to shake some sense into both at them; to tell them how stupid they were, how naïve their hopes and dreams. But this was no time to alienate allies; not with Nathan so obviously on maneuvers.

"Of course he's right. And I will call an Assembly. As soon as we have more information. We've worked too long and too hard to risk everything by moving before we're ready. Facts first. Then decisions."

They didn't look convinced. How long did he have, if he couldn't even count on their support? One day? Two? Any more, and there'd be an Assembly whether he called it or not. And a vote for war. And if he was on the wrong side of that vote, what then? No mystery to that. He'd be out, and Nathan would be in.

Maybe it was a mistake to wait any longer. Maybe he should just go; leave these people, this place, this whole planet, far behind...

"But you know what we really need right now?" he said. "That drink. More than ever. Come on. Let's see if there's room at the bar."

He set off without waiting for an answer. They could follow or not, as they chose.

The inn was a welcome haven. There was no talk of Sanja's death, or the need for an Assembly: not with so many outsiders listening in. He drank, and encouraged his companions to drink; greeted old acquaintances; gladhanded customers and creditors alike. And finally, there came a moment when he was no longer the center of attention, and he slipped away unnoticed.

Outside, the warmth of day had given way to the bitter cold of night in the desert; a welcome relief after the noise and light of the tavern. Sober despite the amount he'd drunk, he made his way through the cluster of buildings and on to the top of the rise, where his house stood alone. It wasn't much to look at: the first and smallest building in the settlement. They'd built it together, just the two of them, all the way up here, an impractical distance from the oasis. That was Judith's decision. She'd loved this spot, and the view over the valley. She'd spent endless hours tending their small garden. It was barren, now. Nothing but weeds and rocks. He wound his way up the familiar path, reached for the door handle... and stopped.

Something was wrong. What?

Reflected firelight flickered red-orange in the window. Someone had lit a fire in his hearth.

But who? Not Sanja. Not this time, and never again.

Eve, perhaps? Come to make up with him? No. She was too firmly in Nathan's camp.

So. Not Eve. Not Sanja... Sanja's killers? Was it his turn tonight?

He reached into his jacket and took out the small pistol he kept hidden there. There was no point in running. He wouldn't get very far without the contents of his strongbox. And he couldn't risk going for reinforcements; not until he knew who was waiting for him. There were too many things he couldn't afford his friends to know.

He cocked back the hammer. The click was loud in the stillness. Too loud. He pressed himself flat against the wall, gun ready, breath held. And waited.

And waited.

Nothing happened. The door remained closed. There was no sound from inside, no shadow disturbing the firelight in the window. He let out a long, slow breath, lowered the gun and made his way to the back of the house.

It wasn't Sanja's killers. Of course it wasn't. No assassin would have risked lighting a fire to advertise their presence. But he kept the gun at the ready. Whoever it was, they'd come uninvited, at a dangerous time.

The back door opened all but silently. The kitchen was

empty. He crept through to the inner door, and carefully opened it just wide enough to see inside.

Someone was sitting in the armchair in front of the fire, boots stretched out towards the fireplace. Familiar boots. Boots inlaid with a fantastical pattern of loops and whorls picked out in brilliant gold. And tapping against the boots, an elegant cane.

Samuel pushed the door open and strode over to the fireplace. He waved the pistol in vague, ambiguous, greeting. The Gallaskian didn't respond. He was staring at his boots, seemingly lost in thought. His long brocade jacket was dark green, and decorated with yet more garish golden spirals; his pony-tail was draped over his left shoulder at just the right careless angle. Samuel snorted, went over to the sideboard, and poured himself a generous glass of casabey from the waiting bottle. But he did so using only one hand, and without setting the gun down.

Jimawn's stick ceased its regular tapping. The sudden silence was intense, and strangely unsettling. Samuel froze with the glass half-way to his lips. The off-comer sat up and rested his hands on the cane's sculpted silver head.

"It crossed my mind," he said. "That maybe you killed Sanja."

Samuel drained the glass in one swift motion. The words hung there; not an accusation, but definitely, if indefinably, a threat.

"Why would I do that?" he said. "Sanja was a friend of mine."

Jimawn said nothing. His face was unreadable.

"He's no use to me dead, Moyem."

"That's true."

"I had no reason to kill him."

"Now that…" Jimawn took one hand off the cane, and relaxed back into the chair. "That's not true. You had plenty of reason. Pride. Fear of your associates discovering who you really worked for…"

"I don't know what you're talking about."

"Yes, you do. You're a liar, Samuel. And a traitor to your own people. But I don't think you killed him."

Samuel poured himself another drink, walked past Jimawn, and sat down in the chair he usually offered to guests. "What makes you so sure I didn't kill the mother? I thought about it often enough."

"But that's just it. You thought about it, and yet he went on living."

Samuel stared at his glass. Jimawn was right. There was a time he'd only have had to think about it once. Something vital had been cut out of him; and Judith had wielded the knife.

Jimawn stood up. "I'm not going to waste time with threats, Samuel. If I thought you'd killed Sanja, or that you weren't any more use to me, you'd be dead. I suggest you strive to ensure that I never do think that. Not even for one minute. Do you understand?"

Samuel said nothing. Jimawn nodded, taking his silence for assent. "Good. We've worked together happily in the past, you and I. I never objected to your relationship with the Gwahnals, not even when I learned how selective your targets had become. But Sanja's death changes everything. You belong to me now. And I have something I need you to do."

He paused; waiting for objections, perhaps. None were forthcoming. What was the point?

The off-comer reached into a jacket pocket. "This is for you. It's a jammer…" He tossed a fist-sized ball of white fluff into Samuel's lap. Samuel glanced at it, and recoiled. It was a cocoon. A *scraping* cocoon.

He flicked it to the floor, shuddering.

"Careful with that. I went to a lot of trouble to get it for you. It jams Commonwealth communication systems. Not for long. It won't live for more than an hour once you let it out, but it'll jam everything for up to half a mile. And an hour's plenty of time for what you need to do. Just be careful when you cut the silk. The antennae are very sensitive. Damage them, and it won't work anywhere near as well."

Samuel stared at the thing with loathing. He made no move to pick it up. "Okay. So, what am I supposed to do that takes less than an hour?"

Jimawn smiled. Again, he reached into his jacket. "That's where this comes in. And this... I'm not going to throw. This one's dangerous."

Samuel flinched. The Gallaskian was holding up a hive the size of a toddler's head; a green, cone-shaped monstrosity, welted with ugly pustule-yellow bumps.

"Here's what I want you to do," he said.

Samuel listened in silence. He felt no emotion: not fear, not horror; not anticipation. His mind was made up. He had wealth enough, thanks to Sanja. All he needed now was time, and opportunity. Then Jimawn could give all the orders he liked. Samuel wouldn't be around to obey them.

CHAPTER 9

*I solemnly swear to be faithful to the ideals of the Service, to be
truthful, honest and diligent in the pursuit of my duty, to obey the legal
orders of my superior officers...*
– From: The Regulator's Oath, (Revised "Anatol" Version)

Jodan looked in on the boys' room. Hesas had climbed
in with Evershem, and the two were curled up together on
the pad. Evershem's left arm was around his little brother,
his right on the coverlet. His hands were so small and so
perfect; the nails neatly clipped; the fingers and palms well-
scrubbed. What had Jodan's hands looked like when he
was six? Not so clean, he could be sure of that. Nor so
soft.

His children were lucky. They wouldn't have to fight
for candlelight to work by, for every scrap of paper, for
attention from teachers who didn't care. They would have
everything they needed, because they had a father. He
would be there for them, ready to push when necessary,
rewarding success and punishing laziness. How far might
they go, his sons? What might they become? However
high they rose, nothing could make him love them more
than he loved them at this moment. He leaned forwards,
brushed the fair hair from Evershem's forehead and kissed

him. His son shifted in his sleep, but didn't wake. Good; it was too early for the children to stir. Too early for Jodan himself, after such a late night. But he had no choice. He yawned and turned to go. Errina was standing in the doorway, a finger to her lips. He crept out to join her.

"They couldn't settle last night," she whispered. "Not without you to tuck them in."

She was at her most beautiful like this; her hair all tousled from sleep, her skin clean of make-up. How did she look so fresh, when she'd waited half the night for his return? He reached over, pulled her to him and kissed her warmly on the lips – making up for last night, when he'd been too tired to do anything but sleep.

"I'm sorry," he said. "I would have called but…"

"I know. I saw the news. That poor child. The Gwahnals…"

"It's going to be a tough few weeks, Rina. Long hours. Short nights."

She nodded acceptance. "Was it murder, then?"

"Sorry, Rina. I can't talk about it. Commissioner Hozefa's taken over the case. There are… bad things happening. Things that have to be stopped before they get much, much worse. Not just here on Noyan – all over the Commonwealth. I've got to go into the office now, and I don't know when–"

"You'll let me make you breakfast first?"

"I can't, Rina. Really, I can't. Hozefa–"

"Would prefer you to be able to think straight. There's no point going in early if you're no use to anyone when you get there. Come along, it won't take me a minute to fix you an oat-mash. And then I'll know you're set up for the day, and I won't worry about you so much."

He gave in. He couldn't refuse her. She was his wife, the mother of his children – the woman who'd cost him a year's wages in fees to a Caliban marriage broker. And she'd been worth every last credit. Their wedding had been the best day of his life; better even than when he graduated from the Academy. It had been a final vindication of all the years of hard work. No one questioned his lack of a certificate of genealogy. His background hadn't mattered – not beside his Commonwealth credits, and his prospects. And it still didn't matter – not to Errina. She'd stayed loyal to him through all the setbacks and disappointments that followed.

He wolfed down the breakfast, kissed her goodbye, and hurried to the garage and the waiting vehicle. It set off at once, the 3-V already projecting the embassy call sign. He took the call, but it was nothing urgent – just progress reports from the night before; and most of those unnecessary. They were working late. Fine. He already knew that. Pointless reports didn't impress him. He'd have to have another talk with the team about time-wasting.

He dismissed the connection and stared out at the passing scenery. Dawn was giving way to clear morning light, revealing the ugliness of Noyan architecture in unforgiving detail. Row after row of soulless, square buildings stretched into the distance, devoid of life and individuality. Noyan technology was inferior in every respect; not just utility, but aesthetic. No wonder so many Commonwealthers were willing to breach the embargo. They didn't just want the convenience. They ached for the comfort of soft, familiar, organic curves.

But just because he understood them, didn't mean he forgave them. Not when he knew the consequences. Not when it led to what he'd seen at Sanja Gwahnal's house. And when he found out where the boy had acquired that house brain, he was going to…

Wait. The progress reports. One was missing. He'd heard from everyone *except* the team at Hotep's house. Either they were too busy gathering evidence to waste time on make-work, or they hadn't reported in because they didn't understand the importance of what they were doing. If so, he'd make it his business to ensure they never, ever made the same mistake again.

"Car: put in a call to–. No, cancel that. I'll call from the office."

He'd already arrived. The dull angular world of native streets had given way to a green and growing fairyland: the Commonwealth embassy. He drank in the sight. There was nothing like it, and no better place, anywhere on Noyan. The embassy was a dream landscape of living domes and graceful minarets; a paradise where buildings and nature merged and became one; where leafy, delicate bridges spanned scented gardens of Homeworld vegetation, and winding paths led past tranquil pools teeming with multicolored life.

"Car: let me out here."

He needed this: needed to walk through the grounds, and refresh his soul. The car could park itself in the garage until needed.

It was cold outside. Not Caliban cold, but the lingering nighttime chill of a climate cursed by too-hot days and too-cold nights. He set a brisk pace to keep the chill at bay, striking out across the bright plaza before veering off down a winding path beside a small stream. It took him through colorful flower gardens and sunken grottos, past gentle waterfalls, and ended where sunlight sparkled on the fountain in front of the Ambassador's minaret…

…and shabbily-dressed natives congregated in shared misery. Some were old, ancient even; some were surprisingly young. They wore rags and cast-offs; scraps of Commonwealth clothing pulled over drab native homespun. No two were dressed alike. But all of them had the same unsightly tattoo disfiguring their foreheads: a large blue oval; a zero to mark their shame.

These were the Family Court's victims. Outcasts. Un-people. Living ghosts. Parents who refused to die at the whim of their ungrateful children – children who rejected the very thing he'd spent his entire childhood longing for: a mother and father of his own.

He opened his wallet and pressed credits into limp

hands. The outcasts didn't cluster around, didn't pester for alms, or embarrass him with thanks. They were the most passive beggars he'd ever known; utterly conditioned to expect nothing but hostility. He continued until his wallet was empty, and then hurried on towards the green spire that housed the Office of Regulation.

The front door opened at his approach, but he declined the invitation. It was too fine a morning to take the cramped paternoster up to the office. Far better to stay outside, ascend the spiral walkway, and marvel at the profusion of flowers wreathing the safety railing.

The office was busy, despite the hour, but there was no sign of the usual crowd gossiping at the building's main trunk. That was as it should be in a time of crisis. Everyone was heads-down, either in conference with workers in the field, or consulting the vast resources of the embassy brain itself. Far from being the first in, he was one of the last. He hurried to his desk, a quarter turn around the circle, and told the 3-V to put in a call to Hatcher.

The boy appeared; blinking, bleary-eyed. He didn't look like he'd slept at all. Well, good. His was an important task. The fact that Jodan had only assigned it to him to keep him away from Mito was neither here nor there. The 'report' for the Family Court had to be convincing. Commissioner Hozefa himself had briefed the boy on what he wanted it to say.

"Good morning, Hatcher. How's the report coming?"

"Uh… it's almost finished, sir. I just need to–"

"Good. Good. I want it on my desk by lunchtime."

"I'll do my best, sir."

"See that you do. And don't cut any corners. The natives don't have access to bi-technicians, but they do have some surprisingly sophisticated amateurs. They're going to push back if we insult their intelligence."

"Yes, sir. I was thinking I'd go with the car as the source of infection. He took it everywhere with him.

Someone could have poisoned it any time it stopped to feed. What do you think, sir? Will that work?"

Jodan smothered a smile. The boy reminded him of Evershem: so eager to please.

"I don't see why not. The car makes sense as a transmission vector. That's why we checked it out in the first place. And feeding's a good angle."

"Yes, sir. Only, I know we're supposed to blame the fungus from the roadroots attack, but I'm worried that narrows the window too much. Everyone saw how fast that happened. If it turns out the racer hadn't left the house recently, no one's going to buy that it took that long to kill the house…"

"True, but… No. I don't think it's an issue. We can just say it took longer because cars aren't roadroots. They can hardly question that."

"No, sir."

"Tell me, Hatcher. Do you find this task distasteful?"

"Sir?"

"Lying in an official report. Does it concern you?"

"Um…"

"If it doesn't, it should. We wouldn't lie to anyone, even the Family Court, if there were any alternative. But the commissioner's right. We have to deal with that brain right now, before word gets out. Nothing else matters. But that doesn't mean we have to like it. Understood?"

"Yes, sir."

Jodan wasn't at all sure the boy did understand, but hopefully he'd planted the thought, at least. And that reminded him… "Good. And one other thing. I want you to push the line that the fungus looks like an accidental byproduct of bad buds circulating on the black market. That's likely true, and it'll help keep pressure on the dealers. The commissioner wants us to blame terrorists, but there's no reason we can't advance the long-term mission along the way."

"Yes, sir. Of cour–"

Jodan cut the connection. Something was going on by the 3-V in the refreshment area. A crowd had gathered, and a colleague was beckoning him over. "Hey, Hyrom. You're on the Gwahnal case, aren't you? You've got to see this."

He went reluctantly – and stared open-mouthed at the appalling news. The Family Court had carried out dawn raids throughout the city. The elite of Commonwealth society – or at least those of their offspring who were known friends and associates of Sanja Gwahnal – were being rounded up for questioning. Those who resisted had been arrested; and if they refused to surrender, threatened with deportation for breach of Custom.

It was an outrageous affront to good relations between Noyan and the Commonwealth. And a message: the Family Court wasn't buying the 'terrorists' cover story.

Hozefa wasn't going to be happy. And saying 'I told you so' wasn't going to help. He'd better double-check Hatcher's report before it went out and make sure it was as strong as it could be, or no doubt he'd end up taking the blame when the natives rejected it. He was, after all, still nominally in charge...

Which led to a serious question. Why was he only learning about this now? And from the 3-V?

He was really starting to hate that Family Court creature. First, she snatched Hotep out of his custody. Now she ...

Hotep. He still hadn't heard from the team at Hotep's house.

He hurried back to his desk and put in a call. The house answered. Not his people. The house. It politely informed him that the team from the Office of Regulation had left yesterday morning, and could it help with anything else?

No wonder Mito tried so hard to get him to reassign the team. He'd needed Jodan to put a seal of legitimacy on something he'd already done. Except it hadn't worked.

And now Mito was in deep, deep trouble.

He knew Homeworlders were loyal to each other, but this… This was insane. Career-ending. And Jodan would be more than happy to testify against Mito at the court-marshal. In fact, he'd start the process right now, and suspend the degenerate from duty, with immediate effect. It didn't matter how short-handed they were. Better a gap in the team than someone undermining the mission from within.

He put in the call, and found himself staring at the embassy call sign.

"I'm sorry, Regulator Hyrom. Regulator Mito is unavailable. Would you like to leave a message?"

Regulator Mito? Since when?

"No, I don't want to leave a message. Where is he?"

"Regulator Mito is in a meeting with Commissioner Hozefa."

Commissioner Hozefa. Yet another Homeworlder.

"Is he now? Is he really?"

"Yes. Regulator Mito is in–"

"Put me through to them. Right now."

The call sign was replaced by Hozefa's assistant, Mino Cherayn. "Regulator Hyrom. What can I–?"

"I need to speak to Mito. Urgently."

"I'm sorry, Regulator, but the commissioner gave me strict instruct–"

"I'm sure he did. But as I said: this is urgent."

"Yes, Regulator Hyrom, but the commissioner was very specific. I can't put anyone through under any circumstances."

"You'd put the ambassador through."

"Yes, of course."

"So, you can put me through…"

"I'm sorry, Regulator Hyrom. Perhaps you'd like to leave a message?"

"No. End call."

He stormed over to the central trunk and stepped into

the paternoster. It carried him to the top floor, and Hozefa's office. Cherayn rose sleekly to intercept him. And, surprisingly, ushered him meekly inside.

Hozefa and Mito were standing together, two chubby peas in a pod, pouring over a tabletop contour map. They straightened up, smiling. Hozefa was positively avuncular. "Regulator Hyrom. How can I help you?"

Something was wrong. They shouldn't be smiling. They should be angry. He'd just barged in on their meeting. And why was the contour map sinking into the table? Like it was something he wasn't supposed to see.

"Uh... I need a word with Mito, sir."

"Regulator Mito, can you spare Regulator Hyrom some of your time?"

"Of course, sir."

The oh-so-careful politeness, the use of Mito's entirely unmerited new title... It was all much, much too formal.

He shouldn't have come here. It was a mistake. A big one. But there was no way to back out now.

"Mit... *Regulator* Mito, why did you go against my direct orders and discontinue the search at Beynan Hotep's house?"

Hozefa put up a restraining hand. "I can answer that, Regulator Hyrom. Those men were reassigned on my orders."

"Your...?"

Of course. He should have known. Homeworlders looking out for each other as usual, come what may.

Mito was smirking, outright smirking. Didn't the man understand the significance of what they'd found at Sanja Gwahnal's house? Mito wasn't a political appointee. He had no excuse. And now it was down to Jodan to make the commissioner understand.

"You have to send them back, Commissioner. Hotep's our only way of tracing that house brain back to the dealer. We need–"

"No, Regulator Hyrom. *We* don't need to do anything.

I am doing something. Something less obvious than sending bi-technicians to stomp all over Hotep's house. Something that won't have every dealer who ever sold contraband to Sanja Gwahnal going into hiding. That's why I took over this investigation. I have access to… let's say more *specialized*, personnel. People who know how to be discreet. People who are already hard at work, and whose job is going to be difficult enough without us getting in the way. So, we're going to leave it to them. Understand?"

"Yes, sir."

Jodan's cheeks burned. He could only imagine how red his face was. And all because he'd let his resentment of Homeworlders get the better of him. Hozefa knew what he was doing. He understood the seriousness of the crisis.

"Yes, sir. I'm sorry, sir. I'll leave you to it…"

He backed up, attempting to retain what little was left of his dignity. Hozefa nodded a dismissal and turned his attention back to the table. Instantly, the contour map began to reform.

And Jodan stopped.

They'd called off the search in the morning. Before they found the brain. Not after. Before.

"You knew. You knew Sanja's house had a replication-capable brain before we ever got there. That's why you called them off. You already knew."

The contour map sank back into the table. Hozefa was looking at Jodan. And he was no longer smiling.

"A replication-capable brain, Regulator Hyrom? On Noyan? Don't be ridiculous. Regulator Mito, did you find anything like that in Sanja Gwahnal's house."

"No, Commissioner. Nothing remotely like that."

Was the sheen of sweat on Mito's forehead a sign of embarrassment? Or purely a marker of his addiction?

"That's what I thought." Hozefa nodded sagely. "No, Regulator Hyrom. This was a simple terrorist murder. We've even received a note from the League of Free

Noyim, claiming responsibility."

This couldn't just be about protecting Beynan Hotep. There had to be more to it. Was Hozefa corrupt? Was that why he wanted the investigation ended? Because someone was paying him off?

"It won't work, Commissioner. There's no way you'll be able to keep a lid on something this big. It's bound to come out. When do you want to admit what's going on? Now, while we can still do something about it? Or when it's too late, and Noyan makes Nephrate look like paradise?"

"Nephrate? Regulator Hyrom – you're overwrought. You've been working too hard. You need to stop and think. Why don't you take a few days off? And when you're ready, we'll have a talk about your future. You're a family man, aren't you? And long overdue promotion. A little extra money would be nice, I'm sure. Some extra vacation? Why don't you go home and take a little time. Think about it."

"And just let you—"

"Please, Jodan, let me finish. I was going on to say that, once you've had time to think, you'll understand there's nothing to worry about. Let's suppose, just for a moment, that the embargo truly had been breached. Don't you think I'd do everything in my power to repair it? And don't you think I'd prefer to use discreet, possibly even unofficial, means to do so?

"There's nothing for anyone to worry about. Provided they do as they are told. On the other hand, should a regulator take it into his head to disobey his superiors, then that might be a cause for concern. Should such a regulator start to imagine all sorts of conspiracies where none exist... Well, we might have to consider whether such a regulator was perhaps suffering from some kind of psychiatric disorder, brought on by overwork. Hard to overstate the consequences for a man like that. For his career. His family. The shame of it... Go home, Regulator Hyrom.

Get some sleep. Take a little time to think, and then we'll talk. Mino will see you out."

Cherayn escorted him out of the office, and stayed with him all the way down to the garage, deep in the building's root system. Jodan was dimly aware of the man speaking, but the words slid past him, lost in general numbness. He climbed obediently into his official vehicle, and made no protest when Cherayn ordered it to take him home. Where else could he go? What else could he do? Hozefa was a well-connected Homeworlder. And Jodan had no evidence. Resistance wouldn't achieve anything, except to ruin his career and destroy his children's prospects.

Could he do it? Could he sit back, keep silent and accept promotion? Would it really do any harm? Hozefa had to heal the breach in the embargo – if only to save his own neck. And really, was it any surprise that the commissioner wanted to do so without exposing his own culpability? Was that really so bad? And higher pay would be nice, as would the chance to see more of his family...

Errina welcomed him back with an affectionate, if puzzled, kiss. The children ran from their playroom to greet him. He shooed them away, and immediately felt guilt overlay his other emotions. They had done nothing to earn his rejection.

He told the house to ready a tub, and headed for the bathroom. Alone once more, he stripped off his clothes, stepped into the hot water and tried furiously to scrub himself clean.

CHAPTER 10

The superiority of our system of morality lies in its understanding that obligation only ever flows from choices we make.

In less enlightened societies, children are born indentured, forever indebted to the parents who brought them into existence. We reject this utterly. Individuals are not born with obligations; they can only acquire them through choices they make. It is the parents who made the decision to create a life; therefore, it is the parents who are obligated, not the child.

This understanding — that only choice begets moral obligation — is why ours is the first truly moral society.

— From: Collected Speeches, *Justice Jeremiah of Deep Mine*

Beth awoke to familiar, crushing disappointment.

It had all been a dream. She wasn't really twenty, garlanded, about to make her Choice of Life. She was old, and tired, and all too alone.

Of all dreams, this was the worst. After a nightmare, she at least awoke to a better world. From this dream, she awoke to reality and the awful truth; there was no Choosing ceremony for her, nor ever had been. She could never make the Choice of Life, never show the world how much she loved her mother, never express her gratitude to the woman who chose to bear her, to endure a nine month — no, a lifetime's — extension of rape; just so that Beth might live.

Her alarm clock was ringing. Loud. Insistent. She reached out wearily to shut it off.

And dissolved in agony.

It was worse than ever; a dreadful, unimaginable pain running from her neck to the base of her spine. The pain was her whole world. It absorbed her, possessed her, denied the possibility of anything outside of itself. She screamed and went on screaming, not for relief or in the hope of being saved, but because she could do no other.

Eventually – a minute, an hour, a lifetime later – the agony subsided. She lay there, breathless, gasping; afraid that the slightest movement would bring it back. Time passed. An insect crawled slowly across the vaulted ceiling. She watched it, envying its freedom, slowly building the courage to try again.

The insect took wing, shaming her inactivity. She risked raising her right arm. Nothing. No pain, at least; only stiffness. She set it down again. Then raised the left, and the shoulder this time. Again nothing. She closed her eyes, summoned all her will-power, and levered herself upright. Her back was tense, sore, but there was no repeat of the earlier agony.

She swung her legs onto the floor and hobbled, achingly slowly, across the room. Was the sink always so far away? The medicine cabinet so hard to reach? From now on, the pills stayed by her bed. She opened the bottle with fumbling, anxious fingers, and swallowed two of the small pink pills. Then she stood motionless by the sink, waiting for them to take effect.

Half-closed blinds filtered the sunlight, casting striped shadows on the wall – and on her reflection in the cabinet's clouded mirror. She stared at herself. Somewhere underneath that mask of wrinkles was the girl she used to be; the girl she'd been in her dream. She was getting old. How could she continue to function as a Justice when she needed pills even to get out of bed in the morning? Maybe it was time she quit the court and returned home.

She missed everything about Marshtop. She missed the trees and the green fields, the people; the smell of the sea. And most of all, she missed her mother. Why not go back and live among people who respected her, people who honored Custom and the Family Court?

But to go back was to be surrounded by reminders of the one thing that separated her forever from friends and neighbors. She'd attended their Choosing ceremonies; even officiated more than once. She'd seen them declare their love of family, watched them joyfully affirm the bonds of community and kinship. And not even for one moment had she ceased to be conscious that she would never be able to do the same. How could it be otherwise, when her mother had had no choice in her conception, and her father was put down before she was even born?

One by one, her peers had gone through the ceremony that marked the true transition to adulthood. Then their children had done the same. And now, even grandchildren. But there would be no ceremony for her, no affirmation of love and gratitude. It was easier, and less painful, to remain here in her chambers, solitary, far from home and the illusion of belonging.

There was a knock at the door: three firm taps. Her privacy was so rarely invaded these days, not since Justice Malachi died. None of the other Justices lived in chambers anymore. At best, one or two would stay over when some duty ran late, and it wasn't worth going home.

Whoever it was, they weren't welcome. She didn't want to see anyone yet. Not until she had the strength to change out of her nightgown.

Another knock; more urgent this time, and accompanied by a familiar voice. "Justice? Are you all right?"

Ethan. The very last person she wanted to see her in her night clothes. "I'm fine!" She took an angry step towards the door... and her legs started to give way. She clutched at the sink, and just managed to stop herself from falling.

"No. I'm not. You'd better come in."

The door opened – slowly at first, and then quickly when he caught sight of her. "Justice. What's wrong? Let me help." He hurried to her side, strong hands gripping her left arm, holding her up.

Why did it have to be Ethan? She glowered at him. His clothes were rumpled, his chin unshaven, his eyes red. He looked almost as bad as she did.

But not as old. Nowhere near as old.

"The toilet," she said, aware of a sudden urgency. He helped her out into the corridor. On one side, the cloister and the inner courtyard; on the other, empty chambers. And at the far end, the communal bathroom. She shuffled towards it, wanting to go faster, but wary of losing her footing despite Ethan's supportive arm.

"Is it your back, Justice?"

"Of course it's my *scra...* Yes. It's my back." She hated this feeling of vulnerability. And his sympathy was worse.

"Should I fetch a doctor?"

"No. Just open the *sc...* Open the door, please."

He pushed it open and helped her through. It was embarrassing to be so dependent; and yet at the same time there was something surprisingly pleasant about leaning on his strong arm.

"No doctor," she said. "I'll be fine. I just need time."

Their footsteps echoed in the emptiness of the bathroom. It was large enough for ten Justices, but only Beth used it now.

"Do you want me to start the interviews, Justice?"

The interviews? Of course. The immediacy of pain had overwhelmed everything, even duty. No wonder Ethan came looking for her.

"No. They can wait. We'll be there soon enough."

He helped her to the nearest cubicle; would have helped her inside, but she pushed him away and entered on her own. This time, her legs held up. She closed the door on his worried face.

Lifting her nightdress was easy enough. Lowering herself onto the seat was more daunting, but proved less difficult than she feared. The pills were finally kicking in. She sighed contentedly, as much from the simple relief of emptying her bladder as the prospect of regaining her strength.

"What's it like down there?" she asked.

Ethan's laughter bounced off the walls. "Total chaos, Justice. Spoiled young off-comers in every holding cell, lawyers demanding access, reporters swarming the front entrance. I've never seen anything like it."

"Good. Maybe I'll leave the questioning for this afternoon. Let the pressure build."

"I don't know, Justice. I'm not sure we can hold them that long. The 3-V's full of talking heads complaining about 'harassment of Commonwealth citizens'. Their embassy's lodging a protest with the Assembly. A lot of powerful people are real unhappy with us right now."

"I don't care. What about the Michael investigation? How's that going?"

"It's not, Justice. I've got Jude's team running surveillance, but there's nothing for them to keep tabs on. Michael's people all left the streets yesterday afternoon. It's like he's shuttered his entire operation. You'd think there was a turf war going on, but nothing's happening. No businesses getting shot up. No fires. No one getting killed."

"Except Sanja."

"Yeah. Except Sanja."

She rose from the toilet. "So, we'd better see what Sanja's friends have to say, then."

A quick pause to adjust her clothing and flush the toilet, and then she was exiting the cubicle. Ethan offered his hand, but she waved him away and walked stiffly across to the row of basins.

"Head back to the Auxiliary Court, and keep a lid on things there. I'll join you as soon as I'm dressed. Oh, and drop in on the registrar's office on your way – let them know I'm unavailable for any Choosing ceremonies until further notice."

"Of course, Justice. You're sure you don't need my help?"

"I'm sure."

If she couldn't dress herself, she'd go back to bed and let someone else lead the investigation. Especially if the alternative was letting Ethan help.

It took her twice as long as usual, but by the time she emerged from her chambers she was ready to face the world. Her dress was the simplest she owned: pale light-brown cotton covering her from neck to ankles, and a pair of open-toed sandals on her feet. She'd hung her gun, sundries bag and wallet on a broad leather belt, and slung it around her shoulder like a bandoleer. It wasn't the most elegant look, but it allowed her to function, and that was all that mattered.

She walked the long way around the cloister, avoiding the fierce sunlight in the sandy courtyard. The central sculpture – Levi's final, sublime masterpiece 'Choice Accepted' – seemed almost to shimmer in the heat. With so few Justices remaining in chambers, it was long past time the piece was relocated to Main Square, where more people could appreciate it. But she didn't have the heart to suggest the move. She'd miss it too much on her quiet, meditative walks around the cloister.

Her car was waiting outside. She ignored it. The Auxiliary Court was within walking distance, and while she was confident of climbing behind the wheel, she wasn't at all sure she'd be able to climb down again. A little exercise would help her back recover, and avoid any potential embarrassment.

She knew it was the wrong decision as soon as she turned the final corner and saw the crowd of reporters besieging the court entrance. She'd never seen so many in one place: Noyim in brown homespun carrying big boxy cameras; off-comers in their gaudy clown-suits. But it was too late to back out now; she'd already been spotted. Reporters swarmed her, off-comer cameras hovering overhead, competing to get the best pictures. Her simple, practical clothing no longer seemed like such a good idea. The loose shift, jury-rigged bandoleer – and worst of all the gun in plain sight – did not represent the image of the Family Court she wished to project.

She pressed on, refusing to break stride. Noyim reporters fell back respectfully, while off-comers took their place and bombarded her with hostile questions. She ignored them, and the scuffles that broke out between off-comers and outraged Noyim. Only when she reached the entrance did she turn to face the jostling crowd. The temptation to vent her irritation was almost overwhelming, but she resisted it. This wasn't the time for emotion; nor for game playing or provocation. She politely declined to comment, informed the reporters she had an active investigation to run, and retreated into the safety of the building.

She took the elevator to the second floor – and almost went straight back down again. Ethan hadn't been exaggerating. If anything, the scene was even more chaotic than he'd described. Auxiliaries, off-comers, lawyers and clerks were milling around in noisy confusion.

She pulled back the metal lattice of the inner-gate, and stepped out of the elevator. A bubble of silence spread through the room. It reached the 3-V, where a tiny version of herself stood on the outside steps delivering her brief no-comment. Then the noise resumed, louder than ever. And, to her astonishment and outright fury, a blue-green bird-thing flew across the room and hovered just out of reach. Its wings were a blur of motion, its grotesquely outsized and disturbingly intelligent jet-black eyes focused unwaveringly on her. She snatched at it, but the thing skipped effortlessly out of range.

An auxiliary was talking to a familiar-looking off-comer at a nearby desk. "You," she snarled. "Get that thing out of here before I wring its neck. This is a murder investigation, not a press conference."

The auxiliary jumped to obey and made a bee-line for the bird-thing. It rose a little higher, staying out of reach. And still its unblinking gaze never shifted from her face. She itched to draw her gun and shoot it, but there were too many people around. The danger of an accident was just too great – especially with other auxiliaries already hurrying to help. One retrieved a broom and tried to swat the thing out of the air, only for it to fly still higher. Then, suddenly, it was diving down in response to a call.

"Wattles! Here Wattles." It was the familiar-looking off-comer, now standing and holding out his left hand. The bird-thing flew straight to him, and perched on a finger. The off-comer smiled, seemingly entirely unfazed by her fury, or the milling group of angry, embarrassed auxiliaries.

"Who are you?" she asked. "And what's that camera doing here!"

"Dil Mahtal, Justice. Perhaps you know me from–"

"No. What are you doing here?"

"That's what I was going to ask you, Justice. You had me arrested, so–"

"You're a friend of Sanja Gwahnal?"

"Yes, of course."

"Then you're a witness and potential suspect. And you're illegally recording the proceedings of the Family Court. Get that thing out of here before I have it destroyed."

"Poor Wattles." The off-comer shook his head with mock weariness. "No one's ever glad to see him these days. Very well. Wattles, wait for me outside."

The creature flitted to an open window, and was gone. Beth looked the off-comer up and down. He seemed to enjoy the inspection. She did not. His pale skin and yellow hair were unpleasantly foreign. There was something else, too – a preening self-confidence, an expectation that he'd be recognized...

"Where have I seen you before?"

"On my 3-V show, I expect. Dil Mahtal's the na..."

"I prefer the wireless."

"Really? How quaint."

Beth glanced back at the window. There was no sign of the camera hovering outside, but nor was there anything to stop it returning. She beckoned to the nearest auxiliary. "Bring this man to my office. I'll interview him there."

She only realized her mistake when she saw Sanja's pamphlets lying spread out across the office table – with the most extreme pamphlets still at the top. The off-comer was right behind her, complaining loudly that there was no need for the auxiliary to hold his arm. She hurried to the other side of the table and scooped everything into a drawer. What had the off-comer seen? More than she wanted, that was for sure.

"What did you say your name was again?"

"Dil. Dil Mahtal."

"Dil Mah..."

"Mahtal. It's usual in the Commonwealth to have two names. The second is a patronymic that–"

"I'm familiar with the concept, thank you." She sat down, and indicated the chair on the other side of the desk. The off-comer shook himself free of the auxiliary and sat down. He crossed his legs with studied, and not entirely convincing, nonchalance

"Sanja Gwahnal," she said. "How well did you know him?"

"Reasonably well. I mostly deal in 'human interest' stories. And humans are generally interested in the rich and powerful. He was good material."

"Well enough to know who'd want to kill him?"

The off-comers eyebrows shot up. "Well, yes. The

terrorists who murdered him, presumably."

"Those would be the traditionalist 'terrorists' who somehow use off-comer tech so sophisticated it can destroy roadroots and houses? Those 'terrorists'?"

Mahtal frowned. She smiled, enjoying a small victory.

"So," she said. "Leaving aside those very unusual 'terrorists' for a moment, who else do you think might have wanted to kill Sanja Gwahnal."

"Nobody, Justice. Not anyone who knew him, anyway. There were plenty who thought he could do with a good hiding, but that was about it. He was only nineteen."

"And what about you? You bore him no ill-will?"

"None whatsoever. I'm always on the lookout for good material for my show, and Sanja was *very* good material."

"I see. And you'd be happy to provide us with details of your whereabouts on the night of the murder?"

"Oh course. It's hardly a secret. I was at the Mitchesons' gala dinner, along with everybody else. I can let you have a copy of my report, if you like. It was the event of the season – though it's been overshadowed since, of course."

"And what about the Gwahnals?"

"Like I said. Everyone was th–"

"You misunderstand me. I meant: might the Gwahnals have wanted to kill Sanja?"

Mahtal froze. "Of course not! Why would you even think that?"

"Why would I not? Sanja was murdered. The killers were clearly off-comers, or had access to sophisticated off-comer tech. Where else should I look for suspects, when someone's killed just short of his twentieth birthday?"

"What does that have to do with anything?"

"Everything – if his parents were afraid of the Choice of Death."

The off-comer gaped at her. And began to swear. His reaction was, if anything, even more extreme that Hotep's.

Were all off-comers this arrogant? Did they really think they could live on Noyan and yet not be subject to Custom? That their children wouldn't be able to avail themselves of Choosing?

She barely listened to the man's tirade. It was obvious she would get nothing from this interview, and there was definitely no point asking him to help with her investigation; he and his audience would be irredeemably hostile.

His audience... Anything she said to this man would go straight out on 3-V. So, what story did she want him to tell? The truth – that she was floundering, confused by Sanja's contradictions? Hardly.

No. Misdirection. Use him to put the killers at their ease. Convince him she was entirely focused on the Gwahnals. They were still suspects, after all. Not *likely* ones, with so many loose ends and inconsistencies in Sanja's life – but they might still be guilty. And she could always apologize to them afterwards, if they were innocent.

By the time she let Mahtal go, he was practically shouting. She had no doubt what the topic of his next show would be; hopefully the killers would see it, and become complacent. She needed every edge she could get.

The following interviews were more prosaic. Rich young off-comers paraded through her office: each and every one of them sullen and resentful at having been dragged down to the Auxiliary Court. And all of them seemingly convinced that Sanja had been every bit as naïve and vapid as themselves. None of them knew – or admitted to knowing – anything of Sanja's interest in traditionalism. Sanja Gwahnal had clearly been living a double life. And that, surely, was what lay behind his murder.

So: she had a likely motive. And she knew the means. The question was: who had both?

Maybe her misdirection wasn't a misdirection at all. Maybe the Gwahnals found out about their son's double-life, and panicked?

Whoever the killers were, she was wasting her time interviewing Sanja's friends. They were dupes, believers in his cover story. She needed to look elsewhere for the truth.

There were only a handful of people remaining to be interviewed. She picked up the list, ready to hand it over to Ethan and tell him to manage the rest. Then one of the names caught her eye: Zachariah of Westway. A Noyan name. And a famous one. Zachariah's mother was the founder of the Westway retail empire – and wealthy enough, evidently, for her son's Noyan background to be forgiven by his off-comer friends.

She told them to send him in, but frowned when the auxiliaries returned with a young off-comer instead; a dandy whose Chameleon-clothes flowed with ever-shifting colors. She opened her mouth to snap at them; and closed it again. This wasn't an off-comer. It was a Noya in off-comer clothing. He slouched over to the waiting chair, reached for it, frowned in puzzled silence, and then pulled it back. Was he expecting the chair move on its own?

Of course. That was exactly what he was expecting. Beth shuddered.

"Zachariah of Westway?"

"I prefer Zach, actually. Zach Westway." He lowered himself onto the resolutely unhelpful chair. Aside from his clothing, he seemed a perfectly average young Noya.

"Do you? Well, Zachariah, I'm Beth, Justice of the Family Court. And I'd like you to tell me about Sanja Gwahnal."

The young man blinked. "Tell you *what* about him?"

"Everything. What kind of person was he? Bright? Thoughtful? Did you like him?"

"Like him? Of course I liked him. We were friends."

"Interesting. Do you have many off-comer friends?"

Zachariah sat up straighter. "Yes. Some of us aren't prejudiced."

Beth sniffed. And wished she hadn't. Something was

irritating her nose, a strange chemical smell... Was he wearing perfume? She couldn't bring herself to ask. "And what about Sanja. Was he prejudiced? What did he think of us?"

"Us?"

"Noyim."

Zachariah shrugged and looked away. "I don't think he thought about 'us' at all. He didn't care where people were from. He just wanted to have a good time."

"Really? Then you'd be surprised to learn he had traditionalist sympathies?"

"No way! Commonwealthers hate trads. Like I said – he only cared about one thing: having a good time."

"Even if that meant using a lot of black market off-comer technology?"

Zachariah licked his lips. "Maybe, but that doesn't breach Custom."

There was a knock at the door. Beth looked up, scowling. Someone was about to learn a painful lesson about not interrupting while she was interviewing. Except that this was no mere team member; it was Ethan himself, carry a candlestick telephone in one hand, its speaker in the other, and trailing the wire behind him.

"Justice. It's Ruth of the Assembly for you. She says it's urgent."

CHAPTER 11

I am often asked how I brought myself to eat 'real' meat. There are several answers I could give: that for me it was a rite of passage; that everyone should do so once; that an excess of politeness can lead one to do the most astonishing things. The honest truth, however, is that I was so drunk at the time, I was barely aware of what I was doing.

— From My Time on Noyan: Memories of a Youthful Exile, *The Rt. Hon. Beynan Hotep na Massowic*

The nipple was as big as Bey's thumb, and the same shade of pale grey-green as the rest of the kitchen wall. He touched it, and a drop of white pap oozed from the tip.

House pap was no worse than honey, really, when you thought about it. Better, in fact. Honey came out of an insect's ass, and was meant to feed grubs. House pap fed wholesome things, like cars and cleanerbugs. And people. Poor people.

Very poor people.

He turned away. He was hungry, but he wasn't starving. Yet.

He opened the fridge, now marked with a regulator's stamp identifying it as contraband, and took out the last bottle of native ale. The moldy cheese was gone. Either the refrigerator had finally integrated with the waste disposal systems, or the regulators had disposed of it for him. Or taken it away for testing. Who fucking knew? The way his luck was going, they probably thought it was the source of the roadroot fungus.

He held the bottle up to the light. The contents were black and treacly. Not exactly his idea of a decent breakfast, but it was better than nothing. He twisted off the cap, one of the many new skills he'd acquired in exile, and sniffed at the top. Yeast and molasses; this wasn't alcohol, it was liquid bread. He drank, deeply. It helped. A little.

He was so fucking hungry. He'd only had one meal all day yesterday – at the Gwahnals' house, waiting to be interviewed by the Justice. After that, nothing.

Well, not nothing, exactly. There'd been plenty of bowel-loosening terror. He'd known Michael wasn't the kind of person you crossed, but... FUCK. The man was terrifying. If it hadn't been for the Justice showing up...

And what was all that about? How had she even known where to find him? And all those heavies, backing off. Why? Just because she was from the Family Court?

Whatever – he owed her one. The way Michael had been looking at him, just before she showed up... He'd never been so scared.

He wandered into the living room. The regulators had been through here as well. Every item of furniture was tagged with a regulators' mark; even the 3-V had a little label suckered onto it, passing it as legitimate. His everyday clutter was pushed into a corner of the room; a pyramid of empty ale bottles, garish cardboard wrappers from native food stalls, fruit-rinds and nameless things he couldn't even identify. The rest of the room was spotless. Bey had to laugh. There couldn't be many places that looked better *after* the regulators had been over them... It was useful, too: the clean areas gave him a good picture of the extent of the regulators' search. They'd only been through half the downstairs, and hadn't touched upstairs at all. His stash remained undiscovered and unmolested beneath the bathroom floor.

Where had the fuckers gone? It was like they'd just upped sticks and left, right in the middle of turning his place over.

He'd expected to be arrested the moment the auxiliaries dropped him off. He hadn't even minded the idea that much. The regulators were scary, but not Michael-scary. And at least he'd be safe with them. And he wouldn't have been fucking starving.

He belched loudly and threw the empty bottle onto the pile with the rest the trash. That had taken the edge off, no doubt. But he was still hungry as fuck.

What to do? He had to eat. So, either he headed out in search of supplies, or he sucked on that green nipple.

The nipple was a nonstarter, so that left going out. There was a native bar not too far away. He'd eaten there once or twice. They did three different kinds of spiced meat, roasted on skewers over an open fire. He'd stopped going when he found a piece of bone on his plate, and understood what he was actually eating. But right now, he didn't care. He was practically drooling.

It couldn't be that dangerous, could it? This was a nice, safe area, so far out in the suburbs it was barely part of Spate at all. Michael's people wouldn't be looking for him out here, would they?

Why not? The fuckers had to know where he lived. It wasn't like it was any kind of secret.

At least the house was some protection. It wouldn't let people in without his say-so; and would immediately call the embassy if anyone tried to break in.

He told the house to activate the 3-V, and slumped down bonelessly onto the sofa. He barely noticed it molding comfortably around him. All his attention was focused on the 3-V and a full-size projection of his dead friend.

Poor Sanja. It was still hard to believe he was dead.

Yesterday had been far and away the worst day of Bey's life – worse, even, than his fourteenth birthday, when Grandfather Massowic caught him *in flagrante* with an aphrobug.

Sanja wasn't the only familiar face projected into his living room. An endless parade of friends and acquaintances followed: all of them under arrest and helping the Family Court with its enquiries. The report segued into a potted biography of Sanja, and finally his own image appeared in a brief cameo. How strange to see himself from the outside; not the hero, but a minor player in someone else's story.

Then it was back to the news report. The Justice was still insisting Sanja had been murdered. But now, amazingly, the regulators seemed to agree. Yesterday, Regulator Hyrom couldn't have been clearer: Sanja's death had been a terrible accident; he'd been killed by black market bi-tech, and it had all somehow been Bey's fault.

Now they were admitting the Justice was right.

Was that why the regulators had stopped mid-search? Because Sanja wasn't killed by illicit bi-tech? How pissed off must Regulator Hyrom be, robbed of his chance to harass an innocent Homeworlder?

And what about Michael? If the regulators weren't blaming black market bi-tech, Michael couldn't still be worried about Bey talking, could he? Not when they were saying it was terrorists…

But *fuck*, the Justice was right about it not making any kind of sense. Native terrorists, with the know-how to do something like that to Sanja's house? And the fungus attack on the roadroots? No way. They'd have used axes, explosives, guns – and got nowhere. They didn't have – didn't fucking want – the expertise to make a fungus like that. They hated everything that came from outside, especially bi-tech.

So, if it wasn't an accident, and it wasn't terrorists, who was it? Who would have wanted to kill Sanja? And why?

And did they have anyone else on their list? Like Sanja's best friend, perhaps.

Because if they were capable of doing *that* to a house that was designed by the Gwahnals for their own son and heir, what chance did Bey have, stuck in this outdated hovel?

He had to get out of here. But where to go?

He'd tried calling friends; last night, when the Justice's men dumped him here. Not a single house had admitted to knowing their owner's whereabouts. No one wanted anything to do with him. He'd attracted the attention of the regulators, and no one needed that. And he'd pissed off the Mitchesons by making that big scene at their reception. And who knew what the Gwahnals thought about him? They'd lost their son. They'd be looking for someone to blame; someone other than themselves. And no one wanted the kind of trouble that came from ticking off the likes of the Gwahnals. He couldn't blame people for deciding to lie low and keep him at a nice safe distance.

Safe for them, maybe. Not for him. He was fucked.

Where could go? He needed to get away from everyone: Michael, the Gwahnals, the Mitchesons – and most especially, from whoever killed Sanja...

Of course! He jumped to his feet and hurried to the garage. His sad excuse for a car was busily exercising on its treadmill. A regulators' tag on the top declared it permissible within the terms of the embargo. No shit. A car like this would have been an antique in grandfather Massowic's day. But it was functional enough. The carapace was dented at the back, and more waxy than iridescent in places – he wouldn't have been seen dead in it, back on Homeworld – but it was basically sound.

On the other hand, it wasn't built for the desert. Sanja had always used one of his parents more rugged vehicles for the journey. Bey didn't have that option. The trip was going to be painfully slow, and seriously uncomfortable, but was worth it to get safely away from here. Anything was preferable to sitting around and waiting for Sanja's killers to come pay him a visit.

"Come on, car, you saggy old mold magnet. Open up. We're going out. Give me full opacity, and no lights. I might as well sleep on the way."

The car left the garage with him safely cocooned in a bubble of interior darkness, and the seat busily reconfiguring itself as a sleeping pad. He told the car to prioritize comfort over speed, and use the roadroot system wherever possible. Then he settled down to go back to sleep. With any luck, he wouldn't wake up until he was safe in the familiar, hospitable surroundings of New Beginning.

CHAPTER 12

Do you wonder, then, that we consider it a great evil to impose incurable mortality upon yet another generation of conscious beings? You who oppose us cannot claim to be indifferent to that mortality. You reckon it a great evil when a child dies before its parents. And yet the parents knew all along the child must die. Why this horror at something that was inevitable from the moment of procreation? Is it because you cannot bear to face up to the consequences of you actions? That you refuse to acknowledge that when you create a life, you cause yet another needless death.

– From A Moral Manifesto, *Isaac the Seer, Third Prophet of Nullism*

The bar at the Spateside Inn was packed with lunch-time drinkers. Beth headed for the snug at the back. Even that was full. A group of boisterous young women, settlers by their clothing, were occupying every bit of space around the booths. She tried to push through them, and met unexpected resistance. The women weren't hostile: far from it. They were laughing, smiling, slapping her on the back. There was even scattered applause. She was still struggling through them, mystified, when Ruth came to the rescue, taking her elbow and leading her through the jostling crowd.

"You can't blame them, Beth," she shouted, fighting to

116

be heard above the crowd. "That's what happens when you make an exhibition of yourself."

"What?"

"Here we are." Ruth pointed to an empty booth. There was no sign of the promised contact – just two half-eaten meals, and a pair of empty beer mugs. Ruth moved down the padded bench to make space for Beth. "David's ducked out until the fuss dies down. He doesn't like too much attention."

"Neither do I."

"Really? After the performance you put on?"

"What?"

"You don't know? You had a starring role in Mahtal's 3-V show. Never threaten to wring the neck of a bi-tech camera, Beth. Not unless you want the whole world to see you do it. Repeatedly. In full-color. It's not a good look."

A rare blush spread across Beth's cheeks. A camera. That grotesque bird-thing, in the Auxiliary Court. She should have shot it.

"How bad was it?"

"Bad. And the camera wasn't the worst of it. You shouldn't have let Mahtal anywhere near your investigation. People listen to him. Not just off-comers, either. And he's telling everyone you're a traditionalist sympathizer. That your office was full of 'extremist literature'. I assume you showed him Sanja's stash?"

"Not deliberately."

"Scrape, Beth. It's a good job we voted on jurisdiction last night. I'm not sure we'd win if the vote happened today…" A short, dark-skinned man slipped silently into the seat opposite. He was around forty, black hair peppered with grey, handsome in a weather-beaten settler way. "Beth, this is David. David, Beth the Justice."

He offered his hand. Beth took it. "David of…?"

The man withdrew his hand, frowning. Ruth filled the awkward silence. "David's agreed to answer your questions about Sanja's involvement with the traditionalist…

'movement'. I think he'd prefer to keep it at that."

The man nodded, reached for his empty mug, and set it down again, disappointed. Ruth hurriedly signaled a waiter for more.

"Understood," said Beth. "Did you know him well?"

David gave her a long, considering look. "I wouldn't say 'well'. We had... mutual friends."

"Friends who put out pamphlets?"

"Could be."

She glanced at Ruth. Her friend was biting her lip, willing this 'David' – if that was even his real name – to be more forthcoming. Why was he being so evasive? It certainly wasn't fear of being overheard: the noisy crowd gave them perfect privacy. Why agree to this meeting, if he wasn't willing to answer her questions?

"It didn't bother those friends of yours that he was an off-comer? What his family does?"

"I'm sure it did. At first. But money talks."

"So, it wasn't just a casual interest? He was an active supporter?"

"He was bank-rolling half the movement. There are a lot of unhappy people out there right now, wondering what they're going to do for funding."

A waiter arrived at their table, jug in hand. He refilled Ruth's and David's mugs, and produced a fresh one for Beth. "This one's on the house," he said, grinning. "I've always wanted to wring the neck of one of those cameras myself."

Beth scowled, which only broadened his grin. She waited for him to leave, then turned back to David. "None of Sanja's friends mentioned any of this."

"I imagine they didn't know. I don't suppose he wanted his parents to know, either."

"Or the embassy," said Ruth, quietly. "Except they had to have known. Or their spies are really bad at their jobs."

Beth took a swig of her unsolicited beer. It was pleasantly refreshing, if overly yeasty. "That depends," she said. "On how long this was all going on. When did Sanja start getting involved?"

David shrugged. "Two years ago? Something like that. Jimawn brought him to a meeting over at the Grain Hall."

"Jimawn?" An off-comer name, but not one she recognized.

"Moyem Jimawn," Ruth supplied. "He's with the Gallaskian Mission. He's meant to promote cultural ties between us and Autarchy. I suppose that's one reason for mixing in traditionalist circles..."

"And he introduced Sanja Gwahnal to traditionalists? What were the two of them even doing fraternizing in the first place? I thought Commonwealthers and Gallaskians didn't get along?"

"On a personal level?" Ruth shrugged. "Who knows? The Commonwealth and the Autarchy are enemies, sure. But individual people? That's different. Still, I wouldn't have figured Jimawn for a friend of Sanja Gwahnal's. They don't seem like they'd have much in common... But then, it doesn't look like Sanja's public image was the whole picture, does it?"

"No. It doesn't. And if the embassy knew he was financing traditionalists, and was involved in some way with this Gallaskian..."

David was nodding. "It makes no sense for traditionalists to kill him. He was too useful."

"And they wouldn't use bi-tech to do it," said Ruth.

David snorted into his beer. "No. Kind of difficult to persuade him to supply his own murder weapon, don't you think?"

Beth leaned forwards. "So, he wasn't just giving them money. He was giving them off-comer tech as well?"

David's face froze. He sat back, and took another swig of his beer. Beth did the same. The yeastiness wasn't too bad, now she was getting used to it.

Ruth filled the silence. "The way he died is the problem. Militants don't have that kind of bi-tech. The embassy does, but they'd never do anything to cast bi-tech in a bad light. And why kill him? Why not just arrest him? Or quietly ship him off planet to avoid a scandal?"

Beth nodded. Ruth was right. It didn't make sense. Even if the embassy knew about Sanja's involvement with traditionalists, why wait two years and then suddenly kill him? It was so... unnecessary. "I don't think it was planned," she said. "I think it just happened. Someone panicked. The question is: who?"

"But that's your question, not mine," said David. "You wanted to know what I knew about Sanja. Now you do. We're done." He stood up and drained his mug.

"Please, don't..." Ruth reached out to stop him. He shook off her hand.

"No. We're even now. No more favors. Don't call me again." He slipped out of the booth, and was gone. Ruth stared after him miserably. Why was she so upset? Unless....

"Were you and he ever...?"

"A long time ago. People change. Their politics change... Did he help, at all?"

"He did. You were right to call me."

Ruth smiled. She reached for her beer and made a visible, and unconvincing, effort at joviality. "Good. Now it's your turn. Are you going to tell me who did it?"

"Of course." They clinked mugs, toasting each other. "The parents, definitely. They killed him because he was a traditionalist. And so did the embassy. Which is odd, because the traditionalists also killed him, but they did it because he was an off-comer agent. And then there's Michael. I'm not sure why he killed Sanja yet. Maybe he was working for the regulators? It's a really easy case this. Everyone did it."

"So, an arrest's imminent?"

"Oh, absolutely..." She took a sip, and set the mug down. "Except I don't even know where to begin. Everyone's telling me a different story. Sanja Gwahnal was a good little off-comer, but he financed the traditionalist underground. He's pro-Noyan, but he loves off-comer technology. He–"

"Couldn't he be both? Maybe he wanted the best of both worlds: our way of life, but their technology."

"Right. So why wasn't he financing your faction instead of giving money to the people who hate off-comer tech?"

Ruth sagged back on the bench. "I don't know."

"No. Neither do I. But at least I've got an idea what to do next. I'm going to go and see this 'Moyem Jimawn', and ask him what a Commonwealther was doing associating with a Gallaskian official. And what that Gallaskian was doing introducing him to traditionalists... So, you need to tell me everything you know about our Gallaskian friends, and especially Moyem Jimawn. Drink up: there's work to be done."

CHAPTER 13

The Noyim, handicapped as they are by a soil unsuited to the cultivation of vines, have no native wine-making tradition. Their standard alcoholic beverage is a kind of beer (they call it 'ale') which varies greatly from region to region, being light and clear in the south, dark and heavy in the north. Other than beer, they produce rough spirits and a surprising variety of fruit-based liqueurs, the most notable of which is 'casabey', a syrupy white spirit derived from the fruit of the native casab tree. Casabey tastes much as honeysuckle smells, has many uses in cooking, and makes an excellent mixer.

– From My Time on Noyan: Memories of a Youthful Exile, *The Rt. Hon. Beynan Hotep na Massowic*

Bey woke with a start, and immediately panicked.

He'd never experienced an earthquake before, but he knew one when he felt one. His sleeping pad was rocking from side to side, tilting at an outrageous angle… And then slowly settling back down again.

Then he remembered, and blushed in the darkness. He wasn't at home, and it wasn't an earthquake. His poor excuse for a car was just struggling to cope with a desert track.

"Car: reduce opacity. Slowly. That's good. A bit more. Stop. And now I want to sit up."

The pad moved backwards and upwards; became a

seat. Sky and ground reorganized themselves, and began to make sense. He was far out in the desert, on something that barely qualified as a road, even by native standards. Two deep ruts, interspersed with still deeper potholes, climbed a steep hill in a series of sharp switchbacks. His poor old junk heap of a car wasn't made for conditions like these. What if it broke down, or became stuck? And wasn't that just a lovely thought to have all the way out here in the desert. Could it even call for help this far out? He could ask, but he wasn't sure he wanted to know the answer. There wasn't a lot he could do about it at this point.

Then the car was cresting the hill... and there it was: New Beginning, a small, dusty hamlet beside an insignificant oasis in the middle of a shallow desert valley. It couldn't be more than ten minutes away; and maybe an hour's walk, should his car fall victim to an especially predatory pothole. He sighed and sank back into the seat, vast unacknowledged tension oozing out of him. He was, for once, truly glad to be here.

New Beginning wasn't bad, as native settlements went. The locals were friendly, which wasn't the case everywhere. There was one girl who was *especially* friendly, and didn't even want paying afterwards, which *definitely* wasn't the usual situation; she was about the only thing that had made it tolerable to come all the way out here just so Sanja could pursue his incomprehensible enthusiasm for native pottery. She was probably still around somewhere. That'd be a major bonus. There weren't exactly a lot of things to do out here in the middle of nowhere. Not that it mattered. This wasn't about having a good time. He was here because it was the perfect hideaway: somewhere he could count on a friendly welcome, and where neither Michael nor the regulators would ever think to look for him.

There was no sharp dividing line where desert ended and settlement began, just a ragged encroachment of humanity – a pile of stones here, an abandoned piece of farm machinery there – and then somehow open desert had given way to dry, dusty fields. They were barely recognizable as cultivated land. Plants should be green, not sickly brown. And fields should be lush and full of life. Here, unhealthy-looking plants grew in thin lines on dry, ungenerous soil. A few peasants labored over the scanty vegetation – and stopped to stare blankly as his car passed by. How sad to lead a life so dull that an outdated bi-tech vehicle was a source of fascination.

The settlement itself was a cluster of grey, flat-roofed buildings built around a central square. The sole splash of color came from the oasis, where rainy-season flowers flourished year-round in the shade of yellow-leaved casab trees. A yard-long wilted leaf was drifting across the empty square, tumbling in the breeze. The car parked itself beside a lonely tractor and unsealed, allowing the baking heat of day into its cool interior.

Heat, and the smell of shit.

It didn't matter how much he braced himself, it was always a shock. A dry, desiccated place like this shouldn't smell of anything very much. But the self-sufficient settlers used human excrement to fertilize their crops, and the eye-watering smell pervaded everything. For once, it wasn't unwelcome: it reeked of safety. No one would think to look for a refined Homeworlder in a slum that smelled of shit.

The Inn was across the square. His stomach already growled in anticipation of a long-overdue meal, despite the ubiquitous smell. Last time he was here, Sanja had dared him into sharing a spit-roasted desert hare, and it had proved surprisingly palatable… He climbed out of the car and hurried towards the Inn's heavy wooden door.

And remembered, just that split-second too late, that native doors didn't open themselves.

His nose took the worst of it; that, and his right shoulder. The shoulder didn't hurt. His nose did.

He reeled back, swearing, and felt for damage. It didn't seem to be broken. There was no blood, amazingly, and pain was rapidly giving way to embarrassment. He glanced around the square, glad to see no potential witnesses. Then he noticed the door handle. And gulped. The vicious-looking metal bar had come within an inch of ensuring Grandfather Massowic could forget about great-grandchildren. He swallowed hard, opened the door and stepped inside.

And was greeted with instant silence.

The room wasn't full. There were only a few grubby-looking natives sitting at the tables. But they'd been talking happily enough when he walked in. And now they weren't.

He barely glanced at them. The back of the inn opened onto a courtyard – and right in the middle of it was a whole goat's carcass, turning over an open fire. Or, at least, it was supposed to be turning. Right now, the boy with the handle was staring at him open-mouthed. Bey didn't care. The smell of roasting meat was driving him crazy. His rumbling stomach was the only sound in the entire room.

The first time Sanja brought him here, he'd had to fight down nausea: the combined smell of stale beer, sweaty bodies, roasting animal flesh, and the all-pervasive shit, had been overwhelming. Now he was drooling.

But the silence was worrying. Someone should have called a friendly greeting by now. Someone always did.

He made for the bar. The steward had been staring at him like everyone else, but now he was suddenly busy drawing fresh tankards of ale for an elderly couple sitting at the bar. And taking a very long time about it.

What was wrong? The last time he was here, he and Sanja hadn't had to buy themselves a single drink. And the village girls had been all over them. Didn't they recognize him?

Oh fuck. The girl couldn't be pregnant, could she?

No. The natives took contraception *very* seriously. Even the youngest girls he'd fooled around with had been extremely careful.

Still, you never knew. His eyes scanned the room in search of an outraged father, but found only a forest of backs. He didn't know what he'd done to offend them, but clearly, he'd done something. Coming here had been a huge mistake. Maybe he should just leave...

"Beynan! What a lovely surprise! Let me get you a drink." Samuel, good old Samuel, was standing in the doorway. "Daniel – a bottle of casabey for me and my friend Beynan!"

At last, someone was offering what he needed most in all the world – a friendly smile. Instantly, the atmosphere in the room lightened. Conversations resumed. People were drinking again. Bey was no longer the center of attention. He could barely speak, he was so moved – but Samuel didn't seem to notice. He marched up to the bar, clapped Bey on the back, and guided him to a table. "It's good to see you, Bey. I was worried, after what happened to Sanja... Are you okay?"

"I'm fine. All the better for seeing you."

He couldn't remember the last time he'd been so glad to see anyone. Fuck, but he must be desperate. Not that he minded Samuel. The man was warm and friendly, and even managed to look distinguished, for a native. It was probably his thick white hair that did it.

The barman arrived with a bottle of casabey and two earthenware mugs. Samuel seized the bottle, and poured two generous measures. "Good. Good. Now, let's have a drink – to friendship, and to Sanja."

"To Sanja," he echoed. Casabey wasn't his drink of choice (it was too strong, over-sweet, and gave him terrible hangovers) but just now he could imagine nothing better. He downed it in one, feeling it warm his throat and his heart.

By the time he'd drunk two more, and had a plateful of the goat with bread on the side, he was feeling a lot better. It helped to unburden himself, to have an audience who was genuinely interested in, and sympathetic to, his tale of woe. It had been days since he talked to someone who didn't want anything from him; someone who knew Sanja as a friend, and shared his sense of loss. Someone who was completely sympathetic to his desire to lie low for a while… until he mentioned the Family Court. Then Samuel's expression suddenly became opaque, unreadable.

"Who are you hiding from? The regulators, or the Family Court?"

"What? No. Not the Family Court. They're fine with me. They dropped me off at home. The Justice… she helped me. It's weird. One minute she seems nice, and then the next you realize what she…"

Samuel's bushy eyebrows were crawling upwards. Bey hurriedly stopped talking and took another gulp of casabey.

"Go on," said Samuel. "The next thing you realize what?"

"It's nothing. It's just… I'll never understand the Family Court, how you people tolerate it."

He knew it was a mistake as soon as he said it – but, Samuel didn't seem offended. If anything, he was amused. "We don't 'tolerate' it," he said. "We celebrate it. We're *proud* of the Family Court."

More casabey appeared in Bey's mug. He drank greedily, and waited for Samuel to refill it.

"You know what the trouble with you Noyim is, Sam? You don't even realize how weird you are. Anywhere else, killing your parents is just about the worst crime you can commit. And here on Noyan, you actively encourage it!"

"No, we don't, Bey. Only the Advocate of Death claims to want that – and nine times out of ten, no ninety-nine out of a hundred, and more – that role's purely ceremonial. I bet you've never attended a Choosing Ceremony, have you?"

"Atten… att…" Bey was struggling to speak all of a sudden; his words tripping over each other.

"Are you okay, Bey? You seem a little... out of sorts."

Samuel was peering at him with a curious intensity. Bey tried to answer, but no words came. Had he really drunk that much? And why was it suddenly so dark? Maybe he should...

CHAPTER 14

There are those who would have us emulate the Commonwealth, and enrich ourselves through trade. Others would rather see us copy the Autarchy: embrace self-sufficiency they cry. I agree. And we should begin by expelling every single off-comer. They talk of progress and prosperity, but what they really mean is change. And I don't want Noyan to change. I want us to remain forever true to ourselves, and to the moral foundation of our society.

– From: Collected Speeches, *Justice Jeremiah of Deep Mine*

Beth tried to understand. Why hadn't the Gallaskians built something more in keeping with their surroundings? Why create this brutalist glass cylinder at the center of a sterile grey wilderness? What was she even standing on? Plastic? Ceramic? It covered every inch of the Mission grounds; a vast oil slick that somehow was as unyielding as stone underfoot.

Why do it? Why create something so utterly alien in the heart of the city? Was it a statement of power? Were the Gallaskians showing they didn't care if they offended their hosts? Hardly. Elsewhere, the Autarchy were assiduous in cultivating the Noyim – and blackening the name of the Commonwealth. Perhaps she should ask Moyem Jimawn to explain.

She trudged towards the featureless building. It wasn't

129

truly made of glass. It couldn't be: there were no panes, no structural elements. Whatever the material was, it was seamless; a single perfect mirror, visible only through reflections and discontinuities: sheared off buildings; bisected clouds.

The closer she came, the more her reflection grew. Finally, she stood within touching distance of herself, and stopped: she'd arrived.

There was no sign of a door, but she'd been warned not to expect one in these flawless walls. Her reflection scowled back at her; old, tired, and irritated. "My name is Beth, Justice of the Family Court. I'm here to speak with Moyem Jimawn."

Movement, to her left; ripples in the surface of a liquid mirror. A section of wall melted away and revealed – or created – a precise, rectangular opening. The invitation was unmistakable. She squared her shoulders and marched towards it.

Beyond the opening was a corridor: blank, translucent walls ending, incongruously, in a conventional wooden door. Was that meant to reassure her? If so, it wasn't succeeding.

How little she knew of them: glass that was not glass, technologies she couldn't even begin to guess at, motives that were utterly opaque. Was it a mistake to come here? Should she have made Jimawn come to her? Or was it better to be reminded of the sheer scope and depth of her own ignorance?

The door opened. A man was on the other side. He was older than she expected – maybe fifty or so, and dressed in absurdly elaborate off-comer clothing; a froth of white lace at his throat; blue waistcoat embroidered with complex silver whorls and curlicues.

"Justice, please–"

"You're Moyem Jimawn?"

"No, Justice. I'm his valet." The man bowed an apology and gestured sweepingly to invite her inside.

"Please, do come in. Hetman Jimawn will be with you momentarily. Perhaps I can offer you refreshment, in the meantime?"

The room looked like the parlor in a prosperous Noyan home. The walls were painted white, and hung with landscape paintings — not of some alien world, but familiar desert and lush southern marshes. They compensated, a little, for the absence of any windows. There was another door on the far side of the room: a twin to the one she'd just come through. But the *valet* — whatever that was — pointed at a pair of wing-backed chairs either side of an ornamental fireplace.

"Please sit, Justice. You'll take tea?" A silver tea-service sat atop a lace-covered occasional table.

Beth shook her head. "No. But you can tell me what a *valet* does. Apart from serve tea."

The man's eyes had a peculiar fold; it leant an alien quality to what were otherwise handsome features. "Of course, Justice. A valet is one who performs personal services."

"Personal services?" She lowered herself into the chair furthest from the doors. "Such as?"

Once again, the man looked at a loss. "Such as helping a gentleman dress and shave, Justice."

"You mean Jimawn can't dress himself?"

"I wouldn't know. I've never had to try." And here, finally, was Moyem Jimawn himself, entering through the far door. He bowed, and favored her with a self-deprecating smile. If anything, his clothing was even more absurd that his valet's. From his long crimson frock-coat — overlayed with intertwining golden whorls — to his polished shoe-buckles and ridiculous silver-topped cane, he was like a caricature of off-comers at their most ridiculous.

"Hartan's been with me since I was a boy," he explained. "As he was with my father before me. And as *his* father was with my grandfather." He sat down in the other chair, elegantly sweeping his over-long frock-coat aside in an obviously well-practiced maneuver. "Thank you, Hartan. I'll take it from here."

The valet bowed and disappeared through the far door. Beth waited for it to close behind him. "He really shaves you?"

"Indeed. And an excellent job he does, too."

Jimawn was much as Ruth had described him: a tall man, around thirty, who might easily have passed for a Noya, were it not for that same odd off-comer fold to his eyes. And, of course, no Noyan man would ever dress like that. Or wear a pony tail. And a Noyan cane was a practical tool for walking, not a foppish silver-topped fashion-accessory.

"You're not embarrassed that you can't even shave yourself?"

"Quite the opposite. I'd be embarrassed to deprive a craftsman of his trade. Skilled craftsmen – and women – are the bedrock of the Autarchy. We're not like the Commonwealth. We don't seek to replace people with devices."

He was altogether too smooth, this diplomat. But she wasn't here to trade niceties. She wanted answers.

"Why did you destroy this entire block?"

"I beg your pardon?"

"Why did you level the whole block? You can't be using more than a quarter of the land the Assembly gave you. Why didn't you do something with it? Why create that wasteland out there?"

Jimawn's brocaded shoulders lifted in shrug. "Out of an abundance of caution."

"Caution? Why? What are you afraid of?"

"The Commonwealth, of course. Aren't you?"

Interesting. Why had that never occurred to her? She knew the off-comers were enemies, but the idea that the Gallaskians might be actively afraid of the Commonwealth... that was a revelation. It opened up a whole new way of thinking. She'd only ever considered off-comers in relation to Noyan. But that wouldn't be how they saw each other. To them, Noyan would only be a small part of a much bigger game.

"Why? What is about the Commonwealth that frightens you so much?"

"The same thing that frightens the Noyim, Justice. The Commonwealth think everyone wants to be like them – or would, if they only knew better. And they're growing. Thirty years ago, they had no presence in this cluster. Now, Noyan's practically a Protectorate. The Autarch doesn't want the same thing to happen to us."

He was exaggerating. Playing her. Why?

"So, you created a wasteland in case... What? They launch an attack?"

"Hardly. The Commonwealth doesn't go in for open warfare, Justice. Neither to do we, for that matter. No one wins an interstellar war. It's easier to destroy planets than to conquer them; and what's the point in that? The whole thing is ruinously expensive, utterly immoral, and only leads to mutual annihilation. No, they won't attack us. Not openly. They want to destroy us economically. And since their whole society revolves around individuals competing to enrich themselves at the expense of others, with no thought for the good of society at large, they are regrettably well positioned to do so."

He was enjoying himself. He was playing her, and he was enjoying doing it. She'd come here with entirely the wrong question in mind. She shouldn't have asked herself why Sanja befriended Jimawn; but why Jimawn befriended Sanja.

"And what about the Autarchy? How does your society work?"

Jimawn didn't hesitate; not even for a moment. "Honor, duty, and self-sufficiency. The three pillars of society. We aren't citizens. Every Gallaskian is a subject of the Autarch. We don't compete for power. We compete for honor. And the path to honor lies through duty. Duty to the throne, to the Autarchy, to the whole. And for the whole to be valued, every individual must be valued: not discarded because someone's found a more efficient way to make a profit. Every subject has their place, and the policy of self-sufficiency protects that place from unfair competition. It's a noble system, a system that provides society with a moral base. Unfortunately, in crude material terms, it's less efficient than the alternative."

The white wall behind Jimawn looked like painted plaster, but what was it really? The fireplace, tea service, walls and doors: how much of it was real? How much was fake? She looked at Jimawn, and wondered the same.

"I'm told you have an aristocracy. Is that true?"

Jimawn shrugged. "We can quibble about terms. But it's true that a minority of Office Holders inherit their positions."

"Did you?"

"Mine is not an imperial office. So, no."

"But others do. And that's not a moral basis for anything Not if children are born unequal."

Jimawn seemed more amused than offended. "But we are equal, Justice. Everyone in the empire is equally subject to the Autarch. The Commonwealthers claim equality, but they don't really have it. Like all democracies, they fall into faction and oligarchy; a handful of families rule the Homeworld, and the Homeworld rules the Commonwealth. But our Office Holders don't rule. Only the Autarch rules. Inherited office merely reflects the great honor earned by their ancestors. And that inspires others to follow their example, and seek to earn similar distinction for themselves and their descendants. It's a virtuous circle."

"But this is Noyan," said Beth. "And there are no ruling families here. Nor Office Holders."

"No. But there are elected representatives, and there are factions. And where you have factions and representatives, you have oligarchy in the making."

Beth relaxed back in the chair. Thankfully, it made no effort to accommodate her. It might be fake, but at least it wasn't alive.

"No," she said. "You overestimate the Assembly's influence. The settlements are largely independent. And there's no danger of faction or oligarchy there. Everyone gets a say. The settlements are true democracies."

Jimawn was fiddling thoughtfully with his cane's sliver head. "Maybe so, Justice. But true democracy never lasts. It requires too much unity of outlook, and too small a population. Of course, were Noyan to join the Autarchy, the settlements could continue to function as they always have. His Majesty does not interfere in the internal affairs of his dominions. But if Noyan joins the Commonwealth, they'll remake you in their own image. And that will be the end of your independent little settlements, and the end of the Family Court."

"Over my dead body."

"Very possibly so, Justice. I may have given you a misleading impression earlier. It's true that open, interstellar warfare is a nonsense. But there is one form of warfare that persists. The proxy war. Who do you think would win a Noyan civil war? Your democratic settlements? Or their enemies, armed with biological technology?"

He was clever, this off-comer. But perhaps a little too obvious. "We're straying from the point. I came here to further my investigation into the death of Sanja Gwahnal. Do you know who killed him?"

Jimawn's eyebrows rose; ironic, cynical. "I understood from the Commonwealth's excellent, if slanted, news service, that Sanja was killed by terrorists."

"And you believe that?"

"Is there any reason I shouldn't?"

"The method, for one."

"Yes. The method." His expression was suddenly

guarded, appraising. Either she'd surprised him, or he wanted her to think she had. "It is a contradiction, isn't it? Hidebound traditionalists don't seem likely possessors of sophisticated bi-tech weaponry."

"You still haven't answered my question, Jimawn."

"Call me Moyem, please. As for your question... I don't think anyone killed him. I think it was a terrible accident. Of course, the Commonwealth would rather blame terrorists than admit that. Anything to protect their precious bi-tech industry."

"Is that right? So why were they determined to say it was an accident, until I started investigating?"

"Fascinating. That's not like them at all. They'll normally do anything to exonerate bi-tech..."

"They were blaming it on contraband."

Jimawn laughed. "Of course! All is explained. And no doubt they planned on pressing for still greater powers for their regulators on the back of it. Poor Sanja. No greater love hath a Commonwealther than this, that he shall lay down his life for their colonial ambitions."

"Sanja Gwahnal didn't lay down his life. He was murdered. And I'd hoped that as his friend–"

"His friend?" Jimawn looked down at his cane. "I suppose you could call me that... I associated with him, certainly. I was amused by him and his little friends. And he had a remarkably good eye, for someone who was otherwise so dissipated. Yes, I suppose we were friends, after a fashion. But I'm afraid I have no idea who could have killed him."

"A 'good eye'? For what?"

"Our shared passion: Noyan arts and crafts. Sanja has... had quite a collection."

"A collection... You mean the pottery, in his bedroom? Perhaps you could take a look, see if anything valuable's missing?"

Jimawn snorted. "I'm sorry, Justice. None of it's worth stealing, never mind killing for. Noyan art is still a matter of taste, not profit. And I'm afraid it's never likely to take off in the Commonwealth. They dislike you too much."

"And the Autarchy?"

"We're more open-minded."

"Open-minded enough to think the Gwahnals might have feared the Choice of Death?"

Jimawn stared at her. Then he burst out laughing. She frowned. "I fail to see the humor."

"I know," he replied, tearfully. "That's what's so funny. I'll bet you've been putting that question to Commonwealthers haven't you? You know what the single most endearing thing about Noyan is, Justice? The way you simply don't understand how anyone can object to Choosing... No, Justice, I don't imagine for one moment that the Gwahnals feared Sanja's Choice. Have you asked them?"

"I have."

"Dear God. How did they react?"

"They claimed not to have considered the possibility."

"I'll bet they did."

"And you think they were telling the truth?"

"Yes, Justice, I do."

"Even though Sanja supported known traditionalist extremists?"

There was a moment of silence. Jimawn brushed an imaginary piece of lint from his cuff. "Surely not," he said.

"I believe you introduced him to them."

"Then you've been misinformed, Justice. Sanja and I attended a couple of public meetings together. And I suppose I may have introduced him to one or two people who might be considered Noyan chauvinists. It seemed appropriate. The boy had a naïve attraction to all things Noyan – but extremists? Ridiculous. Who would be the targets? Himself and his family. Unless, of course..."

He stopped, seemingly struck by a stray thought. She didn't believe it for a moment. If Jimawn had a sudden inspiration, he'd keep it hidden until he could examine it for possible advantage. Whatever was coming was entirely calculated.

"What?" she said.

"It's just a thought. Have you tried looking for patterns in recent militant attacks? They do seem to have become a lot more sophisticated, don't they? There have always been small acts of sabotage, but since when did native terrorists have access to the kind of bi-tech that can do serious damage to Commonwealth interests? I wouldn't begin to know how to destroy a roadroot, but that's what just happened. They seem remarkably well-informed about bi-tech vulnerabilities. Maybe that's why the Commonwealth thinks traditionalists killed Sanja. If they can destroy roadroots, they can definitely kill a house."

"But you don't think they did?"

"No, Justice, I do not. And nor do I think his parents killed him. I'm sure they had no reason to think that Sanja was anything other than a loyal and loving son. Of course, some at the embassy might have thought otherwise. The Commonwealth can be ruthless, Justice. If they were worried that control over the Gwahnals' bi-tech assets might be about to pass into the hands of a traditionalist sympathizer, then perhaps..."

And there it was. He wanted her to blame the embassy. But that didn't necessarily mean he was wrong.

"I'll take that under advisement. But what I'm interested in right now is your movements on the night of Sanja's murder."

"Of course, Justice. They're well-known. I was at the Mitchesons' reception."

"And afterwards?"

"Afterwards, I returned here and reported to his Excellency the Nuncio. After that, I retired to bed. I didn't kill Sanja, if that's what you're suggesting."

"I wasn't suggesting anything." The wing-back chair had good solid arms; they made it easy for her to get to her feet. "I was merely asking questions. And now I have other questions to ask elsewhere. But I shall expect you to remain available for further questioning. And I warn you, if I find that you haven't been entirely frank with me… Well, please remember: there's no diplomatic immunity from the Family Court."

CHAPTER 15

There is no politics in a settler assembly, for there are no politicians; no one to 'represent' anyone else and speak on their behalf. Here, all are equal, everyone has a voice, and all share in decisions over the settlement's future. Here is democracy at its most authentic and vital.
— From: Feature Article, *The Noyan Gazette*

The only light in the Assembly Hall entered via the door; a single beam cutting a bright path to the middle of the floor, and casting the rest into shadow. Dust motes spun lazily, sparkled briefly in the spotlight, and disappeared back into darkness. Samuel's shadow stretched ahead, an elongated black presence. He walked forwards, following his shadow to the very center of the packed hall. Then he stopped, oppressed by the presence of so many people; the weight of them; their warmth; the cacophony of ignorant conversation. Even the topmost tier of benches was occupied; eager settlers taking any seat they could find, blocking the few high windows in the process.

Heads turned. A high-pitched child's voice rang out as other voices quietened. Then the child too fell silent. If only Samuel could turn around and walk away. But he couldn't. Not yet.

A bead of sweat trickled down his neck. It was even

warmer inside than out; the thick mud-brick walls had turned the interior into an oven. That should keep the meeting short, at least.

John was waving to him; an empty seat beside him in the inner tier – Samuel's customary place, facing the entrance. It was no larger or more comfortable than any other seat, but it was the fulcrum of the hall.

Samuel scanned the room, looking for Nathan.

There: in the inner circle, a quarter turn to the right. A well-chosen position: a place of equivalence. And he wasn't alone. His hangers-on filled the seats around him. Amongst them Eve. Smiling. Excited.

They thought they'd won. That they'd forced him to call this Assembly. That he was here reluctantly. Excellent.

He turned and walked towards them. Only Nathan managed to hide his consternation, and even he couldn't mask sudden tension, anticipation of an imminent confrontation. A confrontation that Samuel had no intention of provoking.

He smiled blandly, and carried on straight past them, threading his way upwards through rows of concentric benches until he reached the outermost level, home of youngsters and those too nervous to put themselves forward. His young neighbors hurried to make space for him. They were striplings, no more than twelve or thirteen, dressed in smaller, dirtier versions of the same clothes Samuel wore – so very different from Hotep's spotless off-comer clothing. There hadn't been a speck of dirt anywhere on them. But Samuel had still washed his hands after stripping them off him. Even the feel of them made his stomach churn; that, and the way they resisted him. But he'd had no choice. The clothes, and the vehicle, had to go. The off-comers' technology was vile, but it was also potent. Who knew what devices it might conceal?

Nathan was craning over his shoulder, mystified. Samuel smiled down at him. Equals indeed. It was all he could do not to laugh.

The hubbub returned. The audience was confused, rattled. He hadn't taken his usual seat, hadn't started the meeting. He sat back, letting them talk. Letting the anticipation build. Letting Nathan wonder. Nathan who would have to turn and look up at him, any time he spoke. Nathan who still had so much to learn.

The noise continued to build. People were peering at him, trying to understand what he was waiting for; why he was so far from the center of things. And yet they never asked themselves what they were waiting for. They didn't need him to start the meeting. He was just another settler, no different from any of them.

Except it wasn't true, and they all knew it. New Beginning was *his*. He and Judith had built this settlement, and this movement. It had been their entire life. Did Nathan really think Samuel was going to give it up without a fight?

But then, wasn't that exactly what he was going to do? Walk away and never look back? But not today. Today he would please everyone – his followers and his secret sponsor alike – and buy himself time.

He rose to his feet, and waited for silence. "Brothers and sisters, thank you for joining in Assembly. We have matters to discuss, and a committee to assign. But first, ware strangers! Look to your left. Look to your right. Are all present known to us? Is anyone here not a tried and trusted member of our community?"

Heads turned, looking searchingly at their neighbors. This time, it was no empty ritual. If any outsider was present, they'd regret it. He waited for the ripple of motion to settle, and spoke again, barely needing to raise his voice to be heard throughout the silent hall. "So, brothers and sisters. What shall we do with the off-comer?"

He sat down again. There was the briefest of silences, and then, cacophony. Words were lost, but not the undercurrent of fear.

Nathan turned around, craning to look up at him.

Confused. Suspicious. He hadn't been expecting this; not at all. Samuel smiled down at him, and at Eve, staring at him in blank astonishment. She didn't understand him at all; she never had. She thought he was in trouble; that Hotep was a problem. Silly girl. Hotep wasn't a problem. He was an opportunity.

He got back to his feet. The noise level began to drop away. A voice rose into the emerging quiet, offering the simplest solution of all: "Kill him!"

The uproar returned, louder than ever. Fierce shouts of approval vied with angry protests. Hotep was known here, and not universally despised.

Samuel spotted the speaker: Silas, an old friend, sitting just behind and to the left of John. The reserved seat was long gone, but John was still looking to him for an explanation. Why had he chosen to sit so far away, to spurn the seat John saved for him? He shook his head reassuringly: don't worry – I know what I'm doing. It's just politics.

Allies were allies, and had to be mollified, no matter how little he cared what they thought or felt. Or if they lived or died.

He raised a hand, shouting into the hubbub. "We can't kill him, brothers and sisters. Not yet. Not until we know more. Like why he's here. And if he's working for the embassy."

The silence returned, ominous and fearful. And Nathan finally rose to speak. "You think he's an agent?"

"I think he's an idiot." He waited for the laughter to subside. "But we won't know for sure until we 'talk' to him."

"So, talk to him!" someone shouted, to cheers and stamping of feet.

Samuel smiled ruefully. "I wish that I could, brothers and sisters. But he'll be out for hours, maybe days. I wouldn't have put so much in, if I'd known he was going to drink like that."

There was some scattered laughter, but none from Nathan. "You shouldn't have drugged him at all," he said. "Then we could have been 'talking' to him right now."

Nathan's cronies shouted agreement. Many in the crowd joined them. A popular opinion, then.

"True. But if I hadn't drugged him, he might have tried to leave. And if we used force to keep him here, there'd be no point calling an Assembly to decide what to do. We'd have no choice. We'd have to question him, and kill him. Maybe we will anyway. But that's not my decision to make. That's up to this Assembly. Right now, we still have the option of telling him he drank too much, and letting him go. I know what I think we should do, but it's for you, all of you, to decide what happens next."

He sat down again. A ripple of approval spread around the room. Nathan's expression turned carefully neutral. Silas again filled the silence. "I still say kill him. He's not going to tell anyone anything if he's dead."

"Including us." Samuel didn't bother to stand up.

The silence returned; thoughtful; afraid. And Nathan spoke again – but this time he didn't crane his head to look back at Samuel. This time, he faced forwards, addressing the Assembly.

"So once again we're asked to wait. As we're always asked to wait. What does it matter if Hotep's an agent? If he is, they already know about us, and we need to act now. If he's not, we have a window of opportunity, a chance to act before they find out about us. Either way, the answer's the same. It's time to stop waiting. Sanja's dead. Murdered. Because he was one of us, off-comer or no. And still, we do nothing! They killed one of us. We should kill ten of them! Starting with Hotep. It's time for action, not words. No more waiting!"

There was no denying it: Nathan had timed his intervention well. The benches shook with stomping feet. The crowd was with him. Samuel stood up.

"I agree," he said.

The room erupted in pandemonium. Where they'd stomped for Nathan, they cheered for him. Even Nathan's cronies joined in. Only one face was aloof from the celebration: Nathan's, looking back, knowing he'd been outmaneuvered. Samuel suppressed the urge to wink.

"Brothers and sisters... Brothers and sisters... Sanja's death hurt all of us. Worse, it hurt the cause. He helped us turn the off-comers' own weapons against them. Now, they think they've beaten us. They think we can't hurt them anymore. But they're wrong. They care about Hotep. Because of who he is. Because of where he's from, and who he's related to. It'll hurt them, when we kill him. Hurt them badly. But we can do much more than that. Killing is easy. It's quick. And it's over. Let's hold him hostage, make demands. Make them sweat. Then kill him. And when we kill him... Then the off-comers find out we still have some of Sanja's weapons left. And they really start to fear us."

He sat down, resting his back against the wall and ignoring the roar of approval. Why bother acknowledging it? He'd won. The cheering echoed deafeningly around the hall, cutting off any possibility of further debate. His shirt was sticking to him, slick with sweat. The room had become unbearably humid; another reason for the debate to end. The decision had been made. Only details remained. Hotep's vehicle and clothes still had to be disposed of, for fear of tracking devices. Hotep himself would need to be questioned. Not that there was any chance he worked for the embassy... but he might have told others where he was going. They needed to be sure – and come up with a plausible cover story, should anyone come looking for the off-comer. Then there was the question of what their demands should be, and how long to wait before killing him. As for the manner of his killing... Jimawn's hive of horrors would see to that.

It was a win, a definite win. At a stroke he'd fended of Nathan's challenge, kept the settlers on his side, and arranged for Jimawn's atrocity. Everything had gone perfectly.

He closed his eyes. He couldn't wait to be gone from this place.

CHAPTER 16

The rapidity of the decomposition, especially at the cellular level (as highlighted in Figure 14), is strongly indicative of a link between the two attacks. In each case, the perpetrators introduced a foreign pathogen that caused irrecoverable damage to the host. The fact that two such similar attacks happened on the same night leads to the inevitable conclusion that they were perpetrated by the same group, most likely the organization styling itself The League of Free Noyim.

— From: A Report on The Recent Attacks, *The Office Of Regulation*

The crowd was jostling, hostile. It wasn't just the off-comers at the back — even the Noyim at the front, reporters from *The Gazette* and *The Recorder*, were shouting angry questions.

Ethan was right. She should have stayed in the Auxiliary Court, not come out to talk to the press. But *scrape* the regulator's report was infuriating. What was she supposed to do? Just sit there quietly and let them get away with lying to the Family Court? Never.

A camera flashed, dazzling her and filling the air with acrid metallic smoke. She wafted it away and tried again. "The reason I don't give it any credence is because it doesn't deserve any. It's a travesty: an insult to the Family Court, the Assembly, and all Noyim. The attempt to blame

Noyan traditionalists is—"

"They've claimed responsibility!"

"Not for the murder, they haven't. Only for the roadroots—"

"When are you going to stop harassing innocent Commonwealth citizens?"

She recognized that voice. There he was, towards the back with the rest of the off-comers: Dil Mahtal. And overhead, the familiar, detestable shape of his blue-green bird-thing, watching her every move.

"No one's being harassed. This is a murder investigation. It's normal for the victim's friends to help with enquiries. You were there. I asked you questions, released you, and now here you are, asking me questions. That's hardly harassment. Unless you object to helping us catch Sanja's killers?"

"What about Beynan Hotep?"

"What about him?"

"Why are you holding him? He can't still be 'helping you with your enquiries'?"

"Haven't you already broadcast enough nonsense for one day? I'm not holding him. And those traditionalist pamphlets you've been telling everyone about belonged to Sanja Gwahnal. So maybe it's time you – all of you – put your preconceptions about this case aside, and started asking the regulators difficult questions. Like why they're prioritizing lies and propaganda over catching Sanja's killers. Now, if you'll excuse me, that's as much time as I can spare. I have an investigation to run."

And with that, she fled back into the Auxiliary Court. This whole impromptu press conference had been a stupid mistake. She knew better. Only ever talk to the press if you have a specific goal in mind; not because you feel the need to vent.

The auxiliaries closed the doors behind her. She nodded a thank you, and took the elevator back to the second floor. It was much quieter than it had been that morning. There were no off-comers complaining at their treatment, no bird-things waiting to ambush her as she left the elevator. Sanja's friends had all been interviewed and released, and most of the auxiliaries were out on assignment. She glanced around for Ethan, saw no sign of him, and told a junior to send him in when he returned. Then she hurried past the blaring 3-V and on to her requisitioned office.

The regulators' report was lying open on her desk. It was so tempting to throw it straight into the trash, but she resisted the urge and dropped it into the filing tray instead. It might still come in useful, if only as evidence when she charged Regulator Hyrom with intent to mislead the Family Court. In the meantime, she had more important things to do: like unpicking the many threads of Sanja Gwahnal's complicated life, and finding the one that led to his murder.

Her in-tray was full again: at the top, the report on Sanja's bedroom. It was a thick document, full of photographs. There were shots of all four walls, ceiling and floor; closeups of Sanja's body, of the globeflower, of every piece of pottery – both individually, and in context. She flipped through them until she reached a large photograph of the globeflower, overlaid with red and yellow outlines. Callouts named continents and seas, and identified the planet as Anapkir, a long-standing member of the Commonwealth – and the Gwahnals' home world.

Would a young man who was rejecting his off-comer heritage really have such a thing in his bedroom? Probably not. Quite the opposite, in fact. How did that fit with the pamphlets, and his support of militant traditionalists? Or, for that matter, the collection of Noyan pottery. It too had been carefully photographed and labelled. The annotations supported Jimawn's claim that the pieces weren't valuable. They were simple, well-designed, everyday earthenware. The only distinctive thing about them was the particular yellow clay used in their production, which suggested most of the items came from a settlement called New Beginning. That was curious. New Beginning was a mid-sized settlement to the north of the city, and if she remembered correctly, one founded on explicitly traditionalist principles... Interesting.

"You wanted to see me, Justice?"

Ethan was poking his head around the half-open door. She waved him in, and watched, enviously, as he collapsed into the chair opposite. It must be nice to be able to slump down like that, and not worry about your back.

"That's right. Your interviewees, this morning. Did any of them mention a Gallaskian called Moyem Jimawn?"

Ethan's brow furrowed. "A Gallaskian? No. Why? Should they have?"

"I'm not sure yet. It depends..."

"On what?"

"On who Sanja's real friends were. The ones we interviewed this morning, or the ones he didn't want people to know about. This morning's lot – what did you make of them?"

"Pretty much what you'd expect, Justice. A bunch of spoiled rich kids."

"I agree. Anyone stand out as different?"

"Mahtal, maybe?"

"True. But he's a reporter. He had professional reasons for mixing with them. And I agree, the rest of them were very much like Hotep. Spoiled. Not too bright. No great focus or ambition. So, what was Sanja doing with Moyem Jimawn? Jimawn's no fool. Far from it. And he's no friend of the Commonwealth. What was Sanja Gwahnal doing associating with someone like him?"

"I don't–"

"I have another job for you. Those pamphlets? It turns out Sanja wasn't just reading them. He was financing the groups behind them. And he'd been doing so for a while – ever since this 'Jimawn' brought him to a traditionalist meeting. So, I went to the Mission to see him, and he said something very interesting. He said we should look for patterns, in the recent attacks."

"Patterns? What kind of patterns?"

"I don't know. Not exactly. But I'm sure there's something there. Jimawn's not the type to make off-the-cuff suggestions. He knows we'll find something, if we look. I'm guessing it'll be to do with how sophisticated the attacks have been getting, how they're using off-comer tech. Do you suppose Sanja might have been supplying them with it?"

"I don't know, Justice. He'd have the access, but the risk of his parents finding out…"

"Yes. Exactly. Imagine how they'd react? They manufacture the stuff, and he's paying people to destroy it? People who might also want him to take over his parents' business. People who'd likely encourage him to make the Choice of Death? What would they do, when they found out? And here we are, investigating his murder, which just happens to have been committed using the kind of tech made in his parents' factories…"

Ethan's lips were pursed. He took a deep, thoughtful, breath. "I don't buy it, Justice. If he had that kind of access to his parents' production lines, why would he ever have bought from Michael? But we know he did. And not in a small way."

"I don't know. It depends what he was buying. Maybe he didn't want to risk his parents finding out what he was up to, so he went to Michael for the tools his pet traditionalists needed."

Ethan shook his head. "No way. Someone like Michael, the very last thing he'd ever do is help traditionalists. They're the very worst thing for his business."

"Okay. So maybe Michael's just another a cover story. Something to throw his parents off the scent. The same reason he was friends with the likes of Hotep. And speaking of Hotep… Mahtal seems to think we still have him in custody. Your people did drop him off at his house, didn't they?"

"Of course."

"And there's no way Michael could have picked him up, afterwards?"

"No. Hotep's house wouldn't let anyone in without his say so. And even if it did, Michael has to know he'd be the first person we'd look to, if anything happened to Hotep. Besides, Michael's not doing anything right now. None of his people are."

"So why does Mahtal think we're holding him?"

"Who knows? Maybe the regulators picked him up. You took him away from them. Maybe they wanted him back."

"I do hope so," said Beth, happily. "We've still got jurisdiction. If Hyrom's got him, then he's interfering with a Family Court investigation. That's a clear breach of Custom. I'd love to arrest him for it. Check it out for me."

"With pleasure, Justice."

Ethan's grin really suited him. It brought out his dimples.

CHAPTER 17

...the situation remains fluid, but authorities appear confident in the effectiveness of the current heightened security measures to protect the public while they track down the perpetrators of these heinous crimes. In the meantime, Commonwealth citizens are advised to remain vigilant, and reminded not to allow their vehicles to feed at any shared facilities until further notice.

— From: Noyan News Hour, *a division of Commonwealth Information Services*

"Come to bed, love..."

Errina was standing in the doorway, naked save for the robe snuggling protectively around her. It was cold here in the living room. He hadn't noticed. How long had he been sitting alone in the dark, staring silently at the wall?

"Come on, Jo. You need your sleep."

He reached for his glass. It was empty. So was the bottle beside it. He didn't remember finishing either of them.

"Go back to bed, Errina."

She joined him on the sofa, cuddling against him, her legs tucked up on the seat. Her robe flowed over them both, trying to keep out the chill. She always chose the eager ones, keenest on keeping her warm. Personally, he preferred it cold at night; it helped him sleep. But he didn't feel like sleeping now.

He put an arm around her and pulled her close. She'd been a good wife to him. The matchmaker had chosen well.

"Please, Jo. Tell me what's wrong."

"Nothing. Go back to bed."

She stiffened at his side. "It's not my place to sleep when my husband's awake."

"But it is your place to tell your husband what to do? Save that for the boys."

"You know they cried themselves to sleep?" Her tone was penitent, but the words were an accusation.

"They did? Why?"

"Because their father wouldn't talk to them, wouldn't read them a bedtime story, wouldn't even kiss them goodnight."

"I'm sorry."

Jodan blinked back tears. It wasn't enough that he was a failure as a regulator; he was a failure as a husband and a father, too.

"Your worries are my worries, Jo. Maybe I can help. Maybe just talking will help."

"Not this time, my love." He leaned back and stared at the grey-black blankness of the ceiling; all detail was lost in the darkness, except for over by the window, where the darker dots of quiescent glow-bulbs were just visible in the moonlight.

"I'll make you something to eat. You'll feel better with something inside you." She made to get up, but he tightened his grip on her shoulder and pulled her back down.

"No. The house needs time to build up more gas. Save it for the morning. The children need to eat. I don't."

And there it was again: another mark of his failure. Other parents didn't face such choices. They bent the rules. They upgraded their houses with modern, embargoed equipment; efficient catalysts and waste converters to ensure they never ran out of fuel, or warmth, or any of life's small necessities. But not him. He'd believed in the embargo, believed in the Office of Regulation and its mission. What a fool.

"They've been laughing at me," he said. "All this time, they've been laughing at me."

"What are you talking about? No one's laughing at you, love. Just come to-

"Yes, they have. Hozefa, Mito, all of them. Laughing at the silly little colonial who actually believes in the mission. In progress. In helping primitive worlds rise out of poverty and ignorance. I was so proud to be a regulator. And all the time, they were thinking: what an idiot. Or maybe they thought I was just pretending, going through the motions like everybody else. Maybe they've only just realized how stupid I am."

"Jodan. Stop it. You're scaring me."

He wasn't leaning back anymore. He was bent forwards, head in hands, elbows on knees. And Errina had her arms around him. When had that happened?

He straightened up. He wasn't one of the boys, in need of comfort and support. He was a man. It was time he acted like one.

"I have to resign. It's the only honorable thing to do."

"Why? You've done nothing wrong."

"But I have, Errina. I should have seen what Hozefa was up to from the first. I should have gone straight to Maitland, or the ambassador, when I had the chance. Now it's too late. And if I stay in the service, if I go along with it, then I'm as guilty as they are. Maybe I can't stop them, but I don't have to be part of it. It's resign, or be complicit. What choice have I got? I have to resign."

Errina stood up. Moved away. Was she angry? Probably. It was hard to be sure, with her face hidden in shadow. Then she spoke, and removed any doubt.

"And what happens then, Jodan? The regulators lose a decent officer. How does that help anything? How does it

help this family? How do we feed the boys? We'd be trapped here on Noyan. Is that what you want? Your children growing up as natives?"

"No. Of course not. But I can't just stand by and watch Hozefa trying to save his own neck, and damn the consequences. If they lose control of this... If they don't put the embargo back together, this planet's going to hell. And soon."

"And how will your resigning stop that? Will it make any difference to anyone at all, except you? And your family?"

He shook his head. She was right. Either Hozefa managed to cover up his failures and restore the embargo, or he didn't. Jodan's resignation would make no difference to that. But the difference for his boys would be incalculable. They'd be trapped here. Even at best, it might be years, decades, before Noyan joined the Commonwealth and slowly became more civilized. At worst, he'd be condemning them to live out their lives on a world descending ever deeper into darkness.

He stood up, decision made. "I'll put in for a transfer, then. We'll start again somewhere else."

Errina stepped into his arms. He leaned down and kissed the tip of her nose. Her robe, sensing their mood, opened to envelope them both.

This was what mattered. His wife. His children. His family.

He hated to let Hozefa and Mito win, but what choice did he have? He couldn't fight them. Not without proof of the severity of the breach. And what could he do, stuck at home? He was wasting his time, caring what happened on this world. Hozefa and the Noyim deserved each other. Why not just leave them to their fate?

CHAPTER 18

A State of Emergency is not the whole solution. It won't put a stop to terrorist attacks. But it will at least limit the terrorists' freedom of maneuver. And that, surely, is a precondition for finding a solution. We at the Gazette wholly support the motion: a temporary inconvenience, surely, but a necessary one.
— From: Editorial, *The Noyan Gazette*

Samuel ran his hands over the freshly sanded spoke. It was too light, the grain too open, large knots and other flaws all too apparent. Casab was far from the ideal wood for the job, but needs must. He fitted it carefully into the tractor wheel's empty slot and looked to see how Luke was getting on, preparing the next one on a hand-lathe. It was uncomfortable work, carried out under a temporary and very inadequate awning on a blistering hot morning, but the tractor was lying broken mid-harvest, and they had no choice. Hotep could wait, the harvest could not.

A sudden gust of hot, dry wind blew sawdust in this face, setting him coughing and spluttering. He turned aside, spat the dust from his mouth and wiped his nose on his sleeve. The sooner the rainy season was here, the better... But no. He'd be long gone by the time the rains came.

Across the square, a small group was picking over a freshly woven rug, searching for imperfections. His gaze moved on... and snapped back: Judith, his Judith, was sitting there, working with her friends. He couldn't mistake that smile, her hair, the way she held her needle...

Except it wasn't Judith. It was Eve. Just Eve.

Something in his chest melted; warm despair trickled down and pooled in his belly. He wanted to stop time, to undo the last few seconds. He would give the rest of his life to return to that brief moment of possibility, when Judith was sitting there, as much a part of the world as the tractor and its broken wheel.

He picked up another spoke, still rough from the lathe, and reached mechanically for sandpaper to begin the work of smoothing it down. Across the square, Eve was talking intensely with the young man beside her. At least it wasn't Nathan. Her lover was long gone, off at dawn with the group disposing of Hotep's vehicle and clothes. They wouldn't be back for hours yet.

"Scrape!"

That would teach him to pay attention to his work. A large splinter had embedded itself painfully in the ball of his thumb. He sucked at it to soothe the hurt.

He hated carpentry. But the settlement had needed carpenters, and Judith insisted he set an example. So, he'd taken it up, learned well, and consoled himself with the pleasure she took in his hard-won proficiency. There was no pleasure now. Just bitterness. And another reminder of what he'd lost.

He blew on his thumb and extracted the splinter with his teeth. Blood welled up. He sucked at it to avoid staining the wood.

A noise. Out of place. Unexpected. An engine, but not the truck returning. No blacksmith made that engine. It was too smooth and regular. Mass-produced. An outsider.

It wasn't market day. What was a stranger doing here?

There it was: a battered black car, chugging into the

square. One side of its canvas roof flapped loose in the breeze. It drove over to the group squatting around the rug, and came to a halt. The engine fell silent. So did the square. No one was working, no one was talking. Everyone was waiting.

The driver climbed down – a slow, awkward process. She was small, middle-aged, her features obscured by driving goggles. She lifted them away, but by then she'd turned to face the weavers, her back to him. He saw, but didn't hear, the brief conversation. It ended with Eve pointing towards the inn.

He waited until the woman disappeared inside. Then he hurried over to Eve.

And learned that the stranger had asked for him by name. He glanced at the inn, and then at the car. It was utilitarian at best. An official vehicle. Not someone's prized private possession.

He nodded his thanks, grateful that Eve had had the wit not to point him out. Then he followed the stranger to the inn. The door was wide open. Inside, a handful of settlers were watching in tense silence as the outsider talked to Daniel at the bar.

She turned at the sound of his entrance. There was something familiar about her...

"Ah, Samuel," she said. "Just the man I wanted to see."

"I'm sorry. Do I know you?"

"Oh yes," she said, confidently. "I rather think you do. By reputation, at least. My name is Beth. I'm a Justice of the Family Court."

Of course. He should have known. He'd seen her picture in the Gazette. But she looked so different with the goggles on her forehead, and two dust-free patches around her eyes.

"Justice Beth! What a pleasant surprise. The Family Court is always welcome here. If there's any way I can be of assistance..."

"You could tell me where Beynan Hotep is."

Scrape. She knew the off-comer was here. How?

Or did she?

"Who, Justice?"

Her eyes narrowed. She tilted her head to the left. "Is everyone here going to deny knowing him?"

She knew. There was no way she'd be pushing this hard otherwise.

"Of course I know him. He used to come here all the time with Sanja Gwahnal. I just wasn't expecting–"

"Used to?"

"Well, he can hardly come with him now, can he?"

She wasn't amused, but he didn't care. He'd amused himself, at least. It was a small, bitter consolation. His plan was falling apart, and there was nothing he could do about it. He was surrounded by loyal comrades-in-arms who'd back him against anyone, and anything.

Except the Family Court.

"So, he's not here?"

He smiled guilelessly. "Hotep? Of course he is."

"And yet your friends" – she waved a hand, encompassing everyone in the room – "denied all knowledge of him, just moments ago."

"Of course they did. Daniel – did you know that you were talking to a Justice of the Family Court?"

"No, I–"

"Of course you didn't. You see, Justice: they were just being protective of a friend. Hotep came to us because he was worried for his safety. They weren't going to give him up to the first person who came along. Of course, if they'd known you were from the Family Court…"

"So where is he?"

Why was she so hostile? She was supposed to be sympathetic to traditionalism. She should feel at home here.

Unless she knew, or suspected, the real reason for Sanja's visits…

Thank *scrape* for the broken wheel. If it weren't for that

tractor, the ransom note would already be on its way to the press. He might even have started questioning Hotep. And that would have left marks he couldn't explain away.

"I don't know, to be honest. Daniel, why don't you go and find out where he's sleeping it off? I'll get the Justice a drink. You must be thirsty after your drive. What can I get you? Some casab tea? It's a little early for anything stronger…"

The Justice ignored him. She was watching Daniel hurry for the door. Was his relief as obvious to her as it was to him?

"Tea, Justice?" He went behind the bar, pulled two cups from the rack and plonked them down noisily beside the urn.

"Sleeping what off?" she said.

"I beg your pardon."

"You said Hotep was 'sleeping it off'. Sleeping what off?"

"Oh, I see." He filled both cups. "Look, Justice. Nobody holds it against him. We all understand he was upset. But he really overdid it last night. I imagine he's feeling pretty rough this morning. And more than a little embarrassed. Assuming he remembers anything."

He offered her a cup and, when she made no move to take it, placed it on the bar between them.

"Really? What did he do?"

"Oh, just what you'd expect when a young man can't hold his drink. Fighting. Propositioning women. That kind of thing."

The Justice stared at him silently. Then she took off her goggles and sat down at the bar. But she still didn't touch the tea. He sipped his own. It was lukewarm, but very welcome on a dry throat.

The moment stretched. The other customers fled in ones and twos until only the Justice and he remained. And still she said nothing. She seemed content to sit and wait, but the longer the silence went on, the more self-conscious he became. New Beginning was a small settlement. If the Justice hadn't been suspicious before, this long delay would surely make her so now.

"Tell me, Justice," he said. "How did you know Hotep was here? I thought he didn't tell anyone where he was going."

Her shoulders went down a little, her posture became less stiff. "His house," she said. "It knew where he'd gone."

"His house? You spoke to his actual house?"

"No. One of my assistants. It told him where to look."

Samuel grimaced, telegraphing his disgust. And held onto the bar to support legs gone suddenly weak.

Hotep's house. His *scraping* house. It would have led the regulators straight to them. He'd come so terrifyingly close to making the worst – and last – mistake of his life. If it weren't for that broken tractor wheel, and this interfering Justice, it would all have been lost. The settlement. The League. His plans for escape. Everything.

The front door opened. Daniel, John and Hotep were silhouetted against the sunlight. Hotep's feet were dragging. The other two were holding him upright, his arms draped over their shoulders.

"Hotep, are you all right?" The Justice hurried towards them.

"Justice? S'up?"

The off-comer was swaying to and fro, trying to bring the Justice into focus. And making it even harder for Daniel and John to keep him on his feet.

"Where are his clothes?"

The question was addressed to John, but it was Daniel who answered. "His clothes, Justice?"

"Yes, his clothes. That isn't how he normally dresses."

Hotep looked down, and frowned to find himself wearing worn but serviceable homespun in place of his off-comer clown-clothes. Samuel hurried over.

"He got rid of them, Justice. I told you. He was out of

control last night. Stripped off right in the middle of the square, in front of everyone."

"I did wha...?" Hotep's speech was slurred, but his appalled astonishment was unmistakable.

"It doesn't sound like he remembers doing that, does it?" said the Justice.

"I told you he might not."

"Yes," she said, flatly. "You did. But taking off his clothes last night doesn't explain why he's not wearing them now."

"He threw them in his vehicle, Justice. It took off with them. I don't know where he sent it. Could be anywhere by now. Maybe it went home without him."

"No, it didn't go home. His house lost contact with it somewhere north east of here. Some kind of accident. You'd think if it was clever enough to drive itself, it'd be clever enough not to drive off a cliff, wouldn't you?"

Samuel shrugged. "Who knows, Justice? I hate their technology. We don't allow it here."

"No? But you let Sanja Gwahnal visit regularly enough. And I doubt he came here in one of our cars."

"No... But Sanja was different."

"So I'm learning. Tell me, Samuel. Who do you think killed him?"

"I have no idea."

"Really? I thought you might have some idea, given he was funding your group."

He managed, just, to keep his expression serene. Daniel and John were less successful; but at least they were out of the Justice's eye line.

"I'm afraid not, Justice. The Movement for Tradition and Continuity has many sponsors who help us cover the costs of leaflets and so forth. None have ever been killed before."

"Mov... Movement?" Hotep was looking more confused than ever.

"The Movement for Tradition and Continuity," the

Justice helpfully explained. "Didn't Sanja tell you about that? Strange, given that that was why he kept bringing you here. He never thought to mention it?"

Hotep shook his head, vehemently. The Justice turned her attention back to Samuel. "Don't you find that strange? Why, do you suppose Sanja would be so very keen to keep his involvement with your group secret. All you do is hand out leaflets, isn't that right? And yet he wouldn't even tell his best friend why he kept dragging him out here. Doesn't that strike you as odd?"

"Not really. I assume he didn't want his parents to find out."

"I suppose not. They wouldn't have approved of their son supporting Noyan traditionalists. Especially if he was coming up to the age of Choosing."

"No. I expect not."

"Did he ever suggest to you that he intended to exercise the Choice of Death?"

"Now that you come to mention it, I believe he did say something about it. Once or twice."

"So, he hated his parents?"

"He did."

"N…No. Didn't…" Hotep was indignant but still very slurred. The Justice didn't even spare him a glance.

"So, there's no chance that he was just a go-between? That it wasn't him, but his parents who were really funding you?"

Samuel froze; only for an instant, but it was enough. She noticed. Worse: so did Daniel.

"What? No. Of course not."

"Of course not. Why would they? The Gwahnals are the largest off-comer tech manufacturers on Noyan. They'd have no interest in funding an organization like yours, would they? Let alone any groups involved in sabotage. It wouldn't make any sense. Why fund the people who want to attack you? Come on, Hotep. Time to go."

She separated the off-comer from John and Daniel, and led him towards the door. He staggered along beside her, barely managing to keep up even with her slow pace. She paused in the threshold and looked back.

"There is one thing that's strange, though," she said. "The Gwahnals are such obvious targets – and yet over the last 18 months, they've suffered fewer losses to sabotage than any other bi-tech manufacturer. Isn't that odd?"

Samuel shrugged. "I suppose so. But they've lost something much more valuable, haven't they? Their son."

"Yes, they have. But I doubt traditionalists inflicted that particular loss. And if I were you, I might be worried about who did it, and who their next target might be."

He followed her outside, as much to avoid talking to John and Daniel as to watch her leave. He wasn't ready for that conversation. Not yet. He needed time to think, and to plan. Because the Justice was right. He was in danger. Maybe from Sanja's killers – but definitely from his loyal followers, thanks to the deadly information she'd just let loose.

The square looked very different now. Before, it had been nearly empty. Now, it was lined with settlers, all watching the Justice as she guided Hotep towards her car. The off-comer seemed oddly reluctant to climb into his seat. She leaned over and said something too low to be heard by the watchers. Then she pushed him back towards the car. This time he scrambled inside. Had she told him how much danger he'd been in? The danger he'd continue to be in, if she left him behind? If so, she knew altogether too much. And so might others.

There was a brief flurry of activity – a cranking handle held out, a call for help. Eager youngsters hurried to assist. She chose the largest, passed him the handle, and climbed behind the wheel. She paused a moment to put her goggles back on, and then nodded to the bending youth. The engine caught on the third attempt. The youth hurried to return the handle, and accept a coin in payment. Then the Justice was on her way, taking Hotep with her. And leaving Samuel with a huge problem. Daniel must have understood the significance of what she said about the Gwahnals. Even John would get there eventually. Would either of them believe he hadn't known how the Gwahnals were using them? He had to convince them somehow, and soon. Before they told anyone else. Because if word began to spread through the settlement...

So. First – he was as much a victim as they were.

Second? What would he be doing, right now, if he hadn't known? If it was as much a surprise to him, as to everyone else.

He'd want revenge, that was what.

It was time for the League to target the Gwahnals. Not personally – too dangerous, especially for him if Fange or Amaya had a chance to talk – but something that belonged to them.

Or better, *someone*. At one at the same time, he'd allay his followers' suspicions, and give Jimawn his atrocity.

And buy himself the time to escape.

CHAPTER 19

I say yes to bi-tech, and no to yet more off-comer interference in our affairs. Does anyone really believe Noyan would be irreparably damaged if the Commonwealth condescended to allow us a few more crumbs from their table? That we couldn't cope with comforts that are taken for granted elsewhere? Do you suppose the regulators believe their own stories? Or is it all just a means to control us, to keep the 'natives' down?

– From: Minutes of the Noyan Assembly, *Representative Ezra of Bridgetown speaking*

The heavy blast curtains in front of the windows were spoiling Michaels' view. It was infuriating; an admission of weakness, of vulnerability. And so unnecessary.

He marched over, pulled them aside and stared out over the city. Rank upon rank of geometrically ordered stone-built streets stretched into the distance. Down there, business was still being done. Goods were being fenced, protection was being paid, product was being moved. But not by him. Michael wasn't supplying anyone. Not in the Old Quarter, and not out in the bi-tech suburbs. That was where his best customers were to be found: plush, comfortable areas where better-off Noyim and wealthy off-comers lived side-by-side in living houses. And every last one of them in need of embargo-breaching comforts.

And all currently getting them from Mordecai.

The *mother* probably couldn't believe his luck. One day he's a small player; the next he's the only game in town. And the longer that went on, the harder it was going to be for Michael to take back what was rightfully his.

And it was all so totally scraping unnecessary. The regulators weren't after him at all. This wasn't about him, or his product. It never had been. All this time he'd thought he was under attack, and he was nothing but collateral damage.

He had to put Mordecai back in his box. But how? The regulators might be off chasing terrorists, but the Auxiliary Court were all over him, like lice.

The intercom buzzed, demanding his attention. He stepped away from the window. "Yes?"

"We're all set." Mary's voice emerged, thin but clear. "He's coming in now. Through the kitchens."

"Good. How'd he take it?"

"Not well. He didn't like being summoned. And he really didn't like arriving in a sack."

"Yeah? Tell him he's leaving that way, too. And if he's really lucky, we won't sew up the top and dump it in the desert."

He turned to stare at the wall of 3-Vs. Very little was happening yet; mornings were always quiet. Then Mary appeared, moving through the lobby on the way to the kitchens. A moment of stillness, and she was back, Representative Ezra in tow – and clearly still unhappy: all square shoulders and offended dignity. Until Mary spoke. Then he deflated; a popped bubble, ashen-faced. Better. Much better.

They rode up in the elevator together; Mary casual and relaxed; Ezra nervously biting his lip. But then the elevator arrived at Michael's penthouse and he was instantly transformed. The nervous functionary evaporated, replaced by a leader of men. It was in equal parts impressive, and laughable. The representative strode confidently out, marched across the foyer into the office and offered Michael his hand. Michael pointedly ignored it. Ezra didn't even blink. He lowered his hand without a hint of embarrassment. "Michael. How are you? You wanted to–"

"Sit down, Ezra."

"–see me? Oh. Yes of course."

Mary all but pushed him onto the couch. Michael went to stand over him. The last remnants of Ezra's smile, already more ingratiating than confident, disappeared.

"Tell me, Representative, what do I pay you for?"

"I beg your–"

"It's a simple question. What do I pay you for? All the money I've given you over the years. What's it for?"

"Um… Well. There are all sorts of expenses connected with elections. And then there's the office to maintain. Your contribu–"

"Yeah, yeah. And all those little comforts your salary doesn't stretch to. Don't forget those. It all adds up. But I'm not asking you what you spend the money *on*. I don't care. I'm asking why I pay you."

Ezra swallowed. A bead of sweat appeared in his hairline. "I've always assumed you made your… contributions because you felt my faction was best positioned to ensure there were no unnecessary impediments to the natural flow of business."

"The natural flow of business…" Michael smiled. Ezra was worrying about the wrong things: listening devices, and careful phrasing. What he ought to be worrying about, was walking out of here alive.

"How's the family, Ezra? Wife and children good?"

"Yes thank–"

"Let's keep them that way, shall we?"

It took a moment for the threat to register. Then Ezra's eyes widened, his bottom lip quivered; he opened his mouth, but closed it again without saying a word.

"Listen to me, Representative. There is no 'natural flow

of business'. Not with the Auxiliary Court watching my every scraping move. I've got product ready to ship, and I can't sell any of it. Pretty soon now, it's going to rot. So, I'm wondering why I've paid you all these years, if you can't do your scraping job and keep the auxiliaries off my back?"

"The aux.. aux… What? They're… what?"

"They're watching me, Ezra. Me, and everyone that works for me. Why the scrape do you think we had to smuggle you in? For the fun of it? Those mothers are all over me, and you didn't even know?"

"No, I… How? Your… business is nothing to do with… Why? Are you sure? What would–"

"Am I sure? Did you just ask me that?"

"No, no. Sorry. I meant… Why? It doesn't make any sense. My people at the Auxiliary Court know not to…"

"Do they? I've got rotting buds that say otherwise. It's time you had a word with 'your people'."

"Yes. Yes, of course. I'm so sorry, Michael. I had no idea. It just doesn't make any sense. There's no reason for the auxiliaries to go after you."

"No, there isn't. Get that Family Court mother off my back, Representative. Right now."

Ezra swallowed hard. "The… The Family Court? Michael. I can't… I don't have any… The Family Court. It's not like the auxiliaries. I don't have anyone at the Family Court. I can't. I just can't."

The man was terrified. And he was still saying no. This wasn't defiance. It was the truth. And if there was nothing Ezra could…

"That's not true though, is it?" said Mary.

"It is… It is true."

"No, it's not." Mary had taken out her revolver. She checked the cylinder, spun it, clicked it back into place. "The Family Court can only investigate where it has jurisdiction. And jurisdiction's a matter for the Assembly."

It was a simple, elegant solution. Why the scrape hadn't

she suggested it to him beforehand? Why now, in front of Ezra? Was she trying to annoy him? But still, it was a good idea...

"Here's what you're going to do," he said. "The Commonwealth wants jurisdiction. You're going to give it to them."

"But... But the regulators. All these years, we've been working to limit their authority, and now you want them in charge?"

"The regulators aren't the problem. Not right now. They're busy chasing terrorists. And I can deal with regulators if I have to. The auxiliaries are different. I can't do a thing with them watching. So yes, I want you to give this one to the regulators."

"But... I can't just... It's not up to me. It'll take a vote in the Assembly. I can't guarantee they'll vote my way. I can't even guarantee my own faction. Not for something like this. Our whole platform is about keeping the regulators off people's backs. I can't just turn around and ask them to vote for the exact opposite."

"And yet that's exactly what you're going to do. I pay you to deliver votes in the Assembly, Representative. Now, either you can do that, or you can't. And if you can't, well then, all that money I've given you over the years, that was on the back of a lie. And I really don't like it when people lie to me."

Ezra swallowed. He licked his lips. But for the first time, there was a hint of calculation in his eyes. That was promising.

"It'll take time," he said. "I can't just order them. The Assembly's not like your... organization. I've spent years being pro-bi-tech, I can't turn around just like that. Not if I want to take my faction with me."

"You've got three days. No more. After that it's too late. For my business. And for you. Understand?"

Ezra nodded. Why wasn't he arguing? Fear? Or because three days was too easy? Maybe, but he couldn't go back on it now: three days it would have to be. Indecisiveness was a sign of weakness.

"Okay. You know what to do. Now get out of my sight."

Mary hauled the wrung-out representative to his feet and dragged him out of the office. Michael waited until they were back in the elevator, then returned to his picture window. The blast curtains were ruining the view, and it was a totally unnecessary precaution. He wasn't under attack. Sanja's killers hadn't been trying to get at him. They hadn't considered him at all.

In a sudden fury, he grabbed the curtains with both hands, and tore at them until the heavy material pooled at his feet.

CHAPTER 20

How long, then, before these living houses are more intelligent than their owners? How long before we exist to serve them, not they to serve us? If, that is, they have any use for us at all. How much more likely is it that they will see us as parasites, and take steps to remove the infestation?

— From: Vegetal Intelligence: The Threat, *The Union of Concerned Citizens*

"Please, Justice. Let me help you up."

"No. I'm fine…"

"It's no trouble."

"I said 'no'." Beth glowered at the offered hand. She waited for the young auxiliary to withdraw it, then climbed into the passenger seat. Just because she didn't feel up to any more driving didn't mean she was some kind of invalid.

It turned out to be a far shorter drive than she expected; so much so, she regretted not driving herself. The Mitchesons were nowhere near as rich as the Gwahnals. They lived just beyond the city in a wealthy suburb that had only recently been reclaimed from the desert. Theirs was no vast lakeside estate, but it was still a substantial property. And a surprisingly appealing one. The gardens looked to be full of familiar Noyan trees and shrubs, and were surrounded by a traditional stone wall. Perhaps this encounter wasn't going to be so unpleasant, after all.

But no – the moment they drove through the wrought iron gates, the gravel road was gone, replaced by the smooth wrongness of a roadroot. She signaled to the driver.

"That'll do. Pull over. I'll walk from here."

The mansion was only a short distance away, on the far side of a row of tall casab trees. But the roadroot didn't go straight there. It swept to the left, a giant alien tongue taking visitors on a pompous, looping tour of the grounds before bending towards the house itself. She preferred the direct route.

She climbed down to the roadroot – not without a shudder – and hurried to the edge. It was only a small roadroot, and the lip was easily low enough for her to step over, especially with no great drop down to the rockery on the other side. Either the Mitchesons had dug down before planting their drive, or they'd raised the soil level once it finished growing. Probably the latter. She'd seen what growing roadroots did to nearby vegetation. Even the casab trees wouldn't have been able to compete. They must have been moved here, fully grown, after the roadroot was bedded in.

She walked through the row of trees into a well-planted, well-watered garden centered around a circular pond. And wafting from it, a hauntingly familiar childhood smell: Swamp Truegolds. She couldn't resist going over to look. She hadn't seen Truegolds in years. They were common around Marshtop, but rarely grew this far north.

Not that this display compared with what she'd seen growing up. Here, a few well-schooled plants grew decorously to one side of the pond, broad yellow flowers open to soak in the sunshine. But Truegolds shouldn't be decorous. They should be everywhere, growing in wild profusion, spilling out of the pool to colonize the land around. This garden was, in its own way, as unnatural as the roadroot drive. And yet she wasn't revolted. She longed to take off her shoes and sit dangling her feet in the cool water. Instead, she turned and headed reluctantly towards the house.

The building was another pleasant surprise. It was the least alien off-comer building she'd ever seen – a tall, rectangular structure, six or more stories high; white stone walls inset with huge windows. The central doors were massive, and flanked by enormous ornamental columns. The design was still somewhat outlandish – no Noya would use so much glass, or such an excess of ornamental detail – but at least it looked like a building, not some kind of cancerous growth.

She reached out to knock on the double doors.

And recoiled, when the house spoke to her.

"This is the Mitcheson residence. The trade entrance is to the rear."

This building was a lie.

At least the Gwahnals' domes, the embassy's jungle, didn't pretend to be something they were not. This building might look like a thing of stone and glass, but it was as disturbingly alive as any other off-comer building. Its conventional appearance was a pretense, nothing more.

And now she had to talk to it.

She should have brought the auxiliary along to do the talking.

"I'm Beth of Marshtop, Justice of the Family Court. I'm here to see Constantine and Angelica Mitcheson."

"All visitors require appointments. Would you like me to connect you with the Mitchesons' social secretary to make an appointment?"

"I'm here on Family Court business: no appointment is

necessary. You'd better tell them I'm here."

"The Mitchesons are not currently receiving visitors. Would you like me to connect you–"

"Inform them that unless they see me immediately, they'll be charged with obstruction."

"Very well, Justice. Please wait."

Silence fell. Beth retreated a step. She didn't like being so close to the building. The rows of windows loomed over her like the many-faceted eyes of a giant insect. The outsized double doors reminded her of a predator's jaws. This must be how a fly felt, when it stepped onto a spider's web.

The doors swung open. There was no going back now, not without vast loss of face. A moment of hesitation, a deep self-conscious breath, then she stepped over the threshold into a vast entrance hall. Huge crystal chandeliers hung from a ceiling that was fully forty feet high. Tall gilt-framed mirrors caught the light and reflected it onto white marble sculptures lining the walls. At the far end, a broad staircase rose to the next floor; and descending that staircase was the house's owner, a green napkin at his neck. He was dressed entirely in white; except for his right shirt-sleeve, where a purple vine was slowly growing upwards from wrist to shoulder. He reminded her of a short version of Undersecretary Maitland; pink-brown skin, slim face, and an aquiline nose. Then he scowled and all resemblance disappeared – Constantine Mitcheson was made of far coarser stuff than the refined Undersecretary.

"Well?" he said. "What do you–"

"Where's Angelica?"

"–want?" The off-comer's scowl deepened. He screwed up the napkin at his neck and threw it aside. "My wife is looking after our guests. If you have anything to say, you can say it to me."

"No. I want to speak with both of you."

Something small and beetle-like scuttled out of an

alcove. She flinched and reached for her revolver. And stopped, embarrassed. The creature wasn't attacking. It scurried over to the napkin, folded it, and disappeared back into its hole. Beth swallowed. And wished, fervently, that she was somewhere, anywhere, else.

The off-comer stopped, three steps from the bottom of the stairs. "Well, you can't," he said. "In fact, unless you get to the point very soon, you won't get to speak to me, either."

And suddenly, everything was so much simpler.

"On the contrary. If you don't start cooperating, I'll arrest you both, and interview you at the Family Court."

The off-comer let out a short, barking laugh. "Really? And just how're you proposing to do that? Lady, you can't even fart in this house without my permission. I designed this place. Do you have any idea what it can do, if I want it to?"

"No, I don't. Do you have any idea what I can do, if I decide you're obstructing the Family Court? Now, are you going to answer my questions, or do I have to arrest you?"

The off-comer's face turned red. He glared at her. But he didn't turn back. And he didn't call on his house for help. Should she insist on Angelica's presence? Or take the win?

Take the win. For now.

"Where were you on the night of the fifth?"

"What?"

"Where were you on–?"

"I heard you. The night of the fifth? I don't... No. That was the night of the banquet. Our celebration dinner. Why?"

"It was the night Sanja Gwahnal was murdered."

The off-comer blinked. Then he spoke very slowly, as though to a child or a simpleton. "You think I had something to do with that? You're insane, aren't you? Really, truly insane. But even you can't argue with a hundred witnesses. I was at the banquet. Ask anyone."

"All night?"

"Until the attack on the roadroots, yes."

"Where did you go then?"

"Where do you think? To the site of the attack."

"Were you alone?"

"No. I was with Ambassador Ashef. He and Undersecretary Maitland flew me there in an embassy autocopter. They good enough witnesses for you?"

"Interesting. Don't you think it's a little suspicious that Sanja Gwahnal was murdered at the precise moment when the person with the best motive for killing him was surrounded by senior dignitaries?"

The off-comer's mouth opened, but no words came out. The vine had finished climbing his sleeve. It reached a purple tendril across his shoulder... and disappeared, leaving the entire sleeve purest white. For a moment. Then a hint of purple reappeared at the wrist.

"Me?" he said, at last. "You think I'd kill some spoiled brat because his friend made a scene at my banquet? What kind of motive is that?"

"Not the one I had in mind."

She retrieved Ethan's list from her jacket pocket, and offered it to him. He stomped down the remaining three steps, took the neatly folded paper, and looked it over.

"And this is?"

"A list of attacks carried out over the past eighteen months by an organization calling itself the 'League of Free Noyim'."

"So?"

"Notice anything?"

"Should I?"

"Oh yes. Very definitely yes."

"Well, I very definitely don't. What's this got to do with Sanja? With the Gwahnals?"

"That list comprises every significant attack on

off-co… Commonwealth interests over the last eighteen months."

"Yes?"

"How many of them were aimed at the Gwahnals?"

"I don't…"

He stopped talking. Blinked. Then focused intensely on the list. If he was acting, he was very good at it.

"Aren't the Gwahnals your largest manufacturers?"

He nodded. And carried on reading.

"You'd have expected at least one act of sabotage against their interests, wouldn't you?"

He looked up. "There have been attacks. They're just not on this list."

"Successful attacks? Attacks that caused real, significant damage? Like the damage to your roadroots."

"No. Not like my roadroots." He drew himself up to his full height. He was taller than her. Just. "And, yes. The Gwahnals are big. Bigger than the rest of us, put together."

"And this 'League', which is far the most active militant group, hasn't attacked them. Not even once."

"Apparently not. So, what are you suggesting?"

"That there's a pattern."

"Evidently. And you think someone noticed? And then what? Killed Sanja? And you think that someone was me?"

"Your company is the Gwahnals' largest competitor. I'm told your losses dwarf everyone else's."

He nodded thoughtfully, no longer hostile. "That makes sense. If I were you, I'd probably be here too. But the thing is, I didn't have any idea this was going on. And even if I'd known, I still wouldn't have killed the boy. Or Fange. Or Amaya. Or anyone else. I'd have gone straight to the embassy. The regulators would have… Now there's a thought…"

"What?"

"The regulators. They should have spotted a pattern like this a mile off. If the Family Court can spot it, then…

No offence. But the regulators should have picked this up a long time ago. It's downright negligent. It's their job to be on top of things like this. And negligence means liability, compensation. I won't even have to go to arbitration. They'll settle something like this right off, just to save the embarrassment... Thank you, Justice. Thank you very much indeed."

Suddenly, he was all smiles, hostility forgotten. The vine on his sleeve was once again half way through its climb to his shoulder.

"Be that as it may, you'll have to wait until I've concluded my investigation before you pursue any claims. The information I've given you is confidential. The Gwahnals have other competitors. You're not to talk to anyone about this, especially the regulators, until I give you permission."

"And if I don't? Wait, that is."

"Then I'll sanction you for interfering with a Family Court investigation, and perverting the course of justice."

She held out a hand for the list. He returned it with only the faintest show of reluctance.

"Far be it from me to pervert the course of justice... But I don't think my keeping quiet is going to make any difference. Even if you're right and someone spotted that pattern, and decided to do something completely insane instead of just alerting the authorities... Even then, how are you going to prove it? Establishing a motive isn't enough. You need evidence."

Beth sighed. How long had the off-comers lived on Noyan? And still they knew so little of Custom.

"No, I don't. Not as you understand it, anyway. All I need is to be certain."

"Really? And are you certain about me yet? Or do you still think I murdered him?"

He was smiling at the obvious ridiculousness of the question. She didn't smile back.

"Tell me," she said. "Why did you make your house look like a proper building?"

His smile wavered. "A proper building?"

"Straight lines. Glass. Stone. Or something that looks like stone."

"Ah. I see. I'm from Marion. We're a… traditional people. Just because we're Commonwealth now, that doesn't mean we have to change everything. This is what my grandfather's house looked like. Or would have, if he was rich enough. You like it?"

Beth gazed at the sumptuous hallway. All its gilt and glass were nothing but a veneer. What lay beneath was just as alien, just as disturbing, as any other off-comer building. She looked back at him, and shook her head. And was irritated when he gave every appearance of being delighted by her response

"Why don't you get back to your meal?" she said. "My office will be in contact when I wish to speak with you again. And next time, I'll expect to see Angelica as well."

He escorted her to the door and made a show of opening it for her. Didn't he realize she'd already seen it open itself? Or was this some strange form of off-comer courtesy. If so, it was wasted on her.

Outside, afternoon was giving way to evening. She headed back through the garden to her waiting car. The young auxiliary hurried to light the lanterns. Beth took advantage of the opportunity to climb into the driver's seat. She was in no mood to be driven. At some point in the interview, she'd come to a decision. Constantine might keep quiet about the Gwahnals' attacks on their rivals, but someone would talk, and soon. She'd feel much happier if the Gwahnals were safely under lock and key when that happened.

CHAPTER 21

You will understand, dearest cousin, that while I am personally loathe to press the matter, Ronjan is adamant that unless Fange provides satisfactory answers to the board's questions, he will have no choice but to withdraw his support. Your husband's position is weakening by the day. Too many junior branches of the family see an opportunity for elevation should Fange be removed as our Factor on Noyan...

– From: Private correspondence, *Marhey Atchek to Amaya Gwahnal*

It was easy to dream in the primary dome. Here, Amaya was no longer on Noyan; she was home on Anapkir, sitting beside a moss-fringed pool deep in the heart of a lush rain-forest. Red-filtered sunlight poured through a gap in the canopy, bathing the pool in vermillion light. Flitterbugs hovered over the water; some little more than moats of floating dust; others as large as her index finger, bright sparkles of orange and gold hunting their smaller cousins. And at the water's edge, shaded by the roots of a large tree-fern, a medusa waited – three delicate eye-fronds lurking just above the surface, blue-black feeding tubes twitching in the shallows. A flitter dipped unwisely into feeder-range, and yet flew on unmolested. The medusa wasn't interested in thin, chitinous flitterbugs;

not when Amaya's presence promised richer fare. But she had no treats for him today. She was staring at the glittering surface of the water, lost in a dream of other times.

Sanja was four years old, naked, splashing happily in the shallows while the medusa – smaller, younger, its eye-fronds barely uncurled – looked on resentfully at the noisy intrusion. Sanja's serious face was split in a wide, wet grin. His skin gleamed; his eyes sparkled like hidden violet gems. He was the most beautiful thing on this world, on any world: her son, her future, and the future of her House.

"Amaya."

There it was again. A voice: intrusive, insistent, unwanted. Speaking to her from a world where her son was dead. A world she rejected.

She smiled, happy to see Sanja playing so innocently in the pool that had been made just for him. He would grow up far from home, but with–

"Amaya!"

The voice would not be denied. It dissolved the dream. Sanja was no longer playing in the shallows. The medusa was alone in the water, feeding-tubes questing in search of non-existent tidbits.

Maybe, if she closed her eyes, she could go back there, to that golden time when both Sanja and the medusa were very small. Everything had been different, then: full of possibilities. Sanja's arrival had unlocked everything. Even Uncle Ronjan's long-standing resistance had crumbled. Sanja could not be denied the advancement they so begrudged Fange; not her son; not an heir of the blood.

The choice of Noyan had been an insult, but a welcome one. It freed her of any obligation. And there were fewer jealous eyes so far from civilization; fewer rivals to pounce on the least mistake. And in the end, opportunities undreamed of: the chance to create their own fiefdom, to break with a family that refused to give them their due. Here, they could rule. Their son would grow up on Noyan, but he would never be *of* Noyan. This was where he belonged, in this garden of home they had built for him, and his children, and his children's children.

But now there would be no children, no future.

Her son. Her beautiful son...

Stop. Go back. The boy in the pool; a perfect moment. Better not to think; better to dream. Water on smooth skin; white teeth; glittering violet eyes...

"Amaya!" Fange was standing over her, arms folded, glowering. "Amaya, you can't just leave her there. Think of the consequences."

Consequences? She should care about consequences? The strangeness of the thought brought her back, irrevocably, to the present. And to Fange: this strange, incomprehensible Fange who didn't understand that nothing mattered now, nor ever would again.

"Please, Amaya. Release her. We can't afford to antagonize the Family Court."

The medusa's primary feeding-tube was curling out of the water. She should have brought it something. Sanja would never have come here empty-handed.

"Please, 'maya."

Why was he doing this? Didn't he understand she wanted to be left alone?

"Never. The bitch can rot."

"Please, Amaya. She's not worth it. We can't afford another enemy. Not now."

The medusa's feeding-tube flexed open in anticipation. The thought of its inevitable disappointment cut her to the quick. She couldn't stay here like this, tantalizing the poor creature. She stood up and brushed loose dirt from her culottes. Damp, black-brown soil smeared across her right knee. She watched it fade until only pristine ivory remained. Fange was staring at her, waves of tension pulsing off him.

"House," she said. "Unseal the garden maze."

Fange's shoulders dropped; his arms unfolded. He

reached out to take her arm, but she shook him off. She had no interest in presenting a united front with him – not for the benefit of some monstrous un-woman from the Family Court.

Were those her footsteps? Already? Yes. The bitch was approaching. She had never been far away. The dome was large, but the forest was only an illusion, a clever construct, where seeming-depth deceived the eye. The ever-shifting maze relied on dense foliage and deception, not scale, to keep out unwanted intruders.

There she was now, emerging from the trees. Short. Old. Devoid of grace. Dwarfed by the two native men behind her; both of them hot and flustered, beads of sweat visible on their repulsive brown skin. The old bitch was sweating, too; damp patches spreading disgustingly under her armpits; primitive dress making no effort to adjust to the humidity. She should wear trousers, not a dress. Everything about her was masculine, including her coarse native features. She was as ugly as her calling.

The woman nodded. "Fange. Amaya."

"Justice." Fange nodded back, weakling that he was. Amaya was silent.

The woman was holding a pair of metal bracelets linked by a small chain. So was the man to her right. What strange pieces of jewelry. Were they some kind of badge of office? She had so little contact with the natives, and none at all from choice.

The woman was speaking again. She had an oddly formal tone, as if repeating something by rote. "...accused of murdering your son, Sanja Gwahnal. How do you plead?"

The words made no sense. Amaya looked to Fange. His mouth was flapping open, face flushing red.

"Plead?" he stuttered. "What do you mean 'plead'? We're not in court. This is our home."

"I'm a Justice," said the woman, pityingly. "The Family Court isn't a building. It goes where I go."

The bitch. The arrogant, *evil* bitch. To come here, and accuse her of killing her own son? The rage was all-encompassing. She was shaking. Actually shaking.

She never should have unsealed the maze. But that mistake was easily remedied. She would leave. The bitch would not. The maze worked both ways.

She went to push past the three natives.

And stopped, appalled. The woman had grabbed her wrists and bound her hands. Finally, much too late, she understood the bracelets' purpose.

Only the Noyim could be so brutal, so barbaric, as to bind soft flesh in unyielding metal.

She closed her eyes. Sanja was four years old, splashing in the pool, warm red sunlight streaming in to illuminate him alone...

"How dare you? Get these things off me!"

Fange was shouting, interrupting her dream. Why couldn't he just let her go? Why did he have to keep dragging her back to the present? To cold, hard metal biting into her delicate white wrists. To a world where Sanja was dead.

Still Fange wouldn't shut up. "Who do you think you are? You're monsters. All of you. The Noyim are a damned people, dead to all natural feeling."

He was raging, furious. And ineffectual. The Justice was unmoved. "I'll take that as a not guilty plea, shall I?"

Amaya worked her jaw, building saliva, readying herself to spit. And was dragged away before she could launch it. The natives manhandled them, forcing them back down the path and through the crawler-vine screen that masked the exit. Did the natives wonder at how quickly they'd reached the corridor? Did they understand how the trails shifted at her whim? Perhaps. But it was of no significance.

The air was different beyond the dome. Drier. More alien.

She didn't want to be here. She wanted to be back beside the pool. With Sanja.

But the man was so strong. And the bracelets hurt her wrists when she resisted. It was time for the house to deal with these people, to teach them what it meant to lay hands on a Factor's Lady. She had only to open her mouth...

Fange was craning his neck, desperate to catch her eye. What was he trying to tell her? Why was he shaking his head? Did he guess what she was planning? Probably. Did she care? Not at all.

But nor did she have the strength to act. She was drifting, lost – nothing but flotsam, dragged down corridors and through domes until, between one step and the next, it was too late. She was outside. Outside, and powerless – and finally able to see the horror awaiting her: a convoy of native automobiles, spewing pollution in an evil vapor.

She dug in her heels, but was dragged on regardless. Never in her most baroque nightmares had she imagined traveling in monstrosities like these. But there was nothing she could do about it; not for herself, and not for Fange, who was already being bundled into the back of a large black automobile. She screamed, shouted, protested, but was forced effortlessly into a second automobile. Another native was waiting there. Her captor climbed in behind, trapping her in the middle of the rear seat.

She shrank into herself, disgusted by the stench and the greasy feel of the seat. It looked like... No. It couldn't be. Surely, not even the natives would cover a seat with the flayed skin of a slaughtered animal.

The primitive automobile lurched into motion, carrying her away from home and safety, picking up speed; yet still the sides remained wide open. There was nothing to hold her in place, nothing to save her should the automobiles collide, or simply topple over as they sped unsteadily forwards. She huddled down, fear overriding even her disgust at the charnel-house seat.

And then they were rounding the lake, and she was

faced with a still greater horror: Sanja's house. Night was falling, but the ruined building was clearly visible against the skyline; a grotesque, twisted husk. The stench of decay rolled over the convoy, adding to the industrial stink of the automobiles. Obscene images rose in her mind's eye: images of Sanja – rotten, decomposing, at one with the filth that was his house. The beautiful little boy of her dreams had died alone, trapped, choking; calling desperately for help that never came.

Calling for her.

She buried her face in her bound hands, but the image remained, insistent, accusing – until a sudden, sharp jolt slammed the metal bracelets into her chin and hot, sharp pain dragged her back to the present. She looked up. They hadn't – yet – crashed into another vehicle. The jarring had marked the transition from roadroot drive to native road. The ride, already uncomfortable, became unbearable. Even the natives seemed aware of it. The convoy came to a sudden halt. But no, they weren't responding to the intolerable discomfort. People were jumping down and hurrying to light boxy yellow lanterns at the front of the automobiles. They cast only pale, watery light ahead of them. How could anyone, even natives, trust their lives to such puny illumination?

The convoy set off again, moving through a night that was ever darker and colder. Her shirt collar tightened; the sleeves rolled themselves down; but there was little her culottes could do to keep out the bitter wind. She shivered continually, as much from fear as cold. The journey had turned into an endless nightmare. Threatening shapes loomed suddenly out of the surrounding dark, and passed swiftly out of sight, only to be replaced by the next emerging danger. The convoy was a tiny island of illumination surrounded by a vast, ominous ocean of darkness that sought to snuff it out.

Then, at long last, another island of light came into view. Small at first, it grew rapidly, became intricate, complex, artificial – filling the horizon with the ugly regularity of native streets. Sickly yellow-orange streetlight drew them into a hell of stark, angular roads, devoid of greenery; lifeless spaces where harsh, synthetic light illuminated dead roads paved with stone. Finally, they emerged in a large, open plaza, surrounded by tall, ominous edifices of stone and glass whose upper stories were lost in darkness beyond the reach of puny native streetlights.

A large crowd waited on the broad steps in front of the largest, ugliest building of all: the Family Court. The crowd surged towards the convoy. A line of militia hurried to interpose themselves between the mob and the slowing automobiles. And Amaya finally understood the true depths of the Justice's malice. The bitch wasn't content merely to arrest them; she planned to parade them before the mob.

She grabbed the back of the seat in front and gripped the foul thing with all her strength, fighting the natives' attempts to force her from her seat just as fiercely as she had their efforts to force her into it. And as ineffectually. She was hauled out and dragged through the baying crowd. Everywhere she looked, hostile faces were shouting questions: dark natives and pale Commonwealthers alike, all seemed alien in the unnatural yellow-orange glow of the streetlights.

Bright, white lights flashed as she passed, dazzling and disorienting. The crowd roared, individual words lost in the noise; questions shouted over questions; eager natives holding archaic notebooks; horrified Commonwealthers with cameras hovering overhead. All was noise and confusion; but in the midst of it, the militia was acting with purpose, forcing the crowd back, and dragging Fange and Amaya up the steps.

More militia were waiting at the top. They moved aside, and reformed behind her to hold back the crowd. The Family Court loomed over her, a great cliff of stone. One immense block protruded from the wall, overhanging the entrance. She cowered beneath it, terrified of so much weight seemingly resting on nothing more than a thin wall of glass.

The Justice stopped to address the crowd, but she and Fange were dragged on towards the glass wall. Her feet scrabbled for purchase. She screamed in protest, but no one was listening. The glass filled her view. She saw her terrified reflection, the cruel determined guards. One thrust out an arm, oblivious to the danger. And the glass swung away. It was a door; a strange, alien door, so primitive it couldn't even open itself.

The immediate danger was over – but the ever-present threat remained. She was being forced deeper into a dead building. Thousands of tons of lifeless stone were pressing down above her head. There were no systems regulating this unnatural space; no house brain working to maintain its integrity. Nothing to prevent catastrophic collapse.

All the energy drained from her muscles. She sagged down in the arms of her captors, no longer resisting; barely able to walk. She was alive. But for how long? They were trapped beneath a flat stone ceiling. How could something so impossibly heavy be supported by such distant, inadequate walls?

Her vision was blurring; her heart pounding. She was hyperventilating, desperate for air. The walls swayed in and out, rippling like waves, but her captors pulled her onwards into the nightmarish structure, impelling her forwards into a narrow corridor.

Someone was shouting. It was Fange, close on her heels, and a world away.

Claustrophobic, box-like corridors turned through bewildering right-angles, and transformed into sharp-edged stone stairways, plunging steeply downwards. Every step piled yet more primitive masonry above their heads.

She was going to die here. It was a miracle this building stood at all. One small shock – a tremor, an earthquake, a fire – and the whole edifice would come crashing down on her head.

The final corridor was rock, not stone. Here, at least the ceiling was arched; but that was scant comfort with so much weight bearing down above. Ahead was a wooden door. Solid. Rectangular. Metal grill embedded at head height. A prison cell.

One of their captors opened the door, revealing the tiny, claustrophobic death trap on the other side. Amaya retreated. She was somewhere far away, watching herself, observing the frenzy, the biting-kicking-screaming. The pain in her wrists. The too-tight grip on her arms. Her legs flailing as they carried her bodily inside and threw her onto a primitive native cot.

Something was done to her wrists. The metal bracelets were gone. She surged upwards, and sank back down, despairing. The door was already closing.

Fange was sitting on a second cot against the other wall. Staring at the red marks on his wrists.

Her gaze flickered around the room. Windowless. Low-ceilinged. Closet-small; more truncated corridor than room.

There was a bucket against the rear wall, and a dim native lightbulb above their heads. Someone was at the door, speaking through the grill. Was it the Justice? It didn't matter. The words washed over her, unattended.

The bed was too close to the stone wall. She crawled onto the hard floor and sat in the middle of the room, hugging her knees. Fange joined her, wrapped his arms around her. She buried her face in his shoulder; gave way to tears. The grill snapped shut. Silence fell. They were trapped in a terrible stone coffin, huddling together in search of simple animal comfort.

An endless time passed. Amaya's tears dried. Muscles stiffened. Discomfort penetrated even her misery. She shifted position, shrugged off Fange's arm, and then sought it out again.

Twice the grill opened. The second time, a different voice spoke. A familiar voice. "What are you doing down there on the floor? Surely it can't be comfortable?"

"Moyem?" Fange struggled to his feet. She followed him. Jimawn was no fellow prisoner. His arrogant, smiling face was proof of that. And his presence on the *other* side of the locked door. Did he have agents even here, in the Family Court?

"You have to get us out of here, Moyem." Fange was ashen-faced, his forehead glistening with sweat.

"Why? This is perfect. The Commonwealth and Noyan are at daggers drawn, and we didn't have to do a damn thing to bring it about. The Justice has done it for us, all by her fanatical self."

Fange said nothing. She pushed him aside. "Get us out of here, Jimawn. Now. This building's dead."

"It was never alive, Amaya dear. And there are advantages to dead buildings. No one can poison them. You're safer here than your own home. And don't worry about the Family Court. The embassy won't let them harm you. All you have to do is sit tight and wait for the ambassador to come to the rescue."

"You don't understand. We can't wait. Not here. You have to get us out."

"You're right. I don't understand. We need you here. The longer she holds you, the more intense the crisis becomes. All you have to do is sit tight–"

"We can't!"

"Yes, you can. This building's perfectly safe. Give it time. You'll get used to it."

"No, we won't. We won't have the chance. You're going to get us out of here, and I'm going to kill that Family Court bitch."

"Really? That would be most unwise. This is a golden opportunity. Always get out of the way when your opponents are making mistakes. And you couldn't be more out of the way than where you are right now. Just be patient. That's all I ask."

Fange's hand was on her arm, importuning. "Please, Amaya. He has a point..."

She shook him off. "Our son is dead. Nothing else matters. I don't care about all your clever plans. I don't care about anything, anymore."

"Our plans, my good Amaya. Ours."

"Not mine, Jimawn. Not now. All my plans died with Sanja. I need to get out of here. And I need that bitch dead."

"You're not thinking straight, Amaya. I know you're upset, but try to be rational. Your arrest suits our mutual purposes. You understand that, don't you, Fange?"

"Of course I do! But Moyem, it's hard. This building..."

"Don't worry, it won't be for long."

"No, it won't," she said. "Because if you don't get us out of here, I'll be forced to tell the Family Court everything. About you. About our joint venture. Everything. You understand me, *Moyem*?"

Jimawn's expression was distant, appraising. He nodded. "Yes, Amaya. I understand. Very well, if I can't persuade you, I suppose I have to bow to the inevitable. I'll get you out, but it's going to take a little time to arrange. You will try and keep your mouth shut until then, won't you, my dear?"

"That depends on how long you keep us waiting."

"Understood. Goodbye, Amaya, Fange. Sleep tight."

The grill closed. They were alone once more. Claustrophobia descended again, stronger than ever. She hammered at the door, begging to be let out. Fange reached for her, but this time she pushed him away. She wanted nothing from him, not even animal comfort. She sank down and closed her eyes.

Sanja was four years old, naked, splashing happily in the forest pool...

CHAPTER 22

...Ambassador Ashef has lodged a formal protest with the Assembly demanding the immediate release of Fange and Amaya Gwahnal. All aid projects and joint ventures have been suspended with immediate effect and will remain suspended until the local authorities take appropriate action to defend Commonwealth citizens against arbitrary and outrageous infringement of their liberty...

– From: Noyan News Hour, *a division of Commonwealth Information Services*

Little Jodan was cold. They never heated this wing of the orphanage. The only fire was in the usher's room, and Jodan was unwilling to pay the price of sharing it. He slipped out of bed and tip-toed over to the window. The world beyond was hidden behind a veil of frost. He lifted the hem of his thin nightshirt and cleared a small circle of glass. Peering out, he saw a world transformed. Gone were the brown fields, the muddy roads, the scrawny trees. Everything was soft, white and welcoming. It was worth being cold to see this. He pulled on his too-tight shoes and hurried downstairs, eager to be the first to leave footprints in the snow.

The cobbled courtyard lay concealed under a white blanket. He ran across and pushed on the tall gates with all the strength of his skinny arms. They refused to move. He saw the padlock – huge, half as big as himself, an insurmountable obstacle – and began to cry. Only, somehow the sobs weren't his own...

Jodan opened his eyes. He wasn't in the orphanage. He was at home, lying on his own familiar sleeping pad, staring up at the gently curving ceiling.

But someone was still sobbing.

Errina was standing in the open doorway, one hand on the wall, the other covering her face. He scrambled to his feet and hurried to comfort her. "What is it, Rina? What's wrong?"

She reached out for him, tried to speak, but no words came. Her face was wet with tears. He pulled her to him, burying her head in his chest. And waited patiently for her to compose herself. When she finally spoke, the words were halting, and raw.

"The Gwahnals... The Family Court..."

"What about them? What's happened?"

"They... They... The Family Court. They've arrested the Gwahnals."

"What?"

"She's... She's blaming them, Jo. Says they killed Sanja. It's madness. That poor woman. To lose her son, and then this..."

The 3-V was still projecting in the living room, oblivious of its abandonment. And what it showed was worse than anything he'd imagined. He'd known the Justice was a fanatic, but to see the Gwahnals bundled into the Family Court, and hear the woman's gloating press conference on the steps of the court...

This was his fault. He'd let her take over the case. He had, no one else. He should have taken away the old bitch's gun and shot her with it; or died trying.

Errina was back. She was no longer crying, but her eyes were still red-rimmed, raw. He put an arm around her shoulders. "It's all my fault," he said, bleakly.

"No, it's not, Jo. It's..."

"Yes, it is. I shouldn't have let that bitch get anywhere near the Gwahnals."

"You didn't have any–"

"But I did. Maitland was right. I should have let her shoot me."

"And leave me a widow? Your children orphans? Don't be ridiculous."

He shrugged an apology. She was right. But so was he.

"It's not just that. We can't prove she's wrong. Not without telling the truth. And the embassy's not going to do that. Hozefa's going to let the Gwahnals die before he risks his own skin. And I helped him!"

"No, you didn't. You tried to stop him."

"I did. I helped him. I told Hatcher how to put that report together. Encouraged him to tell lies. And that Family Court bitch knows it. She knows we're lying. She knows terrorists didn't kill Sanja Gwahnal. So of course she's blaming Sanja's parents instead. It's madness – but in her crazy world, it makes sense. She thinks their vile customs apply to everyone, even Commonwealthers. She's convinced herself that Sanja wanted a Choosing ceremony. That the Gwahnals killed him to protect themselves. She's going to murder them, and there's nothing anyone can do to stop her."

"Yes, there is. There has to be."

"How?"

"By telling the truth."

"No one's going to listen to me. Not without evidence."

"So go out and get some!"

"It's not as simple as that…"

Except that… maybe it was. Because, if not him, then who? He was a regulator. It was his duty to uphold the embargo: his duty to the Commonwealth, to his regulator's oath… and, more than anything, to that poor grieving mother, trapped in a native prison cell, in jeopardy of her life. He couldn't abandon her to the mercy of the Family

Court. He had to save her. And there was only one way to do it. He had to show the world what really lay behind Sanja Gwahnal's death: illegal bi-tech, and a shattered embargo.

There had to be a way...

"Beynan Hotep," he said.

"What?"

"He and Sanja were thick as thieves. They must have used the same dealer. I had a team investigating, before Hozefa called them off. I'm still a regulator. I've still got my tool bag. I'm going to do what the Office of Regulation *should* be doing. I'm going to tear Hotep's house apart, find every last bit of black market bi-tech he's got until he has no choice but to tell me who his dealer is. And then I'm going public. Everyone will know who the real killer is: the dealer who sold Sanja the crap that destroyed his house. And once the truth is out, even that Family Court monster is going to have to back down and let the Gwahnals go."

CHAPTER 23

In short, the Assembly should trust in the Family Court. Those representatives who fail to back Beth the Justice against these and other off-comer slanders are disgracing themselves and the people they represent. When off-comers cast aspersions against the court, our representatives should rise as one to defend it.
- *From:* Editorial, *The Recorder*

Beth woke, heart pounding, ears ringing. A claxon was wailing outside her chambers; echoing other, more distant sirens throughout the court.

An alarm. But not the fire alarm. Something was wrong. But what?

It was dark out; the middle of the night. What could...?

The Gwahnals? Was the embassy staging a rescue?

No. Not even off-comers would be that insane.

She switched on her nightlight, shuffled to the edge of her bed, and sat up – just as the claxons fell silent with a final, despairing wail. Her clock showed four in the morning. She'd been asleep for barely three hours.

Maybe she should just lie down again and go back to sleep...

Her eyes drooped. Closed. And snapped open again. Someone was hammering on her door. She tried to call out permission to enter, but was overwhelmed by a coughing fit. It had the same effect; the door opened. She looked up, expecting Ethan, and saw a wide-eyed, broad-shouldered woman from the night team. Agnes? Abigail? Anna? That was it, An–

"The Gwahnals, Justice. Their cell's empty. They're gone."

She was half way to the door before she realized she'd risen without help, or pills. Adrenaline really was the best medicine – but not, perhaps, so good for sound judgement. There were prisoners on the loose, and she'd left her revolver on the nightstand. She went back, retrieved it and rejoined the auxiliary, nightdress flapping, gun in hand.

"How long have they been gone?"

"I don't know, Justice. But they're not in their cell."

"Has the building been sealed?"

"I think so, Jus–"

"Run and make sure. Who's in charge?"

"Sarah. She's–"

"Tell her I want to see her at the Gwahnal's cell. Right now. Go!"

Five minutes later, she was staring unhappily at the empty cell. It was ten feet long by eight feet wide, windowless, with walls and ceiling of solid rock. There was a bed on each side, neither of which showed any signs of being slept in, and a lavatory bucket at the back. The only illumination came from a single naked bulb in the middle of the ceiling. There was nothing here to go wrong. It was impregnable – the perfect cell, deep in the bowels of the Family Court, and totally secure. And yet the Gwahnals had escaped. But how? They hadn't battered down the door or tunneled their way out. They hadn't even picked the lock.

The answer was obvious, and utterly devastating. Someone had set them free. There was a traitor in the court. Not a Justice – that was unthinkable – but someone with access to the most secure areas. A clerk, perhaps?

No. If she couldn't trust the Family Court, she couldn't trust anyone. It had to be an auxiliary. Sarah herself, maybe. She was the shift supervisor. Who better to engineer an escape?

"How long have they been gone?"

"I don't know, Justice."

Sarah's voice, normally so confident, was faint with embarrassment. Or fear. Beth turned to face her.

"You weren't doing regular checks?"

"No Justice. There was no need. It's the Family Court…"

"Yes."

What could she say? This was as much her fault as anyone's. More so. The Gwahnals were her prisoners. She should have given explicit instructions, made sure they were kept secure.

"How did you find out they were missing?"

"One of the guards looked in on them. Saw they weren't here."

"Which guard?"

"I'm not sure. I can find out, but everyone's out searching right n–"

"Who's coordinating the search?"

"Um. I'm not sure anyon–"

"Get me a floor plan. I'll be in the main foyer. I can coordinate from there. And Sarah. Make sure the building's sealed. No one leaves. For any reason."

"Yes, Justice."

"And I want roadblocks. Call out the militia. All vehicles to be searched until further notice. Especially off-comer vehicles. I want those prisoners caught. And send for Ethan. I need him as quickly as he can get here. And a team of auxiliaries with him. The more people we throw at the search, the better. Well? What are you waiting for? Get to it."

Sarah scuttled off, eager to obey and escape Beth's

displeasure. Beth followed wearily, entirely certain the Gwahnals were already far away, and safely out of her reach.

She supervised the search from a trestle table by the main doors. A clerk brought a desk lamp, plugged it into a distant wall socket, and used it to weigh down one end of the unrolled floorplan; the other end was held down by her revolver. Twice, the lamp almost went flying when auxiliaries snagged the trailing wire.

It took ten minutes to organize the searchers into teams. After that, progress was more systematic, but just as slow. Things improved a little when a group of clerks arrived. They lived in shared accommodation within claxon-range, and had hurried in to help. She set them to guard secured areas, freeing up auxiliaries for the search.

Shouts outside heralded new arrivals. Not Ethan's team, but reporters, drawn by the claxons – or tipped off about unusual activity at the court. She sent clerks to keep them at bay, and had the trestle table moved further into the building. It wouldn't suit the dignity of her office to be seen in her nightdress.

Then, finally, Ethan was there, a squad of auxiliaries in tow. There was no twinkle in his weary eyes, and no hint of a smile on his face. But at least now she could safely delegate. She took him aside for a quick consultation, and then retreated to her chambers, leaving him in charge. She would have gone alone, but Ethan insisted – understandably, but irritatingly – on an auxiliary accompanying her and standing guard while she freshened up. Everyone had to be careful with prisoners on the loose, even her.

Every light in her chambers was on. Searchers had been through it, and made sure to leave no dark corners for off-comers to hide in. She allowed the auxiliary to give the room another swift once-over, and then sent him outside. As soon as he was safely on the other side of the door, she methodically turned off all the lights except the overhead, reclaiming the space as her own. Necessary as the search had been, she hated the thought of people in her chambers when she wasn't there.

There was no point in hurrying now: the worst had already happened. And Ethan was safely in charge. She took her time washing, dressing, and putting on her makeup. Then she opened the medicine cabinet and reached for her pills. And put them back. Her back hurt, but not too badly. Better to leave the pills for when she needed them.

She arrived back in the foyer just as the search was wrapping up. It had proved every bit as futile as she'd expected. There was no sign of Fange and Amaya, and no clue as to how they'd escaped. Her clever ploy of arresting the Gwahnals now risked completely derailing the investigation. Instead of focusing solely on tracking down Sanja's killers, she was going to have to divert precious resources to hunt for the escapees.

Dawn was breaking outside. She led Ethan to the middle of the Justices' courtyard, safe from prying eyes and ears under the statue of 'Choice Accepted'. He smiled at her wearily, dimples finally making an appearance. She only just caught herself in time to avoid returning his smile. Behind him, sunlight was slowly spreading across the golden-pink cloister roof.

"Jude came in early," he said. "I've got him coordinating the roadblocks. But at this point..." He shrugged. "Other than that, I'm not sure there's much we can do. They got away."

"They did. But not on their own. They're off-comers. They don't know the first thing about unlocking our cell doors. Someone let them out. Someone on the inside."

Ethan's dimples disappeared as if they'd never been. "You really think so? One of us? Helping off-comers against the Family Court? Why?"

"That's an extremely good question. Money's the obvious motive. But where would they spend it? They'd have to know they'd be caught if they turned up rich..."

Ethan shook his head. "I don't buy it, Justice. I suppose if someone was in debt to the wrong people, they might... We can check it out. But even then... I don't care how rich the Gwahnals are, how big a bribe they could offer. They didn't have the time. They didn't even spend a single night in the cells. It's just too quick. Unless they already had someone on the inside. And I don't buy that, either. Not off-comers. Now, if it was traditionalists who'd escaped, then maybe. A lot of people have traditionalist sympathies: auxiliaries, clerks. Maybe even Justices."

"Not the Justices," said Beth, flatly. "And it'd take more than just sympathies to do something like this. But if the Gwahnals really were the main backers behind traditionalist militants, or if enough traditionalists thought they were... Do you think the militants have followers in the Auxiliary Court?"

"I don't want to think it... but it's possible. Someone helped, and if not traditionalists, then who? It wasn't Michael, that's for sure. I was watching his place all night. There was nothing. No excitement, no unusual activity. Nothing."

"You were watching? Yourself? Not just your team?"

"I was. My people were there too, but I took my turn."

So Ethan's team could vouch for him. He couldn't be the traitor. A tension she hadn't even recognized eased from her shoulders. She made an effort to focus. Ethan was still talking.

"...could be the embassy, I suppose. Maybe they've managed to get an agent into the court. One of us, but working for them. You want me to look into it, see if I can find the traitor?"

"Yes. But not you personally. Someone working for you. Someone you trust. Jude, maybe? We have to keep our priorities straight. Catching the Gwahnals is important. Finding the traitor even more so. But nothing's as important as catching Sanja Gwahnal's killers."

CHAPTER 24

The Noyim do not see beauty in the natural shapes and sensuous curves of our architecture. They see something rendered ugly, even grotesque, by magnification: much as we might view an insect grown suddenly to the size of a horse. Bizarre as it may seem, the Noyim prize unnatural symmetry and artificial regularity as their highest aesthetic.
   – *From:* My Time on Noyan, Memories of a Youthful Exile, *The Rt. Hon. Beynan Hotep na Massowic*

He awoke to the realization that he was alive. It was a profound, almost spiritual, revelation; one moment he was dormant, hibernating, the next a small, frail spark of life emerged somewhere beneath his breastbone. It spread outwards from there, growing to fill his chest and warm his arms and legs until his fingers and toes tingled with pins and needles. Where life returned, pain soon followed. He was lying on his front, left arm twisted uncomfortably beneath him. His head ached. His eyes stung. His mouth was parched and filled with a taste of unparalleled staleness. And his bladder was full to bursting.

There was no doubt about it: at some point in the recent past he'd drunk far, far too much alcohol.

So, he was alive. And he had a hangover. What else did he know?

He rolled onto his back and opened his eyes. The ceiling was green, padded, and dotted with glowbulbs. It curved downwards and merged with the floor. He was inside a soft green bubble devoid of doors or windows: a prison cell.

He closed his eyes. Memories fell into place. He was Beynan Hotep of the family Massowic. And he was in trouble. Again.

How and why he'd ended up in this cell eluded him. It was worrying, not knowing. He needed to get his story straight before grandfather came to collect him. Hard to do that, when he didn't even know what he'd done.

Now, what was the last thing he could remember...?

He sat bolt upright, eyes wide open.

Grandfather Massowic wouldn't be coming to bail him out. Not this time. Grandfather was far, far away on another world. Bey was on his own.

What the fuck was he wearing? No wonder he was so fucking uncomfortable. His suit – his modern, sophisticated suit; the one luxury he still had on this toilet of a world – was gone. He was dressed like a fucking native. And he stank. There was a dark stain around his groin, like he'd wet himself and the trousers were doing a terrible job of processing it.

So, odds-on they'd thrown him in here for being drunk and disorderly. Probably very drunk, and very disorderly. Ordinary everyday drunkenness wouldn't be enough for him to end up in a cell. Not him. Not a Massowic. His lack of memory was probably a blessing.

At least it wasn't a native prison. The room was modern, if plain: aside from the bright dots of glowbulbs, there was nothing to break the monotony of padded walls and ceiling, or to show where one ended and the other began.

He stood up. The soft floor instantly solidified into a hard, supportive surface. He lay down again, and it softened to something more yielding. He reached out to the wall. It was hard when touched, soft and fleshy when (rather gingerly) punched.

"Water, please," he said, and a nipple extruded itself from the wall. He stared at it unhappily. This was the embassy. Had to be. Bi-tech this sophisticated was illegal everywhere else on Noyan.

He leaned over and drank until he couldn't drink any more. Then he called for a toilet and took care of the second most urgent necessity. Feeling somewhat better, he returned to the middle of the floor and lay down again.

So, he'd been drinking. But where? It couldn't be anywhere salubrious; not given the clothes he was wearing. He had a vague memory of a bar, and some casabey...

And Samuel. He was definitely drinking with Samuel...

A door opened in his mind, and memories flooded in: Sanja's death, Jodan Hyrom, the terrifying encounter with Michael, fleeing to New Beginning. And sitting down to drink with Samuel. After that, nothing. Except somehow, he was certain the Justice had been in the bar with them... And he had the weirdest feeling she'd rescued him again – not from Michael this time, but from Samuel.

Which just made no sense at all.

But she'd definitely been in New Beginning. And he thought maybe he'd left with her. So how come he was here, in the embassy? How did that work out?

Time passed. His stomach growled. He was hungry. Very hungry. He hadn't eaten since... when? The last really decent meal he could remember was the Mitchesons' banquet. How long ago was that? It felt like years, with everything that had happened since.

Pride be damned: he had to eat. He stood up and demanded food. A second green nipple emerged from the wall. He suckled on it without hesitation. The nourishing secretion was warm and sweet, a bland syrup that soothed his throat and filled his belly. It was wonderfully, disturbingly satisfying. Sated, he retreated shame-facedly to the middle of the room. At least no one had been there to see him, Beynan Hotep of the family Massowic, sucking on house pap like a pauper.

Immediate wants satisfied, he had time for other, lesser discomforts. His right leg was sore, below the knee. He peeled back a greasy trouser leg, and found a large purple bruise on his shin. Had he been in some kind of fight? Maybe. But what about the bruise on the inside of his left elbow? How the fuck had he done that? He had no clue. There were definitely still gaps in his memory. Big ones. And what he did remember was all messed up, a bewildering mix of hazy memory and alcoholic dream.

But the more he put things in order, the more certain he became of one thing. Beth the Justice had rescued him not once now, but twice.

He lay back, closed his eyes and began to drift off again. Now that he'd eaten, he was suddenly very, very...

"Wake up, Hotep."

He did so, with a start. Someone was talking to him. A familiar voice, but who? His eyes were sticky with sleep. He opened them – and saw Undersecretary Maitland peering down at him.

Maitland. Of course. Who else but the Ambassador's fixer to deal with an erring Massowic?

"Undersecretary." He clambered to his feet.

Maitland looked him up and down very slowly, and very disapprovingly. "Have you any idea how embarrassing it is for the ambassador to have you in the cells?"

"Ashef knows?"

"Of course he bloody knows. You think I wasn't going to tell him we had a member of the Massowic family in the cells? That you'd disgraced your family name, again? And that this time, you'd been dumped on us by a Justice of the Family Court. And not just any Justice. The very one who's busily giving him heartburn at the moment? Yes. The ambassador knows."

"What did he say?"

"What do you think? He wasn't pleased. Not pleased at

all. This is the very last time he's going to bail you out. If you ever end up in trouble again, you'll regret it. Do you understand?"

Bey wasn't at all sure that he did.

"You mean, you're letting me go?"

"That's right. We're letting you go. And we don't want you to come back, ever."

"No."

"No? What do you mean 'no'?"

A good question. Had he really meant to say that? Yes, on balance, he really had. He didn't want to go anywhere. He was safe here. Leaving meant being out there – along with Michael, and Samuel, and who knew what other friendly face turned suddenly hostile and dangerous.

"I mean I don't want you to release me. I want to help the authorities. I'll tell you everything I know. I know who supplied Sanja's bi-t... Ow!"

"Shut up!"

What the fuck? Maitland had slapped him, hard, around the head. His ears were ringing! He'd never seen the undersecretary like this. The man looked positively feral.

"It's not enough for you to drag your family's good name through the mud? Now you want to tarnish the memory of that dead boy as well? I'm not going to let you do it. I don't want your pathetic little confessions. 'Please, sir, I've been a naughty boy. I've been breaking the embargo, sir...'. I don't care. No one cares. We've got a war to fight. Terrorists are attacking our people. Leading citizens are being 'disappeared' by the Family Court. The Gallaskians are playing games. And you think this is a good time to confess? No. You've wasted too much embassy time already. You're going to go home, sit tight, and not embarrass the Ambassador ever again. Got it?"

He did. He really did. He so wanted to do whatever this new, scary version of Maitland said. But he couldn't. Because there were scarier people than Undersecretary Maitland out there. Much scarier.

"You don't understand," he said. "Micha–"

Agony – appalling, unbelievable agony – exploded in his groin. The pain squeezed the air from his lungs, and all thought from his head. He folded in on himself, a slow-motion collapse that ended with him lying gasping on the floor, astonished by the enormity of the hurt.

And still more astonished that Maitland had done this to him – Beynan Hotep, a Homeworlder and a Massowic.

Somewhere far above, Maitland was talking. "I told you to shut up, Hotep. Message finally getting through, is it?"

Bey nodded, desperately. And was hugely relieved when Maitland snorted and stepped away. "Excellent. Now be a good boy and do what you're told. Go home, and stay out of my way."

A door opened in the wall. Maitland stepped through, and was gone; but the door remained open.

Bey lay unmoving on the floor. He remained there, whimpering, long after the pain had faded to a dull background ache. He was still summoning the courage to rise when a guard entered the cell, grabbed him by the upper arm and hauled him to his feet. He protested, but the guard didn't seem to hear him. Considering he was dragging Bey out of the cell, he was doing a remarkable job of appearing unaware that Bey was even there.

They emerged in a long, curving corridor, its walls as smooth and featureless as the cell they'd just left. The guard hurried him along until they reached an exterior door. It was dawn outside. Pink-tinged morning light illuminated the embassy gardens. It was a beautiful sight, but he had only the briefest glimpse of colorful blooms and delicate running water before he was thrust into the back of an official vehicle. The door closed, sealing him in a miniature mobile cell. He couldn't even see out: the windows were fully opaqued, and the vehicle was wholly unresponsive to his commands. It reminded him, miserably, of his childhood, when particularly egregious misbehavior had led, inevitably, to confinement in his room. Then, as now, he'd responded by tearing at the door; and now, as then, the door remained obstinately shut.

The car set off. He felt it in a shift of his weight and a familiar, subtle vibration. But there were no clues as to the direction of travel, or his eventual destination. Four times the vehicle came to a complete stop, but the doors remained closed and his increasingly angry questions were met only with silence. The fifth time, he just stayed slumped in his seat – until the carapace opened. Then he glanced outside, and understood. He was back in his own garage. He clambered out and watched, miserably, as the door closed behind the departing embassy vehicle. Only then did he notice his own car was missing.

"House: where's my car?"

"Vehicle is currently offline or out of range, sir. No location information available."

"Well, fuck."

Still, he couldn't stay here. Michael knew where he lived. Samuel could find out. Anyone could.

Would his house protect him? Sanja's hadn't protected him. And Sanja's house hadn't been a useless, backwards vegetable.

It didn't matter how scary Maitland was: Bey had to confess. He needed the regulators to arrest him. It was the only way to be safe.

"House: get me the embassy. I need to speak to Regular Hyrom."

"Unable to comply, sir. External communication systems have been disabled by order of the Executive Office."

"Of course they have. Okay, house: what do I need to do to get comms back?"

"Requests for reconnection must be made via Undersecretary Maitland."

"Right. Put me through to him."

"Unable to Comply. External communications–"

"Shit. Fuck."

Okay. He couldn't talk, he couldn't drive... Fuck it. He'd walk. "House: open the garage door."

"Unable to comply. All external doors are sealed by order of the Executive Office."

"FUCK!"

That was it. He was trapped. The bastard had him under some kind of unofficial house arrest, and he couldn't even tell anyone.

But Maitland didn't know about his stash. There had to be something in his little stockpile of black market bi-tech that would help him escape; or failing that, allow him to communicate with the outside world.

He ran upstairs to the bathroom. And saw a huge scar running across the floor. He told the hidden compartment to open, and watched miserably as the wounded muscle struggled to comply – and, when it was finally done, revealed nothing but yawning emptiness. A fly emerged from the hollow compartment and buzzed around his head. He didn't even bother to swat it; just sat down on the bathroom floor, too spent and miserable even to cry.

He remained there for a long time, wallowing in misery. Eventually, sheer discomfort forced him to move. He was sore all over, his skin itched and his clothing was soiled and sticky. But at least there was something he could do about that. He stripped off his clothes – not without difficulty; they weren't at all helpful – and told the house to run him a bath. A pool molded itself out of the floor and began to fill. He sank into the warm water until only his face poked above the surface. The sensation was so pleasant that it was almost possible to forget about his predicament, and just drift in the soothing water...

He awoke, coughing and spluttering in cold, scummy water. He surged upwards, went to climb out... and thought better of it. He hadn't washed yet; and, really, what else was there for him to do? He was helpless. Maitland had seen to that. He slumped back down, and ordered the house to cycle the water and clean him properly. It chimed instead, and made an announcement that took him back, nightmarishly, to the morning of Sanja's death.

"Regulator Hyrom to see you, sir."

CHAPTER 25

The Commonwealth embassy has categorically denied any involvement in the Gwahnals' escape. Their public statements are cautiously neutral, but off-the-record briefings given by senior personnel make it clear that the embassy has serious doubts about the Justice's version of events.

– From The Update, *Noyan Wireless News*

"What's it like out there, Ethan? Any chance I can just slip away?"

"Not a hope, Justice. The front steps are crawling with reporters. Those flying camera things are everywhere."

"Of course they are."

Beth leaned back in her chair – until a sharp spike of pain knifed upwards from her kidneys to her shoulder. She managed – just – not to cry out, but it was a wasted effort. Ethan was already hurrying over, ready to fuss. His strong hands lifted her into a more comfortable position, and lingered supportively on her shoulders. She hated how good that made her feel.

"Did you take your pills this morning, Justice?"

"No. I had other things to worry about."

"I'll go and–"

"No, you won't. I can function. And you can stop that,

213

right now." She shrugged away his hands, scowling. "Go and sit down."

He did so, smiling tolerantly. For some reason it didn't irritate her as much as usual. Which was in itself a source of irritation.

"You'll have to carry on without me," she said. "They won't follow you. It's me they're after."

"True. But our suspects are all off-comers. They're not going to talk to me. They won't even let me in the door. I'm not Family Court. Refuse you entry, that's a big deal. Refuse me? Not so much."

The phone rang. She grabbed it and yanked the earpiece from the hook. "Yes, what's so im–?"

"Is it true?"

Beth rolled her eyes, mouthed 'Ruth' at Ethan, and settled back in her chair. "If you mean, 'did the Gwahnals escape'? Yes, it's true."

"Scrape. I was hoping… What happened?"

"We don't know yet. Someone went to check on them, and they weren't there. That's all we know so far."

"This is really bad, Beth. The embassy's talking about 'death squads' and 'disappearances'. Apparently, you're trying to set up a Family Court dictatorship, if you can believe it."

"No, I can't believe it. And nobody else will, either. Now, if–"

"Some will. And a lot more will worry about the embassy believing it. The pro-Commonwealth faction is latching onto this with everything they've got. They're pushing for an impeachment. They won't get it, but they're gaining ground. I need something, Beth. Something I can push back with. Don't you have any idea how they escaped?"

"All we know right now is we put them in a cell, and they weren't there when someone went to check on them. But they must have had inside help. Which means we have a traitor in the court."

"The *Family* Court?"

"Let's hope not. An auxiliary, I expect. And we'll find them, don't worry."

"In the next hour?"

"No, but–"

"Then it'll be too late. The Assembly's in emergency session and there's every chance they'll agree to a debate on handing jurisdiction to the regulators."

"They can't do–"

"Not yet, no. They haven't got the votes. But give it time, and who knows? The Commonwealth's cordoned off the street outside their embassy, and I can't even get a protest motion on the floor. Too many reps are falling over themselves to throw the off-comers a bone. People I normally rely on, people who've been solid, are suddenly all in for giving them jurisdiction. And the real off-comer lovers – the ones who want us to be a Commonwealth protectorate – are out-and-out calling for a State of Emergency. Give me something I can use, Beth. Anything."

"I'll do what I–"

"Thank you! Got to go. There's a vote coming up on the floor. Speak to you later."

"But– Ruth...? Ruth...?"

The line had gone dead. She put the earpiece back on its hook, and set the phone down. Ethan was looking to her expectantly.

"It gets worse," she said. "The Assembly's letting the off-comers walk all over them. So, not only do we have to worry about recapturing the Gwahnals and finding a traitor, now we have to give Ruth something she can push back with. And all while staying focused on catching Sanja's killers. Any ideas?"

In the end, she came up with the solution herself. Twenty minutes later, she was barreling out through the front doors, surrounded by a protective squad of auxiliaries. The waiting mass of reporters surged towards her, shouting questions. She ignored them, and concentrated on staying with the auxiliaries as they forced their way through the crowd. Off-comer cameras flew overhead; Noyan cameras clicked and flashed.

"Out of the way," she shouted. "I'm on urgent Family Court business. Move!"

All around, Noyim began to give way. The off-comers did not, until auxiliaries shouldered them out of the way, leading to much outraged squealing. Mindful of the cameras, Beth was careful not to smile. She carried on shouting for the crowd to give way until the moment she reached the bottom of the steps, and the waiting car.

Ethan was in the driver's seat. He offered a hand to help her up, but gave in with good grace when she pointed for him to shift to the passenger side. He slid across, and she climbed behind the wheel. The crowd flowed around the car, shouting their insistent questions.

"The emergency bell's under your seat," she told Ethan. "Get ringing."

His dimples made an appearance; the only sign of a smile he was otherwise suppressing. He pulled out the heavy brass bell, tested its weight, and swung it wildly out of the side of the car, scattering reporters and ugly bird-cameras alike.

"This is a hot pursuit," she shouted, gesturing angrily at the reporters blocking the road. "Get out of the way."

The result was chaos. Noyim backed off again, only for off-comers to fill any available space. She squeezed the car horn furiously, but its honking was barely audible above the crowd. Ethan's enthusiastic bell-ringing was louder, but no more effective in clearing the way. There was nothing else for it. She put the car into gear and started edging forwards. The off-comers scattered, but not quickly enough. A young woman cried out and fell backwards, holding her foot. Beth eased off the accelerator, and all but snarled as the reporters immediately crowded in again.

Everything was working out just as she'd hoped. But

that didn't make the crowd's lack of respect any less annoying. And they were giving her just the excuse she needed for escalation. She took out her service revolver, poked it out of the side of the car and fired a warning shot into the air. The resulting stampede finally cleared the road sufficiently for the car to make some progress.

Too much progress.

The reporters were still scattered in panic. If she wasn't careful, she'd leave them behind. Useful for the investigation, perhaps; but not so very helpful for Ruth.

She took her foot of the gas and made a show of struggling with the gears. The car slowed to a fast walking pace. Reporters were running for their vehicles, trying to catch up. She had every intention of letting them.

Ethan was no longer ringing the bell. He turned to say something, but she hurriedly gestured a warning: they were clear of the crowd, but off-comer cameras were still flying alongside the car. Those cameras recorded sound as well as vision, as she'd found to her cost. One was flying directly ahead, its head turned through 180 degrees to fix monomaniacally on her face. She accelerated in the hope of hitting it, but the creature easily kept pace. So did the repulsive off-comer beetle-vehicles that were leading the pursuit, leaving a small flock of Noyan cars struggling to keep up.

The first roadblock was less than five minutes from the court. The militia had done a solid job: furniture was piled across the road, with a cart blocking the middle, ready to be rolled aside at any time to allow traffic through. Ethan readied the bell to ensure safe passage. She signaled him to leave it. A delay here would give the straggling reporters a chance to catch up.

Clearly spooked by the approaching convoy, the militia filed out defensively behind the barrier. Long guns were laid nervously across the top. And then removed, hurriedly. Someone must have recognized her. She slowed down and shouted that they were in hot pursuit, and to open the barricade. The militia scrambled to remove the cart. She drove forwards slowly, allowing the reporters to form an orderly line behind her... and sail unchallenged through the roadblock as part of her motorcade.

The next roadblock didn't even attempt to delay them. The first must have called ahead and alerted them to the approaching procession. She shouted her thanks, and carried on.

There were no more roadblocks after that; not until they turned a corner and saw the embassy's alien green spires towering arrogantly over their surroundings. And yet for once the embassy itself was not the most offensive off-comer presence on this street. Three insectile vehicles were parked across the road, iridescent carapaces split down the middle and spread to either side like beetle-wings, closing off access to the street. And sheltering behind the protective wings were hard-faced, uniformed off-comers.

Beth accelerated towards the living barricade. The off-comers took up defensive stances – some with hands outstretched, pointed straight at her. Weapons? Probably. She slammed on the brakes. The point was to make a scene, not to get herself shot.

The squeal of protesting tires gave way to silence, and the smell of burning rubber. She spared a quick glance to make sure the hideous flying cameras were on hand, and leaned out of the vehicle to shout furiously at the waiting off-comers.

"This is a hot pursuit. Move those vehicles now!"

Hands were lowered. Off-comers looked at each other, at Beth, at the convoy rapidly spreading out behind her, at the hovering cameras. Three of them held a rapid, inaudible discussion, and then one stepped forwards. A single beetle-wing lifted to let him through. He approached the car, a picture of wary reluctance. She had them off balance. The trick was to keep them that way.

"Get out of the way before I arrest you!"

The off-comer stopped dead. Bafflement gave way to hostility. "Arrest me for what?"

"Illegally blocking the highway and interfering with a hot pursuit. Aiding and abetting fugitives. Do you *want* the Gwahnals to get away?"

"What?" Of course he wanted the Gwahnals to get away. Unfortunately, he was wise enough not to say it. "We're not interfering with anyone. We're just here to protect the embassy. Turn your automobile around and take a different route. No one comes through here. Not you. Not the Gwahnals. No one."

"That would be easier to believe if this illegal barrier" – she waved at the obstructing vehicles – "was not so obviously designed to help the Gwahnals' evade justice. I'm in hot pursuit, and you're in my way."

There. She was no politician, but that was good. Wait until that went out on the news broadcasts. If Ruth couldn't do something with it, she was in the wrong line of business.

The off-comer's right hand was to his ear. He was frowning, distracted, staring into the distance. Suddenly, he was in motion, backpedaling and signaling to his companions to move aside. "I'm sorry, Justice. My orders are to allow free passage to the Family Court. Please carry on."

The nearest vehicle closed its beetle-wings and reversed out of the way. Beth hardly spared it a glance. "That's just not good enough. You never had the right to deny anyone free passage in the first place, let alone the Family Court. You need to remove this illegal roadblock in its entirety, right now. It's a clear offence against Custom. You say the Gwahnals haven't been through here. Very good. In that case you won't mind helping me search the embassy. I'm sure your familiarity with off-comer technology will be very beneficial. I hereby officially request and require you to take temporary service in the militia. You may join us in this vehicle."

The officer's reply when it came, was deeply satisfying. He was a soldier, not a diplomat, and the sheer effrontery of the suggestion had driven all thoughts of public relations from his head. He told her what she could do with her request, with the militia, with the Family Court, and with the whole....

He stopped; mouth snapping shut in mid-sentence. His face, already red with anger, shaded towards purple.

"Is that so?" said Beth, dryly. "Thank you for being so clear. Let me be equally so. You have deliberately obstructed a Justice of the Family Court performing her duties under Custom, and refused to accept the request of a duly authorized official to serve in the militia. I have no choice but to make an official protest, and to request that the embassy release you into my custody for Judgement at a time of my choosing. I shall be petitioning the Assembly to respond appropriately to this illegal roadblock, and the presence of unaccompanied armed foreign nationals on our streets. Now clear this road immediately before I raise the militia and clear it by force."

There was laughter behind her. Reporters were abandoning their vehicles and crowding around for a better view. The Noyim amongst them, at least, were amused. The off-comer officer was not. He glanced at the surrounding reporters, the hovering cameras, and all expression drained from his face. He stepped aside, a belated study in impassivity. Beth put the car back into gear and drove very slowly towards the embassy, her retinue of reporters following close behind.

The embassy frontage lacked its usual open aspect. New living barriers had grown up; a thick green tangle all along the perimeter. It wasn't overtly hostile – there were no threatening barbs, and the twisted green limbs were strewn with red and blue flowers – but it was tall and dense, and left only a single point of entry; which in turn was defended by a pair of off-comer vehicles. They blocked any access by vehicle, and funneled pedestrians towards a group of uniformed men. And standing there, waiting for her, was Undersecretary Maitland.

She stopped short, set the carriage brake – carefully using both hands to avoid straining her back – and climbed out of the car. Ethan slid over into the driver's seat. She wondered, idly, if any of the reporters noticed the engine was still running.

The undersecretary waited patiently, arms folded. His smile was part amusement, part sardonic condescension. The expression gave her pause. Maitland wasn't anything like the officer she'd just humiliated. This was a professional diplomat, entirely comfortable in the world of politics and public relations. She was on his territory, in more ways than one. She stopped at the point where solid Noyan pavement gave way to alien vegetation.

"Undersecretary Maitland."

"Justice Beth. To what do we owe this pleasure?"

She was surrounded by reporters, many of them hostile. This was a time to be very, very careful.

"I have reason to believe the Gwahnals are hiding inside the embassy. I take it you have no objection to my searching the premises?"

Maitland's smile broadened. "Very droll, Justice. As I'm sure you're aware, not only is your wild accusation completely baseless, but the Family Court has no jurisdiction here."

"On the contrary, Undersecretary. Nowhere on Noyan is outside the jurisdiction of the Family Court."

"But that's precisely the point, Justice. We're not on Noyan. This is Commonwealth territory." He pointed exaggeratedly at the alien green foliage matting the ground beneath his feet. And carefully held the gesture long enough for even Noyan cameras to record the moment.

Beth jerked a thumb at the beetle-vehicles once again blocking the road behind her. "Those aren't. That's an incursion on Noyan territory. What's the diplomatic word for that, Undersecretary? Occupation? Invasion?"

"Hardly, Justice. I think the word you're looking for is 'traffic'."

"Traffic moves, Undersecretary. That's a roadblock."

"Let's not argue semantics, Justice. Can we just agree it's a traffic calming measure. And a temporary one. You see, while you claim to have reasons for this intrusion, *we* have received real, verifiable threats against the embassy. We'd prefer to avoid a mass casualty event, if at all possible."

Now it was Beth's turn to smile. "In that case, Undersecretary, you should petition the Assembly for protection. Your 'traffic calming' measures are a clear breach of Custom, obviously designed to delay pursuit and allow the Gwahnals to go to ground in your embassy."

Maitland ran a weary hand through his hair. "Really? I'd be delighted to see any evidence you have for that statement."

"I'm sure you would, Undersecretary, but I can hardly risk compromising my informant's safety."

"Your informant's safety? What about your prisoners' safety? We only have your word for it that the Gwahnals escaped. All we know for certain is that you took them into custody, and now they're missing."

Angry muttering spread through the Noyim in the crowd. The undersecretary's gaze flicked from her, to the surrounding reporters, and back. Beth kept any satisfaction from her face.

"No, Undersecretary. That's not all we know. We know — because we've all just heard it — that you feel free to insult our most revered institutions. We know that you expect to have armed officers on our streets, but refuse even minimal cooperation with Noyan authorities when off-comers are accused of the most heinous of crimes. I'm sure the members of the press would be fascinated to hear you justify that double standard... Do any of you have questions for the Undersecretary?"

The last was addressed to the reporters. They didn't

disappoint. Questions rang out, swiftly growing into a cacophony. Maitland was forced to turn his attention to them. Beth took a cautious step backwards, allowing more reporters through. Off-comer cameras flew past her, eager to record Maitland's responses. She took another obliging step backwards, and glanced over her shoulder. Ethan was ready and waiting.

It probably wasn't the kind of help Ruth had in mind, but it was the best she could do. Now, to execute the second part of her plan. She hurried to the waiting car and climbed into the passenger seat. Ethan immediately accelerated away. Their departure was not entirely unobserved. Several reporters set off in pursuit. No matter: either she made a clean getaway, or they'd ditch the reporters at the next roadblock..

And then, once they were free of pursuit, she could carry on with what really mattered: working through her list of possible suspects. She still had a murderer to catch. Everything else was just noise.

CHAPTER 26

It should be your first priority to familiarize yourself with the embargo as it applies in your jurisdiction. Even quite mundane devices may be restricted in some localities out of respect for indigenous religious or ethical sensitivities; conversely, a world may be so mechanically advanced that we are forced to release exceptionally sophisticated bi-tech in order to compete...
— *From:* The Regulator's Handbook, *5th Edition, Chapter 7*

"What? You want me to… What?"

"Get me out of here, Regulator Hyrom – please."

It didn't make any sense. He'd come here to bully Hotep, not help him. So why was the spoiled brat treating him like some kind of savior?

It was a joke. It had to be. Hotep was mocking him. Why else would he be standing there, dripping wet, an absurdly small towel wrapped around his waist, begging to be rescued? The aristo brat was laughing at him.

"Okay funny man – I've had just about enough of your…"

And Hotep started to cry.

Jodan stared. And unclenched the fists he hadn't even been aware of making.

It wasn't an act. The boy was sobbing.

His anger evaporated, washed away by pity. Which was ridiculous. How had he ever got himself into a position where he, Jodan Hyrom the Caliban orphan, felt sorry for a Massowic? The man was everything he despised – privilege without responsibility, wealth without class – and yet here he was, feeling sorry for him. The man's sobbing was just too pathetic; too childlike.

He'd have to find another outlet for his frustration. He couldn't take it out on Hotep. The man wasn't responsible for the cover up at the embassy. It wasn't his fault the Family Court arrested the Gwahnals. Nor was he anything to do with their disappearance.

But he wasn't innocent, either. He was guilty of breaching the embargo. And he remained the key to it all: the only lead to Sanja's dealer – and from there, to exposing Hozefa, and saving the Gwahnals from the Family Court.

If they were even still alive.

This was no time to be soft. He grabbed a handful of the boy's wet hair, dragged him to the nearest chair, and dropped him into it. "Shut up, sit down and don't move. I'll deal with you later."

Hotep sat there, miserable and passive, while the chair molded itself around him. His towel squirmed downwards in a failing attempt to preserve what little modesty he had left.

What the hell had happened to the arrogant little bastard? Not that it mattered. Jodan had a job to do.

His tool bag was by the door. He reached inside for the stasis bulb. The petals hadn't closed as tightly as they should, but the seal was still good, and it looked healthy enough. There was no coolant leakage, no roughening of the smooth grey-green skin, no pulpiness to the rounded base. It should still work.

Gripping it firmly in his left hand, he tapped the narrow tip with his right. A flush of silver began to spread, achingly slowly, through the petals. It was old kit, like so much else in his tool bag... But there it was; the petals were opening, releasing a cloud of pheromones into the room.

At least, he hoped so. The bulb had been sitting unused in his bag for months. It had to be running low by now. There was no knowing how long the bulb, or its paired surveillance bug, would last. He'd hate to lose it, but he'd needed to know when Hotep returned. Otherwise, all the effort he put into searching this garbage dump of a home would have been completely wasted.

He'd never seen a home so filthy. The furniture was greasy, the lily-pad flooring ingrained with dirt; there were even piles of rubbish just left lying around. Only the bathroom had been clean – and that because the floor doubled as a bath... and, as it turned out, a secret hiding place. Not that there was much worth hiding. For all Hotep's arrogance and swagger, his collection of embargo-breaching comforts would have been more at home in a teenager's bedroom than a rich young man's house. It was all rather pathetic.

Except for one thing: the prize that made all Jodan's diligent searching worthwhile; a single, somewhat shop-worn, but still highly illegal, hallucinobug. It was exactly what he needed. Hallucinobugs were illegal everywhere, not just on embargoed planets. Possession of one was the kind of thing that could get anyone – even a Massowic – transported, if he were unlucky enough to come before an unsympathetic judge.

If that kind of trouble didn't make the cocky little bastard cooperate, nothing would. Except it didn't look like he needed anything to break Hotep's resistance. He was already broken.

Something flickered at the edge of Jodan's vision; a small black blob descending haphazardly on tiny gossamer wings. The pheromones had done their work. The bug was coming home. He held the bulb steady until it settled safely back inside. Then he tapped the petals. For a worrying moment, nothing happened; then they slowly began to close. He waited for the bulb to revert to the reassuring grey-green dullness of stasis, then carefully stowed it away in his bag. Even the smallest and most primitive pieces of equipment had to be preserved now that he was on his own.

He went to stand over Hotep. The boy didn't move. His tears had dried up, but he was still sitting slumped in the chair, gaze fixed miserably on his lap. There was bruising on his legs and arms, signs he'd been brutalized at some point. But the damage was minor: not enough to explain the slump of his shoulders, the despairing hollowness of his eyes.

"Okay, Hotep. What have you got to tell me?"

Hotep swallowed hard. When he spoke, the words came out as barely more than a whisper. "You have to help me. Please, Regulator Hyrom. I can't stay here. It's not safe."

"So, leave."

"I can't!"

"Don't be ridiculous. Of course you ca—"

"I'm under house arrest!"

"For what?"

"I don't know. Maitland didn't tell me."

"Maitland? You mean Commissioner Hozefa?"

"What? No. Maitland." The boy sat up, suddenly full of feverish energy. "He didn't even tell me he'd done it. He just... assaulted me and sent me back here, and now I can't get out. And Michael knows where I live. He's going to come for me. Please. We have to leave. Now."

If Hotep was acting, he was very good. But he wasn't making any sense. Maitland? Assaulting a Homeworld aristo? No way. And why was he so afraid of this 'Michael'? Did he mean....

"Michael? Are you talking about—?"

"Michael the restaurateur. You must have heard of—"

"Of course I have. I know who he is. And what he

really does. But why would he want—?"

"He's Sanja's dealer! I tried to tell Maitland, but—"

"Michael? Michael was Sanja's dealer?"

"Of course he was. Sanja always wanted the best. And Michael can get you anything you want, if you have the money."

"Including a replication-capable brain?"

"What? No. Of course not! Anything within reason. Who'd dare smuggle a...? You mean someone *has* smuggled one?"

"No. Someone's building them. Right here on Noyan."

"That's impossible."

"We found one in Sanja Gwahnal's basement."

Hotep blinked. There was something new in his expression, alongside the fear. Hurt. "Sanja? But he couldn't have. He would have told me... But then, he didn't tell me about Samuel."

"Samuel? Samuel who?"

"Samuel of New Beginning. He's... He *was* a friend of ours... of Sanja's, anyway. I went looking for somewhere to hide out, after Beth rescued me from Michael."

"She did what?"

"Rescued me from Michael. I've never been so scared. He was so... so... He was going to kill me. I know he was. But she got me out. And then Samuel... She says he's a 'traditionalist'. And Sanja knew. But that doesn't make any sense. Traditionalists hate people like Sanja and me. And he was always so friendly... But he was lying. Like Michael. They're not really friendly, either of them. Please, Regulator Hyrom. You have to get me out of here. Arrest me. Get me somewhere safe."

Jodan walked away. He was drowning in information. He'd come here to beat the truth out of the boy – and now Hotep was hurling it at him so fast he couldn't keep up.

Hotep called after him, plaintively. Jodan ignored him. He was pacing, thinking, sorting, filtering: trying to make it all make sense.

The Justice rescued Hotep? Not once, but twice? How had she even known where to find him?

Unless she was watching him.

But that didn't make sense – not when she was so certain the Gwahnals killed Sanja. Why would she bother having Hotep tailed?

Unless it was all a bluff, a smokescreen. Was she only pretending to blame the Gwahnals?

"Why did she arrest them?"

"Who?"

"The Justice. Why did she arrest the Gwahnals?"

"What? Seriously? She arrested them? For what?"

"Murder."

"Of who? Not Sanja…"

"Who else? But why was she keeping an eye on you? And if you're so scared of Michael, or this Samuel – what the hell were you doing sitting at home taking a bath? Why are you here at all, if you're so convinced people are out to kill you?"

"I told you. I'm under house arrest."

"So, call the embassy. Hell, if Maitland won't listen, call Ashef. He'd take your call. You're a Massowic."

"I tried! I can't call out. My comms are blocked. I'm stuck. Please. Get me out of here."

"Wait, what? Who blocked your comms?"

"Maitland, I told you."

"Maitland. Right. But… Listen up, Hotep. This is very important. What exactly did you tell Undersecretary Maitland? Does he know about Michael?"

"I… I'm not sure. I tried to tell him, but…"

"Did you, or did you not, tell him that Michael was Sanja's dealer?"

"I don't think so. I wanted to, but he wouldn't listen. Please, Regulator Hyrom, can we talk about this at the embassy? We have to get out of here."

"Think, Hotep. It matters."

If Maitland knew, and did nothing, he was as corrupt as

Hozefa. But if he didn't know… Then he probably hadn't taken Hotep seriously. And who could blame him?

"I don't remember. I'm sorry. He was—"

"Never mind. Go get dressed. I'll call the undersecretary. He'll listen to me."

Hotep glanced down, saw how little the towel was concealing, and fled. Jodan put in the call. "House: get me Undersecretary Maitland."

"Unable to comply. External communications have been disabled. Beynan Hotep has been placed under a Restriction Order."

"House: I am Regulator Jodan Hyrom. I have taken Beynan Hotep into my custody. The Restriction Order is hereby suspended until such time as I release him from custody. Please call the undersecretary."

"Your authority is recognized and accepted, Regulator Hyrom. Complying."

That was a relief. He hadn't been absolutely sure Hozefa hadn't suspended him.

A 3-V on the wall projected the embassy's call sign. "Undersecretary Maitland is not available, Regulator Hyrom. Please hold for Duty Officer Boullivant."

Jodan's protests died on his lips. He was already looking at an unfamiliar, space-black face.

"How can I help you, Regulator?"

The man had an oddly nasal accent. What planet did he come from, with that skin and that voice? Not that it mattered. "I need to speak to Undersecretary Maitland."

"I'm afraid the undersecretary is unavailable. Can I help?"

"Unfortunately not. It's a highly confidential matter. I can only speak to the undersecretary himself."

"I'm sorry, but that's not going to happen. Not until this situation with the Gwahnals is resolved. Perhaps Commissioner Hozefa can help?"

"No!" Jodan took a deep, calming breath. "I'm sorry. What I've got to say is for the undersecretary's ears only."

"I see. Perhaps you can tell me a little more? Something I can use to justify passing you up the chain?"

Jodan hesitated. He didn't know this man... On the other hand, wasn't that a good thing? If Jodan didn't know him, he wasn't in the Office of Regulation. And that meant he wasn't one of Hozefa's flunkies.

"Okay. It doesn't look like I've got much choice. You ready for this, Duty Officer Boullivant? Someone's been making replication-capable house brains, right here on Noyan. And now I know who's selling them. So, will you connect me?"

"Of course. But wouldn't it be better for you to speak to Commissioner Hozefa about this?"

"I can't. Hozefa's compromised. He knows about the breach. He's doing everything he can to cover it up."

"I understand. How long have you known about this?"

Boullivant was sympathetic. Not shocked. Sympathetic. Something wasn't right.

"Not very long. A day maybe."

"Before you went on leave?"

"Yes. Definitely."

How did Boullivant know he was 'on leave'? He hadn't mentioned it.

And his supportive manner. It felt wrong. Boullivant wasn't acting like a normal duty officer; someone sitting in the chain of command. He reminded Jodan of something else...

That was it. The time Evershem had a fever, and they took him to see an actual human doctor...

A doctor.

"I see." Boullivant was nodding. Compassionately. Supportively. "I completely understand why you want to talk to the undersecretary. I think you should come in to the embassy, speak to him face to face. I'll send someone round to pick you up. I take it you're calling from home?"

"That's right. When should I expect them?"

Boullivant glanced off to one side. Someone was there,

providing guidance. Hozefa himself, perhaps.

"In around ten minutes."

"Good. In that case, I'll see you soon. House: end call."

Poor Errina. If they were only ten minutes away, they were already on their way. And he couldn't even warn her. If they were going to treat him like he was paranoid, he'd better start acting that way. And be a lot more careful. It was pure luck Hotep hadn't been sitting behind him when he made the call.

As of right now, there was only one priority – getting out of here. They had ten minutes, at most, before Hozefa's people realized he wasn't home. After that, Boullivant only had to ask the embassy where he'd really called from…

He set out for the stairs, and encountered Hotep on his way back down. The boy hadn't even bothered to dry himself. His clothes were doing their best to deal with the moisture, but couldn't do anything about the wet hair plastered to his forehead.

"All right, son," he said. "It's time for you to help with enquiries."

He wasn't sure where they were going yet, but somewhere out there was the evidence he needed to send Hozefa to the gallows. And one way or another, he was going to find it.

At least he wasn't on his own anymore. Hotep might not be much use, but you never knew.

He might make all the difference.

CHAPTER 27

The Gwahnals flight from justice is yet more proof of off-comer contempt for our most revered institutions. This cannot, and will not, be tolerated. The Gwahnals have 24 hours to surrender themselves to the custody of the Family Court. Should they fail to do so, they – and they alone – will be responsible for the deaths of the hostages.
  - *From:* Ransom Note, *The League of Free Noyim*

The roadroot wasn't anywhere near as hard as Samuel expected. It wasn't exactly soft, but it had a leathery springiness that made lying there far easier than he'd feared. He wasn't as resilient as he used to be, and he'd dreaded having to lie on the hard surface and play dead.

But, no. The problem wasn't the hardness of the surface. It was the small hairs that dotted the roadroot's living flesh. He hadn't even noticed them when he lay down, but now they were all he could think about. They itched. And worse, they were a constant reminder that this road wasn't something that people had built; it had grown here – a hideous lab-grown perversion of nature, planted here by off-comers intent on remaking Noyan in their own twisted image. He was skin-to-skin with a monstrosity. But even that nauseating thought wasn't enough to break the endless cycle of worry – worry about the Gwahnals,

Jimawn, his own followers. All of them threats. All of them weighing on him as much or more than the immediate danger.

Mother, but there was one hair pricking the skin by his right eye. It was infuriating. And alarming. What if the foul thing scratched his eyeball? It couldn't be poisonous, surely? No matter how sickly green the roadroot glowed in the dark, it couldn't be dangerous. Off-comers used these highways too.

So, he had to just lie here, endure the discomfort, and wait for his victims to fall into the trap. He could feel them approaching, sense their presence at an animal level, even without any helpful vibrations from the impervious roadroot. Were they all coming to look? Or did some stay behind? If so, the assault team better be ready. That vehicle couldn't be allowed to escape.

He hated having to trust Nathan. But Joshua was elsewhere, preparing the getaway truck. And these days John lacked the necessary drive and fire for this kind of work. Nathan had plenty of both. Perhaps too much. If he let himself get carried away and moved to soon...

Voices, behind him. But not anywhere near as close as he'd thought.

So much for his animal senses. He could have moved; should have, while he had the chance. It was too late now. The trap was nearly sprung.

The off-comers were anxious, fearful. He couldn't make out the words, but the tone was unmistakable. And reassuring. They should be upset, coming across such a horrible scene. They knew nothing of car crashes. How could they, when their own vehicles didn't even need lamps to see in the dark, and were no more likely to collide than two sand-cats prowling through the desert?

If only he'd positioned himself facing the other way. Then he could have watched them approaching. Instead, his entire view was filled with the artfully posed crash: a mangled motorbike, a stolen truck skewed just-so across the road and wedged against the swollen edge of the roadroot – a vast endless lip disappearing into the gloomy distance. And hidden behind it, the assault team.

"Are you all right?"

A young woman's voice, just behind him, so close he could feel her breath on his neck. There'd been no advance warning, no vibration from the roadroot. But they were here: his rescuers; his victims.

But that was no off-comer accent. What was a Noya doing, so close to the Gwahnals' factory? This trap was meant for off-comers, not passing Noyim. And why hadn't he heard her car? Why no engine noise, no warm yellow headlamp light?

He groaned in pretend pain, and turned over. The woman was older than he'd guessed – around 30 or so – but he'd been right thinking she was no off-comer. Her hand went reflexively to her mouth; she was shocked to find him alive.

"Quick," she called out. "Get on to the Factory. Tell it to send help. He's not dead!"

Her companions were a few feet behind her: three off-comer men standing in a nervous huddle – dressed, like her, in slick, sheer vat-grown fabric. A bird silhouette was flying languidly across her chest, completely at home on the glossy alien wrongness of off-comer material.

So that was it. A collaborator, as guilty as the rest. More so. They were off-comers; she was a traitor. There was no need to change the plan on her account.

Besides, she'd seen his face.

"I'm trying," said a strained off-comer voice – the oldest of the men, his hand to his ear. "I can't get through."

So, Jimawn's jammer worked. It was worth unwrapping the foul thing. The whiskery antennae had been every bit as delicate as advertised, but the body was worse: a fat, malformed caterpillar, covered in pustular red nodules. He'd itched to stamp it out of existence, but deposited it on the stolen truck's dashboard instead. At least he didn't have to look at it that way.

He groaned, and made to get up. The woman instantly tried to stop him. "No, wait. Prii, run back to the car. Send it to the factory. Please, sir. Don't move. We'll get help."

But he was already on his feet, revolver in hand. "No," he said. "You won't. And Prii. Don't move."

The youngest of the off-comers – Prii, presumably – ignored him and ran for the vehicle. But stopped when Nathan and the assault team surged over the side of the roadroot. They spread out across the road, using the vehicle's reluctance to harm pedestrians against it; penning it in. Four of them jammed a long wooden pole beneath the panicked vehicle, and flipped it with practiced ease. It was no longer a threat; just an oversized beetle trapped on its back, wheels spinning uselessly.

"Over here." Samuel herded his prisoners towards the truck. The woman stumbled to obey. The off-comers followed more slowly, babbling questions at him and their pet Noya. The woman stayed silent, obedient to the menace of his gun. She understood what it was, even if the off-comers didn't.

"You. Prii. Get with the rest of them."

The young off-comer turned and saw the gun. His brow furrowed. Hadn't he ever seen a revolver before? Possibly not. Many off-comers lived parallel lives, and had little contact with Noyim. Normally, that was to be welcomed, but right now it was an unnecessary inconvenience.

He aimed the gun at the off-comer's feet, and pulled the trigger. The shot went wide, but the deafening report was enough to make the young man freeze; that and the ping and whine as the bullet ricocheted off the roadroot. The off-comer's face was a mask of appalled confusion; but he understood enough to know he was in danger. He moved to join the other prisoners.

Samuel gestured with the gun. "Into the truck. Now."

The off-comers hesitated, then complied. That was a relief. He didn't want to have to shoot any of them. It would only slow things down. Besides, his ears were still ringing. Did his hearing always take this long to recover? Or was he just getting old?

John was in the back of the truck, burlap sack at the ready. He gave a visible start when the woman appeared, but recovered soon enough when the off-comers followed. He held up the sack and barked out orders for them to strip and place everything inside. It would all have to be burnt. There was no knowing what off-comer clothing and accessories could do.

There were protests. Samuel cocked his gun, silencing them. Even then, it was only when the Noya began to strip that the others did the same.

The assault team arrived, rocking the truck in their eagerness to clamber aboard. Samuel headed further in, forcing the hostages before him. John confirmed that everyone was onboard, and thumped the back of the cab. The engine coughed twice, roared into life, and they were backing up, ready to depart.

Samuel glanced at his watch. Less than ten minutes had passed from the trap being set to their fleeing the scene. It couldn't have gone better.

The woman was down to her underwear and shoes now, and intent on going no further. She glared at him defiantly, arms folded. He gestured for her to carry on. She scowled, but complied. People usually did, when he pointed a gun at them. Not that he planned on using it inside the truck. He'd be deafened for days if he pulled the trigger in a confined space like this.

The truck was crowded, noisy and stank of sweat. Behind him, the assault team was celebrating its success; ahead, the off-comers were undressing, and struggling to stay on their feet. John stumbled around them, carefully stowing each discarded piece of clothing in his burlap bag. There was a sudden change in vibration; they'd taken the offramp. Samuel finally began to relax. It wouldn't be long now.

The trip became rougher, the shaking more pronounced. They were speeding down a desert track, putting distance between themselves and the attack. A sudden stop sent a fat, naked off-comer stumbling into him, squealing. He shoved the man onwards, encouraging him on his way with a malicious slap to vulnerable flesh. The assault team joined in enthusiastically, forcing the reluctant prisoners out into the cold.

The settlement's own familiar truck was waiting in the concealment of a small stand of trees. Samuel left it to the others to stow the hostages inside. He stayed with John and reached for the burlap sack. "Leave that to me. I need you to make sure the youngsters don't get too carried away with the hostages."

The old man's brow furrowed. "But I'm supposed to burn the—"

"I'll see to it. Don't worry." He helped John out of the back, then emptied the sack onto the floor of the truck; he needed the bag for something more important than clothing.

The jammer was sitting where he'd left it, a maggot-thing polluting the dashboard. He threw the sack over the top and used it like a large, clumsy glove to pry the thing free. Then he carried it over to Nathan, who was busily stuffing a kerosene-soaked rag into the stolen truck's gas tank.

"Don't light that until you've soaked the clothes in the back. And this." Samuel held up the burlap sack. "We need to make sure everything burns."

Raucous laughter drew him to the settlement's truck. The assault team was enjoying a new spectator sport: watching the off-comers attempts to dress themselves. He joined in, hooting along as the captives tried to pull on cast-off shirts and threadbare trousers. Their Noyan pet was helping them, but it was slow going. The off-comers couldn't seem to grasp that sleeves and trouser legs wouldn't wriggle themselves up; and buttons and laces were a complete mystery to them.

He pushed his way past the struggling off-comers and sat down on the bench seat behind the cab. The truck shook as a door slammed shut: Nathan had joined Joshua in front. Time to go. The gears crunched, the engine snarled, and the truck was moving; slowly at first, but soon quickly enough for Joshua to shift up through the gears. And then, an endless time later – so much later, he'd begun to doubt it would ever come – a loud crump announced the end of the stolen truck.

The drive became even rockier. Joshua was pushing the truck to its limits. The off-comers bleated and clung to each other. Their Noyan pet sat next to them on the floor, arms wrapped around her knees, face set. She saw Samuel looking, and glared back, more confident now that she was no longer naked.

"Why are you doing this?"

He was tempted to ignore her, but answered on a whim. "We need hostages."

"Why? We're not rich. None of us."

"We're not after money."

"What, then?"

"Justice. Your employers killed their son. They need to give themselves up and face the consequences."

"You don't know they killed him."

He laughed. Not mockingly, but because she was completely and utterly correct. And it mattered not at all.

"They'll never give themselves up," she said.

He looked away. She was right. At least, he hoped so. But even if she was wrong, it made no difference. Samuel would simply issue new demands. And keep on issuing them until he found the line the off-comers wouldn't cross. Jimawn would have his atrocity, come what may. But better she didn't know that. The hostages needed to have hope, lest they become fractious and difficult to manage.

And right now, he had better things to do than waste time talking to someone with no future. He finally had a little breathing space in which to think, and to plan. The Gwahnals had escaped: now it was his turn.

CHAPTER 28

In this, Noyan merely followed the classic pattern of primitive worlds coping with a sudden influx of modern technology. First, the richest natives flee the city for bi-tech mansions in the countryside – a flight facilitated by the introduction of a decent roadroot system. Next bi-tech suburbs appear, drawing the professional classes outwards, and leaving the city center increasingly the province of the poor. And if, on Noyan, that center became more corrupt than most, it was a difference of degree, not of kind.

    – *From:* My Time on Noyan, Memories of a Youthful Exile, *The Rt. Hon. Beynan Hotep na Massowic*

Bey opened his eyes to another day, and another ceiling. This one was off-white, with smears of black fungus spreading from three of the four corners. He'd become unpleasantly familiar with it during the night.

He hadn't truly slept, just dozed fitfully. The native bed was unbelievably uncomfortable, and neither he nor Hyrom had been able to get the windows to opaque. Anywhere else, that wouldn't have mattered – he'd been so very tired after whatever-the-fuck happened in New Beginning – but they were somewhere in Spate's Old Quarter, home of restaurants, bars and less respectable entertainment. Garish artificial light flooded in all night long from neon signs and streetlights, painting the ceiling in shades of red and yellow, and turning the fungus blue.

He didn't really mind the fungus. At least it was natural, alive. The room itself was dead; a disturbingly symmetrical box whose walls and ceilings intersected at unforgiving right-angles, without a natural curve in sight. The sheer wrongness of it set his teeth on edge.

Was the place even structurally sound? The skin had rotted away from the walls in places, exposing the mysterious materials beneath. How long could it survive like that without the whole building collapsing?

How could any Commonwealther, even a colonial like Hyrom, stoop low enough to rent a hovel like this? Bey never should have agreed to it – wouldn't have, if he hadn't been so overwrought. Today, things were going to be different.

He glanced at the other bed. It was empty. Hyrom still wasn't back. So at least he wouldn't have to brave the appalling communal bathroom at the end of the hall. He could just piss in the sink instead. Once he found the energy to get up.

He yawned and scratched his chest. He'd been doing a lot of scratching in the night. The coarse blanket was a torture device. He itched all over. Twice in the night he'd discarded it, only to manhandle it back into place when the cold became worse than the itching. Now he threw it back again, glanced down, and…

FUCK!

Small black somethings were crawling all over him, scurrying for cover. He threw himself from the bed – and screamed as his left knee crunched painfully into the hard floor. Suddenly, the insects didn't matter, not beside the waves of hot pulsing pain from his knee. He clutched it, and cursed the stupid fucking floor that hadn't even tried to cushion his fall.

He rolled away from the bed and lay flat on his back, panting, waiting for the pain and panic to subside. Eventually, the pain receded to a dull throbbing and he clambered to his feet. There were nasty red spots all over his arms, legs and chest.

And some of the small, black bugs were still crawling through his body hair.

The next minute was spent in a frenzied leg-stamping dance as he desperately tried to rid himself of the infestation. Then he remembered the sink. He ran over and bent his head under the faucet.

"House: water, now."

Nothing happened.

He tried again, louder, rubbing his fingers through his hair and waiting for cleansing water that never arrived. A single black bug dropped into the sink. After that, nothing. He straightened up, swearing, and took savage satisfaction in pissing on the solitary bug until it disappeared down the drain.

The immediate needs of his bladder satisfied, he stood back, still twitching, and carefully checked to make sure he was bug free. Then he looked around for his clothes.

Aside from the two beds — neither of which he was going near, ever again — the only furniture was a small square table at the end of the apartment, flanked by two mismatched, rickety chairs. Hyrom's work bag was under the table. It was just about big enough to hold Bey's clothes. He dragged it out and tried to persuade it to open. It remained firmly shut: he didn't have the proper authorizations. Was this Hyrom's way of making sure he couldn't leave? If so, it was an unnecessary precaution. This place might be a revolting dump, but where else could he go?

And for that matter, where exactly was he? The Old Quarter was a big place, and he hadn't been paying much attention yesterday. It was embarrassing, looking back, how pathetic he'd been. The last few days had been an endless cycle of terror, confusion, panic and exhaustion. He'd been pretty close to breaking down before Hyrom arrived and rescued him.

Except… this didn't feel like any kind of rescue. He'd spilled his guts, told the regulator everything he knew. He should be safe and sound in an embassy cell. But Hyrom brought him here instead. And ditched his vehicle for a native taxi first. And made the driver avoid main roads.

What the fuck were they doing, sneaking around like secret agents? Last night, he'd been too out of it to register the weirdness of it all. He hadn't much cared what Hyrom was up to, or where the regulator was taking him. But that was yesterday. Now it was time to take stock.

He sidled self-consciously over to the window – he didn't have a stitch of clothing on, and native windows worked *both* ways – and poked his head past the frame. The street outside was surprisingly broad; a grand avenue fallen on hard times. It must have been tree-lined once. Now only a few stumps remained, dotting the sidewalk at regular intervals. There were other signs of decay: outcasts sleeping in doorways, even walking unmolested down the sidewalk. That was a sure sign of a sleazy area. He scanned the row oppose: tall, stonebuilt houses loomed over street level bars and restaurants.

No wonder there were so many flashing signs to keep him awake. One or two of them looked quite famil…

Fuck!

He dropped to the floor, not caring if he hurt himself again.

Michael's restaurant. They were directly across from Michael's fucking restaurant.

Double fuck.

No wonder Hyrom had confiscated his clothes. Nothing could have kept him here, otherwise.

What to do? He could wrap himself in a bug-infected blanket and run for it, but the thought of even touching that thing again made his skin crawl. He could try running for it stark naked… but no. Forget the embarrassment: too conspicuous. He wouldn't last two minutes before Michael's heavies grabbed him and dragged him across the street.

So that left one option: waiting for Hyrom. Then he'd get his clothes back and make a run for it. Right now, his only priority was staying away from the window and out of sight.

He crawled along the wall until he reached the table, glanced back to make sure he wasn't visible from the street, and levered himself up onto one of the rickety chairs. The seat was hard and uncomfortable, but it was better than the floor.

Time passed. The sun rose higher in the sky. The street noise grew from an occasional passing automobile to a constant stream of traffic. Still there was no sign of Hyrom. Bey got back to his feet. He couldn't sit there any longer.

Fuck Hyrom. Was the man insane? Did he *want* to get them killed?

He paced backwards and forwards. It helped. As long as he was careful to stay away from the window…

Footsteps – out in the hall. Approaching the door.

He glanced around for something, anything that might serve as a weapon. There was nothing. He was alone and naked with nowhere to hide. The door was opening… and Regulator Hyrom walked in, carrying a large sack. He kicked the door closed behind him and strode across the room, nodding a greeting. Bey glowered back, but the man didn't even seem to notice. He was busy emptying a jumble of mismatched native clothing onto the table. Only then did Bey register how the regulator himself was dressed.

"What the fuck are you wearing, Hyrom?"

"A lot more than you are… Here – try these on."

He handed Bey a pair of plain grey trousers. Bey didn't put them on. "I want my own clothes, thanks. They weren't much" – certainly compared to his best set, which he doubted he'd ever see again – "but they're better than any native crap."

"I'm sure they are. But these are what people wear around here."

"No, Regulator Hyrom. These are what natives wear around here. And in case you hadn't noticed, we're not natives."

"Not yet," said Hyrom, blandly.

"What?"

"It's these or nothing, Hotep. It's up to you, but I'd get dressed if I were you."

Bey didn't really have a choice. He shook out the trousers and tried to put them on. It took a while. He kept having to grab them to stop them falling down. The ones he'd woken up in yesterday had been the opposite. They'd refused to come down until he found that weird fastening at the waist…

Yes – there it was: a small metal disk, and a matching slit in the material. Ten seconds of frustrated fiddling later, and the trousers were finally securely in place. He felt a lot less vulnerable wearing them. He folded his arms and glared at the regulator. "Well? When exactly were you planning on telling me?"

Hyrom didn't even look up from sorting through the pile of clothes. "Telling you what?"

"That we're right across the street from Michael's place?"

"I wasn't. I thought you already knew."

The regulator held up a white shirt. Bey snatched at it.

"No, I did not."

The shirt was even more complicated than the trousers. The first sleeve was easy enough, but reaching for the second strained his shoulder. And the front was a nightmare – split from top to bottom, with six of the little disc-fasteners on one side; not metal ones like the trousers, but some kind of bone or polished shell. Each one had to be threaded through a matching slit on the other side. He gave up after the bottom three. That should be enough to avoid attracting unnecessary attention when ran for it. And thinking about running, he wouldn't get very far in bare feet...

"Where are my shoes?"

"Same place as your clothes. Somewhere they aren't going to give us away. I'll get you some local ones next time I'm out. Here, take a look at this."

Hyrom handed him a battered black cube the size of his head. The revolting thing was finished in leather; the actual skin of a dead animal; but since he'd already touched it... What the fuck was it, and why had Hyrom given it to him?

The cube was lighter than it looked, and flimsier. It was clearly a box of some kind. Two of the sides were solid; the other four were just skin stretched over some kind of framework. The two solid sides were opposite each other, so top and bottom? A metal tube protruded from the middle of one, so that would be the top. But why was the other one thicker? Was that a slot, for something to lie flat on the bottom?

"What is it?"

"A camera."

Of course it was. There was some kind of lens in the metal tube. He'd had dozens of the things pointed at him, but he'd never seen one this close up before. The slot must be for their archaic photographic plates.

He tried to hand it back. Hyrom shook his head. "No. You keep it. You're going to need it."

"I am?"

"Yes. You're taking pictures of everyone who goes in and out of Michael's place."

"What? No fucking way!"

"You said you wanted to help. This is how you help."

"Like fuck it is. I'm a civilian. I help with enquiries. That's what I do. What the fuck has this got to do with helping with enquiries?"

"Well, let me see... I'm making enquiries into Michael, and you're helping me. See? You're helping with enquiries."

The bastard was smiling. Actually smiling. Like he thought he was funny.

"I want to go to the embassy. Right now."

"And yet you're helping me instead. You know how to use one of those?"

"What? No."

"You'd better learn fast, then."

"No, Regulator. You'd better take me to the embassy. Civilian, remember?"

"Correction: you were a civilian. I've conscripted you. Think of it as your chance to give something back to society."

"Sorry, not interested. Look – just take me to the embassy. I promise I'll tell you everything I–"

"I can't do that, Hotep."

"Why not?"

"Because..." Hyrom sighed, stopped talking, and sat down. For several long seconds he sat staring silently at Bey. Then he looked away.

"Because I'd be arrested the moment we walked through the doors. Or sooner. There are people at the embassy who... don't want this investigation to happen."

Bey sat down, hard, on the other chair. Yesterday's events – so hazy and unconsidered at the time – came into much sharper focus. So did the sack on the table and its primitive contents.

He wasn't under the protection of the embassy, not even marginally. He was right in the heart of Michael's territory, in the company of a lone wolf regulator with so few resources he was reduced to using a native camera to gather evidence.

"Arrest you for what, Regulator Hyrom?"

"Well, maybe not 'arrest' as such. They'd call it something else. Protective custody? Compulsory psychiatric assessment? Something like that."

Bey put the camera down. He rubbed his fingers

absent-mindedly on the rough fabric of his trousers. "Psychiatric assessment... I see. And why would they want to do that, Regulator Hyrom?"

"Because the embargo's been breached, and it's their fault. They'll do anything to save their skins. There's too much gone too badly wrong. It's not just Sanja's house anymore. There was another terrorist attack last night. Four people kidnapped, and no alarm call from their vehicle. That's two attacks in a week, this one and the roadroots, which only make sense if the natives have access to embargoed bi-tech. It was bad enough, Sanja having that house brain. But natives? The worst is, it's not being smuggled in. It's being manufactured right here on Noyan. It's a disaster. And the people who're supposed to be dealing with it are doing everything they can to prevent the ambassador from finding out."

"So, call him up!"

"You think I haven't tried? They won't even let me talk to Maitland."

"So let me. I'll call Ashef. I'm a Massowic. He'll take my call."

"He won't even know you tried. Your house will have told them we left together. They have to be worried about what you know. They'll intercept your call before it gets anywhere near the ambassador. And then they'll arrest us both. Or worse. It depends how desperate they are."

Of course the embassy was against him. Everyone else was. Why should the embassy be any different?

A native truck went by outside. Bey waited for the roar of its engine to fade into the distance. "What about the media? Call Mahtal. He likes a scoop."

"He'll want proof. Evidence."

"You don't have any evidence?"

"Not yet. But I can get some, now I know who's breaking the embargo. That's why we're here. We're laying a trap. I'm going to buy up every bit of black market bi-tech I can lay my hands on. You're going to take pictures of everyone going in and out of Michael's place. All we need to do is tie one of the dealers to Michael, and that's it. I know regulators. Most of them take their oaths seriously. Right now, the honest ones believe Hozefa's lies. But once I've proof Michael's dealing in home-grown bi-tech, Hozefa's cooked."

Bey glanced at the camera. "Where are the plates?"

"Plates?"

"For the camera. You know. For the pictures."

"I... didn't know."

Hyrom's weirdly pink skin became even pinker; almost red. Was he blushing? It was a disturbing sight – but far worse was the realization that the regulator was going to get them both killed.

"You have no idea what you're doing, do you?"

"Of course I...."

"No, you don't. Is this what you normally do? Going undercover?"

"Well, no, not normally. But I've been fully trained for these kinds of operations."

"Really? Take a look at yourself, Regulator. You put on some native clothes, and you think people are going to believe you're a native? Have you looked in a mirror recently?"

"That's why I have this." Hyrom held up a small, round metal container. He struggled with the lid, succeed in opening it, and passed it to Bey. It was filled to the brim with a brown waxy substance, and smelled like essence-of-native-vehicle

"What is it?"

"Something the natives use on their shoes. It won't be as good as a muto-viral, but it should work. I just have to put it on any exposed skin, and make sure I don't get too close..."

"You just... Tell you what, Hyrom. I've got a better idea. Stick to blind dealers. Everybody else is going to spot you a mile off. It's not just a matter of color. Your face is the wrong shape. Your cheekbones stick out. And your nose is too big."

"It's a risk I have to take."

"Or you could try thinking instead. No way can you pass as a native. So, try something else. Ditch the native costume — it'll only give you away. And maybe get you killed. If the dealers don't die laughing first. Get yourself some decent clothes and go in as a rich Homeworlder, looking to buy a bit of luxury... Can you do a Homeworld accent?"

"You mean laak this?"

"No, I definitely don't mean like that. Where the fuck are you from, Hyrom?"

"Caliban — it's a—"

"Never heard of it. But nobody else will have either. So if anyone asks, tell the truth. It'll be easier to remember. The dealers aren't going to care where you're from. They *want* to sell their stuff."

"Okay. I suppose that makes sense. And what about you, Beynan? Are you going to help me, or not?"

"I'll help. But I can't do anything without plates for the camera. And I need shoes"

"Deal. I'll go back out right now."

The regulator got up to leave. Bey nodded his approval, happy to be left alone to do some thinking. Was he really going to help... or should he make a run for it instead?

CHAPTER 29

I understand the embassy's desire to protect Commonwealth citizens, but I fear that a State of Emergency would be counter-productive. Those who champion the motion are playing into the hands of extremists, allowing them to portray the presence of armed Commonwealthers on our streets as a vindication of their darkest suspicions. The motion for a State of Emergency must be rejected – not because it is wrong, but because it is ill-advised.

–From: Minutes of the Noyan Assembly, *Representative Ezra of Bridgetown speaking*

"It's not about you, Beth. It's about the prestige of the court."

"I know that, Justice Bartholomew, bu–"

"You say that, but I don't think you really understand how serious this is. The Gwahnals' disappearance–"

"Escape."

"Yes, yes. The Gwahnals' *escape* has put you in a very vulnerable position. Your fellow Justices want to support you, but the Family Court has to be seen to be above politics, and you seem to be going out of your way to antagonize the off-comers."

Beth pulled the telephone so close, her lips were brushing against the microphone. "Are you suggesting–?"

"No, of course not. But perceptions matter. You're

252

constantly giving your enemies more ammunition. At some point, a motion to impeach really will make it to the floor. And at that point, it doesn't matter whether you win or lose–"

"Of course it matters if–"

"It matters to you. To your investigation. But in the big picture, what matters is not whether it succeeds, but simply the fact of the Assembly voting on a motion to impeach. Once that happens, the relationship between the Assembly and the court is changed forever."

"It won't come to–"

"Won't it? Wake up, Beth. We're almost there now. Think of the damage to the court! Please, I'm imploring you. Hand the case over to another Justice. It doesn't matter who. Choose whoever you think will do the best job. Right now, you're a lightning rod for criticism. You're emboldening the very worst factions in the Assembly. Please, Beth. For the sake of the court."

"Thank you, Justice Bartholomew. I'll take it under advisement. Now, if you'll forgive me, I have an investigation to run."

She slammed the earpiece back onto the hook. Bartholomew wasn't the first Justice to urge her to withdraw. He was the third. And Ethan had been there for all three. He was wisely keeping his expression oh-so-carefully neutral.

"Where were we?" she said.

"I was agreeing with you, Justice. They all knew. The Mitchesons must have talked."

She sat back in her chair and stared up at the ceiling. The fan was spinning lazily, doing nothing to cool the room. A fly buzzed around it, battering itself against blade and ceiling.

Had she read Constantine correctly? He'd seemed genuinely surprised when she told him about the lack of attacks on the Gwahnals' interests. But he was an off-comer. Who knew what really went on behind those unsettlingly foreign faces?

On the other hand, she'd been able to read yesterday's interviewees well enough. And they'd only been pretending to be surprised. Had Constantine told them? Surely not. He couldn't possibly have any interest in protecting the guilty. Not when he and his wife were the most obvious suspects.

"It was the killers," she said. "Has to have been. They tipped everyone off – made sure they all knew before we got there. They didn't want to be the only ones faking surprise. Gave themselves a smokescreen."

"Possible." Ethan shrugged. "So, if we can find out who tipped everyone off... Do you suppose they called Constantine as well? Maybe you should talk to him, ask if anyone tried to tip him off."

"I doubt he'd even take my call. Not with the Gwahnals missing. And it's not like I can make him. That's what comes of letting off-comers control their own technology. The regulators should never–" She sat up straight. "The embassy. They must have realized the Gwahnals were using militants to sabotage their competitors. You don't suppose they..."

"Tipped everyone off?"

"...killed Sanja?"

Ethan's eyebrows shot up. "No, Justice. Why kill the son, not the parents? And why kill him at all? Why not just arrest him?"

She sat back again. He was right. Unfortunately.

"True. So, we're back where we started. Someone we interviewed yesterday is probably guilty. But who? Maybe we should put watchers on everyone we interviewed, see if anything shakes out. They might be worried, with the Gwahnals on the loose. Maybe we should look for someone acting like they think they're a target."

"We don't have the people, Justice. We've already run up against service time-limits with the militia. I've been putting some of our own people on the roadblocks, just to keep–"

"Stand them down. The roadblocks aren't doing anything useful now. If they ever were. The Gwahnals are long gone."

"I'll get–" Ethan looked up, startled. Jude had barged in without even bothering to knock.

"Justice. The 3-V. You need to hear this."

They hurried into the main office. The 3-V was projecting an unfamiliar off-comer face. An official spokesman? Probably. He was standing in the embassy grounds, and reading woodenly from a prepared note.

"...last night. There is no indication of exactly when the kidnapping occurred, nor if anyone was injured during the attack. A copy of the ransom note was delivered to our offices by regular, Noyan mail. The note is addressed to Ambassador Ashef and purports to come from the League of Free Noyim. Code words within the message testify to its authenticity. The missing are all employed at the campus, and were on their way home when they disappeared. We are currently waiting for a statement from the Office of Regulation, who are in charge of the investigation, and have assu..."

Beth didn't hear the rest. She was already on her way back to her requisitioned office, Ethan trailing behind. She waved him back to his chair, grabbed the telephone, and sat down behind the desk,

"Operator, get me the Commonwealth embassy."

The line hissed and buzzed, and went dead. A female voice filled the hollow silence. "This is the Commonwealth embassy. How may I direct your call?"

That voice. There was something unnatural about it. Not the tone. Not the off-comer accent. Something else...

"Put me through to Regulator Jodan Hyrom."

"Regulator Hyrom is on extended leave and unavailable. How should I direct your call?"

It wasn't the voice. It was the background, or lack of it. There was no space, no room around the woman speaking.

It wasn't a real person. It was the embassy itself. Beth grimaced, and soldiered on. "In that case, put me through to Undersecretary Maitland."

There were no clicks, no sounds of progress. Just dead, unnatural silence. And then another voice. A human this time, but not the undersecretary.

"Good morning, Justice. This is Commissioner Hozefa. How may I help?"

"You can put me through to Maitland."

"I'm afraid the undersecretary is currently unavailable. How can–?"

"Tell him to make himself available. Your regulators are infringing on Noyan sovereignty by investigating a domestic breach of Custom. Unless he wants to be responsible for–"

"If you're referring to last night's outrageous abduction of innocent Commonwealth citizens, Justice – the citizens involved are bi-technicians. Not only that, the terrorists clearly used contraband bi-tech in the course of perpetrating their crime. The investigation falls squarely under the authority of the Office of Regulation."

"No, it most definitely does not! Kidnapping is a matter for the Family Court, and always has been. I'm taking over this investigation as a supervising Justice of–"

"I'm afraid not, Justice. You're too late. This crime didn't happen in your district, and the local Justice – the Justice with actual authority – has already recognized our unique expertise, and ceded control of the investigation to the Office of Regulation."

"Expertise? You don't know the first thing about traditionalists. I do."

"On that we can agree, Justice. I have no doubt you're extraordinarily well informed about these terrorists. Goodbye."

The silence returned; but this time, it wasn't anything to do with off-comer technology. Hozefa had hung up.

She took a deep breath, put the earpiece back on its

hook, and set the phone down. Ethan was craning forwards in his chair. She scowled at him, indiscriminately angry. "Where was this kidnapping?"

"I don't know, Justice."

"Find out."

He scrambled to obey. She massaged her left hand. It was cramped where she'd gripped the telephone. She was still working on it when Ethan returned.

"South east, Justice. Out past Bent Bridge."

"Justice Matthew's district?"

"I think so..."

"Of course. Had to be. None of the other Justices would have been so..." She stopped. Ethan was only an auxiliary, after all. "Justice Matthew has ceded control to the regulators. And by the time the Assembly's reversed him, it'll be too late for us to... What?"

"I'm sorry, Justice. It's just..."

A moment ago, he'd been very obviously itching to speak. Now he was dithering. She glared at him until he continued.

"I'm sorry, but I don't think the Assembly's going take your side. Not against another Justice."

The office door was open. The 3-V was just audible. The lone fly was still buzzing up by the fan. She sat back, and closed her eyes, collecting her thoughts.

"Where were we?" she said.

"Justice?"

"The roadblocks. That was it. Make the call. Stand them down and reassign our personnel to keeping watch on the Mitchesons and as many other manufacturers as we can manage."

"Are you sure, Justice? It's going to look bad, getting rid of the roadblocks now, just after a kidnapping. And the Assembly's probably going to turn around and reauthorize them anyway. They'll want to keep the kidnappers from moving the hostages."

"Let them. Our priority is catching Sanja's killers. I

don't care what it looks like. Leave that to the politicians."

"Of course, Justice. Anything else you want me to do?"

"Yes. Find out who's running the investigation at the off-comer end, now Hyrom's off the case."

"Off the case? What do you mean off the case?"

"As in, he's not running it anymore. He's on leave."

Ethan sat down again. Hard. "The embassy told you that?"

"Commissioner Hozefa."

"Well, the commissioner lied to you. Hyrom's not on leave. He's staking out Michael's place, and he's got Hotep with him."

CHAPTER 30

At the meeting, Ambassador Ashef reportedly called on the Assembly to impose a State of Emergency in order to further restrict the kidnappers' freedom of movement. It's understood that the Executive Committee was divided in their response, and undertook to consult with the wider Steering Committee on a way forward.
— From: The Update, *Noyan Wireless News*

"It's a trap. Has to be."

Michael glared at the tenement building across the street. Hotep was in there; Hotep and the regulator, spying on him from a third-floor window.

"Hotep's bait. They're dangling him in front of us, hoping I'm stupid enough to bite."

It would be funny, if it wasn't so scraping infuriating.

And if everything else wasn't falling apart.

His hands were shaking. Actually shaking. Not with fear. With fury. It would be so satisfying to unleash his anger on Hotep and the regulator. Satisfying, but foolish.

He turned away from the window. The off-comers weren't worth it. They were a minor annoyance; nothing more. They weren't even an inconvenience, merely an insult. Much as he'd enjoy killing them, it would achieve nothing. Nothing good, anyway. He'd be such an obvious suspect.

"Any word from Ezra?"

Mary shook her head. "Nothing. He still doesn't have the votes."

"Maybe he needs some motivation."

"Want me to have a word?"

"No. If it comes to that, I'll do it myself. Be good to get some exercise."

Except he couldn't, or course. Because if he once started on the stupid mother, he wouldn't be able to stop. And Ezra was no use to him dead.

Not that he was being very useful just now. He hadn't even stopped the Assembly from letting off-comers work with the militia. Unbelievable. The regulators alone, he could deal with. Off-comers had no idea how much they didn't know. But allied with locals... That was a whole different level of pain.

And why hadn't the scraper stopped the roadblocks in the first place? Didn't he understand what they meant for Michael's business? And there'd be more of them than ever now. And more off-comers behind them.

The trads were so scraping stupid. They didn't like off-comers. Fine. Who did? But attacking them didn't help. It made everything worse. Every single time the trads acted up, the Assembly gave the off-comer mothers a little bit more of what they wanted.

But scrape, the trads had really done it this time. Kidnapping? Threatening to kill hostages? It was insane. The sooner those bi-technicians were freed, the better.

Forget Ezra. The kidnappers: they were priority number one. He needed those roadblocks gone. He'd solve this. Not the Assembly, and definitely not the scraping off-comers. Trads were a Noyan problem, best solved by Noyim.

The Gwahnals. They were a different order of problem. How had they done it? He wouldn't even have tried to escape from the Family Court – but they'd just walked out like it was nothing. How the scrape did they manage that? A pair of off-comers with no clue how things really worked?

"Where the scrape are they?"

Mary shrugged. She didn't need to ask who 'they' were. "Who knows? Maybe they're in the embassy, like the Justice said."

"Not a chance. She knows it, too. She's just winding them up. The embassy wouldn't move a finger to help the Gwahnals. Suits them down to the ground, Fange and Amaya getting arrested. Gives them leverage. Chance to stir up all their little toadies in the Assembly."

"I don't know, boss. Cherayn says the embassy's going crazy; thinks the Family Court still has them, and it's all some kind of game."

"It's a game all right. But the Family Court's not playing. They've escaped, and the Commonwealth doesn't have them. Which means the Gwahnals have resources we know nothing about…"

All these years, he'd thought it was a partnership – and he was the senior partner. The Gwahnals provided the product; he provided the muscle, and the local knowhow. They were useful, but they'd have been completely lost without him.

Except they weren't. They done something he wouldn't have even attempted. And they'd done it without him.

Maybe he wasn't the senior partner, after all.

Or any kind of partner.

Maybe the Gwahnals had been using him, all along. He wasn't their partner; never had been. He was an employee. A mark.

Wherever the Gwahnals were, they better hope he didn't find them. He had questions.

"Check out projector seven," said Mary.

A tall young woman was moving purposefully across the lobby. She was vaguely familiar. "Is that the new runner?"

"Dinah, yes."

A runner. And headed for the elevator. So, a word-of-mouth message. Either someone knew where the Gwahnals were hiding, or they had a lead on the morons behind the kidnapping.

He cracked his knuckles, eager to release tension in the most satisfying way of all. Mary took out her revolver and began, very methodically, to clean it.

The runner arrived sweating, and out of breath. That was good. Her predecessor had failed to grasp the need for haste, and was no longer in a position to disappoint Michael, or anyone else, ever again.

"Boss." She acknowledged him with a nod, but looked to Mary for guidance. It was understandable; she was used to reporting to Mary. But he didn't like it.

"Well? Out with it."

"Message from Rueben. He's picked up one of the trads behind the kidnapping."

The tension oozed out of him. His shoulders lifted. He smiled – and the runner flinched.

"He's sure?" Mary asked. "It's definitely one of the kidnappers?"

"One of the group. This uh… League."

"And we know that how?"

"Rueben's cousin, boss. He's a trad. Not heavy, but on the fringes. He's come to Rueben a few times, dealing for them. Bought guns, ammunition. That kind of thing."

"Okay. Mary – go bring him in. And give Rueben a message from me. No more dealing with trads. Not ever."

Mary pocketed her revolver. She was half way to the door before he stopped her. "No. Wait. I've changed my mind. Dinah – take a message to Rueben. Tell him to take this trad to the factory. We'll meet him there."

Mary waited until they were alone. "What about the cousin?"

"Nothing, for now. He might still be useful. Find out how close he and Rueben are. We don't need a loose end with a grudge."

He waited an hour to give Rueben time to get to the factory before him, then headed down to the basement garage. His car was ready and waiting, engine purring, driver at the wheel; the whole thing cleaned and polished to shining black and chrome perfection. He patted the hood affectionately. This was the car he'd dreamed of owning when he was a boy; the car designed to impress, to attract attention; the car street urchins ran after, and the authorities followed. The wrong car for today. He sent it on its way, and followed Mary to the discreet side door that led to his second garage; the one hidden in plain sight beneath the neighboring building, and to which none of its tenants had access.

There was only one vehicle here. It was far less imposing than his usual car; a regular, inexpensive model. And yet it was superior in every respect: a living ovoid with the intelligence to know its master, and obey only him. No one would guess that Michael was behind the unassuming carapace, seeing but unseen. This could only be a visitor's car. Bi-tech vehicles couldn't survive without a bi-tech house to feed them. Or, at least, they couldn't without the ugly tuber-like growth that took up a good third of the garage – and the ruinously expensive arc lights that kept it healthy.

The vehicle opened at his command. He climbed inside, waited for Mary, and told it to head for the factory. It detached from the tuber, and set off so smoothly the motion was barely perceptible. He settled back to enjoy the ride, and the anticipation of violence.

And descended into a cold fury when they reached their first roadblock, and the vehicle obeyed an off-comer's casual instruction to open.

One moment, he was basking in anonymity and control; the next he was powerless, exposed. What he wouldn't give to stamp on this arrogant, interfering off-comer who dared... Something was flickering at the man's shoulder: something small, and too fast to see.

Something deadly.

The man was asking questions. Michael left it to Mary to respond. He was focused on the targeting glove on the off-comer's right hand. So – there was the glove. Where was the hive?

There. On his back. Pretending to be a backpack. And crawling out of the top, a tiny, metallic-bright insect. Then it was gone; airborne so quickly it disappeared. He fixed his gaze above the man's head, looking for – and seeing – the tell-tale shimmer of loitering munitions.

He should have brought his favorite car after all. This vehicle stopped being useful the moment the Assembly allowed embassy guards onto the streets. You couldn't fight off-comers with their own weapons. They understood bi-tech too well; and bi-tech understood them, and respected their authority.

He'd been wrong ever to worry about the Family Court. This was the real danger: off-comers, moving in, taking over.

The trads did this. The trads and their provocations.

And one of them was waiting at the factory.

He couldn't wait to meet the mother.

Inspection complete, the vehicle was allowed to continue on its way. Michael barely noticed. His mind was elsewhere, feeling out the shape of this new world, looking for an edge. He'd always prospered at the interface between old and new; Noyim and off-comers. But what if that interface was disappearing? What happened when the off-comers took over? Because it was coming. He saw that now. The trads were right. It was only a matter of time.

And what then? The off-comers could shut him down overnight, if they wanted. All they had to do was end the embargo, and his entire business disappeared.

He had to slow things down. Give himself time to think, to plan, to develop new markets, new ways of staying on top.

So: first, deal with the trads. They were the reason everything was moving so quickly. Stop the provocations, stop the rapid descent into off-comer control. Representative Ezra didn't know it yet, but he was about to become a fanatic for preserving Noyan independence.

The vehicle was slowing down. They were approaching the main gate. He'd been sitting and stewing longer than he'd realized. That encounter with the armed off-comer had really shaken him.

The old man on duty waved them through. The vehicle picked up speed, following the unpaved road along the valley bottom to the inner gate. They waited for the electric fence to be disconnected, and then continued until they reached a large, rectangular ruin covered in corrugated steel panels: the disused mine-head.

The vehicle opened its carapace. Cool, climate-controlled comfort gave way to searing hot desert air and the cloying smell of burning oil. He nodded to Mary to go ahead. She hurried to the rusty steel door, peered inside, and signaled the all clear.

He followed, and warily scanned the echoing space for danger. It was an ideal place for an ambush: a maze of pipework interlaced with rickety latticework gantries. Anyone could be hidden there. But not this time. He strode to the central elevator block, and waited for Mary to press the button.

The doors opened smoothly on sheer, white walls and a smooth, clean floor. The mine-head was a ruin, but the elevator was modern and bright as an operating theatre. There was no attendant. Nor did they need one. No sooner had they stepped inside than the doors closed and it began to descend.

Down below was a different world, where tunnels were lined in living bi-tech, and the light came from glowbulbs embedded in rounded ceilings. The Gwahnals had insisted: no competent bi-technicians would risk their lives down here without bi-tech to reinforce the rough stone walls.

He'd given in to them then. He didn't plan on doing so again.

A waiting guard led the way past barracks and canteens, hydroponics farms and laboratories. The factory was bigger, far bigger, than he remembered. He hardly recognized the place. Yes, the production side had been growing recently – but this much? Everywhere he looked, off-comer bi-technicians were tending trays of immature buds, or laboring over unfamiliar instruments. Was all this product really his? Or did the Gwahnals have other partners he didn't know about? Partners who'd helped them escape…

He'd had the Gwahnals pegged as unsatisfied exiles, wanting a bigger cut of the action. But this place spoke of greater ambitions. There had to be someone here who knew the Gwahnals' plans; perhaps even where to find them. Maybe the trad wasn't the only one he should be interrogating.

Another corner, another sealed laboratory – and finally, a familiar corridor. A line of traditional rectangular doors stretched ahead, incongruous against the rounded walls. The guard stopped at the second door, and opened it.

There were no surprises waiting inside; just a sparsely furnished room. And in the middle, the prisoner. His ankles were tied to the legs of a wooden chair, his arms bound behind him. He was young – somewhere in his mid-to-late-twenties at a guess. And he was angry. More angry than frightened, from the way he was glaring. But then, aside from a freshly split lip, he hadn't really been hurt. Yet.

Michael circled around behind him, leaned over, and whispered in his ear. "Have you any idea how much trouble you and your friends have caused me?"

There was no response. That was okay. Michael wasn't in any kind of hurry.

"Nothing to say? You don't care? But you will. You will."

He strolled back into the prisoner's view. The man's eyes followed him.

"You know, if I were you. I might think about cooperating. You're going to eventually. People always do. There's really no need to go through lots of unnecessary unpleasantness. Not that I wouldn't enjoy it. I have a lot of... issues... I need to work out. But it would save a lot of time, so I'm willing to let it go. It's up to you. What we'll do is, I'll ask a question, and you answer it. And if I like your answer, I won't hurt you. Deal?"

Again, the young man didn't speak.

But someone else did.

"Sorry, but no."

An unfamiliar voice, directly behind him.

He whirled around, reached for his revolver. And stopped.

There was no assassin, no gun pointed in his direction. Just an off-comer in expensive brocade; a pony-tailed Gallaskian, leaning casually on a fancy walking stick.

"Who the scrape are you?"

"My name is Moyem Jimawn. And I would very much appreciate it if you would release my employee."

"Your... You would... Who the scrape do you think you are?"

"I believe I already answered that question."

The man was unarmed. He had to have seen Michael reaching for a gun. Didn't the idiot understand what that meant?

Scrape it. He didn't care. He'd had enough.

"Mary. Kill him."

Mary cocked her revolver. But she wasn't pointing it at the off-comer. She was pointing it at him.

The off-comer smiled. "Let's try this again, shall we?"

CHAPTER 31

Ambassador Ashef declined to comment, leaving it to Undersecretary Maitland to reiterate the long-standing Commonwealth policy of refusing to negotiate with terrorists. Behind the official line, however, it is clear that the embassy is increasingly frustrated with what they see as a lack of urgency on the part of the Assembly, especially its ongoing refusal to declare a State of Emergency.
— From: The Update, *a Noyan Wireless News Report*

Samuel missed the smell of shit; the smell of fertility wrung from barren soil. Familiar. Soothing. Part of the patchwork of everyday experience that somehow added up to *Home*.

There was no such comforting smell here in the desert. Not unless he sought out the section of the cave they'd turned into a latrine. All there was out here was dust, and the spice-smell of sparse native vegetation. And even that was fading as the sun rose higher.

Not that he could go inside right now. He was on lookout. It was better that way. The less he saw of the hostages, the easier it would be when the time came.

He glanced over his shoulder. The motorbike and sidecar were hidden under netting by the cave entrance. They would have fitted inside, but the thought of sharing the cave with Jimawn's hive made his skin crawl. He wasn't alone in that; no one wanted to be any closer to the sidecar than absolutely necessary. Which was why he'd stashed his escape kit under the seat, safe from prying eyes.

A noise. The distant put-put of an engine. Not off-comers, but still a potential threat. He picked up the binoculars and crawled up the slope to a better vantage point.

Nothing. Just empty desert. No. There. A puff of dust, far off to the right. He focused the binoculars. A truck. Smaller than New Beginning's, but just as battered and workaday. Not Nathan, then, but no threat either. It crawled across the landscape, disappearing occasionally behind bluffs and boulders, but never varying in speed or direction.

Someone touched his ankle. He flinched and looked back. Daniel was crawling up to whisper a message. "News is almost on. Thought you'd want to be there."

"Thanks. Nothing happening here. Just a truck." He handed over the binoculars, crawled away from the edge, and stood up. Eve was crouched beside the wireless at the cave entrance. He'd have preferred to take it deeper inside, but they reception died away immediately when they tried. And at least this way the hostages wouldn't hear the news, and become restive.

He bent to listen. A scratchy musical interlude was whiling away the time before the day's first news broadcast. It stopped mid-note, replaced by familiar chimes, and followed by equally familiar news headlines. Nothing had changed from last night. The Gwahnals still hadn't handed themselves in. The Assembly was trying to please everyone, and failing. Auxiliaries and regulators were busily chasing after leads and getting nowhere. The embassy was pompously refusing negotiations – as if he'd ever offered any. Jimawn wanted dead hostages, not useless concessions. Though quite why was a mystery. It couldn't just be hatred of the Commonwealth. That wasn't the Gallaskian's style. It must be part of some bigger scheme – something Samuel would have cared about, if he'd had any intention of sticking around.

The bulletin came to an end. Only one thing mattered. The deadline had expired. Their demands had not been met. He glanced at the sidecar, a few steps away.

Eve turned off the wireless. "It's been more than 24 hours."

"Yes, it has."

"They're not taking us seriously."

He recognized that tight-lipped expression. She was angry, blaming him. For what? Did she think he'd brought them this far to back down now? The temptation to tease her was overwhelming.

"I don't know. They're pushing pretty hard for a State of Emergency…"

"We need to make them do it. Tear the mask off. Show everyone what we're up against. There won't be a settler anywhere that doesn't join us."

And just like that, the joy in teasing her was gone. She wasn't his daughter anymore; she was Nathan's emissary. Both of them young, naïve and fanatically stupid.

The settlements wouldn't rise. They'd be revolted when they saw what happened to the hostages. They'd sit back and do nothing. And the city-dwellers – who were all that really mattered now – would cheer the Assembly on as it ceded yet more extra-territorial control to the off-comers.

He'd been exactly like Eve, once. He'd believed it all so intensely. But not now. He didn't believe in anything, anymore.

"You're right," he said. "But let's wait for Nathan. He shouldn't be long."

That calmed her down. As he'd known it would.

He headed deeper into the cave. It narrowed into a tunnel – tall enough for him to walk through, but so tight he had to turn sideways. After two sharp turns he was forced to use his hands to navigate in pitch darkness. Then he emerged into the cave proper, a candlelit space made up of three scooped-out semicircles, the product of some ancient geological process. The middle scoop was the largest; easily big enough for John and the other guards. The far scoop, nearest the latrine tunnel, was where the hostages waited, huddled miserably together against the wall, hands and feet bound to keep them from causing trouble. The nearest scoop held their scanty supplies. Water, especially, was running low. Nathan would bring more when he came, but they didn't need much. They weren't going to be here for long.

John rose creakily to his feet and hurried over to consult. What was he expecting? A breakthrough? It would be a pleasure to disabuse him. He did so in whispers, keen to avoid alarming the hostages – but unable to prevent John from doing so by looking at them with such obvious regret. The Noyan woman made a deliberate effort to lock eyes first with John, and then with Samuel. He turned away. The off-comers didn't bother him much... but the thought of a Noya, even a collaborator, dying that way...

He patted John's shoulder, and headed to the latrine. Afterwards, he helped himself to a cup of water, joined the other guards in the middle scoop, and lay down to rest.

He awoke suddenly, a hand shaking him by the shoulder. He brushed it off irritably. He hadn't meant to fall asleep.

It was John. And, behind him, Nathan. With a split lip.

"What happened to your face?"

"My...? Oh." Nathan reached for his lip. "Right. Yes. Argument with a windshield. Braked too hard."

"Looks painful."

"It was. So. Eve said you want to talk."

"I do. But not here. Come on."

He led the way back out to the sheltered area in front of the cave. Daniel was still at the edge of the rise, keeping an eye on the desert track.

"So?" said Nathan. "They didn't give themselves up."

"No."

"And the deadline's been and gone. It's time to show them we mean what we say."

Samuel nodded. It was true.

But the woman. He couldn't kill her. Not that way.

No, that wasn't true. He could, if he had to. But there was a better way; one that let him live with himself, afterwards.

"It is. But the moment we kill them, we're old news. Better to string it out a little more. Stay in the headlines. Keep the momentum."

"Or lose it completely. We have to kill the hostages, or they'll never take us seriously."

"They will once they find the body."

"The body?"

"We kill one. Then they know we mean it. And we still have three left. For leverage."

"Which one?"

He shrugged, pretending not to care. "The woman."

"Why her?" Nathan was looking at him searchingly. "Why not one of the off-comers?"

"The off-comers are more valuable, don't you think?"

"Yes…"

"And they're easier to handle. Too reliant on their technology. Especially without her to help them. Come on. Let's get this done."

The inner cave was alive with quiet conversations. They ceased the moment Samuel entered. Everyone knew a decision had been made. The guards were excited and nervous in equal measure; all save John, who seemed merely unhappy. The hostages were shrinking back against the unyielding rock wall. But not the woman. She was glaring at him. He walked over, grabbed her arm, and hauled her to her feet. She struggled for balance with her ankles tied, but he managed to hold her upright.

"I'd like you to do me a favor," he said. "The authorities are refusing to negotiate. I need you to convince them we're serious. Will you deliver a message for me? You believe we're serious, don't you?"

She nodded. Her eyes were narrow, suspicious. But there was a spark of hope, too. That was useful. She'd be cooperative, as long as that hope lasted.

"Good. You should be able to convince them, then."

"You aren't worried I'll tell them where to find you?"

"How? You were blindfolded. You have no idea where we are."

"I know you're in a cave."

"You know we are *now*. You think we're going to stay here, once you're gone? So, are you going to deliver my message? Or would you rather stay here, and leave it to one of your colleagues?"

"I'll do it."

"Good. Nathan, she's all yours."

Nathan cut the ropes around the woman's feet; then blindfolded her and led her back down the tunnel. John watched the whole time, smiling. Did he really think they were going to let the woman go? Senile old fool.

Samuel went to the latrine again; more to be alone than from any real need. It was just a matter of waiting now. It wouldn't be long before Jimawn was satisfied, his followers' bloodlust was slated, the authorities were reeling... and he could finally flee.

It was a risk, of course. The authorities might happen upon this hiding place. The off-comers might get their longed-for State of Emergency, and complicate his plan to be smuggled off-planet.

But risks had to be taken. He'd run out of safe options a very long time ago.

CHAPTER 32

The Noyan distinction between Law and Custom is difficult for outsiders to grasp. At its heart is a view of laws as transitory and subject to change, while Custom is permanent and fixed. Laws can have a moral component; Custom always does – however perverse that morality may seem to us.

– From: My Time on Noyan, Memories of a Youthful Exile, *The Rt. Hon. Beynan Hotep na Massowic*

Well, fuck.

There was a man, knocking on Michael's door. And he couldn't be a waiter, or a restaurant goer: it wouldn't be open for hours yet. A dealer? Maybe. Definitely someone who worked for Michael's *other* business.

Bey was out of excuses. He was going to have to take another photograph. Fuck.

He stepped up to the window, uncapped the lens and started counting to five.

He made it to three before his nerve broke. He was just too exposed. If anyone so much as looked up at the window...

He dived back out of sight. How the fuck had he let Jodan talk him into doing this? It was madness. And a complete waste of fucking time.

He checked the camera lens. At least he'd remembered to put the cap back on this time. And he'd managed a count of three. That was better. But was it enough?

He extracted the plate from the back. It came out easily. It should. He'd had plenty of practice.

The first look was promising. The image on the plate had the usual strange inversion of light and darkness, but it seemed less blurry. The longer count had helped, and so had capping the lens. Maybe this time...

He held it up to the light to get a better view. Yes, it really did look as if he'd finally... But, no: it was happening again. The image, so clean at first glance, was rapidly losing detail, blurring away like all the others until all that remained was a field of solid black.

He flung it disgustedly onto the discard pile; his private shrine to incompetence.

Did it need an even longer count? Did he have to stand in plain sight for five, ten fucking seconds? Or did he need one of those bright flashing lights the native reporters used? Was that what fixed the pictures so they didn't fade away?

Well fuck it. If that was it, Jodan could forget all about his precious photographs. It was bad enough just standing there. No way was he going to throw in come-get-me lights.

His stomach rumbled loudly. He hadn't eaten since Jodan brought that hunk of cheese and a loaf of coarse native bread yesterday lunchtime. How late was it now? Late enough. Pretty soon, he'd have gone a whole day without eating. Again.

Not that he could blame Jodan for that. He could have had bread and cheese for dinner as well. The problem was the consequences.

Drinking was fine. He could always piss in the sink – when Jodan wasn't around to complain. But eating... Taking a shit meant a trip down the hall. And everything about that was awful: the danger of being seen; the sheer horror of native toilets. They had *water* in them. Water that *splashed.*

The very thought of it made his skin crawl.

He headed back to the table, native shoes clunking loudly on the wooden floor. Were their shoes always this uncomfortable? Or was he just a victim of Jodan's cack-handed shopping choices? Still, it was better than going barefoot. You couldn't run far in bare feet, and the way things were going, he was definitely reconsidering running as an option.

He sat down, laid his arms on the table and used them as a pillow. He hadn't slept at all well last night. The floor had been unbelievably uncomfortable – but still better than enduring another night in the infested bed. Maybe, if he just closed his eyes…

He woke to the sound of footsteps in the hallway; a heavy tread, approaching the door. There had been others before. None had come this close. Were they slowing down? Or was that just fear distorting his sense of time? No. The footsteps had stopped. Right outside the door

He waited, heart pounding. A second passed. Another. Then it finally came: the familiar rat-a-tat-tat of Jodan's pre-arranged knock. Bey hurried to let him in. The sooner Jodan was inside and out of sight, the better.

The door was easy to unlock, once you knew how. Like the faucet, it was just a matter of learning the trick. You turned the key *before* you pushed the handle down. Then you pulled it open. He was much quicker at it now, but still not quick enough; the regulator barged in as soon as it began to open.

"What the fu-?"

Bey saw the look on Jodan's face, and closed the door behind him. It was just like the very first time they'd met: the same anger; the same barely suppressed violence. The regulator thrust a folded-up native newspaper at him.

"They're dead," he said. "One of them, definitely. Maybe the rest, too."

The newspaper headline was lurid, and unambiguous: 'Hostage Execution Horror'. Bey looked up, unwilling to read any further. "Which one?" he said.

"The woman. They shot her. In the head. At close range."

"The native? Not one of the Gwahnals' people?"

Jodan's jaw muscles bulged. "She was both."

"Of cour—"

But Jodan wasn't listening. He marched over to the window and stared out across the street. Bey hovered by the door, unread paper in hand. His stomach growled again, loud in the silence. He retreated to the table and sat down. After a little while, Jodan joined him, face unreadable. Bey nodded at the pile of discarded photographic plates.

"I tried again. It wasn't any better with a longer exposure."

Jodan's expression didn't even flicker. "We're wasting our time," he said. "I can't get anyone to sell me any contraband. And you can't take photographs."

Bey shrugged. "Maybe there's something wrong with the camera."

"Of course there's something wrong with it. It's a piece of native crap."

"So maybe if you get me ano—"

"No. We can't go on like this. It's not working. We'll never do this using native—" Jodan stopped. The slumped despondency was gone. Suddenly, he was full of barely-suppressed energy. He ducked down beneath the table and emerged with his work bag.

"That's where we've been going wrong," he said. "We can't do things the native way. It has to be our way. We have to use what we've got. And no more of this waiting around. It's time we took the fight to Michael."

Bey blinked. He glanced towards the window. He couldn't see Michael's restaurant from this angle, but it was still out there, a constant threat.

"You mean…?"

"I mean go over there and plant a bug."

"No fucking way. I'm not going anywhere near Michael. Hozefa's right: you're off your fucking head."

"Not you. Me. We've been going about this all wrong. Forget this native rubbish. We need to play to our strengths. I still have a few bits and pieces that'll give us an edge…"

Jodan rummaged through the bag. There was an eagerness about him; enthusiasm that bordered on mania. It was beyond disturbing.

"You can't go in there, Jodan. Not without embassy back up. You could disappear and no one would ever know."

"Maybe so – but Michael doesn't know that. And I have you. You can let the embassy know if anything goes wrong. Here, you'll need this."

Jodan handed him a small, featureless, green sphere. It looked like a ball from a particularly dull children's game. He turned it over in his hands, mystified. "What is it?"

Jodan ignored him. He retrieved a grey-green bulb from the bag and tapped the pointed end with his index finger. Petals appeared; first as little more than outlines, then flushing silver and curling open. Something small and black flew out.

And Bey's hands disappeared. In their place was a bizarre spherical image a foot wide.

"What the fu-?" His own words came back at him from inside the sphere. Suddenly, the incomprehensible jumble of colors and shapes began to make sense. He was looking at a distorted, inside-out, three-dimensional view of the room, seen from above. Jodan and he were weird, dwarfish characters with enlarged heads – one brown, one pink – staring out of opposite sides of the sphere, though in reality they were face to face.

He glanced upwards, seeking the bug. There it was: near the ceiling. It buzzed towards Jodan. Bey glanced back into the sphere. A warped image of Jodan's too-pink face took up much of its area; his lips a grossly-outsized red slash that rippled as he talked, and echoed every word he spoke.

"The modern ones compensate for the distortion. You really need training to use this type properly. But you don't need to worry about that. Just make sure you don't lose it. The recording's what matters. And that kicked in the moment the bug activated."

One of the pink dwarf's arms moved, flowing upwards to the top of the sphere. Bey glanced up. Jodan was rubbing the open end of the old-fashioned stasis bulb on the top of his head. He saw Bey's expression, and laughed.

"I can't have it buzzing around me when I go in. Too obvious. But if my hair smells like home, the bug'll stay put long enough for me to get inside. And then we'll see."

"Don't do this, Jodan. It's not safe."

"I know. But I don't have any choice. Besides, the bulb can't have many pheromones left. It's use it, or lose it. And I'm going to use it. See – it's working."

The bug was descending in a slow spiral. Bey glanced down at the sphere. The combination of distortion and motion made his eyes water. Then it was still. The bug had landed on Jodan's head. A nightmare landscape filled the sphere: a pock-marked plain, topped by a forest of scaly hairs. Never had baldness seemed so appealing.

"You can't do this, Jodan."

"Yes, I can. I just have to remember not to scratch where it itches. And it's too late for second thoughts now. I've got five minutes, tops, before the pheromones evaporate. I need to be in there before it takes off again. Wish me luck."

"But–"

"Goodbye, Bey."

Bey gave up. Jodan was already on his way to the door.

"Good luck, Jo."

The regulator nodded a thank you, and was gone. The

image in the sphere remained the same, but the audio was changing. Jodan's breathing was getting louder and faster as he hurried downstairs. The 'sky' above the hair forest turned from white to blue. Was he outside? Yes – and marching straight across the street to Michael's place. Then knocking imperiously on Michael's front door.

There was an angry argument, an assertion of right of entry and a demand to see Michael... and then Jodan was inside: the sky was white again, and the sound had an echoing quality. Speech gave way to silence and a distant creaking, overlaid with the sound of Jodan's heavy breathing. The elevator? Yes – there was the clank of the opening doors. Then footsteps. And then a sound that turned his bowels to water: Michael's oh-too-familiar voice.

"Ah, Regulator Hyrom. What an unexpected pleasure! And to what do we owe this visit?"

Bey couldn't see him, but he could still feel the man's visceral presence. Every pore, every detail of the monster's face was etched in his memory, burned there in an instant of pure terror when the bastard frightened the life out of him.

But if Jodan was afraid, he was giving no sign of it. "I think we both know the answer to that question, don't we, Michael?"

"I'm afraid not, Regulator. And I suspect Representative Ezra, here, is equally baffled. Perhaps you'd care to enlighten us? I assume you two know each other?"

"I've seen the representative on 3-V."

A small earthquake shook the hair-forest. Was that Jodan nodding acknowledgement to the representative?

"Regulator Hyrom. What a pleasure. How goes your investigation?"

The image was changing; the hair forest thinning out, becoming a plain of cratered pink. A pool of coarse fabric welled up from the bottom of the sphere. Jodan's collar? The bug was heading downwards. The pheromones must be fading. At least it hadn't flown away. Even the natives would be suspicious of an insect taking off from a regulator's scalp.

Meanwhile, Jodan had given up on pretending to be interested in Representative Ezra. "I'd like to ask you a few questions, Michael, if you don't mind?"

"And if I do mind?"

"Then I'll ask them anyway."

"And if I choose not to answer?"

"In that case I'd have no choice but to arrest you. But I'd rather keep things civilized, if–"

"And on what authority do you intend to arrest me, Regulator Hyrom?"

Michael knew. Shit. Michael knew.

"On my authority as a regulator."

"Interesting. I'm curious how that works. Do you continue to have that authority in some kind of personal capacity? Even when you've been suspended?"

Jodan's answer was just that beat too slow in coming. "That's not a problem. The suspension was just a cover story to put you off guard."

A sudden, bewildering kaleidoscope of colors swirled and melted across the surface of the sphere. Was the transmission breaking up? But no: the picture was stabilizing. Bey shook his head, trying to make sense of a jumble of deformed rectangles and pink and brown blobs.

Then it clicked. He was looking at a truncated, bug's-eye view of Michael's office; one so distorted it was hard to tell where people ended and furniture began. Michael spoke, and the image resolved itself still further; Michael was the circular brown blob on the right – the one with two arms and a pair of projections that looked like breasts, but must be feet.

"Really? And you won't mind if I call Commissioner Hozefa and get confirmation of that?"

"Be my guest." The pink blob had spoken: Jodan. Which meant the third blob, the one with stumpy dwarf legs sticking straight out in front of it, that must be Representative Ezra. Was he sitting down? Was that why his legs looked like that?

"Your guest? In my own place? Hardly. But don't worry. I won't call him. From what I hear, the embassy would love to know where you are. And I don't believe in helping regulators."

"Why? Afraid we'll catch you?"

"Give it up, Hyrom. You're playing out of your league."

"Really? And what about you? A jumped-up dealer, selling things you don't understand and could never make." Jodan didn't seem to know when he was beaten. Bey willed him to get out. While he still could.

"I'm just a restaurateur, Regulator Hyrom, nothing more." There was beginning to be an edge to Michael's voice. Jodan was annoying him. Bey wished he would stop. He'd only seen Michael angry once, but that was too often.

The pink blob moved. Bey couldn't make sense of the direction, or how the blobs related to each other. Was Jodan retreating? Or heading further in? And then Jodan spoke, and he clearly wasn't going anywhere. "Nothing more? No. Something less. Definitely. You sell things decent people won't touch. Not just bi-tech. Dirtier things. If this were a civilized planet, they'd run you in just for being a pimp."

"Is that so? But you know what, Regulator Hyrom? There's a reason pimping isn't against Custom. And that's because prostitution didn't exist here on Noyan. Not until you off-comers came along. It's one of the many benefits of 'civilization' you brought with you."

"Took to it like ducks to water, though, didn't you? How long have you been a pimp, Michael? Ten years? Twenty?"

"Like I said, I'm just—"

"A restaurateur. Right. So, how did that work? You started out as chef? Learning the trade from the bottom up? Because from what I've heard, that's how you learned about pimping. From the bottom up."

Oh shit. Did that mean what Bey thought it meant? Was Jodan *trying* to get himself killed?

But strangely Michael didn't seem annoyed. If anything, he was expansively friendly. "Ah, well… You shouldn't listen to rumors, Regulator. Look, you're a family man, aren't you? I thought so. Don't you worry about what's going to happen to them, once the embassy catches up with you?"

"What?"

"I mean, let's be honest. You're going to get caught eventually. You have to know that, right? The way you're going, I might even change my mind, call the commissioner myself. And what happens then? After he comes to collect you? Who's going to look after your family?"

"The embassy." Jodan sounded puzzled, like he didn't even realize he was being threatened. Bey shouted at the sphere, trying to warn him, but the regulator was far away, and couldn't hear.

"Oh, I'm sure. Very civilized, you off-comers. Like you said. But I was thinking – you never know what happens while you're locked up. I mean – what if terrorists decided to go after your family? You wouldn't be there to protect them, would you, Regulator?"

"But—"

"And there's other bad people besides terrorists. Like you said: pimps. Someone could make a lot of money, selling off-comer ass. Your wife. Your kids. For variety, you know."

"You son of a—"

There was movement in the sphere. The pink blob was lunging away from – or was that towards? – Michael. And suddenly Michael had something metallic in his hand. And Jodan stopped moving, very abruptly.

"Now, now, Regulator Hyrom. None of that. I'm just

trying to give you a friendly warning, that's all. You don't want your wife taking it up the ass. Especially not the way Fange took–… Sit down, Hyrom."

"Fange? Fange Gwahnal? What do you mean? Not 'the way Fange took' what?"

"I said, sit down."

"No, I don't think so. I think I'll be leaving. Fange, was it? Very interesting."

Jodan was moving again. Headed for the door? Probably. The motion was obvious, the direction less so. A stick-like arm stretched out in front of the pink blob. Was Jodan reaching for the door?

"I won't tell you again, Hyrom. Sit down, or I'll shoot you."

"You haven't got the guts."

What was Jodan playing at? Did he really think Michael wouldn't shoot? Didn't he know who he was dealing with?

And then, sickeningly, Bey understood. Jodan *wanted* Michael to shoot him. It was his last throw of the dice, his final chance to gather incontrovertible evidence: the recording in Bey's hands.

A black line cut into the edge of the sphere. The door opening? Jodan was still talking. "Women and children are more your style, aren't they? You should have stuck to selling your own a–"

The shot was appallingly, terrifyingly loud. So loud, Bey dropped the sphere. It rolled away, a rotating dome of color and movement. He hurried after it, snatched it off the floor, and tried to make sense of what it was showing. One of the men in the room was no longer a truncated blob with arms, but recognizably a man. It was Jodan, and he was lying prone on the floor.

"*Mothermothermothermother…*" Bey closed his mouth, but the babbling continued. It wasn't him. It was coming from the sphere.

A red stain was spreading around Jodan's body. Bey stared at it, disbelieving.

"Shut up!" Michael's voice bristled with anger. The babble cut off as if a switch had been thrown. The black line of the door turned into a hole in the sphere. A furious blob stormed in, paused at the sight of the body, and gesticulated with stumpy dwarf arms. "There's something transmitting from in here!"

A woman's voice, and she knew about the bug. Shit.

"What?"

"There's a bug. Your cretins let him in with a bug."

"Scrape! If the embassy..."

"Don't be stupid. We'd never have detected an embassy bug. This thing's old kit. The receiver can't be far away... The boy. He must have left it with the boy."

"So, pick him up! Now."

The woman's blob-head changed shape. Two eyes appeared; a nose. She was looking directly at Bey. She could see him!

No. She could see the bug. She raised her right hand. White mist poured out and filled the sphere. He was holding a swirling ball of cloud. Then, quite suddenly, the mist whipped away in a tumbling blur of confused motion. The bug had fallen to the ground.

All motion stopped. Half the sphere was a close-up view of the floor. The other half was a forest of towering legs. Then a huge booted foot. And then nothing.

Bey was holding a dull green ball in trembling fingers. Three stories below, the front door slammed.

Jodan was dead, and they were coming for him.

CHAPTER 33

The Commonwealth and their intemperate supporters have no evidence for their wild claims and sly innuendos. All their talk of 'disappearances' and hints at foul play on the part of the Family Court are a transparent attempt to obscure the facts. Let us dispense with humbug: the Gwahnals are fugitives from justice, nothing more, nothing less...

- From: Editorial, *The Recorder*

Amaya Gwahnal's eyes were no longer in their sockets. One dangled against her right cheek, held there by a bloody umbilical cord of veins, nerves and arteries. The other lay some distance away on the sand, shriveled raisin-like in the desert heat.

Someone had brought Amaya here, stripped her naked, and tied her spreadeagled to pegs hammered deep into the hard, dry ground. Then they'd inserted a roadroot into her vagina. True to form, the roadroot had grown where it was set, and greenery now packed every orifice. Thick roots grew out of her nostrils, her ears, her distended mouth. Questing shoots emerged from her eye-sockets, reaching out towards Fange, face down beside her, a roadroot protruding from his anus. Both bodies were clamped to the ground by thousands of tiny roots.

Beth turned away, nauseated. She'd been warned, but no warning could ever have prepared her for this. How long had they lain there, knowing what was growing inside them – feeling it grow, even – before death finally took them?

"What does it take?" said Jude, beside her. "I mean, what kind of a sick mother... Sorry, Justice. But, what kind of monster do you have to be to... to...?" He pointed a shaking finger at the prone figures.

"I don't know. But whoever they are, they were sending a message. But who was it aimed at? Michael? Samuel and his friends? We should offer them protection, for what it's worth... But the Gwahnals were my prisoners, and I couldn't even protect them."

"It's not your–"

Jude stopped, distracted by a growing uproar behind them. The militia were shouting, pointing skywards. Beth looked up.

And saw a nightmare approaching.

It flew as an insect flies; floating, indifferent to gravity. But no insect had ever grown so large. It was the size of a truck – a vast, predatory green wasp, six legs dangling beneath its tapered body, bulbous head pointed unwaveringly in her direction.

She held her ground, refusing to be intimidated. There were no giant wasps on Noyan; only off-comer flying vehicles. It was overhead now; wings resolving into rotors, eyes into windows. She signaled to the unseen pilot to land on the far side of the tape. The pilot – if there even was a pilot, and not merely some malign vat-grown intelligence – ignored her, and swooped downwards. Revulsion, and a fierce downdraft, forced her to retreat, leaving the monster free to lift its snout and perch insolently inside the cordon. It flexed its legs to soften the landing, and then was still, rotors folded back, bulbous eyes gazing sightlessly into the distance.

Beth stared at it with unmitigated loathing, revolver in

hand. She had no memory of drawing the pistol, but its solid weight was oddly reassuring. And she needed reassurance. The thing was even larger than she'd thought – fully forty feet from its rounded head to the tip of its spiky tail.

She turned back to Jude. "Get your team together. I don't want off-comers anywhere near those bodies. I'll deal with this."

A hatch opened, sphincter-like, in the side of the vehicle. Emerging from it, an orange tongue quested for the ground and transformed into a set of steps. And smiling down at her from the hatch was Undersecretary Maitland. She pointed the revolver straight at him.

"Stop right where you are. This is a sealed area. I want that vehicle back on the other side of that cordon immediately, with you inside it."

"Do you always threaten first and ask questions later, Justice? I can't believe it makes you popular..."

"Get that vehicle back on the other side of the barrier or I'll have it impounded."

"We always seem to be having the same conversation, don't we, Justice? The Family Court doesn't have jurisdiction here. The Office of Regulation does."

"We'll let the Assembly rule on that, shall we?"

"But my dear lady, it already has."

Maitland stepped aside. Ruth was standing there, looking embarrassed. Beth lowered her gun. "I don't believe it."

Ruth shrugged unhappily and climbed down the steps. Uniformed off-comers poured out of the vehicle behind her.

"Sorry, Beth. There was nothing I could do. I've been delegated to bring you back to face a Committee of Inquiry."

"And Undersecretary Maitland kindly let you share his transport? How very astute of you to accept the offer."

Ruth pulled her away from the stairs. "Actually, it was

my idea. And I'm very glad I came along. If you'd shot him, Noyan would be a Commonwealth Protectorate by midnight."

"I wasn't going to shoot him."

"Then why'd you get the gun out? You know better than that."

"Okay. I'm sorry. It was that thing…" She waved the revolver towards the flying machine. "It shouldn't be here. And it definitely shouldn't have landed this side of the tape. This is a crime scene."

"I know. But Beth, the Family Court doesn't have any say anymore. It's their investigation now… Hold on. I have to stop this before it gets out of hand."

"Stop what? Oh…"

Only then did Beth register the noise of an altercation behind her. Maitland and a phalanx of hard-faced embassy guards were facing off against Jude and the militia. It wasn't an even match. Jude was far too junior to face someone like Maitland, and the militia's anger was no match for the off-comers' professionalism. She holstered her revolver and hurriedly signaled Jude to back off. He mimed disbelief, but stepped obediently out of the off-comers' way. Then Ruth was beside Maitland, thanking the militia for serving and telling them, and a scandalized Jude, that the Assembly had ceded jurisdiction over the Gwahnal case to the Commonwealth.

Beth listened along with the rest. If it had been anyone but Ruth, she might not have believed it; or, believing it, have resisted anyway. But whatever differences they had, there was no questioning her friend's loyalty – to her, and to Custom. She didn't protest when Ruth ordered the militia to disperse; not even when Jude turned to her, furious. "They can't do this, Justice. It isn't right!"

"I know, but–"

"They can, and they have." Ruth cut her off. "It doesn't matter if we think it's right or not. There's nothing you or I or Justice Beth, or anyone at the Family Court can do about it. The Assembly's voted to cede jurisdiction. As far as Custom's concerned, that's the end of the matter."

Beth patted Jude's arm. She understood; she felt the same way. But Ruth was right. Custom was everything; and Custom vested ultimate authority in the Assembly, not the Family Court.

"Leave it, Jude. There's nothing we can do. Stick around. Keep an eye on the off-comers, but don't interfere."

"Yes, Justice." Jude stalked off unhappily, and watched the off-comers remove the tape he'd set up around the crime scene. Beth turned to Ruth.

"Why, Ruth? Why'd they give away jurisdiction?"

"Wake up, Beth! Look around. You arrested the Gwahnals – and look what's happened to them."

"Yes. Look. The killers used roadroots. Their tech, not ours. Off-comers did this."

"Forget it, Beth. It's over. And unless you come back with me right now and cooperate with the Inquiry, losing jurisdiction won't be the end of it. They want to impeach you. And if they succeed, it's only a matter of time before you're expelled from the Family Court. Please, Beth! We have to go."

"Okay. Fine. Come on, I'll give you a lift to the Assembly."

"No. I'll give you a lift – in the autocopter. We're all headed there. Maitland's testifying to the Committee."

"The autocopter?" She stared at the giant insect. It stared back at her malevolently. "No thanks. I'd rather drive."

"We don't have the time."

"I'm not getting in that thing."

"You can't seriously be scared of flying?"

"You know I don't like off-comer tech."

"You *are* scared, you old fossil. Come on, there's nothing to be afraid of. Autocopters can't crash. They're fabulous machines. Those rotors don't even need power once they're in the air, not to stay up, anyway. They create their own lift. Even if something goes wrong, they just land safely."

"And what if it decides to fold those rotors while we're off the ground?"

"It can't. There are lots of fail-safes. Give it up, Beth. There's never been a crash. These things are foolproof."

"So was Sanja's house."

"It's not going to crash, Beth. Stop worrying about the autocopter, and start worrying about what you're going to say to the Inquiry."

Beth wanted to go on arguing, but Maitland was on his way over, and she couldn't bear the thought of appearing weak in front of him. She nodded reluctant agreement, and allowed herself to be ushered up the narrow steps and into the waiting vehicle.

The interior of the autocopter was nothing like the aggressive, insectile exterior. Everything was rounded, curved, cushioned. It was a dream-space, where the padded cell was the universal design standard and sharp corners and angles didn't exist. Rows of over-soft chairs were grouped around a central aisle. Ruth dropped happily into one of four bloated armchairs looking out through the bulbous window-eyes. There was no cockpit; no controls; no pilot. Beth wanted to flee, but Maitland was climbing the stairs behind her, and she had no choice but to follow Ruth.

"You won't believe the view when we're in the air, Beth. It's incredible. Everything looks so small."

Beth sat down next to her, and sank into a chair with the softness of marshmallow. Then she was suddenly much too heavy, and sinking still further; the autocopter had leapt into the air. The rotors spun. The autocopter leveled off. And something far worse than excess weight grabbed her attention: the view through the windows.

The desert floor was shrinking, rushing away at appalling speed. Her stomach lurched. Her hands clutched convulsively at the seat's softness, gouging holes in the unresisting material. Everything about this experience was wrong, impossible, absurd. The ground was too far away; the autocopter too heavy. It couldn't possibly fly. It was going to plummet to the ground, taking her with it.

Ruth, was talking, but the words meant nothing: blind panic left no room for anything else. Beth closed her eyes, but it made no difference. Every change of altitude, every motion, sent tremors through her gut. Somewhere in the distance, Ruth was patting her leg and muttering meaningless words of reassurance. They didn't help. Nothing would. Not until she was back on the ground. And once there, she'd never, ever get in one of these scraping things again.

The landing, when it finally came, was so gentle she didn't even feel it. Only when Ruth stood up did she realize it was over. They'd made it. They were down.

The outside world rushed back in. Words once again had meaning. Sensations other than fear became possible – including pain; her fingers were cramping from their death-grip on the seat. She slowly prised them loose. Then she tried to stand, but the seat was just too deep and too soft. Ruth helped her to her feet; then gave her a surprisingly welcome hug.

"I'm sorry, Beth. I had no idea… How do you feel?"

"*Pregnant*. You should have let me drive." She managed a weak smile. Ruth mirrored it.

"Next time, for sure. But we had to, Beth. You can't be late. This is your one and only chance to turn this around. It never occurred to me you'd take flying so badly. I'm sorry."

"Ladies?   Shall we?" Maitland was gesturing to the waiting steps. His supercilious expression gave no hint that he recognized, or cared about, Beth's obvious distress.

"You go ahead," said Ruth, coldly. "We'll follow."

"As you wish."

Beth made her slow way to the hatch. A small crowd

was already gathering around the autocopter, excited by its novelty. Beyond them lay the Assembly Hall. Beth shook off Ruth's over-helpful hand.

"So, who's on the Committee?"

"There's three of us. Me. Adam – he's the Chair and supposedly neutral. And Ezra. He's the opposition: reliably pro-Commonwealth and a definite vote against you. Concentrate on convincing Adam: he's the swing vote. That's what Maitland will be doing."

Beth nodded. "Come on, then," she said. "Let's get this over with."

CHAPTER 34

It is a continuing source of astonishment to me that so many Noyim survive to a ripe old age. Their houses are death traps. Their automobiles lack even the most rudimentary safety features and require constant supervision to avoid collisions – even with stationary objects. As for Noyan bicycles and tricycles – I can assure you that absolutely nothing could persuade me to venture onto such an insanely dangerous device ever again.

– *From:* My Time on Noyan, Memories of a Youthful Exile, *The Rt. Hon. Beynan Hotep na Massowic*

Bey peered down the stairwell. Three floors below, a hand was skimming the banister. There was no escape that way.

Back into the room? No. That was a trap.

The toilets? Fuck no.

There was only one choice – upwards.

Heavy boots were pounding up the stairs. Bey forced himself to go slowly. His only hope lay in stealth, difficult as that was in native shoes.

He made it up one flight – and ran out of stairs. This was it: the top floor.

Fuck.

It was identical to the floor below: apartment doors; a toilet at one end; a window at the other. Nowhere to hide.

No way out. The window was too high for him to jump down. Climbing was out: a native building couldn't create handholds or footholds. Besides, the window opened on Michael's street. Going out that way would be suicide.

Then he saw it: a door that didn't fit – right where the next flight of stairs would have begun. It couldn't be an apartment. There wasn't enough room. A closet, maybe?

The pounding footsteps stopped. A door slammed open. Shit! He should have locked the door. That would have slowed the bastard down. Now he knew Bey wasn't there. Fuck. He'd run out of time. He yanked open the closet door.

It wasn't a closet! It was another staircase; a spiral one. Made of metal, not wood, and with scary open treads.

He stepped inside and closed the door behind him, cutting off some, but not all, of the light. There must be a window somewhere up there. And a way out. There had to be a door. Why else have stairs?

He tiptoed upwards. Four complete turns of the spiral later, he found the source of the light: a small glass window inset in a wooden door. It was too dirty to see through, but that didn't matter. Staying here wasn't an option.

Shit. What if it was locked?

He tried the handle. It turned. Thank fuck for that.

But it didn't open. No matter how hard he pulled. Was it locked? Or just stiff? He rattled it backwards and forwards. Was that a little give? He pushed, hard as he could... and almost fell flat on his face.

The fucking thing opened outwards. Not inwards. Outwards. That was all. It opened outwards.

He was standing on a flat, gravel-covered roof.

And staring straight up at Michael's penthouse. If anyone so much as glanced out of the window...

What now? He couldn't go back inside. Not with the heavy after him. He closed the door, and weighed his options. The front and back of the building were out. Both were sheer drops, with only a small parapet between him and certain death. To his left was an unscalable blank wall: the neighboring building was much taller. To his right was a parapet-less edge, and another sheer drop – but to the next building, not the street.

He ran towards it and looked over the edge. Another flat roof. That was good. But it had to be a ten-foot drop, maybe more. Well, he couldn't stay here. He sat on the edge, turned around, lowered himself as far as he could, and let go.

The landing jarred his ankles, but he was okay; he hadn't broken anything. He picked himself up, ready to run.

But where next? There was no door on this roof, no convenient staircase. Just two skylights. And the next building was much taller than this one. He was trapped between sheer walls.

He headed for the far wall. There were cracks and missing bricks. Maybe he could climb...

He looked back – just in time to see an athletic-looking native jumping down after him. He seemed vaguely familiar. Not that it mattered. Life was so simple when you didn't have any choices.

He ran towards the nearest skylight and jumped on it, feet first. It gave instantly, collapsing in a shower of broken glass and twisted metal.

He braced for a hard landing, but hit something soft and yielding instead: an empty bed. He tumbled forwards, arms raised to shield his face from a sea of broken glass; then bounced back up to hands and knees, cutting himself badly. But he couldn't worry about that now; someone was screaming. Amazingly, it wasn't him. There was a second bed. Inside it, a fat Commonwealth man and a native girl. The man was glaring at him. The girl was doing the screaming. Bey jumped to his feet and ran for the door.

This hallway was far more luxurious than the one in the rooming house. The walls were brightly-colored and festooned with paintings of scantily clad men and women engaging in acts that left nothing to the imagination. So, it was *that* kind of building.

The stairs were a nightmare, covered in some kind of treacherous fabric. It might have been designed to trip the unwary. He longed to tread carefully and cling to the banister, never mind his bleeding hands. But he couldn't. The noises from above were as unambiguous as the pictures on the walls: his pursuer had followed him through the skylight. He scrambled down as quickly as he dared. It sounded like the couple in the room was putting up more resistance this time. That was good. That should slow the bastard down.

Finally, there were no more stairs. He was on the ground floor. What now?

The front door was dead ahead – but an angry woman stood between him and escape. She was small and white-haired, but she was carrying a truncheon. For a moment they faced off. Then she retreated, shouting for assistance. Bey doubled back down the corridor in search of another way out. Thank fuck for the old biddy! If she hadn't been there, he'd have gone straight out the front door – and into Michael's street.

The back door was locked; the window beside it covered in black paint.

"House: open the window."

Nothing happened. Of course. He reached for the window's small handle. It turned easily, but neither pushing nor pulling did any good. He wrenched at it frenziedly – and suddenly it turned through another 45 degrees, and the window swung open. So simple, when you knew how.

He climbed out into an unfamiliar street. It stretched for hundreds of yards in either direction: an endless row of joined-together native buildings. And some distance away on the other side of the street, a gap where houses gave way to an open market. He set off towards it at a run.

He was half way there when a squeal of brakes made him look up. Something was happening at the end of the street. A purposeful group of men and women were fanning out across the road, closing off any exit.

He skidded to a halt and made to turn back – only to see the athletic native from the roof emerging from the brothel window.

Once again, he had no choice. He ran full pelt for the market. Either there was a way out the other side, or he was dead. But what else could he do?

A loud bang echoed down the road. Something whistled overhead. He flinched, and almost wet himself. Another bang and whistle, and something struck a nearby wall in a shower of sparks and stone chips.

A gun: a native gun – the bastards were shooting at him. He found an extra burst of speed, ran into the market, and dived between two stalls. His entrance and the accompanying gunfire sent shoppers and stall-holders scattering. Angry abuse followed him through the market, but he didn't care. The more chaos he left in his wake, the better. Anything to slow his pursuers down.

He pelted onwards, a locus of panic sending ripples of confusion through the market. Where next? Somewhere to hide? Not a hope. A way out? No. There were more buildings at the back of the market. Unless… Was that a gap? Yes! Right there: a small alleyway between two tall buildings.

He hurled himself over a nearby stall. Fruit went everywhere. The stallholder yelled furiously, and then backed off. Even now, in the midst of his terror, Bey felt a glow of satisfaction. The man was right to be afraid. Bey was bloody and hurt and angry and if anyone got in his way, he'd tear them apart with his bare hands.

The alley was ahead, confusion behind. He had a moment's grace. How to use it?

There: a vegetable barrow – just feet away. He grabbed the handles, pulled it into the alley, and overturned it behind him. Then he ran on. He had to reach the other end of the alley before the posse gained the entrance. They couldn't possibly miss in a shooting gallery like this, not even with native weapons.

The pounding of his feet echoed off the walls, but no matter how hard he ran, the way out didn't seem to get any closer. He was trapped in a tunnel whose exit was receding with every step he took. He could sense his pursuers taking aim, could feel their eyes boring into his back... and then it was over. He was through the alley. He dived to the right, putting solid stone between himself and his enemies.

Then he doubled over, struggling for breath. His legs felt limp and hot and sore, all at the same time. He couldn't go on like this. He had to find a place to hide. But where?

He was alone in a small back street. It was narrow and dark, with native vans and automobiles parked along its whole length. The remaining strip of road was just wide enough for a single vehicle. He scanned up the street. Where to go?

Then he saw it: a big, black tricycle, with twin baskets to the rear, and another between the handlebars. He grabbed the handles and set off at a run. It bounced along beside him, moving easily on its big wheels. This was going to work!

He jumped astride the machine, and almost fell off the other side before righting himself – only to cry out when one of the footrests rammed into his calf. They were appallingly designed, whizzing around with the wheels instead of staying still. What maniac thought that was a good idea? Still, at least his calf had stopped them spinning. He rested his feet gratefully. Finally, he could catch his breath and let the tricycle do the work.

Except it was slowing down. He yelled at it to go faster. It ignored him. What the fuck?

A shot rang out. His pursuers had emerged from the alleyway.

Of course yelling wouldn't work! It was a native machine. There must be an engine. But where? It wasn't in front. Behind? No – not that he could see. And the pursuers were back there, running after him. It must be under the seat. He was going to have to risk standing up.

He did so, and almost fell over the handlebars. The footrests had turned under his feet. He sat back down, hurriedly, legs circling.

The tricycle was picking up speed again.

His legs were moving, and the tricycle was speeding up...

Fuck! The engine wasn't under the seat. *He* was the engine. Him and his tired legs.

But it was better, and faster, than running. And the harder he pushed, the faster his legs went, and the more the tricycle accelerated. He glanced over his shoulder. Michael's gang was falling behind. That was good... Except that they were leveling their guns...

He put his head down and pumped his legs as hard as he could. More shots rang out, terrifyingly loud. His legs hurt. His lungs burned. But he kept going faster.

And then, suddenly, he burst out of the back street. Horns honked. Brakes squealed. He was headed straight across a busy thoroughfare. He'd barely registered the danger before the tricycle was mounting the far sidewalk. He was moments from colliding with a solid stone building. He screamed and twisted to the right, readying his shoulder to take the brunt of a crash... that never came. The handlebars moved with him, and so did the tricycle, skidding up on two wheels before slamming back down onto three. Somehow, he was alive. Alive, and heading in the wrong direction: towards Michael's street.

Fuck. If only the damned thing had turned left. But it hadn't, and there was no going back now. His only hope lay in speeding by before he was spotted. He started pumping his legs again. Pedestrians dived out of his way, protests silenced by renewed gunfire behind him.

The wheels were turning more easily now. Was he getting a second wind? Or was it because he was going downhill? Yes. That must be it. He was picking up speed, going fast. Too fast. It was getting harder to swerve around obstacles, even knowing how the handlebars worked. He had to get off the sidewalk.

He yanked the handlebars to the right, and crashed back down onto the road. Michael's street went by too quickly for anyone to intercept him — but not so quickly he wasn't seen. Angry shouting meant yet more heavies in hot pursuit. But they hadn't a hope of catching him, not now. He was getting away! And doing so very, very quickly…

The downhill was becoming steeper and steeper, and the tricycle was going faster and faster. He shouted at it to slow down. Nothing happened. Of course. There had to be a mechanical way to stop this thing. But how? What would a brake even look like?

The footrests were spinning so quickly he couldn't keep up. He tried to fight back, to make them slow down, but his left foot lost its grip on the whirling footrest and he almost toppled from the seat. He pulled both feet wide and clear, desperate to regain his balance.

Then he saw what lay ahead: heavy traffic, and a major junction. Trucks and automobiles were crossing directly in front of him. Staying on wasn't an option. But how to jump clear, with his feet waving helplessly in the air?

He did the only thing he could: pushed against the handlebars with all his strength, and hoped it would be enough to throw him clear. It wasn't. The rear-left wheel ran straight into him. He barely even registered the pain. It was nothing, beside the bone-jarring impact with the road. He bounced and tumbled helplessly, arms flailing, until the curb brought him to a final, painful, halt.

Somewhere up ahead, he heard the sound of skidding brakes, and a loud metallic crunch. He struggled to raise himself, but could hardly move. He was gulping at nothing; drowning in air. Then, suddenly, his lungs opened and he took in a huge, ragged breath. Nothing had ever felt so good. It almost didn't matter that he hurt all over. He was alive. His head was swimming; his shoulder ached; his hands were crisscrossed with cuts from the broken glass on the bed – but he was alive!

He glanced ahead. The tricycle was lying crushed beneath a truck. He smiled with blissful relief: that could have been him! Then he looked behind him, and the smile died. Michael's people were running towards him.

He struggled to his knees, and then to his feet. He tried to run, but fire in his lungs forced him to stop. It was no use. He didn't have the strength. After everything he'd been through, they were still going to catch him. It didn't seem fair.

Then, just when all hope seemed lost, an automobile pulled up clanking and coughing beside him. The driver beckoned to him. Bey stared at him blankly. It was the athletic young man who'd chased him across the roof and through the brothel. He yelled at Bey to get in.

Bey glanced back towards Michael's heavies. The leading two were already raising their guns. A bullet ripped through the automobile's canopy. There was no need for a decision. He scrambled inside. His would-be rescuer slammed the vehicle into gear and set off, almost sending him tumbling back out again. He clung on for dear life as bullets tore through the roof and clanged against the bodywork. One whistled past Bey's ear and smashed the front windscreen.

Then the automobile was screeching into a turn, and the stalled truck was between them and their pursuers. They were safe. There were no more bullets – or none that could reach them. Bey slumped down in his seat. It was over. They were just another automobile driving along the road; albeit one riddled with bullet holes.

Bey's rescuer turned and favored him with a broad grin. The two of them burst into delighted, near-hysterical laughter: they had survived; somehow, they had survived.

Bey was the first to sober up; laughter hurt too much. "Who the fuck are you?" he said.

"My name's Ethan," said the man. "I'm an Officer of the Auxiliary Court. And you, Beynan Hotep of the family Massowic are the luckiest off-comer mother alive."

CHAPTER 35

Whoever committed this depraved act, the ultimate responsibility lies with the Family Court. Having taken the Gwahnals into custody, the officers of the court had a clear duty of care, no matter how heinous the crime of which their prisoners were accused.
— *From:* Editorial, *The Recorder*

The Assembly Hall was as full as Beth had ever seen it; even the outermost circle was packed. She squared her shoulders and followed the usher to a seat in the inner circle. Across from her, three empty spaces waited for the committee members. Other than that, there didn't seem to be a spare seat in sight, not even in the outer tiers where the public sat. One figure was instantly recognizable by his elaborate clothing, boldly patterned in sinuous golden whorls: Moyem Jimawn. He offered a mocking half-bow and saluted her with his cane. She ignored him, moving on in search of other familiar faces. And finding Maitland, just a few seats down from the Gallaskian. The undersecretary didn't waste time on courtesy, mock or otherwise; he was busy talking to his companions.

The ambient noise changed; all around the room, people were falling silent. The committee members had arrived. Or two of them, at least. Adam strode purposefully to his place, Ruth just behind him. She smiled encouragement at Beth, but couldn't hide the anxious tension around her eyes. Did she really think there was a chance the Assembly would vote to impeach? It seemed impossible. Surely the public wouldn't stand for it... Yet as Beth looked around, very few representatives were willing to meet her eye.

Adam sat down. He was one of the oldest representatives; older even than Beth herself. She knew him by sight, but had only spoken to him once or twice in all in the years he'd served in the Assembly. He didn't belong to any of the popular factions. Was he neutral? Or did he just go where the wind blew? Either way: no Officer of the Family Court had ever been impeached; would he really want to be the first to break the precedent?

Ruth took the seat to Adam's right, and glanced irritably back towards the entrance. Around the room, attentive silence gave way to puzzled conversation. The committee wasn't going to be able to convene without its third member. Adam and Ruth put their heads together for a whispered consultation. Then Ezra was hurrying to his seat, looking suitably abashed and not a little flustered. He muttered something to Adam and Ruth – an apology? – and sat down.

Adam stood up, waited for silence, and began. His sonorous voice, polished by years of public speaking, carried easily throughout the hall. "This Committee of Inquiry is now in session. We will consider two issues: whether to confirm the assignment of Jurisdiction over the murders of Sanja, Fange and Amaya Gwahnal to the Commonwealth Office of Regulation; and whether Beth of Marshtop is a fit person to serve as a Justice of the Family Court. I have been tasked to act as committee chair and with me are..."

It was really happening. After all these years of sitting in judgement on others, she was finally being judged herself. These people had the power to expel her from the court, to strip her life of all meaning, to overturn a lifetime of dedication, to…

"Well, Justice?"

Beth looked up, startled. She replayed the last few seconds in her head, trying to make sense of words that had floated past her, unnoticed. She snatched them back from oblivion, parsed them, and tried to understand what she was being asked. That was it. They wanted an account of her investigation, an explanation – more, a justification – of the actions she'd taken.

She was tired. Her back ached. She was still reeling from the twin horrors of seeing the Gwahnals' bodies and travelling in the off-comer flying machine. And now she had to stand up and defend herself. And if she failed, she would lose the only thing that gave her life meaning.

What would she even do, if she wasn't a Justice? Where would she go? The chambers were her home.

Not that it mattered. If she wasn't a Justice, she wouldn't need a home. She'd have no reason to go on living.

She put her hands on her knees and slowly levered herself to her feet. Everyone was silent, staring at her, waiting for her to speak. It was like the summation at a Choosing ceremony – save that this time, she was defending herself. And she had no option to refuse the Choice of Death.

"Thank you, Chair. Please excuse me if this takes a little while. I haven't had a chance to prepare. I suppose the obvious thing is to start with the death of Sanja Gwahnal. You may remember that when I began my investigation, the Commonwealth were refusing to accept that Sanja had been murdered.…"

She walked them through the events of the last few days, laying out the facts much as she might have done in court. But unlike her courtroom, this audience didn't listen in respectful silence. Partisans on both sides made their feelings known with shouted objections or roars of approval. Only new information – the campaign of sabotage against the Gwahnals' rivals; her ploy in arresting them – was reliably greeted with silence. And the longer she talked, the fewer cheers there were, and the louder the hostile shouting. By the time she sat down, she was utterly exhausted, worn down by the open hostility, and a crushing sense of failure.

Ezra was the first to get to his feet. "Thank you, Justice. I wonder, could you tell the Committee what you thought of Sanja Gwahnal's house?"

"His house? I thought it was foul. It stank."

There was some laughter, a lightening of the mood. That helped, a little.

"I'm sure it did, Justice. But you would have disliked it in any case, wouldn't you? You have an aversion to bi-tech."

As traps went, it was conveniently obvious. She smiled and shook her head. "Not at all. What I have is a reverence for life. Off-comer technology treats living things as resources, as material to be worked with, manipulated, twisted to serve their needs. I think that's profoundly unnatural, and wrong."

"So, you're opposed to this Assembly's policy with regard to the Commonwealth?"

"My views on policy have no bearing on my actions as a Justice."

Ruth was on her feet. She cut Ezra off before he could respond. "Of course not, Justice. And I'm sure Representative Ezra doesn't mean to suggest that Officers of the Family Court are subject to some kind of loyalty test to ensure they agree with current Assembly policy?"

"By no means, I–"

"Quite. So, Justice, why don't you tell the Committee why you investigated Sanja Gwahnal's death in the first place? Was it out of prejudice against bi-tech, or because you'd determined that the regulators were hiding his murder in an attempt to blame his death on black market bi-tech?"

Beth's reply was drowned out by furious shouts from one side, and loud cheering from the other. Adam stood up and raised a hand for silence. It never quite came, but eventually Beth was able to respond without shouting.

"I started the investigation because Sanja's death was murder. And murder is the province of the Family Court." Even her enemies couldn't argue with that.

Ezra smiled, thinly. "Thank you, Justice. And thank you, Representative – though if I were you, I'd be more hesitant in ascribing motives to parties who are not testifying here, and in no position to defend themselves. For my part, I am more interested in Justice Beth's reasons for her actions. And in that vein, Justice, I'd like to take you back to your arrest of Fange and Amaya Gwahnal. Correct me if I'm wrong, but it's your testimony that you didn't really think the Gwahnals killed their son, but you arrested them anyway?"

"That's correct. But I knew tha–"

"So, in fact, you arrested them under false pretenses? Not to put too fine a point on it, on entirely trumped-up charges?"

"Yes, but–"

"And you must have known the damage your actions would do to relations between Noyan and the Commonwealth. In fact, I venture to suggest that that was the real reason you arrested them. You were playing at politics, weren't you, Justice?"

"I'm not interested in politics, Representative. Only in justice."

"Justice? Is that what you call it when you arrest people you know to be innocent?"

"Hardly innocent. I arrested the Gwahnals because they were behind a campaign of sabotage against their rivals."

"With respect, Justice, you don't know that. Your

evidence, if we can even call it that, is entirely circumstantial. And what little there is points at Sanja Gwahnal, not his parents. But you couldn't arrest Sanja, could you, because he was dead? So, you arrested the Gwahnals. And after you arrested them, they ended up staked out in the desert as living fertilizer for roadroots. Isn't that right?"

There was no point in replying. Ezra's final words had been all but drowned out by the audience's anger. And much of it seemed to be directed at her. Adam once again rose and demanded silence. But not for her to reply; for Undersecretary Maitland, who was on his feet demanding attention.

"The chair recognizes Undersecretary Maitland."

The off-comer nodded respectfully first to Adam, and then – amazingly – to Beth herself. "Mr. Chairman, I wish to make it absolutely clear that his Excellency the Ambassador places no credence whatsoever in any rumors of wrongdoing on the Justice's part. We do not accept that there are death squads operating out of the Family Court. Nor do we believe that Justice Beth had anything personally to do with the murder of the Gwahnals, or that she has at any point been in league with terrorists."

Maitland nodded respectfully at her once again, and sat down. Around the room, silence gave way to angry muttering. No one seemed happy with Maitland's statement. She wasn't happy herself. He'd seemed supportive, and at the same time…

Movement, just a few seats away from Maitland: Jimawn was standing up. Adam once again ceded the floor.

"Thank you, Chair." Jimawn bowed to the Committee, a studiedly elegant and profoundly alien courtesy. "The Imperial Nuncio also places no credence in the rumors the undersecretary was so very keen to place on the record. They are obvious, arrant nonsense, promulgated by the Commonwealth's own dirty tricks department.

"No, don't bother to deny it, Undersecretary. Your

motives are, as always, entirely transparent. First, you wish to undermine faith in the most prestigious institution on Noyan, the Family Court. And second, you wish to ensure that the Commonwealth gains control over the investigation into the death of my good friend Sanja Gwahnal."

Jimawn was all but shouting now, struggling to be heard over the furious response from pro-Commonwealth elements in the audience. But not, curiously, from Maitland, who was gazing at the commotion with evident calm.

"Why is that?" Jimawn continued. "Is it because you have something to hide? Are there, in fact, death squads operating on Noyan? But not Family Court death squads. Commonwealth death squads. Was Sanja killed for fear he would exercise the Choice of Death? Are you so afraid of Commonwealthers adopting Noyan ways? And did those same death squads, perhaps, commit this atrocity against Fange and Amaya Gwahnal to silence them, and to bring disgrace on the Family Court?

"Members of the Assembly, you must understand that the Commonwealth is not your friend. Its goal is to absorb you into itself. They will stop at nothing to turn Noy..."

Jimawn could no longer be heard, his voice drowned out by pandemonium. There was fighting in the public tier. Representatives were shouting at Jimawn, and each other. All around the hall, sergeants-at-arms were busy trying to restore order. Except for two, who were making a beeline for Jimawn – presumably following directions from Adam.

It took some time for the room to settle down, even after Jimawn was escorted from the hall. Then Adam rose to ask his own unemotional, factual, and quietly devastating questions. Her replies sounded hollow in her own ears: no, she couldn't account for the Gwahnals' disappearance from the Family Court; no, she had no clear suspect for their murder; no, she was in no position to make any arrests; no, she had no idea when she might be able to do so.

After Adam sat down, Ruth tried to undo some of the damage. She focused on off-comer wrong-doing; the Gwahnals' campaign of sabotage against their rivals; the regulators' misleading statements and failure to cooperate; the Commonwealth's unreasonable demands for extra-territorial authority. Beth answered truthfully, trying to make her listeners understand how much the off-comers despised the Family Court and all it stood for. But the more she spoke, the more she sensed she was losing her audience; especially the one audience that really mattered – Adam.

There were several more speakers. Some were friendly, most were hostile, but she doubted any of them were making a difference. She closed her eyes, letting her mind wander over the events of the past few days. There was so much she should have done differently, so many mistakes…

A sudden silence dragged her back to the present. Adam had risen to announce the Committee's majority verdict. Jurisdiction was awarded to the Commonwealth. Beth the Justice was impeached, and suspended from the Family Court pending a Motion of Expulsion to be submitted at the next full session of the Assembly.

Ruth had tears in her eyes. Beth put her head in her hands, and wept.

CHAPTER 36

The roadblocks are a step in the right direction. Equally welcome is the sight of combined patrols of Auxiliary, Militia and Commonwealth personnel working to protect the public – Noyim and off-world guest alike. But surely the events of the last few days, and the ongoing hostage crisis, should be enough to convince even the most die-hard of traditionalists of the need for a State of Emergency.
– From: Editorial, *The Noyan Gazette*

Samuel took a deep breath. And coughed. And spat. After two days, the cave was starting to smell altogether too much like home.

Someone was coming: urgent footsteps, hurrying down the tunnel. Was it time for a new lookout already? No. Couldn't be. It was less than half an hour since Nathan went on watch…

News, then. Something on the wireless. Important, too, or the footsteps wouldn't be so hurried. Not just more fuss about the dead collaborator. Something new.

Unless… Might Nathan have braved the hive and discovered his stash?

And there Nathan was, standing in the tunnel mouth, skin shiny with sweat in the candlelight. Half of his face was in shadow, emphasizing its angularity, and his long, sharp nose.

"The Gwahnals are dead."

The news was bad; the details were worse. Jimawn's hive was vile – but nothing like as terrible as what had been done to the Gwahnals. Jimawn wasn't going to be happy. His big atrocity wouldn't matter now. Not after this.

Roadroots. That was a definite message. But who sent it? The Mitchesons? No. Too obvious. Had to be Commonwealthers, though. Nobody else had access to that kind of bi-tech.

Except Jimawn.

The jammer. The hive. Were they really just Sanja's left-overs? Or did Jimawn have his own separate supply?

But why would Jimawn want to kill the Gwahnals? Because two atrocities were better than one?

Or because they knew too much?

And if so… What did that mean for Samuel?

It was time to go. No more waiting for the perfect moment. This was it.

"We can't ignore this," he said.

Silence fell. Nathan nodded agreement. "No, we can't."

"Let's do it."

Nathan turned around and led the way back outside. Samuel followed, and John tagged along behind, uninvited.

Nathan hesitated in the cave entrance. Samuel pushed past him. Eve was at the top of the rise with the binoculars; she'd taken Nathan's place on lookout. She glanced back, nodded, and returned to watching the empty desert.

It was hot outside; even more so beside the sidecar. He lifted the netting, and winced when his bare skin touched hot metal. The hive was where he'd left it, wedged in the folds of a rug to keep it safe during transport. Surely, no one would have risked coming closer than this…. Not even Nathan, out here all alone with no one to see…

He had to be sure. He reached past the hive and slipped a hand under the seat. Yes. There was his revolver.

And next to it, the big leather pouch. He had everything he...

Sudden, sharp pain. He flinched back, stifling a cry. Something had stung his index finger. He sucked at it. Then stopped, appalled.

What if it wasn't a sting? What if...?

He stared at the hive. There was no sign of any burst pustules.

What, then? He inspected his finger. There was a red mark, and the beginnings of swelling. Not a bite. A sting. And there were plenty of desert insects with unpleasant stings.

But he didn't put his finger back in his mouth.

Nathan stepped out of the shadows, suddenly solicitous. "Are you okay?"

"It's nothing. Just a sting."

He reached for the hive. It was undamaged, the nodules still sealed. But even so, handling it made his skin crawl.

"It's not... It's not from the hive?" John was standing beside Nathan, and awake – finally – to the danger.

"No. It's fine. Just a tick, or a crawler. The hive's still sealed, see." He held it up. John recoiled.

"Do we have to... do it that way, Sam?"

"After what they did to the Gwahnals? Yes. We do."

"All of them? Couldn't we just..."

"All of them," said Nathan. He turned and headed deeper into the cave. Samuel was sorely tempted to hurl the hive at his retreating back. Nathan had driven him to this. Nathan, and Jimawn.

"Go and fetch a candle, John. I don't fancy carrying this thing in the dark."

John shuffled after Nathan. And returned not long afterwards, face set in misery; but ready with a candle to light the way.

The main cave was much as he'd left it. The hostages were huddled together fearfully in their semi-circular cave-within-a-cave. His comrades-in-arms were scattered around the open space. Then they saw the hive. Those who were seated scrambled to stand up, ready to flee. The hostages, bound hand and feet, had no such option. But they weren't gagged.

"What's that?"

"What are you doing?"

"Please, no."

Of course – the off-comers built things like this. They understood. He was sorry for that, but compassion was of no use to him now. He threw the hive, hard as he could, at the wall behind the cowering hostages.

It shattered, showering them with pith and a mass of small, black insects. The hostages panicked, screamed, squirmed away, elbows and knees forced to do the work of hands and feet.

It was a futile effort. The insects were all over them, swarming on exposed skin. The captives pawed at them two-handed. The insects clung on, claws pricking pale off-comer skin, adding smears of red to the edges of living filigree tattoos, black tracings that mapped out a branching pattern of veins and arteries.

"Please," John pleaded uselessly beside him. "Stop this!"

Samuel ignored him. It wouldn't be long now. It was just a matter of time.

"Please, Sam. Put them out of their misery. Please."

What was he supposed to do? He'd left his gun in the sidecar. And he wouldn't have used it, in any case. The horror was the point.

One stray insect wandered across the floor towards him. He crushed it under his boot. Jimawn had warned him: even a single bite carried the risk of blood clots and thrombosis.

The hostages were twitching, quivering, slowing down. Their movements became stiffer, more awkward. They looked more like automata than human beings. Only their eyes betrayed their humanity. And their suffering.

"Please, Sam."

"It's too late, John. They're dead. They're all dead."

It was true. The off-comers were motionless, frozen in their last agony. The room was utterly silent. Samuel looked around at his followers. Some were horrified, others guiltily excited. Nathan's expression was unreadable. He caught Samuel's eye and asked: "What now?"

"Now? We wait for... that."

The tattoos were breaking apart. Insects dropping like autumn leaves – first by ones and twos; then in a constant shower until only a scattering remained, no longer clinging to their victims, but simply lying where they died.

He walked over and prodded the nearest body with his foot. It was hard as stone – more like a statue than a still-warm corpse.

Judith's body had taken hours to stiffen like this. And there'd been blood everywhere: so much blood, from such a small wrist...

"Okay, they're safe now. We'll move them tonight, when there's less danger of being spotted. Best drop them in three different locations. Sow confusion. Scare the off-comers witless. The more of us they think there are, the better."

Some of his followers were pale and unhappy. Others looked exhilarated. Only John was in tears. He put a comforting arm around the old man's shoulders.

"Okay, Nathan, I'm leaving you in charge. I'll go for the truck. Expect me at dusk. Pick five people to help you move the bodies. The rest should head back to New Beginning. We'll lie low for a while."

He was already pulling John towards the exit, keen to get ahead of any objections, but there were none. Nathan seemed almost amused. Did he think Samuel was afraid of a few dead insects? Fine. Let him. What did he care what any of them thought? He never planned on seeing them again.

John was still carrying the candle. That was useful. It helped them make good speed through the tunnel. He plucked it from the old man's unresisting fingers and left it to burn itself out on top of the wireless.

Eve ignored them, intent on a vehicle making its way along the road below. He settled John into the sidecar. There was no danger of him exploring under the seat; not when he was staring sightlessly into the distance, hands folded on his lap.

The lone vehicle passed by below, and was gone. Samuel kicked the motorcycle into life. Eve looked back and nodded a greeting. He returned it perfunctorily, and set off down the rocky path to the road.

They'd been driving for almost an hour before John realized they were going in the wrong direction. He tugged at Samuel's sleeve and shouted a question lost in the engine noise. Samuel nodded reassurance: don't worry; I know what I'm doing; it's not a mistake.

He took the next side track, following it up a small rise until they were out of sight of the road. Then he pulled over on the inside of a bend and turned off the engine. A small fold in the ground fell away to their left.

John looked up querulously. "I thought we were going home?"

"We are. Just one thing to do first. Come on."

He helped the old man climb out of the sidecar. Then he reached beneath the seat for the revolver. "You know," he said, pulling back the hammer. "If you'd tried to stop it – I mean really tried – you could have. There were guns, in the cave. You could have shot them, put them out of their misery. No one would have stopped you. You let it happen."

The old man stared at him in silent confusion.

And Samuel shot him.

The first bullet took him in the throat; the second struck the small of his back as he tumbled down the slope. He came to a halt against a weather-worn boulder and lay still, blood soaking into the sand. Just like Judith's.

Samuel climbed back onto the motorcycle, dropped the gun into the sidecar and kicked the engine into life. Then he was on his way back to the main road, heading for the city.

The riding was hard going without a passenger to weigh the vehicle down. Every bump set the motorcycle bouncing, jarring his spine. He took his right hand off the handle and flexed it. The index finger was hot and wouldn't bend properly. He'd been too slow to suck the poison out. The hive had spooked him, made him careless of everyday dangers. It was inconvenient, but trivial compared with what could have gone wrong.

Empty desert gave way to habitation. First there were a few scattered homesteads. Then groupings of houses. Hamlets became villages. Villages turned into suburbs. And then he was driving down a major road through city streets. Now all he had to do was head for the Old Quarter and...

A roadblock. Militia, guarding the road. And off-comers with them. Lots of off-comers.

He brought the motorcycle to a sudden halt. The waiting militia, previously inattentive, turned to stare in his direction. Two of them set out towards him. He had thirty seconds, at the most. Did he have blood on his hands? No – he hadn't touched John's body. And the hostages' blood had solidified, not flowed.

What about his clothes? John had been very close when he shot him. He should have checked for spatter before he got back on the motorcycle. It was too late now.

The gun. With two rounds missing. Right there on the seat. Scrape. He shouldn't have stopped. He could have bluffed his way through. Too late for that now. He had their attention. The nearest man couldn't be more than ten seconds away.

He wrenched the wheel around and accelerated away. There was shouting behind him. He glanced back, saw the two men running after him. They were only militia; no threat there. But the off-comers behind them could be dangerous. Best to keep the runners between him and any off-comer weapons. He slowed down, encouraging the militia not to break off their pursuit.

A side-street, just ahead. He swerved towards it. Stupid of him not to use backroads in the first place. Of course, the major arteries were blocked.

He turned the throttle and accelerated away. The running men stumbled to a frustrated halt. There was an awful moment when he was exposed to possible attack, and then he was safely around the corner, and away.

He abandoned the motorbike at a convenient street corner, parking it alongside three bicycles and a car. He'd be better off on foot. The authorities would be looking for a man on a motorcycle, not a pedestrian. But he needed his stash. He reached under the seat. The pouch was too big for convenience. He distributed the contents between his pockets, and jammed the handgun in his waistband. He'd have to get new clothes, and quickly. A shave. A haircut. The less he resembled the man who'd fled the roadblock, the better. Then he'd seek out the man who could get him what he needed; a criminal with no loyalty to Noyan, but plenty of useful off-comer contacts – the kind of contacts who'd sell anything for a price, even a ticket off world.

CHAPTER 37

When people ask whether my exposure to primitive native medicine has had any long-term consequences, I fear my response invariably disappoints. The truth is that, aside from a few barely noticeable scars on my hands, the one lingering after-effect of my time on Noyan is an inordinate fondness for waking up in the comfort of my own bed.

– *From:* My Time on Noyan, Memories of a Youthful Exile, *The Rt. Hon. Beynan Hotep na Massowic*

Bey woke with a start. He was lying in a tangle of native sheets.

In the bed.

With the bugs.

What the fuck?

He tore at the sheets, but his hands wouldn't grip properly. And they hurt. Everything hurt.

The ceiling. It was pristine; white. Where was the fungus? It couldn't just have…

Memory flooded back. He slumped down again.

He wasn't in the Old Quarter. He was in Representative Ruth's house. And there weren't any bugs in the bed. She'd proved it to him last night, angrily, when she helped him into bed.

And it didn't matter – because Jodan was dead.

Nothing mattered very much, after that. Not even the primitive bandages wrapped around his damaged hands. He'd barely protested when they wrapped strips of white cloth – ordinary germ-ridden native cloth – around his wounded hands. Ethan assured him it was safe, and necessary, and he'd given in, too exhausted to do anything else.

That was a mistake, looking back. He should have insisted they take him to the embassy for proper, modern treatment. His fingers were hot and sore. Swollen red fingertips protruded from the white material. He could almost feel infection seeping into the cuts. How long before irreparable damage set in?

What time was it? Not very early. Bright daylight was flooding in through the inadequate, lacy curtains. This room was so different from the other native bedrooms he'd slept in: the tiny, barely-remembered room in New Beginning; the squalid apartment he'd shared with Jodan. This was the residence of an urban sophisticate. The walls were decorated with a repeating pattern of small pink flowers. The hard floor was concealed beneath something soft, green and vaguely fur-like. But it was an illusion. This house couldn't grow fur. It was dead, and so was everything inside it. Only the people were alive.

Unlike Jodan.

It was still hard to take in. He'd been in shock, yesterday. Today... it just seemed unreal. He closed his eyes, and remembered Jodan's distorted body, the deep red of blood pooling in the bottom of the sphere.

The recording! Jodan had given his life for it. Where was it? In his trouser pocket... but where were his trousers? Or the rest of his clothes, for that matter? Not on the floor, or the wooden bureau by the door. Where else...?

Never mind. His clothes didn't matter. There it was, on the bedside table: a dull green ball, out of place in this room, in this house. All the tension oozed out of him. And was replaced by a sudden, urgent need to empty his bladder.

He surged up, fought his way free of the sheets, and scrambled out of bed. There was no sink in the room. He was going to have to brave the representative's toilet. He ran to the door. And stopped dead.

What the fuck? The door handle wasn't a lever. It was round: a shiny metal knob. How was that supposed to work? Grip it, and turn? Great. How the fuck was he going to do that with fucking useless bandaged hands?

He placed one palm either side of the door knob, pressed inwards, and tried to turn it. The fucking thing barely moved. He pressed harder. That worked a little better, but he just didn't have the strength to...

Except maybe he did. Because the alternative was wetting himself. He pushed so hard his hands hurt... and the handle finally turned. He yanked the door open and ran, naked, down the hallway to the bathroom – and a mercifully open door.

This toilet didn't stink like the ones in the apartment building, but it had water in the bottom, just the same. Still, he had no choice. And none of his usual dexterity. How to direct the flow? He could sit down, but only at the risk of being splashed. Or he could stand in front of it, lean over, and hope.

It worked – and gave him a horribly fascinating view of the toilet water slowly turning yellow. He shuddered, and flushed it away – another new and unwelcome skill he'd acquired in the last few days. Then he glanced at his hands. Should he wash them? Were the native bandages waterproof?

"Good. You're up."

He whirled around. And belatedly covered his groin with his hands – much to the representative's amusement. He blushed, embarrassed by his own embarrassment. But he kept his hands where they were. It didn't matter that she'd seen pretty much everything last night, between helping him undress and wash. He'd been helpless, then; barely conscious. Today was different.

"Let's get you dressed, shall we? Breakfast's waiting."

His clothes. She was carrying his clothes. And she'd washed them. More: they'd been mended, and folded. He mumbled a 'thank you' and followed her back to the bedroom.

It was humiliating, needing help to dress – even if the useless native clothes couldn't do anything for themselves. The worst part was when she pulled up his trousers. He looked away, blushing fiercely, and tried to pretend that she wasn't really there – something that would have been much easier if she hadn't insisted on talking to him the whole time. And why ask about his hands in the first place, if she was only going to laugh at him for worrying about primitive native medicine?

He followed her downstairs to the kitchen. It was at the back of the house, and already occupied. He could hear two voices: one male and familiar; the other female, and speaking across the first. It didn't sound like they were arguing – more like two completely different conversations going on at the same time.

Then he entered the room, and understood. The woman's voice was coming from a polished wooden box on the counter: a native radio. The other speaker was Ethan, seated opposite Beth the Justice at a small wooden table by the window.

Except Beth wasn't a Justice. Not anymore. It was all coming back to him now. She'd been impeached. And Fange and Amaya were dead. Murdered in the most horrible way imaginable.

He stumbled over to the table and collapsed into an empty chair. He'd been wrong earlier, when he thought he'd remembered everything. He hadn't. Nothing like.

"Hotep? Are you okay?" Ethan was shaking his arm. Trying to get his attention. How long had he phased out?

"Yes. Sorry. I was just… I thought you'd left?"

"I did. And now I'm back. I've been reassigned. I can't watch Michael anymore. Which means you really *are* the luckiest off-comer alive. If they'd reassigned me yesterday, you'd–"

"Thank you, Ethan," Beth interrupted. "But I'd prefer you reported to me, not Hotep."

"Of course, Justice."

Why was Ethan smiling? He should tell her where to get off. It wasn't like she was his boss anymore.

"There isn't much left to report, anyway. By the time I got back, everything had quietened down. All Michael's people were off the streets, and if Regulator Hyrom came out again, he didn't–"

"Come out again? He's dead. I thought you knew."

"What?"

All three natives were staring at him. Ruth dumped a stack of plates and cutlery on the table. He flinched, imagining deadly shards of porcelain flying in all directions. But miraculously, nothing seemed to have broken.

"You know Michael shot him? No? Why'd you come to save me, then, if you didn't know?"

"I could see all that muscle coming across the street. It was obvious where they were going. I had no idea tha–"

"Wait." The Justice raised a hand for silence. "How do you know Michael shot him? Were you there?"

"No. Jodan had a bug with him. I was watching. I saw... I saw... everything. But they knew. About the bug. That's why they were coming for me. They want the recording."

"The recording? You have a recording of Michael killing Regulator Hyrom?"

"Yes. It's upstairs... The green ball, by the bed." The last words were shouted after Ethan, who'd set off at run.

The Justice was staring at him, eyes wide, intense. In the background, the radio was reporting on the weather: hot and dry, just like every other day this time of year.

"Tell me what happened. Why did Michael kill him?"

"I don't know! He could have just called the embassy. He knew Jo was suspended. There was no need–"

"This it?" Ethan set the green ball down on the table. It rolled gently away and came to rest against a spoon. Ruth picked it up.

"How's it work?"

"That's the receiver. The bug was separate, but they destroyed it after they kill–"

"No. The recording. How do we play it back?"

"Oh. Right. I don't know. It's specialized equipment. And it's so out of date. You don't see things like that on civili... Commonwealth planets."

"Well, there aren't any obvious switches. So..." She raised it to her mouth. "Receiver. Replay mode. Latest transmission... Recorder, playback... Recorder, play... Receiver, play recording..."

His stomach rumbled. He could smell something baking, and it had been a very long time since he'd eaten. The Justice snorted. "Leave it, Ruth. We'll get the specialists to look at it. Ethan's pet off-comer needs feeding."

"Okay. Anyone else want to have a try? What about you, Hotep? It might respond better to a Commonwealth voice." She headed to the other side of the room. Bey shook his head. He'd leave that to the professionals. He wasn't used to seeing people murdered; let alone someone he knew. He didn't want to see it again.

"No," said the Justice. "We'll do this the old-fashioned way. Tell us what happened. And take your time. There's no hurry."

"Okay. Jodan was trying to buy embargoed bi-tech, but no one was selling him any–"

"Embargoed bi-tech? Why?" Ruth was back, with a loaf of fresh baked bread on a wooden board. It smelled wonderful – and even more so when she began to slice it with a large serrated knife.

Beth waved the question away. "It doesn't matter. I

want to know what's on that recording. Everything else can wait."

He started again, trying to explain as best he could, but hardly ever seeming to get out more than a sentence or two without Ethan or the Justice interrupting, demanding ever more details. He wanted to help, he really did, but when a slice of buttered bread appeared in front of him, he couldn't help himself. He forced a pause by the simple expedient of stuffing his face. Even then, Ethan wouldn't let him eat in peace.

"You're sure?" he said. "Michael already knew Fange was dead?"

Bey hurriedly swallowed enough to continue. "I think so. He said something about Fange taking it up the…" He stopped, blushing. There were women present. "You know, like, with the roadroot…"

"Hold on," said Ethan. "This was before you ran for it?"

"Yes. Jodan was—"

"He did it, Justice. Michael killed the Gwahnals. Must have. No one knew how Fange had died. Not then. Except for the people who killed him. If we can get this in front of the Assembly… You're the only one who was ever willing to investigate Michael. They'll have to rescind your suspension."

Beth shook her head. "Not without evidence, they won't."

"No, but with the recording…"

"Which we can't access."

"Not yet, no. Like you said, we need a specialist."

"You need the embassy," said Bey. "They'll be able to access it, no problem. And they can treat my hands at the same time."

The Justice snorted. "Good try, Hotep. But that recording doesn't go anywhere near the embassy. And neither do you. We'd never see it again. The Commonwealth wants me off the court. They're not going to let anything get in the way of that."

"Yes, they will. You don't understand. This is too big for them to cover up. The Gwahnals were important. Really important. There's no way they can just cover it up. They wouldn't even try."

Ruth was shaking her head. "Not normally, maybe. But right now... I don't know. Getting Beth off the court is a huge win for Ashef. Anything that undermines that is going to get buried."

"Including you," said Ethan, dropping another slice of buttered bread on his plate. "You walk into that embassy, you'll end up back under house arrest. You really want that? Michael knows where you live."

Bey stared at his bandages. There were crumbs lodged in the course material, and a smear of butter on his right thumb. Which was worse? House arrest? Or primitive native medicine?

"What if we took it to a reporter?" he said. "I know someone who—"

"Quiet!" Ruth was waving for silence. "Listen. The hostages..."

The woman on the radio had moved on from the weather. "...cording to Commonwealth news reports, two of the kidnappers were captured fleeing the scene. It is unclear at this point whether the third hostage is still alive. Updates will follow as more information—"

Ruth hurried over to radio and did something to make it shut off. "Come on," she said. "There's a 3-V in the front room."

She set off, with Ethan quickly following. Beth had other priorities: she reached for the green ball. But Bey was faster. He scooped it up with his cupped hands. She glared at him, then got up and headed for the door. He tagged along behind, glad to have established his rights over the recording. After everything he'd gone through to save it from Michael, he'd be the one to decide what to do with it.

The 3-V was in the far corner of the front room; not

grafted there – this wasn't a living house – but actually growing through the wall. It was like seeing a dinosaur adrift in the modern world. Somewhere on the other side of that wall there must to be a bloated stalk with its own separate root system. He'd known such things still existed here on Noyan, but to actually see one...

The 3-V was projecting Dil Mahtal's face. Behind him lay open desert, and an area of frenzied official activity where regulators and embassy guards were busy with something on the ground. There was even an autocopter off to one side; a sure sign of senior embassy personnel in attendance.

Mahtal was speaking in a slow, measured tone quite unlike his usual fast-paced gossipy delivery. Only once or twice did his excitement at reporting real news shine through – as when he proudly announced that 'Wattles' had managed to get pictures of the scene before the exclusion zone was in place.

And that was the last thing Bey heard for a while. Because with that, the close-up of Mahtal was replaced with something very different. A dead man was in the room with them. Or what was left of him. His head, right arm and both legs had separated from the body. And yet there was no blood. The man had shattered, like a glass ornament dropped on hard ground. The raw stumps of neck and arm exposed flesh and blood turned crystalline. This couldn't ever have been a living, breathing human being. It was a twisted work of art, gruesome but unreal.

Fuck. Sanja's body had been bad. This was worse.

He turned away, struggling not to throw up the bread he'd just eaten. In the background, Mahtal was still talking. Bey made a conscious effort not to listen, and concentrated instead on trying to stuff the green ball into his pocket two-handed. Then he heard something that made him turn back. Had Mahtal really just mentioned 'New Beginning'?

"Both individuals are reported to be residents of the

settlement, some... 20 miles west of my current location. One is reportedly the daughter of a man authorities are seeking in connection with an incident at a roadblock yesterday evening. Samuel of New Beginning is believed to be hiding somewhere in the city, and to be armed and dangerous. Repeat, he is believed to be armed and dangerous."

Mahtal paused briefly, a finger to his left ear. "Just in: The embassy has released the following images, and is urgently seeking information as to the suspect's whereabouts. Do not approach him under any circumstances. Inform the embassy if..."

Bey wasn't listening anymore. He was staring at the blurred image of a man on a motorcycle. It was definitely Samuel.

He swallowed. Hard. That body, lying shattered in the desert... It could have been him. It could so easily have been him.

"Scrape! Is that Samuel?" Ethan was pointing at the projection. "I saw him. Last night. When I went back to watch Michael."

The Justice spun on her heels. "You saw them together? What were they doing?"

"No. He wasn't *with* Michael. He was just there, in the street. I thought he was just another derelict..."

"You have to call the embassy," Bey interrupted. "Tell them where to find him."

"This was yesterday. He could be anywhere by now."

"So, tell them that. It's a start, isn't it? You saw what the bastard did."

"We saw," said Beth. "But we're not calling the embassy. They'd never catch him, not in the Old Quarter. But we can. Ethan, you have to delay your reassignment. If you can stay on—"

"Sorry, Justice. I can't."

"But—"

"It's no use, Justice. I've already pushed it as far as I

can. Further. Any more, and I'll be suspended, too. And you need me on the inside. Here, Hotep. Let me."

"Hey!" Bey protested. And shut up, embarrassed, as Ethan plucked the green ball from his useless hands and stuffed it effortlessly into the pocket he'd been struggling with the whole time.

"All right," said Beth. "I'll do it myself. It's not like I'm any use sitting around here."

Neither Ethan nor Ruth looked happy about that idea. "Be careful, Beth," she said.

"Of course I'll–"

"No. Seriously. Be careful. We can't afford to lose you."

"I don't know about that. But I do know there's a job that needs doing, and it looks like I'm the only one who can do it."

"Okay. But I have to get to the Assembly. There'll be another push for a State of Emergency on the back of this. Bound to be."

The Justice nodded. "Yes. And Ethan needs to report to the Auxiliary Court. We all need to be somewhere else. Except you, Hotep. You stay here, and keep out of sight."

CHAPTER 38

How much longer can this go on? Time and again, this newspaper has called on the authorities to recognize the seriousness of the current situation. Desperate times call for desperate measures. Had the Assembly acted when first called upon to do so, a State of Emergency alone might have been sufficient to bring the current crisis to an end. But the Assembly chose not to act in a timely manner, and we now have no choice but to call on our friends in the Commonwealth to support us materially and institutionally in our fight against the common enemy.
—From: Editorial, *The Noyan Gazette*

Beth crumpled the newspaper and dropped it on the café table. She would have bought the Recorder for preference, but it was unavailable today, the victim of a mysterious paper shortage that somehow hadn't affected its rival, the Gazette. She regretted the purchase. The publishers had finally given up all pretense of balance. The paper had become what it had always wanted to be: an unrelenting off-comer propaganda sheet. She had no intention of ever buying it again.

She shifted uncomfortably in her seat. A café on the shaded side of the street would have been better, especially with midday approaching, but none of them were as well positioned for watching the comings and goings at Michael's building. So she endured the heat, and sipped at a glass of cold milk that was now, at best, lukewarm. And tried not to think about the unpleasant way her skirt was sticking to her where she sat down.

She fiddled with her sun hat – Ruth's best, with a pretty flower pattern woven into the straw – but even its wide brim was little help in the full heat of the day. Hopefully, it was at least keeping her from being recognized. She felt very conspicuous as the last remaining breakfast patron, with lunchtime fast approaching.

She set the milk down, saw a cartoon on the front page, and laughed out loud. She'd missed it earlier. Two off-comer vehicles were copulating, despite the outraged protests of the startled drivers. It was a borderline heretical dissent from the paper's unrelenting pro-off-comer agenda. She wondered, vaguely, how long the cartoonist would last.

A waiter approached. No doubt he wanted to encourage her move her along and free up the table for lunch. She had no intention of obliging him, but she couldn't really nurse this glass of milk any longer. She surprised the man, and herself, by ordering a glass of casabey.

She'd never been one to drink much during the day. The responsibilities of office were too serious for such indulgence. But the office was gone – likely forever. There was no reason to abstain when she had no position, no role, no responsibilities. No reason for living.

She couldn't blame her fellow justices. But, oh, it was bitter to be refused access to her own chambers after a lifetime of service; to have her few possessions left out for her in boxes, like so much trash.

Three wooden boxes – that was all she had to show for sixty years of life. All sitting untouched at Ruth's house. She couldn't bear to unpack them. To do so would be to admit that her banishment was more than a temporary setback.

Someone was approaching Michael's front door. A

woman. Well-dressed. Some kind of business caller?

"Your casabey, Justice."

She looked up, frowning. So much for not being recognized. The waiter had returned with a loaded tray. He made a great display of lighting a completely redundant candle, and placing it in the middle of the table. Then he put a tall, impractical cordial glass in front of her and set about filling it with casabey.

"Leave the bottle," she snapped.

He did so, eyebrows raised. And retreated. She poured a large measure into the milk. Not bad. Definitely more palatable. But it could still be better. She poured in more casabey, and sat back, glass in hand.

The poor waiter was hovering by the door. She shouldn't have been so cranky with him. He'd only been trying to honor her office; her *former* office. The candle was a sign of support and sympathy, no matter how absurd. She'd apologize, next time he came by.

The business woman was already leaving. Why such a short visit? And why was she walking? Where was her car? She couldn't live or work near here; not looking like that.

A lone outcast shuffled by, and the woman went out of her way to avoid him. That wasn't the behavior of someone who spent much time in the Old Quarter, where the dregs of society congregated. And now the outcast was crossing the street, impeding Beth's view and making her lose sight of the woman. It was impossible to mount a meaningful surveillance like this, without a team to back her up. There was no point even trying. All she could do was keep an eye out for Samuel, and hope.

The outcast shuffled closer. She took another sip of the fortified milk, and steeled herself not to react to the proximity of such moral corruption.

And the outcast sat down at her table.

It was all she could do not to spit the milk out in fury. She scrambled to her feet. Never in all her life had she imagined an outcast would dare…

It wasn't an outcast.

The '0' on his forehead was fake, a badly drawn imitation tattoo – obvious, once one looked closely. But who looked closely at an outcast? Which, no doubt, was exactly what Samuel was relying on.

She downed the fortified milk in one gulp. And sat down again, heart pounding. Samuel looked terrible. Drawn. Haggard. His skin a mass of angry spots; some large as boils. His eyes were red sores. He was like something out of prehistory – a victim of the Black Death transported across time and space.

She glanced over her shoulder, and saw the astonished waiter's openly disapproving expression. She couldn't blame him.

"Justice." Samuel nodded a greeting, his voice a husky rasp.

"Samuel."

She poured a measure of casabey into the unused cordial glass, and pushed it across the table. He ignored it, and reached for the bottle instead. Three long gulps slid past the boil on his throat. He stopped, belched, and wiped his mouth with the back of a trembling hand.

"What happened to you?" she asked.

His only answer was a shrug. He took another swig.

"The off-comers say you were behind the kidnapping. Is it true? Was it you?"

He looked away, refusing to meet her gaze. "I want protection," he croaked. "I'm not saying anything unti–"

The rest of the sentence was lost in a coughing fit. If it weren't for his condition, she'd think he was mocking her. He must be the only person on Noyan who still thought her protection worth having.

"And why would I want to protect you?"

"Immunity first."

"Immunity for what?"

Samuel tried to reply, but broke off into more wretched, dry coughing. He took another swig of casabey.

His hands were shaking so badly he could hardly hold the bottle to his lips. Maybe she should stop this; get him to a doctor – or at least get him out of sight before he was recognized.

"Too many enemies. The off-comers. The League. Jimawn–"

"Jimawn? Moyem Jimawn? What's he got to–"

"Double-crossed the mother. Thought he controlled me. Scraper. Tried to run... Smuggler didn't haggle. Agreed my price right off. Not right. Double cross... Immunity first, Justice. Then talk." He set the bottle down and ran his fingers through his greasy hair, defiant and pathetic at the same time.

"Jimawn," she said. "What's he got to do with you? I thought you worked for the Gwahnals?"

"What? No! Mutual benefit. That's all. After Judith, didn't seem any... That mother Jimawn, he–"

Samuel's eyes bulged. Was he coughing? Or choking?

Something was wrong with the boil on his neck. She blinked – but no, there was no mistaking it: something was moving beneath the skin.

Samuel clawed at his throat. The boil erupted. Black foulness poured out. A swarm of tiny black insects ran through his fingers and crawled over his neck and face. He lifted his hands and stared at them in disbelief.

Then he screamed; or tried to. All that emerged was dry retching. His eyes met hers in appalling mute appeal. He opened his mouth, and a black vomit of insects poured out. Beth wanted to run, to hide, but froze helplessly as he collapsed face-down onto the table. He twitched once, twice, and was still. More insects poured from boils on his head and neck. Some were scurrying across the tabletop towards her. She flung herself backwards, overturning the table and sending Samuel's inert body crashing to the ground. The insects kept on coming, struggling towards her through a fresh lake of casabey – until the liqueur reached the still-guttering candle flame, and Samuel, insects, and table were engulfed in fire.

She staggered backwards, shielding her eyes. The heat was intense; the smell cloying. Someone was screaming in the café behind her.

And in the distance, a siren.

CHAPTER 39

It should come as no surprise that few Noyim choose gardening as a pastime. Leaving aside the poor quality of their soil and the extended periods without rain, their houses are wholly incapable of regulating the land around them, leaving the native gardener to nurture each plant with his own hands – digging and watering the inhospitable soil, cutting back excessive growth, even uprooting unwanted plants called 'weeds'. And after all this labor, there is no guarantee that the resulting garden will grow as intended – or indeed, grow at all.

– From My Time on Noyan: Memories of a Youthful Exile, *The Rt. Hon. Beynan Hotep na Massowic*

Bey had long since tuned Mahtal out. The 3-V had provided company of a kind when the others deserted him, but the reporter's breathless excitement had quickly become wearisome. And definitely less interesting than the state of his own hands.

It was a morbid fascination, to be sure. Were his fingertips redder than before? That had to be a sign of infection, didn't it? How long before there was irreversible damage, and he needed new hands?

The 3-V was about the only thing in this house he could actually control. You needed hands for everything else. He was helpless like this, with fingers that couldn't grip. He'd struggle even to use the bathroom on his own.

They shouldn't have left him alone. It wasn't safe. The representative could have stayed, at least. Native houses like this were death traps. It wasn't just the deadly stuff they were full of; glass and porcelain and who-knew-what else. The houses themselves could burn down. He'd seen it, on the news. Whole houses, burned right down to the ground. And they'd just left him here to fend for himself. With useless hands. And much, much too much time to think.

About his hands.

About Jodan.

And the hostages.

And what Samuel did to the hostages.

And what Samuel would have done to him, if Beth hadn't showed up.

Fuck.

They should have let him call the embassy. Then he'd be somewhere Samuel and Michael couldn't get to him. Somewhere safe. And he'd get proper treatment.

Something changed, on the 3-V. Mahtal wasn't speaking anymore. It was someone else, talking over a confusing Old Quarter scene. People were milling around outside a café. There were native auxiliaries and several heavily-armed embassy guards. Something blackened and burned was lying on the ground; something no one was approaching.

Then he registered what the voiceover was saying. The scene came into sudden focus.

The blackened mass on the ground was Samuel. Or what was left of him.

And Beth was wanted for his murder.

The wording was far less direct – something about her being 'sought in connection with' Samuel's death – but its meaning was clear enough. And what followed was worse. An embassy spokesman was explaining that there was no *conclusive* evidence that the *former* Justice had been in league with Samuel; that, *of course*, it was far too early to speculate about the motive for his murder; that there was no way of knowing at this point whether Samuel had been killed because he knew too much about the Gwahnals' disappearance and murder.

It was all so very skilled, and profoundly wrong. The worst of it was, the man probably believed what he was saying. But Samuel hadn't killed the Gwahnals, and neither had Beth. And she hadn't killed Samuel, either. No way. She'd needed him alive. Talking.

He had to call the embassy. Not for himself, or for the sake of his hands. For Beth. And for Jodan. And for the Commonwealth. Terrorists were bad, but they were a sideshow. The breach of the embargo was what really mattered.

This time, they'd have to listen to him. He had proof. Once they saw the recording of Jodan's murder, everything would be different. Jodan had given his life for that evidence. He *had* to get it to the embassy.

The telephone was in the hallway; a wooden box bolted to the wall, with a funnel-like microphone poking out of the front, and a black earpiece hanging from a hook at the side. He'd never used one of these things, but he knew how they worked. First you lifted the earpiece. Then you talked into the microphone. Easy.

He slipped one bandaged hand either side of the polished earpiece, squeezed... and it squirted straight out of his grip, clattered against the wall, and swooped down towards the floor. It swung there gently at the end of its wire.

He bent down – which hurt, after his fall from the tricycle – put his hands around the wire and followed it to the earpiece. Then he straightened up and put it to his ear. There was a faint buzzing noise, but nothing more. He leaned forwards and spoke into the microphone.

"Hello? Hello?"

There was no answer.

Maybe it wasn't quite as easy as the natives made it

look.

But it had to be. They just spoke into the microphone, asked to be connected, and the phone did the rest…

Except it couldn't, could it? The phone couldn't *do* anything. Not a native phone. Someone must do the connecting – just like their automobiles needed a human being to do the actual driving.

So, the natives weren't speaking to the *phone* when they asked for a connection. They were speaking to a *person*. There had to be someone at the other end of the wire.

But he'd tried talking, and no one had heard him. How to get their attention?

He looked at the box, seeking clues. All he saw was the microphone and the earpiece hook. He'd tried talking into the microphone. So that left the hook; the only moving part in the whole apparatus. He used his elbow to dip it down three times. And almost dropped the earpiece when a tinny voice emerged from the speaker.

"…tor speaking. How can I connect you?"

"Help!" he squawked. Then remembered the microphone, leaned forwards and said it again, directly into the funnel.

"How ca…? Sir, is this an emergency?"

"Yes. No. But it's urgent. I need to speak to the embassy."

"I see." Was that a note of irritation? Definitely a person. "Would that be the Gallaskian or the Commonwealth embassy, sir?"

"Commonwealth, pl–"

"This is the Commonwealth embassy. How may I be of assistance?"

The background clicking and buzzing was gone. There was just the embassy's voice and behind it, nothing. It was profoundly reassuring.

"This is Beynan Hotep. I need to speak with Ambassador Ashef as a matter of urgency."

The silence at the other end of the line changed. It was

no longer a noise vacuum. There was a hollowness, a sense of space. And coming out of that space, a voice – but one too young, and much too friendly, to be Ashef.

"Beynan! Where are you?"

"I'm... Where's the Ambassador?"

"He's tied up at the moment. Can I help?"

"I need to speak to the Ambassador. Who am I speaking to?"

"Assistant Secretary Mino Cherayn. I'm happy to–"

"Listen. This is urgent. I need to talk to Ashef. Right now."

"Understood. But I can't just put you through. Not without more information. We've got an ongoing crisis here."

"That's why I'm calling! Listen. You're going after the wrong people. Beth the Justice didn't kill Samuel. And Samuel didn't kill the Gwahnals. It was Michael the Restaurateur. And he killed Jodan, too – Regulator Jodan Hyrom. I've got a recording that proves it. You know who I am. You know who my grandfather is. I have to tell the Ambassador what I know. Are you going to put me through, or not?"

"You have a recording? Of the Gwahnals' murder?"

"No. Jodan's. He was investigating a breach in the embargo, and Michael killed him. But he had a surveillance bug with him. I have the–"

"Stop right there. This isn't something we should talk about over a native line. I'll get a squad out to you right away. Where are you?"

"I'm at Ruth th–"

Bey stopped. Something hard and metallic was pressing against his temple. A native gun. And Beth was holding it. She plucked the earpiece from his unresisting hands.

"Who are you talking to?"

"The embassy."

"Beynan. Hello, Beynan..." Cherayn's voice was thin and distant, but the concern in his voice was unmistakable.

Then it was gone. The earpiece had been placed back on its hook

Beth stepped away, but she was still pointing the gun straight at him. Or nearly straight. She seemed to be having difficulty holding it steady. She looked exhausted. Her face was drawn and waxy. There were sweat stains under her arms, and disheveled strands of hair were poking out from under the ridiculous hat she'd borrowed from Ruth.

"I was trying to help," he said. "I told them they'd got it all wrong. We need them, Justice. I was trying to help."

"By telling them where to find me?"

"No! I was telling them where to find *me*. You weren't here. I wasn't helping them. I was helping you. I told them you couldn't have killed Samuel. That Michael killed the Gwahnals. Please, Justice – you have to leave. The embassy will know where I called from. They'll be here any minute."

She lowered the gun. "You're right. Come on. Outside. Now. We're leaving."

"Me? No. I have to wait her for th–"

The gun was back up, and steadier this time. His vision narrowed to just the barrel, pointed directly at his face. There was a spiral pattern worked into the metal inside. The strange decoration didn't make it any less intimidating.

"The embassy's not getting their hands on that recording, or you. I don't trust them, and I don't trust you. Come on. Out."

She nodded towards the door. He had a sudden, vivid flashback to the first time they'd met. She'd been holding a gun then, too, and threatening to shoot Jodan. There was no reasoning with her. But at the same time... He owed her. She'd saved his life. Twice. He had to make her see sense.

"Please, Justice. Let me help. I can stop them coming after you. Once they see Michael was–"

"Now, Hotep."

He stopped talking. and moved. He hadn't made up his mind to do so. His body had made the decision for him.

The front door was wide open. She must have left it that way when she saw him on the telephone. He stepped outside, flinched at the harsh midday sun, and came to a halt; only to hurry onwards when the gun jabbed him painfully in the back.

The small front garden ended in a wooden fence, and an open gate. He glanced up and down the unfamiliar street. There were none of the tall stone rowhouses of the city proper. Here, each small house was independent, and different from the next. Some were wooden boxes like Ruth's, made from the bones of dead trees; others might have grown out of the earth itself, rounded-edged cubes with walls the same color as the ground they stood on. Around each one was a small parcel of land. Some were fenced off with yet more dead wood; others bordered by bushes and trees, or simply left as open scrub.

"Which way?"

"Turn right. Head for the main road."

"Why? Where are we going?"

"Away from here, for now. After that... The countryside, I think. Away from off-comer sympathizers. Stop talking, start walking."

The countryside. That wasn't good. There was no. hope of proper medical treatment anywhere away from Spate. If she'd just let him talk to Ashef, he'd be able to clear everything up, no problem. Ashef wasn't like Maitland; he was a Homeworlder. He understood what it meant to be a Massowic. He'd listen.

Besides, it was different now: he had hard evidence. He just needed to show it to them, and everything would be fine. But first he had to persuade Beth, and she wasn't even letting him talk.

The neighboring house had a well-tended garden bordered by a hedge of straggly native shrubs with spectacular red-gold flowers. The next house was more concerned with privacy than appearance. There were no flowers on its hedge, just a dense wall of dark-yellow leaves shutting out the street; the only gap blocked by a solid wooden gate. He'd almost reached it when a sound stopped him in his tracks: sirens, approaching. Not the tinny, clanging bells of local emergency vehicles. Proper sirens, loud and wailing. Cherayn hadn't wasted any time coming to his rescue.

Beth had other ideas. She opened the gate, forced him through and pushed him to the ground. He landed badly, sprawling painfully across a carpet of succulent plants. Beth lay down beside him, breathing hard. A convoy of embassy cars sped by, just visible through the base of the hedge. They pulled up outside Ruth's house, bright reds and yellows strobing warningly across their iridescent surfaces. The sirens fell silent. Troops poured out: eight, nine, ten. He lost count in the confusion of motion. They were so close. All he had to do was call out, and they'd come for him. But he couldn't. Not with the cold, hard metal of the gun once again pressed against his temple.

The embassy troops took up defensive positions. They were treating this like a military operation. Did they think he was being held hostage? Or worse, that it was a trap? Yes, that must be it. Three men stepped forwards, hives strapped to their backs. They spread out and raised their targeting gloves. No one in their right mind would refuse to surrender in the face of that much fire-power. But there was no one in the house to hear any ultimatum. What would they do, when it was ignored?

He itched to shout out; to tell them they were wasting their time, he was over here. But even bi-tech weapons wouldn't be quick enough to stop Beth from shooting him.

The hives began to swarm. Three glittering smoke-trails of insects rose and coalesced into a cloud of darkness. Here and there, bright sunlight sparkled ominously off metallic wings, beautiful and deadly. What did the troops think they were facing that could possibly be dangerous enough to justify three entire hives?

The men's right hands moved in ominous synchrony. The cloud divided into three swarms… And smashed into the house. One tore through the front door; the others through the walls.

Bey blinked, waiting for his vision to clear. For reality to reassert itself. A section of wall exploded outwards. Wood and dust spread far and wide. And amidst the detritus, the flicker of deadly beauty as the swarm reorganized, rose into the air and smashed its way back into the house.

Something clicked by his head. The gun. He felt it as much as heard it.

"Proud of yourself, scraper?"

He swallowed. The world retreated. Nothing was real, except him, Beth, and the gun pressed to his head. Even the noise of destruction was suddenly remote.

"They thought I was in there," he said. "They thought I was in there, and they didn't care."

The moment stretched. The gun pressed painfully tight against his skin. Then was withdrawn.

"That's true," said Beth.

The outside world came back in a torrent of noise and violence The house was still standing, but only just. Windows were broken, or missing altogether. Whole sections of wall had been blown out. And still the swarms smashed through the structure, diving backwards and forwards to weave yet more destruction through the filigree remains of the original structure.

And then, with a final rumble, the building collapsed in on itself. Dust rose, and with it the swarm. Whirling eddies spiraled upwards and coalesced into a single menacing whole. It hovered, glittering above the ruins.

"Hotep." Beth whispered. She was shaking his shoulder. How long had she been trying to get his attention?

"What?" He kept his voice low. The noise of the collapse was already giving way to silence; and the small, random noises of the rubble settling.

"Can you drive one of those things?" She pointed the gun at the nearest vehicle.

"No. Well, yes. Anyone can. But–"

"Come on then, while they're busy checking over the house. Or what's left of it."

"Forget it. Those are embassy vehicles. We get in them, it's over. We have to get of here. The moment they realize they didn't get me–"

"You?"

"Who else? Jodan was right. He said they'd do anything to stop the news about the embargo getting out. I didn't believe him. I thought he was paranoid. But he was right. And I told them I had proof Michael killed him. That I knew the embargo had been breached. I'm so fucking stupid…"

He levered himself up to his hands and knees. It hurt – especially his left knee – but standing wasn't an option; not without being seen.

Beth did the same, much more slowly. He waited for her. They were in this together now, whatever happened. He didn't stand a chance on his own.

She nodded towards the back of the house, slipped the gun into her purse and set off. He followed her, staying low and close to the hedge. The succulent plants were soft, but the ground beneath them was hard and stony. One especially sharp stone dug into his left knee and almost made him cry out. Only terror of the nearby troops – so close, he could hear them talking – kept him from screaming aloud. How Beth was coping he couldn't even imagine. She was wearing a skirt, and her knees were bare.

Or maybe she wasn't coping. She'd veered away from the hedge. Was she trying to find softer going? It wasn't worth it. The cover of the hedge was the only thing keeping them alive.

Then he saw it: a thorny bush directly in their path. She hadn't had any choice.

He looked at the house. Saw a window, right there. Anyone inside would see her crawling by. But it was the middle of the day; the owners were probably at work. He glanced ahead. Beth had skirted the bush, and was once again hugging the hedge. He could see past her into the back garden. It was much larger than the front, and very different. There were far fewer of the low-growing succulents, and many more full-grown bushes; even a few trees. Plenty of cover for their escape. And there was no road at the bottom of the slope for embassy vehicles to patrol; just open scrubland.

He'd been right not to branch out on his own. The Justice knew what she was doing. He followed her around the thorny bush. She was moving more quickly now. The downhill slope was making the going easier, if no less painful. Half way down, she paused and peered back through the hedge. He did the same.

Dust still hung over the ruins of Ruth's house, but it was thinner now, attenuated. The troops were clambering over the rubble, searching. There was no sign of the swarm; the insects had returned to their hives. That was good. Not that they couldn't come out again, but still...

The Justice tugged his elbow. She pointed to a stone-flagged path meandering across the back garden. It was flanked by bushes, and led towards the far hedge. But how to get to the path without being seen? He glanced back towards the troops. None of them were looking in this direction. Maybe, if they were really quick... He turned back to nod agreement. And saw there was no point. Beth had already risen to a crouch and was scuttling away.

He swore silently under his breath, got up off his knees, and ran after her. If one of the troops so much as looked around...

Would there be any warning? Or would the swarm just slam into him and turn his body to pulp?

Fuck! How could this be taking so long? The path was barely a few steps away. How much fucking longer...?

And then he was there, and safe. Or was he? He peered back through the bushes. There was no swarm approaching, no sign the troops had seen him. He swallowed a deep gulp of air and hurried after Beth. She hadn't wasted time looking back. She was right. There was no point. If they were seen, they were dead. The only thing to do was get away as quickly as possible.

Soon there were more bushes, a few trees, even a corner of the house between them and the troops. But this was as far as they could go without crossing the hedge into the next garden – and there was no way to do that without standing up. They'd just have to stay here and hope the troops didn't widen their search.

He turned to whisper as much to Beth, and rolled his eyes in frustration. She was already half-climbing, half throwing herself over the hedge.

Once again, she'd left him no choice. He couldn't stay here on his own.

He looked back. The troops were still there; visible more as movement than clear figures. Would they be able to see him, if he stood up? Enough to want to investigate? Almost certainly. But if he could just make it to the other side of the hedge...

He was going after her. Right now.

Except his legs wouldn't move.

He was so sick of this shit. Or running. Of hiding. Of everyone wanting to kill him.

Yesterday had been easy. There'd been no time to think. Only to run. Now he had choices, and that was terrible.

He wanted to stay right here, To curl up and hide, and hope they wouldn't look for him. But they were so close! If they released the swarm and had it quarter the ground from above...

There was no safety here. He dived over the hedge,

landing awkwardly and nearly hitting Beth. She was lying slumped on the ground, one hand clutching the small of her back.

"You okay?"

She ignored him. He sat up. They couldn't stay here; there was no cover. This garden was just an extension of the scrubland at the bottom of the slope.

"We have to keep going," he said. "Do you need any help?"

She shook her head, tried to rise, and sank back down, hissing. He offered his hand. This time, she took and let herself be helped up to her hands and knees, and then to a low crouch. They set off together, moving more slowly than he would have liked; but at least they were under way again.

The next two property lines were marked by nothing more than a few tall flowers. The third was very different. This wasn't just a well-tended garden; it was luxuriant; an island of green in a sea of ochre. But it was deadly. The house at the top of the slope was neither wooden, nor an earthy cube. It was the twin of his own small house, transplanted to an area where bi-tech houses were few and far between.

Beth didn't seem to notice. She was hurrying on in search of cover. He pulled her back and pointed at the house. "We can't go there. It'll see us."

The Justice stood very still. "Does it know we're here?"

"It doesn't care. We're not trespassing. But if we do, it'll take an interest. And if it decides to report us…"

"Right."

They headed down to the scrubland. The going was easier here. A dried-up creek ran parallel with the street, easy to walk down, but too shallow to offer cover. He glanced back nervously, shoulders itching in anticipation of an attack from behind and above. They weren't visible from Ruth's house, but they were still dangerously exposed.

They passed five more gardens before they came to the end of the street, and there was no way to go any further. A line of bi-tech houses lay across their path. Either they sneaked through the last garden and back out onto Ruth's street, or risked a long detour through the open scrubland. Both routes would leave them suicidally exposed.

They sat down in the shade of a small tree. It was a good place to catch their breath. They were out of sight from the nearest house, the air, and anyone looking this way from the ruins of Ruth's house. Bey stared at his hands. The bandages were filthier than ever; caked with dust and sandy soil. But there was no point worrying about it. The way things were going, he'd be lucky to live long enough for it to become a problem. And luck didn't seem to be his strong suit at the moment.

"Where do we even go?" he said. "If we get away. Where do we go?"

Beth was hunched over, arms wrapped around her knees, head down. She looked up at him with tired, rheumy eyes.

"Marshtop."

"Where?"

"Marshtop. My home. We'll be safe there."

She lowered her head again. He stared at the thin grey hairs on her scalp. Somewhere along the way she'd lost the hat. He couldn't remember where or when.

"How do we get there?"

"I don't know. A truck? Hitch a lift with settlers?"

"What about the roadblocks?"

She shrugged. "Depends who's behind them. If it's just Noyim, we have a chance. If there are off-comers with them..."

Bey looked out over the scrubland. The city would be crawling with embassy personnel by now. They couldn't go anywhere by road. But was the scrub any better? There was no water anywhere out there. Even the creek they'd walked along was dry as dust. How long would they last without water? Maybe it'd be better to be caught. At least the swarm would be quick.

He glowered at the dry river bed. It must be a decent-sized river in the rainy season. So how come they'd built the main road right across its path? Wouldn't all the houses flood?

He got to his feet and headed towards the creek. It was even wider here. An additional tributary had joined a few houses back, coming down out of the scrub. He peered ahead. And understood. There was a culvert, running under the main road. It was four feet across, big enough to cope with a sizable river in the rainy season.

Big enough for both of them, if they went single-file.

He hurried back. Beth's head was down. There was no sign she'd even noticed his absence.

"Justice, where does the creek end up, when there's water? Where does it go?"

She shrugged. "Where they all go, eventually. To the Spate. Then the sea."

"The river. Right... Justice, have you ever rowed?"

"What?"

"You know. Rowed a boat. On water."

She looked up, the picture of impatience. "Of course. Listen, Hotep. I'm tired and—"

"I tried it once. Went in circles. Not my idea of fun at all. Couldn't work out what people see in it."

"Is there a point to this?"

"It's something we have in common, nati... Noyim and Commonwealthers. Liking boats. Not me, but lots of people. Only, for us, boats are all about leisure. We haven't used them for transportation in a very long time. It's not even going to occur to the embassy that we could go that way. And there are no roadblocks on a river..."

CHAPTER 40

It is easy to lose sight of our ancestors' reason for creating the Choosing ceremony. Thanks to this unique institution, we live in a society where every child is a wanted child, and cruel or neglectful parents are mercifully rare. But these are merely happy accidents. Choosing exists not for practical reasons or for the benefit of society, but because it is a moral necessity.

— From: Reflections, *Justice Daniel of Sweetwater*

It was so peaceful sitting here on the veranda, watching the sun slowly sinking over the delta. She'd forgotten how beautiful Marshtop could be: the reed beds; the heady scent of Dreambells with their tiny pink flowers; the bright yellow Truegolds growing at the water's edge; the delicate strands of evening mist rising from a thousand streamlets winding their way to the sea. After so many years in the arid north, the sheer lushness of home seemed almost unreal. How had she ever persuaded herself to leave this place for the dusty heat of the city?

She stiffened, suddenly wary. Movement had caught her eye. But it was only Miriam, strolling hand-in-hand with Bey beside one of the many small rivers. They disappeared into the reeds, laughter echoing in the evening quiet.

She never should have put the two of them together. Wouldn't have, if she'd thought Miriam would fall for him. But Miriam was young. And Bey was exotic; an off-comer with tales of other worlds. A stranger in a place where everyone was known. And, more than that, a wanted man – a dangerous renegade with a price on his head...

She'd made so many mistakes recently: letting the Gwahnals out of her sight; setting Miriam to watch Bey; leaving him alone in the house with the means to contact his embassy; rescuing him from Michael in the first place, perhaps. Except, without Bey, she never would have made it safely home to Marshtop. She owed her life to this spoiled young off-comer. How strange life could be....

She levered herself out of the chair. It was good to be able to move again. The long journey had left her crippled, barely able to stand unaided. She'd still be like that, if cousin Simon hadn't finally managed to secure a supply of her pills. He was always so good to her. And how did she repay him? By bringing an off-comer to seduce his daughter...

She headed inside to her mother's bedside. The old woman rarely left her bed these days. She seemed content to lie there, gently drifting between wakefulness and sleep. This time, she was awake; awake, and smiling at Beth. Her smile had never changed: always so simple, warm and loving, with no thought that anything could ever come between them. It broke Beth's heart.

"Would you like something to drink, mother?"

"No, love. Just sit down and talk to me. How're you feeling? Is your back better?"

"Much. You're sure I can't get you something?"

"I'm sure."

She lowered herself carefully into the rocking chair. Its gentle creaking filled the silence.

Why did she find it so difficult to talk to her mother? Always there was this awkwardness, this inhibition. Ever since she'd understood she could never say the most important words of all: I'm glad you gave me life, mother; I make the Choice of Life.

Why couldn't she let it go? It was always there, gnawing at her, hurting every bit as much as it had on the worst day of her life; the day she realized that she, alone of all her friends and family, would have, could have, no Choosing ceremony.

She had to say something, had to fill the silence.

"Did you hear the news, mother?"

"No, I–"

"There was a riot in Lakeside. The Assembly can declare a State of Emergency all they like. They're not getting very far with the settlements."

"Lakeside, love? I don't think…"

"It's a big settlement, west of Spate. They're forming a standing militia to keep off-comers out. Maybe there's hope for us yet."

"I don't really follow the news, these days, love. It only upsets me."

"Of course. Sorry."

"No, sweetheart. Don't worry. Let's talk about something else… Have you seen Esther's little boy? You remember Esther, don't you? He's teething now, can you believe it…"

Beth let her mother's words flow by; an endless, gentle stream of information about the lives of people she didn't know; people born long after she'd departed for the desiccated north. She didn't remember 'Esther', and she couldn't ignore the news: not when so many representatives were openly calling for Noyan to join the Commonwealth. Not when everything she believed in was teetering on the edge of destruction.

Her mother's chatter was an irritation, a distraction from weightier concerns. And that, too, was a source of guilt. As was the relief she felt when a knock on the door halted the flow of gossip. Simon entered, cap in hand, showing her the respect due a Justice of the Family Court;

refusing, like all Marshtop, to acknowledge her expulsion from the court.

She smiled a welcome. "Yes?"

"Justice." He ducked his head nervously. His letters had always been so friendly, so relaxed – yet in person he was as shy of her now as he had been as a little boy, worshipping her from afar. He shuffled from foot to foot, garbling out a hurried message: a stranger had come to the settlement, and was asking for her. "We would have put him on the next truck. But this here Ethan said he was a friend of yours. And you said..."

"Ethan? What's he look like?"

"He'd be about twenty-five. Maybe a little older. Quite a well set up young man. Make a good field hand. Lots of muscle–"

"Does he have dimples? When he smiles."

"Hard to say, Justice. I wouldn't say as he was in a smiling kind of mood."

"Where is he?"

"We've got him in the Assembly Hall. Should we tell him you're not–"

"No. Let me take a look, see if it's really him."

She rocked the chair forward and used its momentum to help her to her feet. She was half way to the door before she thought to go back and kiss her mother on the cheek.

"Sorry, mother. I have to go."

He mother smiled, eyes already closing as she drifted back towards sleep. Duty done, Beth set out into the gathering dusk, following Simon closely. The broad streets of her childhood were long gone, transformed into a maze of narrow and winding paths. Marshtop was always changing, reshaping itself to house ever more settlers on the same low hill; the one place for miles around that remained above the floodwaters in the rainy season.

Voices called out as she passed by. The pathways might be unfamiliar, but the people were unchanged. She couldn't pass an open door or window without greetings being exchanged; nor see a family sit down to their evening meal without being asked to join them. She waved and walked on, secure in the knowledge that she was as safe here as anywhere on Noyan. These people would never betray her, and no spy could hope to enter Marshtop undetected.

The Assembly Hall was perched on the crown of the hill, a massive eight-sided building; the settlement's heart, and its place of refuge when the waters rose too high. She peered through the nearest window, but saw only empty corridor. Simon led her to a window further along, near the main entrance. A handful of people were seated on the far side of the inner circle. And in the middle, Ethan, surrounded by hostile young men. No wonder Simon hadn't seen him smile.

"It's him," she said, and headed straight for the door. The young men saw her, and hurried to form a protective shield. She waved them aside, and Ethan rushed over, embraced her, and planted a kiss on her forehead. "I thought you were dead! I saw Ruth's house and I thought you were dead."

"Well, I'm not. Calm down."

"No, you're not, are you? Or the off-comers wouldn't be going crazy trying to find you." He smiled, dimples firmly back in place. She found herself smiling back.

"What about you, Ethan? Are they looking for you?"

"No. They don't have anything on me. But they arrested Ruth."

"I heard. The wireless... I still can't believe it. It's an act of war."

"A few weeks ago, maybe. Now, not so much. The State of Emergency changed everything. Did you see what they did to her house?"

"I was there. We only just got away. They weren't looking to take prisoners, Ethan. They wanted to kill us. Bey rang the Embassy, and—"

"Hotep? He's a spy?"

"No. They were trying to kill us both. Him more than me. Come on, let's get you somewhere you can sit down and have a bite to eat. You look terrible."

It wasn't true. He looked tired and disheveled. But that only seemed to make him more handsome, not less.

"I feel terrible," he agreed. "It took three days of scrounging lifts to get here. I could have got here sooner, but I didn't want to lead the off-comers straight to you."

"Any chance you were followed?"

"I don't think so. They don't have any reason t–"

"No, I suppose not. Nonetheless..." She beckoned to Simon. "Ethan's my guest. I want a room for him, and a good meal, as soon as possible. He looks like he needs it. See what you can organize. And while you're at it, I want an eye keeping out for any signs he was followed. And not just by road. Get someone on the rooftops, watching the skies. And send for Bey. Oh – and mother will need someone."

"Of course, Justice." Simon put a hand on Ethan's arm to lead him away. Ethan shook him off.

"I wasn't followed. But it doesn't matter. You can't stay here, Justice. It's not safe. The off-comers are looking everywhere for you. Telling everyone you're a terrorist and he's a traitor. They're bound to search here eventually."

Beth smiled. "They already have. Been and gone before we even got here."

"They'll be back."

"Of course they will. And we'll be careful. But that's not why you came here, is it? You've got something? Something we can use?"

"Not as such, no..."

"But?"

"But I know where to look. I've found Michael's factory."

CHAPTER 41

It is not that the Noyim are blind to immorality, but rather that their moral sphere overlaps so imperfectly with ours. Whole areas of moral behavior are entirely foreign to them; and yet they will agonize over questions of 'morality' that, for us, are not moral questions at all.
    – *From:* My Time on Noyan, Memories of a Youthful Exile, *The Rt. Hon. Beynan Hotep na Massowic*

Bey slipped off his shorts, eager to follow Miriam into the reed-encircled pool. The cool dark water looked so inviting in the moonlight. He stepped into it… and almost jumped straight back out again.

Fuck, it was cold! Much colder than he'd expected after such a hot day. He stopped dead, goosebumps racing up his bare legs. Maybe this wasn't such a good idea, after all.

Miriam had already reached the far side of the pool, and was on her way back. She swam effortlessly, pulling herself through the water with long, leisurely strokes. He stepped forwards gingerly, fearful of slipping before he'd fully acclimatized to the piercing cold.

A loud splash made him look up. Miriam was gone. The only sign she'd ever been there was a spreading pattern of ripples. He waited for her to resurface. And waited. The ripples spread out, flattened, became part of the background surface noise. The silence stretched, unbroken save for the distant, plaintive calls of native wildlife. He shivered, not from the cold, but a sudden horrifying thought: what if they weren't alone in this pond? What if Miriam hadn't dived at all? What if something pulled her under? Was some native predator lurking in the depths, waiting for unsuspecting swimmers...

Something seized hold of his ankle, and pulled. He barely had time to register the attack before he was toppling, shrieking, into the water. He floundered, coughing up water and struggling to free himself. And Miriam emerged, laughing, right hand gripping his ankle.

The cold bit into the still-sensitive cuts on his hands, and forced the air from his lungs. It sucked the warmth from his chest and insinuated itself into every hollow and crevice of his body, leaving him gasping for breath. But it didn't matter. Miriam was bare and wet and beautiful. The sight of her made him forget all about the pain and discomfort, and join her in laughter.

She released him and sank back into the water. Her buttocks broke the surface, twin islands glistening in the moonlight – so smooth, so tempting. He reached out towards them... but she was already diving again, slipping past him into the deeper water. He laughed and set out in pursuit.

He'd laughed a great deal in the last few days. Grandfather was so wrong about the Noyim. They weren't perverse; they were too childlike for that; childlike, and truly, deeply crazy. It was hard to feel animosity towards a people so idealistically democratic that ten-year-olds voted alongside adults. But it was very easy to laugh at them. They couldn't seem to make even the simplest decision without gathering every settler, no matter how young or old, to debate the issue. Even the Choosing ceremony seemed less odious here: it was merely an anthropological fossil, no more to be hated than ritual cannibalism amongst savages – and doomed to go the same way once the natives were civilized. Perhaps Bey himself would be a civilizing influence. He hoped so. The Marshtop settlers weren't bad people. They'd sheltered him and befriended him and shown him nothing but kindness since he brought Beth the Justice safely home again. And most important of all, there was Miriam...

He caught up with her, toes squishing unpleasantly in the soft mud as he scrambled to stand up. He dipped a hand into the water and splashed her as hard as he could. She responded in kind. White water surged between them as each tried, unsuccessfully, to make the other wetter than they were before. Finally, he reached out through the foaming water and pulled her towards him. Her skin was cold and smooth to the touch, and she didn't flinch away.

He'd slept with other native girls, but none like Miriam. She didn't want anything from him except shared closeness, shared pleasure. And she was beautiful; not elegant like a Commonwealth lady, but earthy, wholesome, healthy – an apple-faced peasant girl, browned by the sun. And with an uncomplicated, guilt-free, enjoyment of sex unknown in the Commonwealth. The natives didn't seem to see casual sex as a moral issue at all; for them, only procreation, sex for the purpose of creating life, was a matter for moral concern.

He kissed her forehead. She nuzzled in closer, hand tickling down his stomach and reaching for him even before he was ready. How strange, and how strangely thrilling, to be the seduced rather than the seducer. His body responded eagerly. She laughed happily, nose crinkling in a way that just demanded to be kissed. He lifted her up, hands cupping her buttocks, and turned to carry her out of the pool.

And found himself face to face with her father.

"Hello, Beynan."

Bey's heart stopped. His erection wilted. He gulped for air. "We... we... Uh.... Only swimming..."

"Oh, hello, Da. Is something wrong?" Miriam was

peering unconcernedly over her shoulder. She slipped out of Bey's arms, leaving him naked and exposed. He used his hands to cover his embarrassment, and in the process lost his balance and floundered backwards into deeper water. He'd been in situations like this before, and they'd all ended with him fleeing for his life (or, at least, his capacity to father children). But Simon didn't seem angry. He was smiling at his daughter, entirely unconcerned by her nudity.

"Beth wants to see you, Beynan," he said. "I'm to tell you Ethan's here."

Bey stared at him, uncomprehending. How could the man be so calm, seeing his daughter like this? He would never understand the Noyim. They were beyond rational understanding.

"What? Um, yes. I'll just... get dressed, shall I?"

"Very good. They're at the Assembly Hall. Miriam will show you the way."

"Right..."

He watched, still not quite believing it, as Simon headed back the way he came, leaving Bey alone with his daughter. If he wanted, he could take Miriam back into his arms, and...

"Bey?"

"Huh?"

"You're bleeding again. Best wait for it to stop before you get dressed."

He glanced down at his hands. A thin trickle of blood was leaking from one of the deeper cuts. He waited patiently for it to dry up. Most of his cuts were little more than scars at this point. Native medicine hadn't turned out to be quite as bad as he'd feared; either that, or he'd been incredibly lucky. Still, there was no good reason modern medicine was covered by the embargo. He'd make a fuss about that when he got back to Homeworld...

If he got back. Right now, that didn't look very likely.

He dressed quickly when the bleeding stopped. They

walked back together, Miriam clinging to his arm. He was glad of her warmth: his clothes were clammy against his wet skin, and the heat of the day was quickly receding.

The settlement looked different at night. The dense slum of reed-roofed hovels was transformed into a single organic whole, a living hill dotted with flickering lights, and crowned by the Assembly Hall. It loomed at the top of the hill like an ancient fortification dominating the surrounding countryside. Golden light poured invitingly from its open doors. It seemed so close, so impossible to miss, a beacon to lead the way – and yet no sooner had they entered the maze of narrow streets than it disappeared from view. Whenever he glimpsed it – through a gap between squat, rickety houses here, or at a sharp switchback turn there – it was always a long way from where he was expecting. He clung to his confident native guide as she led him ever upwards through dark, claustrophobic passageways. Then, finally, they reached the top of an alleyway, and the wide-open doors were facing them across a small cobbled square.

They hurried into the Assembly Hall and found it transformed into a bazaar. Folding tables had been set up in rows and settlers were loading them with every kind of necessity – from loaves of bread, to weapons. The crowd parted briefly; and there, inspecting some kind of native long-gun, was Ethan. Bey ran over, Miriam clinging happily to his arm. They reached Ethan as he was raising the long gun to his shoulder. He sighted along the barrel, and pulled the trigger. The resulting click was very loud.

"Too noisy," he said, returning it to its disappointed owner. "Too long range."

The settler nodded his understanding. Bey took the opportunity to step in. "Ethan! It's so good to–"

"You got a decent knife? Only, I really need something for close-quarter work."

Ethan hadn't so much cut him off, as failed to acknowledge his existence. He went on talking to the settler as if Bey wasn't even there. The settler retreated in obvious embarrassment, eyes darting from Ethan to Bey and back again.

"Ethan?"

"Hotep." The auxiliary finally spared him a glance. And immediately turned away to pick up a leather toolbelt from the nearest table.

Bey flushed. Miriam's grip on his arm tightened. He could sense her outrage; but he was merely baffled. And hurt. He *liked* Ethan. Didn't Ethan like him back?

"What's going on? What do you want with a knife?"

"Tell him, Ethan." Beth had joined them; coming to the rescue. As ever.

Ethan looked up. "You sure we can trust him?"

"I trust him."

"Okay, if you say so, Justice..." He dropped the tool belt onto the table, and finally consented to explain. "We've found Michael's factory, Hotep. We're going to go check it out."

Bey froze. Memories clawed at him. An arm around his shoulders. A menacing voice. Cold, cold eyes. And Jodan's blood filling the bottom of a sphere. So much blood.

"We need you to come with us, Bey." Beth's hand was on his elbow. She was smiling like a kindly grandmother. He wanted to slap her.

"Come with you?"

"Yes."

"We can manage without," said Ethan. But it was no more than a token protest. Bey willed him to be more forceful. And when nothing was forthcoming, sought his own way out.

"I don't see how I—"

"We need evidence," said Beth. "Something that proves your embargo's been breached. You'll know what to look for. We won't."

"I might," said Ethan.

"At a glance? I don't think so. You're not an off-comer.

We need you Bey. Grab yourself a bag and start packing. We're leaving tonight."

Miriam's grip on Bey's arm tightened again. Maybe, if she didn't want him to go, he could... But no. Her eyes were shining with excitement. *Of course* he would help Beth – wasn't he the hero who'd brought her safely home again?

He tried not to panic. There had to be a way out of this. There had to be... "I don't understand," he said. "I thought you didn't care about the black market bi-tech?"

"We don't," said Ethan. Someone passed him a knife. He nodded his thanks and unsheathed it, testing its balance. He clearly had no intention of elaborating.

"Ethan..." Beth's disapproval was unmistakable. Once again, Ethan gave in.

"It's not about the black market. It's about getting proof your embassy's covering up a breach in their precious embargo. Once the Assembly knows they're lying about that, they'll want to know what else the embassy's lying about. Like, maybe, you and the Justice being terrorists. All of a sudden, they aren't going be so keen on sitting back and letting the embassy hunt you down. Not without talking to you first. They're going to want to hear what the Justice has to say. And once they're listening... We've got proof Michael killed the Gwahnals, not terrorists – and definitely not you two. And that changes everything. Pretty soon Justice Beth will be back on the Family Court where she belongs, Ruth will be out of jail and back in the Assembly. And you won't have embassy goons looking to shoot you on sight. This is where we stop running and start fighting back."

Bey wanted to spit. He'd been looking for an excuse to say no, not a reason to say yes.

"This factory. I don't suppose it's guarded, is it?"

"Heavily fortified, I expect."

"Thought it might be..."

Ethan slipped the knife back into its sheath, and set about attaching it to his belt. Much as Bey hated to acknowledge it, the man had a point: he couldn't keep running forever. The traitors in the embassy wanted him dead, wanted it so badly they'd destroyed a whole house just to get him, not caring who else might be inside.

And the worst of it was, the traitors were right. They didn't just *want* him dead. They *needed* him dead. Because he wasn't just anyone. He was a Massowic. As long as he was alive, he was a danger to them. People would listen to him, if he lived long enough to get in front of them.

He didn't have a choice. Either he helped bring the traitors down, or they'd keep on looking until they found him, and killed him.

And at least he wouldn't have to disappoint Miriam this way. That was good. He liked how she was looking at him.

"Okay," he said. "I'll come."

Beth patted his arm. "Very good. Choose a bag and start packing."

Ethan put out a restraining hand. "But no weapons. I don't want you shooting me by mistake."

A well-wisher thrust a bag into his hands and disappeared back into the crowd. He stared at the flaccid sack, unsure what to do with it and happy to let Miriam take over. She filled it with food: a small loaf of bread, bags of nuts and dried fruit, and some thin dark-brown strips which he belatedly realized were preserved meat. He might have rejected them, if they hadn't already disappeared into the bottom of the sack. Then, just as he was about to complain about too much weight, someone handed him six full canisters of water – round, leather-bound containers that together weighed more than everything else combined. That was it. He couldn't possibly carry any more. He hurried to close up the neck of the sack. There were two leather strings that were clearly supposed to seal it somehow. He stared at them, trying to work out how they functioned. There was no point telling them to close up, he'd learned that much by now. But how exactly where you supposed…?

Miriam reached over, laughing, and tied the strings into a bow. He flushed, not because she was laughing at him, but in anticipation of her disappointment. The strings had been a much-needed wake-up call. He couldn't do this. It was madness. He couldn't risk his life with this kind of equipment. It was suicide.

"I can't–"

She stifled his protests with a kiss, and hung the bag from his left shoulder by its single strap. The weight dragged him down, equalizing their height. He straightened up, trying to break free so he could explain – and found himself stumbling to stay upright. The crowd was moving, and he and Miriam had no choice but to move with them. Everyone was headed for the exit. Just ahead of him, an unfamiliar face was talking earnestly to Beth.

"It's all set and waiting on you, Justice. The blacksmith's given it a thorough service, and the tank's full. You shouldn't even have to stop."

He couldn't hear her reply. She'd disappeared through the open doors. He hurried after her, but it was hard to make progress with Miriam's arm threaded through his. He tried to talk to her, to explain, but she was busy shouting to someone at the back of the surging crowd, and he couldn't make himself heard.

Then they were outside, part of a river of people flowing downhill. It was a friendly, supportive river – but one that jostled and pushed, and separated them effortlessly at the entrance to a narrow passage. He stumbled onwards, head down, fearful of mis-stepping in the darkness.

The trip downhill was much swifter than the climb up had been. All too soon they were at the edge of the settlement. A truck was waiting, smoke billowing from the back. Ethan was already helping Beth into the cab. Bey hurried towards them, desperate to explain that he'd changed his mind, but two local young men steered him away, laughing. He couldn't possibly travel in front – not an off-comer like him. He'd be spotted in no time.

He was hustled, protesting, into the back of the truck. They'd made a space for him deep inside, hidden between racks of moldy vegetables. An upside-down crate served as a seat. He turned to tell them this was a mistake, that he wasn't going after all. But the rear doors were already closing. He had one last, brief glimpse of Miriam waving goodbye, and then he was alone in the darkness.

He swore loudly and reached out to feel his way back to the exit, and safety. But he'd barely taken a first hesitant step before the vehicle lurched forwards, the upturned crate slid viciously into the back of his knees and he tumbled backwards to half-sit, half-lean against the wall. Something awkward inside the heavy pack dug into his kidneys. He groaned, set down the pack, and rearranged himself as best he could in the darkness. The vehicle was picking up speed. It took a bend and the crate-seat once again slid across the floor, this time taking him with it. His nose made sharp, painful contact with something hard and wooden. A large half-rotten leaf landed on his head and clung wetly to the back of his neck. He barely had time to hurl it away – and for a finger-tip inspection to check his nose for damage – before the truck lurched again. This time he was ready. He wedged himself against the nearest rack and used his arms to shield his face.

Time passed. His arms and legs grew stiff. He longed to sit back, but didn't dare for fear of being thrown around. Eventually, he drifted into an uncomfortable half-sleep peppered with nightmares of Michael chasing him down an endless corridor, roadroot seedling in hand; of Samuel approaching, bearing a hive that buzzed with killer insects; of Grandfather Massowic, Bey's ear in one hand, aphrobug in the other, humiliating him in front of the entire family...

He awoke to stillness, and the sound of the back door opening. The respite was short – a brief midnight halt to eat, drink and defecate in the bushes, and then he was back in his dark uncomfortable prison, wishing for the journey to end, no matter where or how.

Eventually, after an endless, miserable time of wandering dreams, half-sleep and nightmares, light began to seep into the truck. The walls were not as solid as they appeared. Cracks in the paneling painted the interior in bright, thin lines of sunlight. Slowly, the nighttime chill gave way to warmth. At first, he welcomed both: with light, he had the opportunity to arrange his surroundings and make them less intensely uncomfortable; the warmth helped with the stiffness of his limbs. But the heat soon rose from comfortable, to unpleasant, to stifling; and the stench of rotting vegetables became unbearable.

But worst of all was the thirst; thirst, and the knowledge that he had water right there. If he could just open the fucking bag!

He pulled at the strings with stiff fingers, gnawed at them with a dry mouth, wept over them in profound, soul-destroying frustration. Until somehow, finally, the bow gave way. He had no clue how he'd done it, or how to retie it, and he didn't care. He pulled out a canteen, wrenched painfully at the top until it opened, and drank his fill. The water was warm, metallic, and absolutely wonderful.

He drank his way through two full canteens before the next problem presented itself. He needed to relieve himself, and there was no sign of a bucket or anything similar in the back of the truck. No matter. He repurposed the first canteen as a makeshift latrine, and sighed blissfully.

The momentary relief (so short, but so very sweet) soon faded. It was hard to aim accurately in the jolting truck, and urine spilled everywhere. He spent the last few hours of the journey a prisoner in a hot, rancid cell, wishing for anything, even capture, to bring an end to his misery.

He awoke to silence. The truck had stopped. He'd been asleep — truly, deeply asleep. The truck was pitch-black;

outside, night had fallen. He heard voices at the rear of the truck. The doors creaked open. He unbent and struggled to his feet in an ecstasy of pleasure and pain. It didn't matter who was at the door, friend or foe. It was enough that he could finally get out of this fucking truck.

It was friends. Ethan was clambering inside. He hurried over, grabbed Bey's shoulder bag, and helped him stumble out into the chill night air.

At first, Bey barely registered their surroundings. His whole being was focused on the relief of breathing untainted air. Then, slowly, the world became real. Both moons were in the sky, spreading overlapping shadows across a grey desert landscape: dry, mountainous and bleak. There was no sign of a factory, or any other kind of habitation.

Beth was at the front of the truck, pouring over a native map in the light of the vehicle's headlamps. Ethan went to stand beside her. Bey followed suit. She looked up, folded the map, and nodded towards the nearest hills. "The factory's fifteen miles that way."

He glanced back at his heavy pack, still lying where Ethan had dropped it. "Couldn't we get a bit closer first?"

"Not unless you want to knock on the front door," said Ethan. He waved to the unseen driver. Something crunched mechanically under the hood. They stepped aside, and the truck lurched away into the darkness, taking with it their only link to anything approximating civilization. Bey watched it dwindle into the distance, turned to the others... and saw them disappearing into the night.

He picked up his pack and hurried after them. It was still dauntingly heavy, even with two fewer canteens. He would have complained, but the sight of Beth struggling silently with her own pack was enough to keep him quiet. She looked absurdly old to be attempting this hike. If she could suck it up, so could he.

For a time, he almost enjoyed the walk. It was good to

stretch his legs and breathe the clean desert air. Even the danger seemed more theoretical than real. Then they began to climb into the hills. Gentle slopes became steep inclines, the footing more treacherous – and the consequences of a fall more serious. Worse still, the others had native flashlights, but he only had moonlight to show him where to put his feet. Every step took that little bit more effort than the one before. Blisters began to develop, and his thighs were soon chafed raw by the unforgiving native trousers.

An endless time later, the sun rose and colored the desert in shades of ochre. The light helped. But with it, came heat, burning his scalp and searing his lungs. The blisters on his feet became unbearably painful, as did his left shoulder where the pack rubbed. He shifted it to his right, which was soon just as raw as the left.

They stopped at the foot of a small, sheer cliff and drank from their canteens. Bey gulped greedily at the lukewarm water, and licked his cracked lips. His reserves of water were getting very low. He was going to have to ask the others to share, and if they didn't like it, too bad. They chose to leave him in the back of that truck. It wasn't his fault he'd had to drink so much before they even got here. If only he'd stayed in Marshtop where he could drink as much as he liked, and look out over ponds and rivers and brooks and waterfalls and...

He couldn't go on like this. "Listen, Ethan – Beth can't take much more of this. Why don't we find some shade and wait till dark. It'll be easier then."

Ethan nodded. Beth was bent almost double under the weight of her pack. Her breathing was loud and ragged. "Okay," he said. "As soon as–"

"Scrape that! We go on." Beth's voice was remarkably strong, considering. Ethan shrugged. Bey sighed and went back to his daydreams. Somewhere far away, Miriam was swimming naked in a clear pool, and he was plunging his head underwater and drinking and drinking and drinking...

They resumed their journey. Twice more they stopped for water, and twice more Beth insisted they carry on. And then, finally, long after Bey had given up hope that this journey would ever end, they topped a rise and saw their destination: a large, oblong building squatting in the middle of a broad valley. A tall fence surrounded the structure. The building seemed old and dilapidated, but the fence was very obviously in good repair. Bey ducked down, and retreated below the ridge. Beth and Ethan followed more slowly.

There was a hollow, a few yards below the crest. A good place to wait out the remainder of the daylight. Bey sat down heavily; glad to take the weight off his feet. He closed his eyes...

...and opened them again, blinking groggily. The shadows had changed; the sun was closer to its zenith. He'd slept where he sat, propped up by the shoulder bag. Ethan was on the opposite side of the hollow, his back against a rock. Beth's head was cradled in his lap. She was fast asleep. Bey struggled painfully to his knees, slipped the bag from his shoulder and retrieved his last canteen. The stale water was better than any of the expensive wines at the Mitchesons' misguided party...

Had the gala dinner really been such a short time ago? He shook his head, and regretted it; the movement hurt his stiff neck. Ethan nodded to him. It wasn't much of a gesture, but it was better than his earlier hostility. Bey reached into his pack and retrieved dried meat and fruit. The fruit he ate, the meat he gave to Ethan; his mouth was too dry, and native meat was too daunting a prospect when he was sober.

Ethan bit off a chunk of the leathery flesh and grunted a 'thank you'. His right hand was on Beth's forehead, testing it like a parent checking a child for fever. And looking about as concerned.

"My water's all gone," said Bey. "Yours?"

"Not yet."

Bey nodded at Beth. "Does she need a drink?"

"She needs to sleep."

"Yeah, I suppose. So do I. When do we go on?"

"Not till it's dark, and then not for a while. I want them asleep before I go near the place."

"You and me both..."

"Will you two shut up?"

Beth was awake, and glaring. She closed her eyes, pointedly. Ethan grinned, and followed suit. Bey settled down with his bag as a pillow, and despite the heat, and an underlying sense of dread that never quite went away, was soon asleep.

CHAPTER 42

People ask why, if we consider it such an evil to knowingly create new life, we do not simply have ourselves sterilized. The answer lies in the core tenet of our moral philosophy: because to do so would permanently remove the element of choice. Without choice we cease to be moral agents; we become mere animals, acting according to our natures without any consideration of right or wrong.

– Attributed to: Isaac the Seer, *Third Prophet of Nullism*

Beth awoke with cramp in her neck, and slow agony building in her spine. Ethan's lap, so treacherously inviting, had proved to be a terrible pillow. Now she was paying for her weakness. She should have used her pack as she'd intended.

Sitting up was too great a challenge. She grudgingly permitted Ethan to help. He slipped his hands under her shoulders and heaved upwards. It was undignified, but effective, and left her sitting hunched over, elbows resting supportively on her thighs.

Evening was giving way to dusk, leaving the hollow in deep shadow. She stared back over the hills they'd crossed the night before – a stark landscape, but not lacking in grandeur. A distant crag turned from red to gold, and finally to deep black as the last sunlight touched it, and was gone.

Bey was still sleeping. Ethan went to rouse him. He was less than gentle. It was her fault. She shouldn't have told him about Bey phoning the Embassy. Hopefully, when this was over, she'd find some way to make amends.

"Come on," she said. "Let's eat."

The meal was brief, functional, and taken in silence. Afterwards, Beth swallowed double her usual dosage of pills, and a carefully rationed mouthful of water. Her last canteen was half-empty already, and there was no guarantee they'd be able to refill at the factory. It might need to last all the way through tomorrow's return trek.

Ethan and Bey stepped aside to relieve themselves, but she felt no such need. She sat completely still, waiting for the pills to take effect. It was taking longer than usual. She'd walked more in the last twenty-four hours than she had in decades, and her whole body ached.

Ethan returned and helped her to her feet. The three of them climbed up to the ridge and looked down on the valley beyond. It was dark and still, with no sign of life. The bulky shape of the mine-building was just about visible; the fence around it lost in the gloom.

"Well, Ethan? How do we get in?"

"Through the fence. There are people on the gate."

"It's bound to be electrified."

"Bound to be."

"Electrified?" Bey was off to one side, staring miserably at his feet. Now he looked up. "What do you mean, electrified?"

"You know," said Ethan. "Electrified. As in, electricity. Touch it and you fry."

"Fuck...! You mean they...? Shit."

Even in the darkness, the revulsion on his face was unmistakable. Beth shook her head. She'd never understand off-comers.

"There's only one way to find out," she said. "We'll go in where the valley's narrowest – that'll give us less ground to cover once we're inside the fence."

"Makes sense," Ethan agreed. "And be careful on the way down. We don't want to take a tumble and give ourselves away."

"Or break out necks," said the off-comer, dismally. Ethan laughed.

"Yeah. That too. Here we go. Last one down gets to connect the bypass wires..."

This side of the hill was far less steep. The descent should have been easy, but they couldn't turn on their flashlights for fear of being seen, and every step had to be judged just so in the darkness. In some ways it helped. The need to focus completely on where she placed her feet was a useful distraction from all her aches and pains – and the challenges they faced once they reached their destination. Circumventing an electrified fence was no easy task.

Up close, the fence was even more daunting than it had appeared from the top of the hill. They hunkered down in a nearby dry river bed to take stock. Ethan pulled a pair of wire cutters out of his bag. And stopped, frozen.

"I can't move," he said.

"Shit!" said Bey. "Neither can I."

Then she felt it too. There was no stiffness or discomfort, but she couldn't move a muscle from the neck down. She was still breathing. She could turn her head. But that was it. "What's happening?"

"It's a fucking tanglefield."

"A what? How do we get out of it?"

"We don't. That's the whole point. It's a Gallaskian tanglefield. There's nothing we can do. We're fucked. I shouldn't have come. I shouldn't have fucking come. Of all the stupid..."

Beth tuned Bey out. He wasn't saying anything useful. She craned her head a little further and caught Ethan's eye. "Any ideas?"

He managed only the faintest ghost of his usual smile. "I was planning on waiting and seeing. You?"

"I suppose that's as good a plan as any."

She settled her head into a more comfortable position and closed her eyes. Bey was still muttering angrily to himself. She was tempted to join in. There was something especially ignominious about failing this completely before they'd even made it through the fence.

But Gallaskian tech? This was supposed to be a bi-tech factory. Why hadn't they made their own defenses? And how would Michael even get hold of this 'tanglefield'? It wasn't as if the Gallaskians were keen on exporting their technology; not like the Commonwealth.

On the other hand, tanglefields were obviously very effective. Maybe it was just the best tool for the job, better than anything the factory could produce. In any case, Ethan was right. There was nothing they could do except wait and see. And hope there *was* something to see. Because the alternative was sitting here until they died of thirst or heat exhaustion, whichever came first.

"Someone's coming." Ethan was staring past her at something she couldn't see. Bey stopped muttering and craned his head to get a better view. She didn't bother trying. All she'd do was strain her neck.

Light flickered into view – three beams, four, moving rapidly over the ground. Searching. One beam touched Ethan's legs and moved on. Then rushed back, pinning him in green-tinged circle of light: an off-comer device. But the voice that called out was purest Noyan: "There they are! Three of 'em, just like the scope said."

The other beams skittered across the landscape, found Bey and herself, and were still. The same voice spoke again, somewhere over her left shoulder. "Right. Luke and I'll carry the woman, you carry–"

"Carry them? Scrape that! Get Control to cut the field. We'll make the mothers walk!"

"Nobody's calling Control." A female voice this time, authoritative and in command. "Not yet. First, we search them. Then we let them up."

The speaker stepped into Beth's eye line. She was tall, broad-shouldered, in her thirties. Light poured from her forehead, casting her face into deep shadow. Something blinked red at her neck; a grey plasticky collar. Protection from the tanglefield? It had a Gallaskian look. And the woman was moving unimpeded, where the three of them were still immobilized.

Ethan glared at her. "This is an outrage. I don't know who you people are, or how or why you're doing this to us, but–"

"Yes, you do. Let's not waste time."

"Beth's a Justice of the Fa–"

"Former Justice. Like I give a scrape. We know who you are. Now be quiet, or I'll have Luke over there hurt you. He's not a big fan of the Auxiliary Court, are you Luke?"

"No, ma'am."

"No. Now, what have we got in here…"

Ethan watched helplessly as she pulled the bag out of his grasp, carried it away and handed it to someone out of sight. Then she returned and started going through his pockets. When she stepped away, even his belt had been removed, and the wire cutters were no longer at his feet.

She searched Bey next. His belt was also taken, and his pockets emptied. And for the first time, the woman seemed surprised by what she'd found.

"Well, well, well. What have we here? Not one of ours, I think…"

She held up her prize. It was Hyrom's bulb – the one piece of real evidence they had. And Bey had brought it with him, here, to the very last place anyone with half a brain would have taken it: Michael's factory. Beth closed her eyes. She didn't open them again until it was her turn to be searched. The woman was quick and efficient. She hardly seemed to have begun before she was stepping back and giving orders to 'Control' to 'cut the field'. One moment Beth was immobile and insensate; the next her whole body was a mass of pins and needles. Two men grabbed hold of her and dragged her to her feet. Even with their support, it was all she could do to stay upright.

Ethan was more resilient. He launched himself at the men who came for him, bypassing one and downing the other. Then he dropped like a stone. Another man had struck him on the back of the head with a rifle butt. Beth struggled uselessly against her captors, desperate to go to his aid. He was lying very still. The blow to his head had been vicious. But not vicious enough, apparently, to satisfy the man he'd knocked down; he kicked Ethan brutally in the midriff. There was no reaction.

"Is he dead?" The woman in charge echoed Beth's fears. The assailant knelt down to check.

"Not yet. But it can be arranged."

Beth glanced at Bey. He was staring disconsolately at the ground. Had he even registered Ethan's escape attempt?

"No, it can't," said the woman. "They're wanted for questioning. All of them." She turned to Beth. "But if either of you tries anything, I'll make you wish you were dead, understand?"

Beth nodded. She didn't trust herself to speak. The situation was too hopeless. There were seven captors in all; two for each of them, and one left over. And all of them were armed. There was no way she could escape. But if she saw a chance to hurt the man who'd kicked Ethan...

No opportunity arose. They were herded – and Ethan carried – to a waiting truck. Ethan was thrown inside like a sack of potatoes. She was forced to climb. She tried to get to Ethan, but a guard pushed her away. She gave in and slumped against the wall. There was nothing to do now, except wait. Ethan was out cold. Or dead. Bey was forced after her, and sat doubled over, arms around his knees, head in his arms. The flexibility of youth. She took a deep breath, closed her eyes and tried to gather her resources.

The trip ended at the mine-head. They were dragged

inside – Ethan unconscious; Bey whining. The interior was a large, echoing space, its walls and ceiling lost in darkness. There was no sign of any activity. Was this really Michael's factory? It had to be. Why else the tanglefield, and the guards? But...

A light came on. They were surrounded by the rusting paraphernalia of the disused mine. And a single, well-maintained concrete structure right in the middle, complete with spotless elevator doors. The factory wasn't housed in the mine-head. It was in the mine itself.

The doors opened, revealing a large, white elevator. There was no lattice door to be pulled aside, no operator to do the pulling, or to operate the buttons. To all appearances it wasn't an elevator at all, but an antiseptic, windowless white room. More Gallaskian technology...

A push from behind forced her inside. She leaned against the wall, exaggerating the tanglefield's lingering aftereffects in the faint hope of lulling her captors into discounting her as a threat.

The door closed, and became all but invisible; part of the wall. They were inside a blank white box. And it was moving. And moving quickly, judging by the sensation in her stomach and the slight vibration she could just about feel through the floor.

Michael must have gone to vast expense, installing this thing. Why? No bootlegging operation needed this level of technology. Surely the original mine elevator would have sufficed. Was this the Gwahnals doing? They had the wealth, certainly: wouldn't care about squeezing profit as much as someone like Michael. But this definitely felt Gallaskian. Why would the Gwahnals, of all people, use Gallaskian technology?

They were slowing down. She could feel it in her back as her full weight returned. She braced herself for whatever came next... and recoiled, revolted, when the doors opened on a corridor from her nightmares. Ribbed intestinal tubing stretched into the distance. This, finally, was what she'd been expecting.

A guard was waiting, gun at the ready. It was some kind of pistol, but unlike any Beth had ever seen. It was slender and colorful: more like a children's toy than a real gun. And where was the cylinder? The hammer? Off-comer tech, clearly, but not remotely organic. More Gallaskian equipment? Interesting.

The guard lowered his weapon and stepped aside. Their captors chivied her and Bey out of the elevator, dragging Ethan along behind. At least they were all still together. She tried to look back, but was pushed forwards so roughly she almost fell. Bey protested, and yelped at a blow. She gritted her teeth, and focused on memorizing the turns they were taking, just in case.

There were many turns. Michael's factory was much bigger and more sophisticated than she'd expected. This didn't feel like a criminal operation at all. It was too big, too organized, too polished.

They turned into a dead-end corridor. Ahead of them, two armed guards flanked a solid, wooden door. The woman in charge marched to the front, knocked, and entered.

Beyond the door was a spacious office, full of well-made local furniture. To one side was a small table, surrounded by comfortable chairs; at the rear, a large desk. And sitting behind it, his booted feet on the desktop, was Moyem Jimawn.

Suddenly, the Gallaskian technology made sense. Suddenly, a lot of things made sense.

CHAPTER 43

Nullism is, of course, an intrinsically self-limiting creed, but it would be wrong to assume that it is now completely extinct on Noyan. There are new adherents in every generation. I pointed out to one such that, should everyone suddenly embrace her creed, the human race would entirely cease to exist – only to find that she viewed that prospect with apparent equanimity.

– From: My Time on Noyan, Memories of a Youthful Exile, *The Rt. Hon. Beynan Hotep na Massowic*

"Moyem?"

What the fuck?

All this time, he'd been sweating blood, terrified, expecting to see Michael, and now…

What the actual fuck was Moyem Jimawn doing here?

A Gallaskian.

In a bi-tech factory.

Oh shit.

"Beynan! What a pleasant surprise. How are you? You're the last person I expected to see."

Jimawn looked wrong without a brocade coat. Incomplete. Where were all the elaborate whorls signifying who-knew-what status to other Gallaskians? He seemed almost naked like this, hair loose around his shoulders, jacket missing, buttons of his ruffled shirt only partially done up. Naked, but not vulnerable. Arrogant, and very much in charge.

"Now you, Justice. You, I expected so see. And the gentleman who's currently resting is…?"

Jimawn's boots were on the desk. That wasn't like him at all. He was normally so polite; all delicate manners and careful bows: very imperial. Not this time.

"His name's Ethan. He's my Team Leader in the Auxiliary Court."

"I see. And how many other little auxiliaries do you have up there?" He pointed a languid finger at the ceiling.

"There's no one else. Just us three."

"Just you. Of course. And how did you get here? Magic carpet?"

"We walked."

"Through the desert? I don't believe you, Justice."

"I don't care, Cultural Attaché."

"What about you, Beynan? Did you walk here, too?"

Jimawn's smile was as urbane as ever. Bey nodded, not trusting himself to speak. Jimawn frowned and turned to the woman in charge. "What do you think?"

"There are no other hotspots in the valley, Hetman. And no sign of a vehicle."

"So, they really did walk here. How very athletic of you, Justice. I'm impressed. And you, Bey. I never knew you had it in you."

Bey's cheeks burned. Jimawn was laughing at them. To think he'd actually liked the Gallaskian. And all the time Jimawn had been… what, exactly? Not what he pretended, anyway. Did Sanja know? What about the Gwah…

"You killed Sanja!"

The words burst out, unintended. A guard moved ominously behind him. He flinched, expecting a blow, but Jimawn waved a dismissive hand, and it never came.

"As it happens, I didn't," he drawled. "Why would I? He was much too useful. Unlike you, I'm afraid."

"And the Gwahnals?"

Jimawn smiled. And took his feet off the table, no longer remotely casual. "Did they have radios?"

"No, sir. Just wire cutters. Weapons. And the off-comer had this."

Fuck. The receiver. All that effort, everything he'd done to try and make sure Jodan's death meant something... all a complete waste of time, because he was too fucking stupid to leave it with Miriam.

Jimawn inspected the green ball curiously. "What were you planning to do with this, exactly?"

"Nothing. I just had it on me."

"Really? You expect me to believe that? Janet – give this to Mary. I'd like to know what it is. In the meantime, see if Michael can't encourage them to be a little more cooperative. That's supposed to be his specialty, after all."

The room receded. Jimawn was still talking, but Bey couldn't hear him; not over the blood pounding in his ears. "Please, Moyem. I'll tell you everything. The receiver. It was Jodan's. It's a recording. From before. Please, Moyem..."

He gave up. The guards had hustled them back into the corridor, and Jimawn was on the other side of a closed door.

The walk that followed could have been long or short. He didn't notice. His mind was elsewhere, overwhelmed by memories of Michael's eyes and voice; of blood slowly filling the bottom of a sphere; of the Gwahnals pegged out in the desert.

The walk ended at a rectangular native door. The room beyond was nothing more than a walled-off section of the original mine repurposed as a storeroom. Empty shelves lined the walls; a single bulb dangled from the ceiling. There was no bi-tech reinforcement here, just bare rock scored with tool marks. The only thing preventing millions of tons of stone from crashing down on them was primitive native engineering.

They tried to force him inside. He resisted, violently –

until a well-placed blow drove all the breath from his body. Then he was thrown into the room. Ethan, still unconscious, was dumped carelessly beside him. He lay sprawled on his front. Beth hurried over to help, and the door slammed shut, leaving the three of them alone once more.

"Give me a hand here," she said. "We can't leave him like this. He could choke."

Bey took a deep, painful breath and struggled to his feet. Ethan didn't look good. His breathing was shallow. The hair on the back of his head was clotted with blood. Together, they turned him on his side, bringing his knees up to prevent him from settling back onto his belly. At least he could be sick without choking on his own vomit now. Bey had done the same for Sanja once, when the boy was too drunk to move.

Was Jimawn telling the truth when he denied killing Sanja? He'd sounded sincere. And he had no reason to lie. Who were they going to tell, after Michael did whatever he was going to…?

Best not to think about that. Best to think about something, anything, else. But…

"What are they going to do to us, Beth?"

"I've got no idea." She was sitting cross-legged beside Ethan, gently stroking his cheek.

"You don't think they'll… They won't… It won't be like what they did to Fange and Amaya?"

Her hand froze in mid-stroke. "Has anyone ever told you, you talk too much? What if the room's bugged? You want to give them ideas?"

Bey retreated to the other side of the room. He sat down, his back against a shelving unit. Time passed. He closed his eyes, but sleep didn't come. Finally, Beth broke the silence. "What's Jimawn up to?"

"Careful," he said, pettily. "Bugs."

"You're afraid of telling him what he already knows?"

"Maybe I'm afraid of giving him ideas. But it's obvious,

anyway. He's after bi-tech."

"Is that all?"

He opened his eyes. Beth was lying beside Ethan, her gaze focused on the ceiling. She genuinely didn't seem to get it.

"All? It's everything. Bi-tech's what gives us the edge. We understand their technology – it's just a version of what we had before bi-tech came along. We understand their capabilities. They don't understand ours. Or didn't. They will soon enough, now they've got this factory. It's a geopolitical disaster."

Beth's brow furrowed. "But if all he cares about is your technology, why'd he kill the Gwahnals? Especially that way. If all he wanted was to get rid of them, he could have done it quietly. But he didn't. He must have had a reason for stirring up the embassy like that. You'd think that would be the last thing he'd want to do? I'm missing something. Jimawn's not stupid. There has to be a–"

She stopped. The door was opening. Bey's stomach tightened into a sharp knot of fear. But it wasn't Michael – only a guard, bringing a tray with food and water. This was his chance. If he could overpower this one guard, he could... Too late. The man hadn't even entered the room; not properly. He'd just set the tray down and backed out. There was a loud click from the door. Some kind of lock? Probably.

On the other hand, that water bottle looked so good right now. He grabbed it and began to drink.

"I'd go easy on that, if I were you," said Beth. "No toilet..."

He shrugged, took two more large gulps, and passed her the bottle. Then he helped her sit up. True to her own advice, she took only a small sip before handing it back. He desperately wanted more, but couldn't bring himself to indulge in the face of her self-restraint. He closed the bottle, returned to the wall, and sat down. Beth reached out to stroke Ethan's hair. She looked so caring, so maternal – and yet she was a Justice of the Family Court. It didn't make any sense.

"Why'd you become a Justice?" he said.

"What? Why do you ask?"

"Does it matter?"

"It might."

Why did he ask? He wouldn't have cared at all, not so long ago. The Family Court was evil, and so were all the people who worked for it. Simple.

But this was Beth. She'd saved his life. More than once. He liked her, respected her. And yet...

"I can't understand how you do it. You're not a bad person. You care about Ethan. You saved my life. You're brave, dedicated... and part of the Family Court, and everything it does. I don't get it. You're a good person, but you still do what you do."

"And what do I do, Bey?"

"Help ungrateful children kill their parents."

And Beth laughed. And saw the look on his face. And shrugged an apology. "I'm sorry. It's just the way you put it... I've never helped anyone kill their parents, Bey. No Justice has. It's up to the parents. They can choose to accept the Choice of Death, or not. If they accept it, we provide the means. That's all."

"Call it what you like. Morally, it's murder."

"If you say so."

"No! Don't do that. Tell me why I'm wrong. I want to understand."

"Really? So, you're an open-minded off-comer, are you? That's a first. Are you sure you want to have this conversation? Here? Now?"

"We may never have another chance."

"That's true enough, I suppose. Okay, then. I joined the Family Court because I believe profoundly in Choosing. Without it, there's no possibility of moral balance. If I should decide to create a life–"

"Did you?"

"What?"

"Create a life. Do you have any children?"

"No."

"Why not? Afraid they'd make the wrong Choice?"

"No! I didn't have children because I could never be so selfish."

"What?" She had to be joking. But she looked so serious... "Having children is the least selfish thing anyone ever does. It means putting someone else's needs in front of your own. Caring about others, more than yourself."

"Caring about others? Nonsense. Children aren't 'others' – they're extensions of the self. People who really care about others dedicate themselves to looking after the poor, the sick, the disabled. Existing people, with existing needs. They don't create someone specifically to be dependent on them. Creating life isn't done to fulfil the child's needs. It can't be. The child doesn't have any; it doesn't exist. People have children because *they* want them. Because it fulfils their own needs. I can't conceive of anything more selfish that knowingly creating a conscious mind to satisfy one's own needs."

"You couldn't be more wrong. Being a parent is all about unconditional love."

"Unconditional? Really. Except people don't pick a random stranger to shower with unconditional love, do they?"

"No, of cou–"

"So, it *is* conditional. They don't just want to give unconditional love. They want to receive it. And they create someone specifically for the purpose, someone they know will be completely dependent on them, someone they expect to love them unconditionally."

"Not always. People adopt."

"They do. But people don't adopt adults, do they? Why? Because adults are independent. Not helplessly dependent. But I'll grant that adoption is a moral way to fulfil the need to parent. At least when people adopt, they aren't making a decision they have no right to make."

"Having children isn't about a 'decision'. It's the most natural thing in the fucking world. We're *meant* to have children."

"So what? Just because it's natural doesn't make it moral. We have all sorts of 'natural' urges it'd be immoral to fulfil. Human beings killing each other is about as natural as it gets, but we still call it murder. Choosing to create a life means creating a conscious being who's inevitably going to die. How is that any different from murder?"

"It's completely different! That life didn't exist until they created it."

"Neither did its death. The parents are as responsible for the child's death as they are for its life. That death wouldn't happen if they hadn't chosen to have children. Every child is dying from the moment it's born. It doesn't matter when or how. It's going to happen at some point. And it didn't have to."

"Everyone dies, Beth. That doesn't mean life's not worth living."

"Maybe not. Not for you. Not for me. But others disagree. And how can it ever be right to make that decision on someone else's behalf? That's what happens, if you have a child."

"Okay – so they don't want to be alive? They can always kill themselves."

"But they can't choose not to have been born. To become a parent is to create a conscious mind that one day, inevitably, will cease to exist. Once the child exists, the damage is already done, and there's no way to undo it. No one has the right to make that decision for anyone else."

Didn't she have any idea how crazy she sounded? His whole head was pounding with frustration. She was infuriating, impervious to reason. He had to make her understand. "You can't know we cease to exist when we die. What if there's life after death? What then?"

"That's even worse. Then there's no escape from consciousness, not even through suicide. How could you ever make that decision for another person? How could you live with yourself?"

"But... But... if no one had children, we'd all die out!"

"Yes. And?"

"And...? Fucking 'and'?"

"Yes. So, we die out. So what? Morality isn't subordinate to survival. If it were, any atrocity could be justified by necessity. Morality comes first. It has to, or it doesn't mean anything. And there's no way that creating a consciousness can ever be moral. Choosing doesn't change that. All it does is allow a retrospective possibility for a kind of justice. If I'd had a Choosing... Look, Bey. This is pointless. I joined the Family Court because I believed in it, and I still do. Let's leave it at that. You're an off-comer. You'll never understand."

"You're right. I don't under—"

He stopped; angry rebuttal washed away in a sudden rush of fear. The door was opening.

CHAPTER 44

In contrast with the ongoing slump in the housing sector, recent days have seen a mini-boom in consumer bi-tech sales. According to sources in the Office of Regulation, the roadblocks and other measures implemented as part of the State of Emergency have made it all but impossible for black market bi-tech dealers to operate, forcing potential customers to turn to legitimate suppliers.

— From: Noyan News Hour, *a Commonwealth Information Services Production*

Michael couldn't stop grinding his teeth. They hurt, but so what? He deserved the pain.

He was back where he started. Powerless. Pimped. By Jimawn. By Mary.

And he'd let them do it. He was *still* letting them do it.

And everyone knew. Even his own people

Except they weren't his now. They were Mary's. And she was Jimawn's. And so was he; coming running when called. Like a good little puppy.

Something gave in a back tooth. A spike of pain shot up his right cheek. *Mother,* but it hurt.

He turned his head. His own scowling reflection stared back at him from the opaqued window. Were they really on their way to the factory? Or was this summons something else? Something final.

Could he take them? There were only two of them. Janet, one of Mary's loyalists, sitting opposite; Luke beside him. Luke was more of an issue. Not that his size would help in this small a vehicle. And muscle wasn't much use against a gun...

The vehicle was slowing down. No way was this the factory. It *was* a trap.

The carapace lifted. He reached for his gun. And relaxed. It was a roadblock; one of the new random ones popping up all over the place, grinding business into the dust.

He moved his hand back to his lap. Four off-comers were approaching the vehicle. Arrogant. Confident. Armed. Streetlight glittered off the cloud of insects hovering above them. A pair of larger insects floated into the vehicle. One buzzed angrily by his left shoulder. The other did the same by Janet's ankle, and then Luke's waist. So that was where they were carrying. Good to know.

The off-comers were wary, suspicious. Why the guns? Janet was ready with the answer: who wouldn't want to be armed, traveling in a bi-tech vehicle with trad terrorists on the loose? The off-comers lost interest. They waited to be sure their insect spies didn't discover any contraband bi-tech, and then waved them on their way. The vehicle lowered its carapace and resumed its journey.

The sharp pain in his cheek had become a dull, throbbing ache. He smiled at Janet. She didn't smile back.

What to do?

Were they headed to the factory? Or some quiet place in the desert, where his body would never be found?

Maybe he should just shoot them now. He'd get one, at least. With luck, both.

But that would be it. He'd never get a chance at Mary, or Jimawn. He wouldn't live long enough.

It wasn't worth it. Jimawn's summons might still be real. Insulting. Infuriating. But real.

And if it wasn't real, that roadblock had to give them

pause for thought. If his body showed up now, or if he just went missing… They'd be the last people to have been seen with him. Not a good position to be in.

So, he'd go on pretending these two were just bodyguards, escorting him for his own safety. But he'd be ready. Better to die fighting than end up spread-eagled with someone shoving a roadroot up his ass.

How long had it been since the roadblock? Long enough. They should be at the factory by now. Unless…

What was that?

They were slowing down. Either they'd reached the factory, or–

The carapace lifted. Insipid, odorless air gave way to the familiar smell of oil and grease. It wasn't a trap. This was the factory. And Luke and Janet were focused outwards, like proper bodyguards. Janet took point. She hurried to the door, checked that everything was as it should be, and beckoned them over. He nodded to Luke to go ahead. Then he loosened his gun in its holster, and followed.

There was no welcoming party waiting inside; no one ready to grab him as he came through the door. His bodyguards were nothing but dark shapes disappearing towards the elevators. He followed at a distance, more confident than before, but still wary.

They didn't join him in the elevator. That made sense. He wouldn't need bodyguards below. Even so, his gun was out and ready when the doors opened. But there was only a single guard, and she nodded a greeting and stepped aside. Michael holstered his gun and set off down the corridor, shoulders crawling with tension. What better time to kill him than now, when he was off his guard?

But no. Jimawn wouldn't do it here. Too messy. And too upsetting for any poor, pampered bi-technician who happened upon the scene. Even so, he didn't properly relax until he turned the corner and knew he was safe.

There was a guard waiting at Jimawn's door. A

Gallaskian this time, and a hard man despite his soft off-comer clothing. He put out an arm to stop Michael entering.

"You're to see Nathan."

"I was asked to com–"

"You weren't asked. You were told. And I'm telling you Nathan has your orders. On your way."

Michael walked away. It was that, or put his hands around this mother's neck and squeeze the life out of him. But he couldn't. Not yet. He'd made that mistake with Hyrom, losing his temper, and with it Jimawn's respect. He wasn't going to do it again.

But it felt so good to kill the mother: a glorious, cathartic moment. It helped him rediscover himself. He wasn't born for slow, careful revenge. He needed to act. Waiting was for the weak. He'd rather die than be powerless again. But if he was going to die, he wanted to take Jimawn with him; not some functionary standing guard at his door.

Nathan's quarters weren't far away. The trad was a trusted lieutenant now. Maybe he always had been. He certainly didn't act like any trad. Trads didn't wear fancy off-comer dressing gowns. They didn't signal you to wait while they sat in their bed and finished reading through a sheaf of papers like some kind of fussy clerk. Was the man deliberately trying to bait him? Perhaps. If so, he was succeeding. *Scrape* waiting.

"I'm here," he said. "What's he want?"

Nathan sighed and set down the papers. "Obedience, generally. And competence. But right now? He has certain questions he'd like to have answered. Earlier tonight, three intruders showed up, here at the factory. Hetman Jimawn would like you to... interview... them. Were they alone? Are they expecting to be rescued? What exactly were they trying to achieve? You get the picture."

"I do."

"I thought you would. And Michael, do be careful. We

don't want them too badly damaged. The Hetman's planning on giving them a supporting role, when festivities begin. For that to work, their bodies have to tell the right story. Understand?"

"I–"

"Excellent. They're in the storeroom behind the main hydroponics chamber. I assume you know the way? Good. Report back to me when you're done."

It was deliberate. It had to be. The mother was trying to wind him up. Why? Was it some kind of test, to see if he could control himself? The scraper wasn't even looking at him anymore. He was back to reading his papers, like Michael wasn't even there. Like he was no kind of threat at all.

If he was still alive after killing Mary and Jimawn, this one was next.

A guard was waiting beside the storeroom door, slumped down in a chair with her head drooping. If she was asleep... But no, she scrambled to her feet as he approached. At least *she* was still scared of him. That was something.

He gestured towards the door. She unlocked it, pulled it open, and stepped aside. He entered the room... and stopped dead. And ground his teeth furiously until another flash of pain seared up his cheek.

Hotep. And the Justice.

And Nathan hadn't bothered to tell him.

The scraper probably thought he was funny.

Hotep was staring up at him, eyes bright with terror. The Justice was lying next to a third person – someone he didn't know. Not that it looked like it mattered. Unless it was a trick...

He stepped forwards and kicked the stiff in the small of the back, just in case. The Justice glared at him, but the stiff didn't react at all. Dead, or unconscious, then; not a trick. He waved the guard away.

"You can get out. I'm fine on my own."

The guard retreated. And locked the door. That was good. They'd have to unlock it to come in; he'd have plenty of warning of an interruption.

"Hello Justice. Beynan. Long time no see."

The Justice ignored him. She was still focused on the stiff. That was interesting. And possibly useful.

Hotep's eyes were wider than ever. "What do you want? Are you going to... hurt us?"

He smiled. There really weren't many people he wanted to hurt more than this off-comer. Only Jimawn. And Mary. And Nathan.

But they were the ones who wanted him to do it.

"That depends," he said.

The Justice looked up, infuriatingly calm. "There's no need to hurt him. He's terrified. He'll tell you anything you want to know."

"And doesn't that worry you, Justice?"

"Of course. But I see no reason for him to suffer unnecessary pain."

"There we differ, Justice. I can think of at least one good reason. I'd enjoy it. But you know what? It's his lucky day. Scrape Jimawn. If he wants to torture you, he can do it himself."

"You're not...? You're not...?" Hotep looked to be on the verge of tears. But the Justice's expression hadn't changed at all.

"What are you going to tell him?" she asked.

"That's my business."

"You're not worried he has us bugged?"

"I'm not."

Scrape. A bug. He should have thought of that. But it was too late to worry about it now.

"And you're not worried our stories won't match?"

"I don't think that's going to be a problem. I doubt you'll live long enough to talk to him again. The only reason he's keeping you alive is so your bodies stay nice and fresh You're the two most famous trads on Noyan.

Having you two as martyrs to the cause is going to help the coup no end." He nudged the third person with his foot. "Who's the stiff?"

"That's what this is all about? A coup d'état?"

"You didn't know? I'm disappointed in you, Justice. But never mind, you'll be right in the thick of it, when it happens – playing your very own posthumous part helping the cause."

"His name's Ethan," she said, calm as ever. "And he's not dead."

"Yet."

"A coup?" said Hotep. "That's it, then. The Autarchy gets bi-tech, *and* Noyan. Grandfather'll never forgive me."

"I think that's the least of your worries."

"Do you?"

The Justice tried, and failed, to stand up. "Why are you doing this?" she said. "You're a Noya. You can't want this. You have to help us stop him."

He stifled a laugh. Was this really the same woman who'd bullied her way past his people? So much had changed, in such a short time.

"Are you appealing to my patriotism?"

"I suppose I am."

"In that case, I'll tell you exactly what I'm going to tell Jimawn. That you're an idiot. That you and your friends had no idea what you were walking into. That there's no one coming to rescue you. That he doesn't have anything to worry about. And I think this little diversion, enjoyable as it's been, has gone on long enough. Hotep, come here."

"Why?"

"I said, come here."

Hotep crept over; cowering, shrinking into himself. And crumpled, bleating, when Michael's punched him in the eye.

It was so tempting to follow up with more, to administer a real beat-down... but the Justice had somehow found the strength to surge to her feet. Michael danced backwards. Her anger was strangely intimidating, despite her fragility.

"It's over, Justice," he said. "Don't make me hurt you, as well."

"You didn't have to enjoy it."

"Perk of the job." He knelt down and rubbed his knuckles in the blood matting the unconscious prisoner's hair. "Both of you – over here, and get some of this blood on yourselves. I want it to look as though I meant it."

"And if we don't?" said the Justice.

"Then *I'll* have to make it look as though I meant it."

She obeyed without obvious emotion; Hotep with pathetic eagerness to please. His left eye was already swollen. He was going to have an impressive black eye, by and by. If he lived long enough.

Michael made them step back. Then he knocked on the door for the guard. But he didn't turn his back, or lower his guard, until he was safely out of the room. Then he headed back to Nathan's quarters.

Nothing had changed. The scraper was still in bed, still reading through his papers. And still enjoying making Michael wait.

"Well?" he said, finally deigning to look up.

"Well, what?" Two could play the make-them-wait game.

Nathan rolled his eyes. "Do they know about the coup?"

"Of course."

"How?"

"I told them."

Nathan actually smiled, like he appreciated a bit of push back. Michael didn't believe it for a moment.

"Very good. And what did they know before you told them?"

"Nothing. They're a pair of idiots. I don't know about the other one. He didn't wake up. But I imagine he's the same. They had no idea about you, Jimawn, any of it."

"So why were they here?"

"Because they thought this was still my factory. They had no idea what they were walking into."

"And they were acting alone?"

"They were."

"You expect me to believe that?"

"I believe it."

"Do you? Do you really?"

The man was smirking; smug and arrogant as an off-comer. Was the storeroom bugged? Did he know Michael was lying? No. There'd have been a reception committee waiting to jump him the moment he walked in.

"You never really were a trad, were you, Nathan? Did you always work for Jimawn?"

Nathan set the papers down and swung his legs out of the bed. "That's an interesting question. I gather you've been asking a lot of questions recently. Moyem is beginning to be quite disturbed by it."

If Nathan shared that feeling, he wasn't showing it. He walked over to his desk, seemingly unconcerned that he was exposing his unprotected back. Dismissing Michael as a threat.

"Really?"

"Yes. You know, I don't think he entirely trusts you. He may even be wondering whether you shouldn't join your friends in the storeroom on a more permanent basis..."

Michael's throat tightened. Was that a warning? Why? It didn't make any sense.

Unless this was the trap he'd feared all along.

"Why should he think that?"

"I don't know. You tell me. Have you given him any reason to distrust you?"

Nathan pulled open a drawer. Michael tensed. What did he have in there? A gun? No. A flask, and two small glasses.

"Drink?"

Michael nodded. He didn't trust himself to speak.

"Personally, I'd have killed you the moment you realized you weren't really in charge. Moyem's a little too rational sometimes. He forgets other people bear grudges. Do you bear him a grudge, Michael?"

"I'm not that stupid."

Nathan filled the two glasses and offered one to Michael. He took it and put it to his lips. Smelled the brandy. But he was careful not to sip; not even when Nathan drank his freely.

"Tell me, Michael. Do you think our prisoners are well guarded? I mean, if they were to escape – a Justice of the Family Court, a high-ranking Homeworlder... People might listen to them. It could be a real threat to Moyem's plans, don't you think?"

Michael set the glass down on the desk. "What are you trying to tell me?"

"Tell you? Nothing? I was merely asking your opinion on our security arrangements. I think it's important to consult senior personnel on these matters. Especially at a time like this, when we only have a skeleton staff on duty. And there's even an autocopter on the roof, if you can believe it. If they were to somehow get to it... Do you think we have enough security, in the circumstances?"

Michael licked his lips. "No."

"No. Probably not. Thanks for the advice. I'll see something's done about it. In the morning. In the meantime, why don't you go get some sleep. I think Moyem wants you to wait around. Said something about making his mind up..."

"About what?"

"Oh, this and that." Nathan guided him firmly towards the door. "But, before you go... I never answered your question. No. I didn't always work for Moyem Jimawn."

The door closed in Michael's face. He was alone in the corridor. And completely lost.

What was this? Some bizarre loyalty test? Was he

supposed to go telling tales to Jimawn?

Maybe. And maybe he'd already failed by hesitating.

But if it wasn't a test… Why would Nathan want to warn him? And why encourage him to free the prisoners?

There was a game here. A game he didn't understand. He wasn't a player. He was a pawn.

Time to take himself off the board. Time to run.

The prisoners could go breed themselves. Jimawn was welcome to kill them, any way he wanted.

Except Nathan was right. Hotep and the Justice… they were important. They could make people listen. And if people listened, Jimawn was finished.

It wouldn't be as good as killing the mother, but it was better than nothing. And at least this way he'd go out fighting, not naked in the desert, screaming. He'd teach the scrapers he was still someone to be feared.

He retraced his steps to the improvised cell. This time, the guard didn't rise at his approach; she was asleep in her chair. He glanced up and down the corridor. If this was a trap, it was well set.

He crept along, revolver in hand. Still, the guard didn't move.

He didn't use the gun. That was for when he no longer had any no choice. For now, a broken neck was a much quieter – and far more satisfying – solution.

She woke, briefly, but not in time to save herself. He dropped the body, and waited for the trap to spring.

Still nothing. No outbreak of shooting. No command to halt. He was alone; just him, and the body.

Her gun was one of the new Gallaskian models Jimawn had provided. That was good. Off-comer weapons were far quieter than his revolver. The odds just shifted a little in his favor.

He took the keys from her belt and unlocked the door. Hotep looked up, mouth agape. The Justice saw the guard's body, and hurried to help him drag it inside.

"So, you changed your mind?" she said.

"Looks that way, doesn't it?"

They dropped the body in the corner. He straightened up and gestured at Hotep with the gun, more for convenience than to intimidate. "Come on – let's go."

Hotep didn't move. He was staring at the dead woman's twisted neck.

"Hotep! Wake up!"

"Come on, Bey," said the Justice. "You take his left arm. I'll take his right."

Michael looked over. The Justice was kneeling by her unconscious friend. And, unbelievably, Hotep was on his way to help. Were they really that scraping stupid?

"Drop him. We don't have the time."

Hotep looked tempted. The Justice acted like he hadn't even spoken. Between the two of them, they lifted the helpless man off the floor and hoisted his limp arms over their shoulders. Michael raised the gun and pointed it at the lolling head. "I said drop him."

Hotep shrank away. The head dropped a little. So did Michael's gun. But the Justice didn't even flinch.

"We're not leaving without him," she said.

"Drop him or I'll blow his scraping brains out."

"No, you won't."

"Why not?"

"Because if you do, I'll kill you."

"I have a gun."

"True. So, maybe you'll kill me. Either way, we're not leaving without Ethan. Is that really what you want?"

CHAPTER 45

Experts in the field assure me that old-fashioned projectile weapons rarely cause fatal injuries. Supposedly, they are highly ineffective, inaccurate, and as likely to injure the user as the target. I can only say: try getting shot at by one. They seemed horribly effective to me at the time.

– *From:* My Time on Noyan, Memories of a Youthful Exile, *The Rt. Hon. Beynan Hotep na Massowic*

Fuck, Bey's eye *hurt!* He could barely see anything to his left. Just a sliver of corridor, and Ethan's head bobbing up and down. The man might not be dead, but he was still a dead weight dragging them down.

Bey's right eye was still good, but the view wasn't much better: just endless corridor, and Ethan's useless fucking arm continually creeping upwards, forcing him to drag it back down again. And every time he did, it seemed he was taking yet more weight until he felt like he was carrying the man all by himself. He would have complained, but the last time he'd turned his head to look at Beth, she was so bent over it was a wonder she was upright at all.

Where the fuck was Michael? Was he really coming back? Or was this all some kind of trick – a fake escape to give them hope, just so the bastards could crush them that bit more?

But the dead guard hadn't been fake. They wouldn't kill one of their own, just to torture them, would they?

Fucking typical. Michael was a monster. The last person Bey ever wanted to see again. Except for right now. And now he was nowhere in fucking sight.

Fuck, this was hard. Every step hurt more than the one before. His leg muscles were burning. His back and shoulders ached. He just wanted to lie down and die. Or maybe not. But what he wouldn't give to drop Ethan, and go on without him...

It was easier, back in the cell. There'd been no hope then. Only distraction – arguing with Beth to push the fear away. But now there was hope. Hope, oscillating with terror. Every corner was a possible trap. And afterwards, the tension remained: a tight little knot in his stomach, waiting to expand at the least sign of danger.

It was a living nightmare. Anything would be better than this endless flight. Even waking up back in the cell.

His strength was seeping away, his shoulders sagging ever lower. Level floors were becoming an uphill struggle. Each step was harder than the last.

A movement, up ahead. His heart lurched. This was it, the end of all the effort and the hope.

A face. A hated face, but welcome now. Michael, beckoning to them from a corridor branching off to the right. The way out? A trap? It hardly mattered. He just wanted this to end. And no matter how desperate he was to hurry, he couldn't; not while Beth went plodding on at the same slow pace.

There was no trap around the corner. Just the elevator. And Michael. And a dead woman, with blood pouring from a gaping wound in her throat and pooling around her head.

Ethan's weight shifted. Beth was still moving. He'd stopped, but she hadn't. He lurched forwards, struggling to stay on his feet. There was slickness underfoot. He tried not to think about it. The elevator was right there, open, waiting for them. They were going to escape. They were really going to escape.

"Get in!" Michael waved them inside. Beth's pace, so painfully steady for so long, finally picked up.

The elevator was clean, white, antiseptic. This wasn't native tech. Nothing like. He shouldn't have been surprised earlier, when he saw Jimawn. Not at all. Wouldn't have been, if he hadn't been too scared to think straight.

The doors closed. Michael was inside with them. There was blood on his hands, spattered over his clothing.

Bey leaned back against the wall, letting it take some of Ethan's weight. Then everything grew heavier, including himself. The elevator was going up.

Movement, to his left. Was Ethan waking up? He craned his head, and let it slump back again. It was just Beth, gently pushing Ethan's hair away from his face.

The elevator began to slow. He felt it in his stomach, in the easing of Ethan's weight around his shoulders. And saw it in Michael's defensive crouch, a gun in each hand. Where did the second come from? And why now? What did he think was waiting for them?

The doors opened as silently as they'd closed. Michael dived outside, guns at the ready. And cursed, as he stumbled and almost fell. There was something on the ground in front of the doors.

"You've been busy," said Beth, dryly.

Everything snapped into focus. The thing in the doorway was a body. Two bodies – one male, one female – sprawled face down on the floor.

And Michael was confused. Afraid.

Michael was afraid. This wasn't his doing. Someone else had killed them; someone who might be watching right now. Watching, and aiming.

And then Michael was gone, fleeing into the darkness beyond the elevator light.

Leaving them exposed.

Ethan's arm was slithering away. Beth was moving again, taking Ethan with her – and in the process, dragging all three of them to the floor. Bey grabbed Ethan's wrist and staggered forwards. Weight settled jarringly on his shoulders, leaving him off-balance and framed in the doorway: a perfect silhouette for the benefit of any would-be assassin. And Beth chose that moment to slow down and maneuver oh-so-carefully around the bodies. He would have screamed, but his throat was so tight with panic he could barely breathe.

The doors were closing behind them. Bey used all his strength to drag them out of the narrowing rectangle of light.

Darkness fell. No shot rang out. They were alive, but not yet safe. There was another light source: dim native bulbs, somewhere high up towards the ceiling. And in the half-light, he could see Michael crouched behind a squat pillar, scanning their surroundings, guns at the ready. Bey followed his gaze. Half-glimpsed structures loomed threateningly behind a skeleton of metal stairways and gantries. Every wall, every open space, was crisscrossed with pipes and walkways. But there was no sign of life, just the two dead bodies by the elevator.

Michael straightened up. He headed for a wrought iron stairway and started to climb. "This way," he said.

"What? But–" Bey gave up. It was madness heading up instead of out, but Beth had already set off, and he had no choice but to follow.

Michael's footsteps echoed loudly in the hollow space. Bey sped up, forcing Beth to follow suit. They reached the stairs, and stopped. Ethan was a dead weight; Beth a cripple. It was just too much. He longed to drop them both and run up the stairs, but conscience held him back. Conscience, and inertia.

Then the alarm went off.

It was appalling – an ear-splitting howl so loud it

triggered a firework display in his bad eye. And somehow, gave him the strength to haul Ethan up the first three steps.

The burst of energy didn't last. His shoulders and thighs burned with the effort. His lungs couldn't take in enough air. His grip on Ethan's arm began to loosen. He was going to collapse.

A hand reached past his shoulder, grabbed hold of Ethan's collar, and hauled him upwards. Michael had returned. He was helping. Bey went to thank him, and flinched away in the face of raw fury. He hurried to take as much of the burden as he could.

Together, they carried Ethan up flights of stairs and across narrow walkways, while Beth struggled along behind. The whole time, Michael was scanning the shadows, gun in hand. There was no way this was a trick. Michael really was helping them escape.

They reached a final walkway, and a half-open door. Michael slipped Ethan's arm from his shoulder, drew his second gun, and disappeared through the door. Bey staggered backwards, unbalanced by the sudden shift in weight. He tottered helplessly towards the gantry's edge – trying to save himself, but knowing it wasn't going to work. He was going to topple over, and fall to certain death, Ethan beside him.

And then Beth was pulling them back. And taking up her share of the burden once again. Together, they tottered towards the door. The alarm shut off – the sudden silence instantly more terrifying than the noise had been. He surged ahead, forcing Beth to do the same.

Outside, night was giving way to dawn. The dim light revealed a maze of pipework and gantries on a flat roof. Everywhere he looked there were more girders, more pipes, more gantries crisscrossing the corrugated iron roof. In the very center, four gantries came together to form a square. And perched there, atop the railings, was the most beautiful thing he'd ever seen.

An autocopter.

A wonderful, elegant, modern, wet-dream of an autocopter.

It was small – a four-seater, little bigger than a standard domestic vehicle – but it was perfect.

He blinked away tears. An autocopter. Of course. What else? Suddenly, their mad rush to the roof made sense. They were going to make it. He wasn't going to die!

But Beth had stopped. Worse, she'd dug in her heels. What was wrong with her? Seconds from safety, and she just stopped? Was she having a stroke? Her whole body was rigid; eyes wide; gaze fixed on the autocopter.

"I'm not getting in that thing."

"What? Are you fucking crazy?"

Un-fucking-believable. He'd watched her stand in front of Michael, calm as anything, and invite him to shoot her.

And now she was afraid of flying?

He didn't have the time for this. His life – his life! – could be at stake. He used his weight to force her onwards.

Michael hurried back to help. There was some kind of green dot on his forehead. Surely that hadn't been there before? What could–?

The dot disappeared – and with it, the back of Michael's head, blowing away in a silent explosion.

Bey was too shocked even to scream. He turned to Beth. There was a green dot behind her right ear.

He shoved sideways. The dot moved, racing towards him. And Ethan's face ripped apart, spraying blood and brains everywhere as something punched them from behind. Then he was landing, hard, on the unforgiving gantry. A lightning bolt of pain shot up from his left knee, momentarily overwhelming everything, even his survival instinct. Then it was gone, leaving him face-down in warm red horror, trapped beneath the weight of Ethan's body. He struggled to free himself – and then Beth was helping him up. Together they ran, limped, stumbled towards the autocopter. Bey's scalp itched, his skin tightening against the terrible green dot that must be – mustn't be – there.

They were so close! The autocopter stairs were right in front of them. He turned to help Beth through the wide-open door. And she slammed into him, blood blossoming on her right shoulder.

He heaved her bodily up the stairs. Leaving himself all alone, the perfect target. It was almost more frustrating than frightening. To be so close to the promise of safety, but know that any second now, a bullet was going to...

The moment stretched. He threw himself up the stairs and through the open door. And somehow, miraculously, the bullet never came.

"Autocopter! Get us out of here. Now. Emergency! Go!"

The autocopter leapt skywards. Bey was thrown backwards, tumbling over Beth to land awkwardly in a cushioned seat. He lay there, winded, counting the seconds. How long before they were out of range? Would the assassin's bullets recoil from the shell, or rip straight through and send the autocopter tumbling from the sky? He waited, stomach tight with horrified anticipation, for the shot that would send them spinning to their deaths. And waited. The autocopter leveled off. He crawled past Beth and peered out of the viewport. There was no sign of the factory, just dawn breaking over the empty desert. How far had they come? Were they out of range?

"Autocopter: get low! Put some scenery between us and the factory – or whatever you call the place we just left. Now. Move! Top speed. Forget safety margins. This is an emergency."

The autocopter dived again. Bey was thrown backwards. His elbow smacked into Beth's side and, astonishingly, she cried out in pain. She was alive. Her right shoulder was a mess of blood and bone, but she was alive. And complaining. Her voice was barely more than a whisper, but no less vehement for that. "Get us down. Can't stand it. Get us down. Not a flying machine. Walk."

And Bey laughed.

It was wonderful, the funniest thing ever. They were alive.

"Cheer up, Beth, for fuck's sake. I just saved your life. Again."

She didn't respond. Was she trying to be brave? Or just too hurt to argue? It didn't matter. He crawled into the seat beside her. She needed medical assistance right now, and not the primitive local kind. And he needed to warn the embassy about Jimawn before it was too late.

"Autocopter: take us to the Commonwealth embassy."

Beth shook her head. "No... The Assembly... Take us to the–"

Her head slumped back. Whatever last burst of energy she'd found, it was gone. He reached over and patted her good arm. Her priorities were not his.

Outside, dawn was turning into day. The autocopter skimmed the ground, barely twenty feet up. Shades of ochre flew by dizzyingly fast. How long before they reached the city? And what then? How would the embassy react when he showed up in an autocopter?

Shit. Beth was right. They couldn't go to the embassy. Someone there wanted him dead. Would anyone even listen? Or would they just unleash the hives to tear the autocopter apart?

But he had to warn them. And Beth had to get treatment. How?

"Autocopter: change course. Head for..."

If not the embassy, then where? He couldn't give up. He wouldn't be able to live with himself. But who could he turn to? Not Ambassador Ashef, and not Undersecretary Maitland either. He'd never get through to them. The most important news on this or any other planet, and no one was willing to listen...

News.

Of course.

"Autocopter: Head for Zachary Street. We're going to

pay Mahtal a visit. And Wattles, of course. Mustn't forget Wattles."

The autocopter banked, veering right. It rose higher, picked up the line of the Spate, and followed it past small native villages until they reached the outskirts of the city proper. Then it turned north and flew over a dense grid of grim native streets. There were only a few isolated bi-tech houses below, tiny islands of nature in an angular wasteland. Then everything changed. The too-straight roads gave way to sinuous curves and spiral streets fringed with living houses identical to his own little home-away-from-home, so modern for Noyan, so antiquated back on Homeworld.

The autocopter slowed down. They were approaching Zachary Street. What number was Mahtal's house? Never mind. All they had to do was head for the narrow end of the spiral.

"Autocopter: take us to the end of the street, away from the main road. Then land."

Mahtal's property looked different from the air. Bigger. It was three time the size of Bey's own, and on a plot that was larger still. Did 3-V really pay that well here on Noyan? Or was this a marker of Mahtal's semi-official relationship with the embassy? He hoped so. The cozier Mahtal and Ashef were, the better.

The autocopter landed at the very edge of Mahtal's property. That helped. The less distance he had to carry Beth, the better.

He prodded her good arm. There was no reaction. Her face was ashen grey, and smeared with blood. How much was hers? And how much was Ethan's? He inspected her ruined shoulder. The blood was dripping, not pouring. Was that a good sign? Or the worst possible?

Mahtal's mansion was a lot more sophisticated than his own place. It was bound to have some kind of emergency treatment capability – enough, surely, to keep Beth alive until she could get proper treatment. Assuming she wasn't already dead.

He dragged her to the door, let go, and climbed down the stairs. Then he turned, grabbed her ankles and pulled her towards him. She slipped forwards – slowly, at first, and then too quickly. He straightened up to stop her falling; and almost dropped her when she groaned. That hopeful sound was all the encouragement he needed. He knelt down, hoisted her over his left shoulder and managed, just, to stand up.

Mahtal's front door was a few yards, and an endless distance, away. He lumbered towards it, placing his feet with immense care. If he tripped and dropped her now, he'd never be able to pick her up again.

"House: I want to speak to Dil."

There was a short, and deeply worrying, delay. What if Mahtal wasn't in? There was no reason he should be. He was probably off somewhere, recording an item for his show. What to–

"And I'd love to speak to you, Beynan. It's not every day the biggest news story on Noyan just shows up at my door. And in an unregistered 'copter, no less. And with... I presume that's Beth the Justice over your shoulder?"

"It is. Let us in, Dil. She's hurt."

"Yeah, you don't look any great shakes yourself. As for letting you in... Are you armed?"

"No."

"What about her?"

"Armed? She's not even fucking conscious."

"So... Well, my house believes you. Come on in."

The door opened. Bey staggered inside. And ducked instinctively as Wattles swooped in for a close up. Mahtal was waiting at the far end of the entrance hall, sleepy-eyed, wrapped in a dressing gown.

And pointing a small native handgun straight at him.

"Is that really necessary, Dil?"

Bey was past the point of being frightened, but he still had room for irritation. Mahtal ignored him. "God, you're in a state. What happened to you?"

"Any chance of some help here?"

"None at all. Bring her inside. Then we'll talk."

Mahtal stepped back, making room. Bey staggered after him and found himself in a small reception room with a single well-cushioned sofa. He lowered Beth onto it, and straightened up. Then he turned to face the journalist. "Can I at least have a drink?"

"Of course. What would you–?"

And Bey punched him. Hard. In the stomach.

He'd had enough – more than enough – of people pointing guns at him.

The punch was astonishingly effective. Bey's one-eyed vision had deceived him. He'd meant to hit Mahtal – not try and punch right through him. The journalist collapsed in on himself, gasping for breath. Bey plucked the gun from his nerveless fingers. And all the while, Wattles faithfully recorded the scene from above, entirely indifferent to his master's fate.

"Sorry, Dil."

He was, too. That punch hurt his hand.

"Hou... Hou..."

Bey put the gun to the journalist's head.

"Complete that word, and I'll blow your brains out. Think your house can stop me before I pull the trigger? Because I really doubt it."

Mahtal closed his mouth, abruptly. Bey smiled. "Okay, Dil. First, have you done anything stupid like calling the embassy? If you have, better tell me now."

"No. Wanted story first. Then call."

"You're all heart, Dil."

"Not... Not traitor, though."

"Neither am I, Dil. Neither am I. Now listen. You want a story. I'll give you a story. The biggest you'll ever have. Because the embargo's busted to fuck, and Moyem Jimawn's planning a coup d'état. Interested?"

Mahtal nodded. Slowly. He was getting his breath back,

but he was still dazed. Bey's smile widened. "First things first. Beth needs medical attention. Right now."

"Of course. But. Need to talk to embassy first. Immediately."

"Can't. The minute they know I'm here—"

"They already know."

Bey brought the gun back to the ready. "You said you hadn't called them!"

"I didn't! You came here in a fucking autocopter, Bey. They'll have tracked it. Hous—"

"Stop!"

"For fuck's sake, Bey! Put the gun down. I have to call Ashef. It's the only chance you've got."

Bey stared at him. Mahtal was himself again, and looking him straight in the eye... Fuck it. He had to risk it. That was why he'd come here – to find a way to make the embassy listen.

"Okay. But I warn you, the last time I tried to talk to the embassy, they destroyed a whole house just to get at me. And they didn't care who else was in there."

"Fine. Say I believe you. Do you think anyone's going to risk something like that with Wattles around? Useful things, cameras. Hou..." He looked to Bey for approval, then carried on. "House: get me Ambassador Ashef."

The embassy call sign appeared in the corner of the room, and gave way almost instantly to Undersecretary Maitland. "Dil. I wondered when you'd be calling. Perhaps you'd care to explain why an unregistered autocopter is... Ah. Beynan. I should have known. Are you all right, Dil?"

"Fine."

"You say that, and yet he seems to be holding you at gunpoint. Embassy—"

"No, Nicholas. Wait. It's not what you think. Don't do it."

Bey blinked. And swallowed. What could the embassy have made Mahtal's house do to him? It didn't bear thinking about. He lowered the gun. Mahtal visibly relaxed.

"It's not what you think, Nicholas. Bey has something to tell the Ambassador. And Ashef has to listen. Right now. It's important."

"Sorry, Dil. That's not going to happen. Not even for you. Not without running it by me first."

Mahtal started to argue, but Bey shut him off. "It's okay, Dil. We don't have any choice. Undersecretary, I know you think I'm some kind of traitor, but–"

The house chimed, cutting him short. "Attention. Autocopter landing. Embassy personnel disembarking."

Maitland didn't even blink. He'd known this was coming. Bey had to make him understand.

"Undersecretary. Listen. Moyem Jimawn was working with the Gwahnals. He's got a bi-tech factory. You have to stop him. He's planning a coup–"

"Attention. Embassy personnel are entering the building."

Mahtal stepped between Bey and the 3-V. "Call off your men, Nicholas!"

For the briefest of moments, Bey was aware of a strange smell. Then there was only darkness.

CHAPTER 46

...pursuant whereto, our faithful and beloved servant, Moyem Jimawn, is hereby appointed Prefect Provisoriam of the said territory upon its Acquisition and Elevation, and granted sole right, title and interest in any and all resources acquired thereby. Let none hinder him in the pursuit of the said rights and duties under pain of Our displeasure. Given under Our hand in the thirteenth year of Our reign...
    – *From:* A Monopoly on Death: The Role of Imperial Letters Patent in Covert Warfare, *Dr. L. M. Beau*

The honorable Moyem Jimawn, Knight Bachelor, Senior Novice in the Most Noble Order of Grand Imperial Servitors, Worshipful Hetman in the Imperial Navy, Cultural Attaché with the Autarch's Mission to Noyan, Officer, Gentleman and sometime spy was woken by the intruder alarm. He reached instinctively for his swordstick, rolled out of bed and stood en garde in the darkness, waiting.

The moment stretched. No attack came. He moved away from the bed, silent and surefooted in the darkness. He didn't plan on being an easy target for any would-be assassin.

Two sharp knocks on the door; then a delay, and two more. It was the correct signal, but could he trust it? He waited, nerves stretched taut, sword motionless.

"Hetman?"

Jimawn lowered his sword. Hartan's loyalty was unquestioned. He called out permission to enter.

The door opened. Light poured in, but Hartan remained outside. He was focused outwards, gun pointed unwaveringly at the sole entrance from the corridor; a liegeman intent on defending his lord. Any potential assassin would find himself in the sights of a weapon far more sophisticated than any Jimawn allowed his native servants.

The alarm was even louder with the bedroom door open. It echoed up and down the corridor, overlayed with the sound of booted feet.

He sheathed the swordstick, twisting the ornate head to lock it in place. The danger was past. No assassin could hope to get at him now. "Relax, Hartan. Whatever it is, the native cadres can deal with it."

"Yes, Hetman."

Jimawn smiled. Hartan's stance, and focus, were as rigid as ever. Hartan didn't trust the natives, and wasn't about to start doing so now, no matter what Jimawn said. That was the problem with family retainers. They never quite forgot your childhood, and having to favor their judgement over yours on matters of safety. It ingrained an unfortunate habit of disobedience.

He thumbed a control on the swordstick's head. "Operations. What's the alarm?"

A familiar native face – the man's name was on the tip of his tongue, but just wouldn't come – flickered into blue-tinged holographic life above the stick. "The prisoners, sir. They're not in their cell. And Abigail's dead."

The man was staring at something unseen: the surveillance screens, presumably. Good. He wasn't letting the call distract him.

"She was on guard?"

"Yes, sir."

Jimawn frowned. Abigail should have been able to handle the prisoners. Hotep couldn't have killed her; wasn't even man enough to try. The unconscious auxiliary was certainly no threat. The Justice? Had she been faking fragility? No, the old woman was practically a cripple. And unarmed.

But she *was* a Justice of the Family Court, and Abigail *was* a native. Had she hesitated, and died as a result?

No. He didn't buy it. They hadn't escaped. Someone had let them out. "Very well. Inform me when they're caught. And turn off that alarm. It's annoying."

A flick of the thumb, and he was alone with Hartan. "See, Liegeman. Nothing to worry about. Put the gun away and dress me."

There was something pleasantly reassuring about the familiar ritual of dressing; a reassurance he needed. It was a real effort to maintain an air of calm for the benefit of the servants. Because he wasn't calm. Not deep down. He'd been living on his nerves ever since Sanja was murdered. And the closer he came to success, the more an incident like this disturbed him. If anything went wrong now, when everything he'd planned and hoped for was his for the taking…

It was so close. All the years of planning were coming to fruition. He'd traded everything – all his family's wealth, built over generations – for a Letter Patent, and a chance to become an Ancestor. And all because he'd seen what others missed: the unbelievable opportunity in Fange's resentment at his posting to Noyan. They only saw what Fange saw: a primitive backwater world, devoid of resources, irredeemably perverse. But Jimawn had seen a lever.

Fange had been pathetically easy to persuade. What better way to revenge himself on the family that exiled him, than to use their own bi-tech against them? The embargo was a dead letter anyway, honored more in the breach than the observance. Why shouldn't Fange push the limits, weaken the Commonwealth's hold on Noyan, and create his own fiefdom? Better to rule here, surely, than continue to accept the crumbs at his family's table?

It had all gone so smoothly. Too smoothly. Jimawn had begun to take it for granted, to anticipate the glorious day when Noyan and all its resources – including poor, deluded Fange's factories – would belong to him. And with them, the greatest prize of all: a monopoly on bi-tech throughout the Autarchy, backed by an unassailable Imperial Patent. Noyan would go from despised backwater to the most important of all imperial possessions. And Jimawn would be its undisputed ruler.

And then Sanja Gwahnal died.

He'd never doubted it was murder, not from the first. But who killed him? Some rival at the Mission, finally grasping the scope of his ambition and moving to forestall him? Had the Nuncio infiltrated an agent to confound him? No. The Nuncio had the resources, but he'd never betray the Autarch, no matter his jealousy of Jimawn's purchased authority. For all his faults, the Nuncio was no traitor.

And it couldn't be the Commonwealth. If they knew this factory existed, there'd be no subtle infiltration of agents: just an all-out assault to prevent their precious bi-tech from falling into the wrong hands.

His hands.

So, if not the Nuncio, and not the Commonwealth, then who? Some misguided native acting out of loyalty to their noxious Family Court. One of Nathan's fanatics, perhaps?

"The family crest, my lord?"

Hartan was back, jacket in hand. It was much more formal than his usual factory wear; high-collared, made of stiff brocade, intricately figured with the bold loops and whorls of the family device. Perfect. It mattered not at all that only Hartan and he would understand its significance. It was a call to duty, to stoicism, and spoke to him at a level below thought. He nodded his approval.

The alarm finally cut off. Hartan continued his careful inspection for lint, stray hairs and other calamities. Scrutiny complete, he tied off Jimawn's pony tail with a fresh black ribbon.

Jimawn watched the door, swordstick at the ready, unwilling to lower his defenses even in this most secure and intimate of spaces. Hartan stepped back for a final review – more thorough and trustworthy than any mirror – straightened his master's cravat with the lightest of touches, and declared himself satisfied. Jimawn thumbed the controls again. "Situation update."

"Unclear, Hetman. Multiple casualties, including prisoners. Unauthorized autocopter departure."

"Shoot it down."

"Acknowledged. We're trying, Moyem."

"Try harder."

He cut the connection. Hartan was glaring at the space where the holograph had been, outraged by the native's unthinking use of his master's first name. Jimawn sympathized. The natives were simply untrainable. He'd happily swap every last one of them for a single squadron of solid, disciplined Gallaskians. But that wasn't possible. Not until Noyan was absorbed into the Autarchy. At which point, he could bring in as many Gallaskians as he wanted, and replace the Noyim with a more compliant population.

But he was getting ahead of himself. Noyan wasn't his, yet.

And might never be, if that autocopter got away. Who was on it? And what if the idiots failed to shoot it down?

On the other hand… Did it make a difference if they succeeded? The Commonwealth couldn't possibly miss an autocopter being shot down – and by Gallaskian systems, at that. Either way, his enemies would be coming. The time for patience was over. He could no longer afford to wait until every last piece was perfectly positioned. Now was the time to strike.

"Onwards, Liegeman. We're going to Operations."

He hated rushing. It wasn't his style at all. But what else could he do? Everything had been accelerating since Sanja died. This was just another ratchet upwards, a final headlong race towards the finish line, and victory. Or defeat.

The operations room was far busier than it should have been at this time. Many stations had twice their normal complement of personnel, some with tactical gear pulled hastily over nightclothes. That was good to see; a sign of seriousness, for all the lack of discipline.

No one reacted to his arrival. Their focus was on the fleeing autocopter, and the effort to shoot it down.

It was still in the air, then. That was unfortunate.

He sauntered over to his chair, sat down and placed the swordstick in its holder. A good leader kept his doubts to himself, even when the screens on the far wall showed a tiny green autocopter evading all pursuit.

"Refreshments, if you please, Hartan. Waking early does give one such an appetite."

He never should have sanctioned the manufacture of that autocopter – not until Noyan was his. It was an act of hubris, and he was paying for it now, in nerves and sweat. And the effort it took to hide his frustration.

"Tea, Hetman?"

Hartan was at his punctilious best, bowing at just the right angle, heels together, back straight. The delicate yellow cup looked impossibly fragile in his big, warrior's hands. Jodan took it, and sipped appreciatively.

At the very least, he should have had a remote self-destruct installed. Or, better yet, something to force the autocopter to return to base.

The room was quieter now. Fewer people were focused on their screens; fewer still actively trying to target the autocopter. It was just too far away. The tiny green icon was at the very edge of the wall, on the verge of disappearing entirely off the edge of the map.

People were turning to look at him. Not openly. Just quick furtive glances. At least for now. He drained the last of the cup, smiled at Hartan, and asked for another; and perhaps a pastry this time.

The vermin who betrayed him would suffer for this. He'd make an example of them that the natives would remember for generations. Something to make the Gwahnals' death appear merciful by comparison.

The second cup arrived, together with small sugar-dusted pastry. The room was completely silent now. His servants were no longer hiding their glances. They were looking to him for guidance. He took a bite of the pastry, chewed unhurriedly, and washed it down with tea. Then he set the cup aside.

"Well? Who sounded the alarm?"

"I did, Hetman."

The answer came from the doorway; Nathan, a long gun cradled in his arms. Mary was at his side. Both of them were sweating and short of breath.

"You, Nathan?"

"Yes, Hetman."

'Hetman', was it? So formal – unusual in a native, even a quick learner like Nathan. The man was afraid. And with good reason.

"Why you? Why not one of the guards?"

"I was the one who found–"

"Yes, but why? You were checking on the prisoners personally? In the middle of the night? That seems... unusual."

"It is, Hetman. But when Michael took so long to return–"

"Michael."

"Yes, Hetman."

"Ah. Of course. Michael. I presume he's in the autocopter?"

"No, Hetman. He's on the roof. Dead. Him and the

auxiliary both. I clipped the Justice as well, but Hotep got her into the copter."

"Did he now? Did he really? Amazing. You never can tell about people, Nathan. Remember that. I suppose you absolutely had to kill Michael?"

"I did, Het–"

"Yes, yes. Of course." He turned his gaze on Mary. "Well, Mary, it looks like you were right. I shouldn't have kept Michael alive, after all. But there's no point crying over unspilt blood. This is a time for action. Order all the cadres to their assigned positions. Tell them to wait for our signal. We have to move now. Today. Before the Commonwealth has time to react."

"Yes, Hetman. But…" She swallowed, glanced unhappily at Nathan. "We hadn't planned on mobilizing on such short notice. We won't be able to get everyone in posi–"

"How many?"

"Sir?"

"How many units can we get in place by…" He glanced at the clock. How long would it take the Commonwealthers to react? Not long. They could move very quickly when their power was threatened. "…say, noon?"

"Eighty percent. Maybe a little more. Maybe a little less."

Eighty? He'd hoped for more. But this was no time to show weakness, or hesitation.

"Good. That's more than enough. Give the order."

There was no hesitation. Just a quick, "Yes, Hetman," and she was striding to her station. But Nathan hadn't moved. And he was frowning.

"Are you sure, Hetman? No one's going to listen to them. They're fugitives. The Commonwealth'll shoot them on sight."

Hartan was bristling. It was heart-warming, and more than a little amusing. How to respond? Slap Nathan down, and satisfy Hartan? Or indulge the man. For now.

"They might," he said. "But I rather doubt it. Not with an unregistered autocopter flying right at them. They'll want to talk first. Once Ashef realizes their precious embargo's been broken..."

"Fuck. Of course."

"Yes. As you say. Of course."

Jimawn frowned. Something was bothering him. But what? Nathan's impertinence? The need to rush? No. But there was definitely...

"Hetman?"

Hartan was offering another pastry. He reached for it; and saw Mary looking to him for guidance. Was she waiting for him to explain himself to Nathan before following orders? And these two were the best natives in his employ. The sooner he was rid of them all, the better.

"Go ahead, Mary. Give the signal. And Nathan, ready your cadre for action. We strike at noon."

There was a moment of almost total silence. Then Mary was barking orders at her assistants, and Nathan was running back down the corridor. Good. He should run. His fanatics were at the heart of the critical path. The capture of the Assembly must seem like the work of traditionalists intent on overthrowing a corrupt institution, not a Gallaskian takeover. Not until it was too late for anyone to stop him.

He settled back in his chair and took another bite of pastry. His mouth was so dry it was difficult to swallow, but he carried on regardless. It was important to portray quiet confidence at a time like this. There was nothing else he *could* do. He'd given the orders. Now it was down to his servants. His task had been the months and years of planning and preparation. Now he could only watch and wait. His leadership would not be required again until there were setbacks. And there would be setbacks. There were always setbacks.

The room buzzed with activity. Everywhere he looked,

people were hard at work. Plans long prepared were finally being implemented; orders were being passed; screens updating with fresh information. The natives had taken very well to their new equipment – so astonishingly modern for them, so terrifyingly ancient to him.

Michael. Of course, Michael. He'd been a fool to let the man live.

He finished the last of his pastry, patted his lips with the napkin – an elegant piece of spider-silk, with a single fractal whorl spiraling out from the center – and looked across to where Mary was pacing the floor. She was talking intently into her headphones, gaze fixed on the red dots appearing on the master wall map. None had yet turned green, nor would for several hours. He waited patiently for her to end the call.

"Mary. You still sure Michael didn't kill Sanja? This doesn't make you change your mind?"

"No, Hetman." The tone was confident. The body language less so. Was she having doubts? Or simply afraid he was judging her by association? Maybe – and maybe she was right.

"I was with him when he heard about Sanja's death," she said. "He was as shocked as anyone. I don't think he became a threat until after you... took him into your service."

"After I ignored your advice, you mean?"

"I didn't say that, Hetman."

"Didn't you? Don't worry, Mary. I forgive you. You were right. But you're wrong about the Commonwealth killing Sanja. If they had the least suspicion of what the Gwahnals were doing, we wouldn't be sitting here, untouched. And they'd have gone after Fange, not his son."

"Unless the Justice was on the right track in the first place, Hetman. Maybe, if the embassy thought he was going to exercise the Choice of Death..."

He laughed. He couldn't help himself. There was

something almost heroic about the natives' stubborn inability to grasp how foul their customs seemed to others.

"My dear Mary, I can absolutely promise you that it would never have occurred to them. But let's say it did. All they'd have done was ship Sanja back to a Commonwealth world. And if for some mad reason they decided to kill him, they wouldn't have done it that way. The last thing they'd ever do is risk damaging the prestige of their precious bi-tech."

She held up a warning finger: a call was coming in on her earpiece. He waved her away. She had more important things to do than speculate about Sanja's death. They could talk later; if he kept her around. He'd have to think about that. How useful would she be, after he'd won? His chief mistake so far had been a failure to dispose of people quickly enough. Not just Michael. The Gwahnals, too. To think they'd been willing to risk everything just for a petty business advantage... Commonwealthers: they were almost as bad as natives. No honor. He should have killed Fange and Amaya years ago, and installed Sanja in their place.

The morning wore on. A cluster of markers in the bi-tech suburbs turned green. The snatch teams were in place, ready to pick up all those vulnerable family members the embassy really should have thought more carefully about. Now they just had to stay out of sight until the other cadres were ready. That would be a while yet. There was still more red and orange than green on the map. And his self-imposed deadline of noon was fast approaching.

This was all Sanja Gwahnal's fault. Why did the idiot have to get himself killed?

All Jimawn's hopes, his future, his family's future, depended on the outcome of this day. And he was having to rush, to strike before he was ready.

There was no screen at his desk, no commlink. A good commander delegated. His role was to receive information, and make decisions. Hence the wall screens, and the two items on his desk: a 3-V, and what looked like a native radio. But no native device would have worked this far underground.

He checked them both, listening for word of his strike teams – unlikely, but possible if one were discovered prematurely – but most importantly, for news of the autocopter and its notorious passengers. There was nothing. Was it possible he still retained the advantage of surprise?

No. The autocopter might have gone unnoticed by the media, but it would not have escaped the attention of the Commonwealth embassy.

What to read into their silence? Panicked confusion? Or a ruthless pursuit of tactical advantage. There was no way to know. He would hope for the former, and plan for the latter.

Except that there was no more room for planning. All he could do now was react to events as they unfolded.

Noon approached. There was a good deal of green on the map now. The densest clusters were by the radio station and the Assembly.

There was still too much red: useless cadres, scattered across the map. The ones who couldn't be mobilized on such short notice.

The moment finally arrived. Everyone who could be mobilized had been. Mary looked to him for the go-ahead. He gave it with a nod. The room – relatively quiet for the last quarter-hour – erupted in a frenzy of renewed activity. And all across the map, green dots were in motion.

He turned on the radio. The first word of success – or failure – should come from there.

For ten achingly long minutes, there was nothing. The news station was full of the local, the parochial, the trivial. It all floated past him, an endless flow of irrelevant chatter.

Then, abruptly, the station went off air.

He looked up. On the wall map, the radio station had turned green. Mary glanced back, and nodded. The station was his.

Five minutes later, the station came back online. This time, everything was different. Including the announcer. A fresh voice – young, enthusiastic – was calling on loyal Noyim to rise against the off-comers and their corrupt enablers. The Assembly had voted to rescind the State of Emergency and expel the Commonwealth from Noyan. Collaborators in the Assembly had been rounded up and were being held, pending trial for treason.

So far, so positive. There was no need to listen further. This was news he'd helped to script. He turned to the 3-V. A panicked announcer was warning Commonwealth citizens to stay in their homes: terrorists were rounding up innocent citizens and committing atrocities. Hostages were being taken, demands made. People should shelter in place, and trust to their homes to defend them. Embassy personnel were on route to assist.

Atrocities? Hardly. The teams had been warned only to use violence if they met determined resistance.

Unless... Were ordinary natives rising to his call, and proving more militant than his own troops? How long would they last against vengeful embassy personnel? Not long, no doubt. But the more pressure they took off his teams, the better. Even the latest Gallaskian weapons were outclassed by the Commonwealth's bi-tech arsenal, and his cadres had access only to old, long-discarded stock. It was an unfortunate necessity. Gallaskian involvement in the coup must remain deniable. For now. Until the Assembly formally called on the Autarch for help. In the meantime, the more natives who died at Commonwealth hands, the better.

His sword-stick vibrated. Of course. How predictable. He silenced the 3-V with a word, plucked the stick from its holder, and thumbed the controls.

"Excellency?"

The Nuncio's fat face rose from the stick's head, flabby cheeks wobbling with barely-suppressed fury. "What in the

Autarch's name do you think you're doing, Jimawn?"

"Are you really sure you want me to answer that question, Excellency? When others might be listening?"

"If you...? Why did...?"

It was all Jimawn could do not to laugh. The fat old fool had no authority to give Jimawn orders, and he knew it. He couldn't even demand a proper explanation; not when there was even the remotest chance of their conversation being intercepted.

The Nuncio made a visible effort to get himself under control. "Very well. But I insist on a delivery for the Mission garden. I want some... cuttings where they're safe from blight. In case anything should happen to your own plants. Do you understand me?"

Jimawn didn't even bother to hide his amusement. "I'm sorry, your Excellency. But I can't go against the Autarch's express wishes."

Especially when those wishes were so ruinously expensive to secure. If he relaxed his control over bi-tech, the Nuncio would walk away with the titles and glory that were rightfully Jimawn's own.

"Damn you Jimawn!"

"I'm sorry, your Excellency, I have urgent business that requires my immediate attention. I'm afraid I have to go. You understand?"

"Oh, I understand all right! I–"

The Nuncio's face disappeared back into the stick. What should he do with the pompous old bastard, once he'd won? He'd have to think about it. He knew full well what the Nuncio would do to him if he lost.

Moments later, Mary made the announcement he'd been waiting for: the assault on the Assembly had gone off without a hitch. Spontaneous applause broke out. Jimawn bowed his head in acknowledgement, and shared a private smile with Hartan.

For the next hour, the news remained entirely positive. Riots and uprisings targeting off-comer interests were breaking out across the city – and several were genuine, not staged. Some of the injured were Gallaskian, but that was only to be expected. The natives never had been able to distinguish between Commonwealth and Autarchy.

But not everything was going so smoothly. The teams tasked with snatching embassy dependents were meeting far more resistance than expected – both from bi-tech houses, and embassy troops. No families of senior embassy personnel had been secured, and the snatch squads were starting to suffer heavy casualties.

He gave orders to redeploy the teams. They'd do more good helping the cadre at the radio station. Better to consolidate a key success than waste resources on a failed strategy. And the station had been under more or less continual attack since they made their presence known.

The 3-V stayed on all afternoon, a colorful sphere taking up half his desk. He checked in with it frequently, and saw nothing but confusion and incoherence. Contradictory claims followed each other in an endless loop, loud voices claiming it was all a hoax followed immediately by breathless reports of miraculous escapes from rampaging mobs.

Then a new voice came on. Confident. Clear. Authoritative. And completely unexpected. It was Dil Mahtal, the gossip columnist. And he was asserting that the Assembly had not, after all, been captured. That a rebel attack had been beaten back, and the Assembly was meeting in emergency session.

And he was promising a live feed in the near future.

It was a bluff. It had to be.

"Mary! Get hold of Nathan. Find out the situation at the Assembly."

She nodded, and spoke into her microphone. And again, more insistently. Then she looked back, frowning. "The link's down, Hetman. We're trying to reconnect."

But the link didn't come back up. And an attempt to patch through a nearby team failed. Then the line went down altogether. Others followed. Green dots began to disappear from the map. So did red dots, dropping together in a sudden crimson shower. That could only mean wide-spread communication failure. Did that betoken real problems on the ground? Or just interruptions in the information flow.

Hartan was standing ramrod-stiff beside him. It was good to have one thing in this world he could completely rely on. "Liegeman, prepare my room. I think we'll be a long time at this, yet. I might need to take a brief nap, by and by."

"Of course, Hetman."

If Hartan was perturbed by the coded message, he gave no sign. His bow was as precisely measured as always, his departure unhurried. But he would be ready, should the worst happen.

Jimawn sat back and surveyed the room. Mary was shouting into her headset. Her immediate assistants were still receiving information and relaying orders – but elsewhere in the room, people sat in silence. There was nothing for them to do. The people they were supposed to control weren't speaking to them anymore.

"The radio, Hetman!"

Mary had taken off her headset. She wasn't looking at the screen or supervising her lieutenants. She was talking directly to him.

He turned it on. And heard a new voice, a Commonwealth voice, reporting that a small band of extremists and criminals had tried to seize control of the Assembly, but had been beaten back when the Assembly called on the Commonwealth for assistance. The emergency was past, but loyal Noyim were advised to stay in their homes for the time being.

He turned it off. The radio was bad, but the 3-V was far worse. It was projecting the final proof of disaster. Mahtal was reporting from inside the Assembly Hall itself, gleefully relaying the news that the Assembly had passed a

Motion of Incorporation. Noyan was now part of the Commonwealth.

It was failure, and worse than failure. He had sought to win Noyan for the Autarchy, and handed over it to the enemy instead.

Somewhere in his future, a firing squad was waiting.

The alarm sounded: a single short tone, constantly repeated. Not an intruder alert this time. The factory was under attack.

Mary was looking to him for guidance. Should he stay here and salvage his honor by dying in battle?

No. Honor lay in serving the Autarch. And his death today wouldn't serve the Autarch's interests. Not when he had in his gift secrets that would transform the balance of power between Gallask and the Commonwealth. His duty was clear.

He reached for his swordstick, surged out of his chair, and headed for the door at a run. Pandemonium broke out behind him. The corridor was much the same: it teemed with panicked technicians. He used his stick to clear a path, fighting against the flow of people until he reached his quarters.

Hartan's body was lying beside the bedroom door. Someone had been waiting for him inside.

No. Someone had been waiting for Jimawn. Hartan had merely been the one who opened the door.

Someone might still be waiting.

He drew his sword and crept forwards. Then he kicked open the door and dived through, ready to strike. But the bedroom was empty. The assassin had moved on, mission unfulfilled. Jimawn's liegeman had done him one final service, and died in his place.

There was no time to waste. He sheathed the sword, reached under the bed, and suppressed a shudder as the waiting bag reached out and took his hand. He pulled it from its hiding place. Inside this bag were bi-tech secrets that could redeem his honor. It no longer mattered if the

Nuncio claimed credit. This bag and its contents must reach the Mission.

He marched confidently towards the blank rear wall, speaking the code words. The wall melted away, revealing a smooth tunnel sloping gently upwards. He set off at a rapid pace, keen to put distance between himself and any potential assassin. Lights winked on ahead, and faded to darkness as he passed.

Something shifted underfoot. The tunnel shook. He stumbled, righted himself. And stumbled again. Earthquake? No: there it was – the sound of a distant explosion. And another. The lights went out. He was alone, in total darkness. But far from helpless. A quick command, and light poured from the head of his stick. He pressed on; slower now, but steady.

The smooth, straight tunnel gave way to rough stone and a winding natural cave. He began to relax. The final corner was just ahead; and around it, his escape vehicle, a fake bi-tech carapace concealing the Gallaskian roadster beneath.

He turned the corner, and stopped dead. Nathan was waiting for him, pistol in hand. A green light shone from the barrel, straight into Jimawn's eyes.

"Hands up, Moyem."

"But..."

"Just do it."

It was too much. One setback too many. He was floundering. Lost.

Nathan? A traitor?

Or... No. Not a traitor. An agent.

The man's whole manner was different. Professional. And the accent was wrong.

And then he knew what had been bothering him earlier, before Hartan distracted him. Poor Hartan. If he'd picked his moment better, he might still be alive.

"You should have said 'scrape'," he said.

"What?"

"You said 'fuck'." He dropped the bag and made as if to raise his hands. "That's not a native—"

It wasn't much of a distraction – a few words, the sound of the bag hitting the cave floor, the raising of his hands – but it was enough. In one smooth, liquid motion he drew his sword and separated Nathan's right hand from his body. Years of training and practice had their fulfilment in a single transcendent instant where hand and eye and will were one.

There was a heartbeat's pause; empty of motion, full of the sound of Nathan's screams. Jimawn remained poised, ready to strike again. Blood gushed from his enemy's wrist; a glorious sight.

There was a noise behind him. He turned.

"Mary," he said, astonished.

She too had a gun in her hand. Another green light shone directly in his eyes.

But only for a split second.

CHAPTER 47

Does it matter how long it takes a murder victim to die? If they live for an hour or a day, does that in any way lessen the crime? Of course not. What if they live for a week, a month, a year? No, the length of time is immaterial: it is the cause of death that matters, not how long it takes for the consequences to manifest themselves.

How is having children any different? Without birth, there is no death. With it, the victim may live for sixty, seventy, even a hundred years, but the eventual result is the same. In the end, death is certain.

– From A Moral Manifesto, *Isaac the Seer, Third Prophet of Nullism*

"How long will it take?"

"She should be waking up now, Excellency."

The voices were far away, faint echoes in her darkness. Who were they? Off-comers by the accents, but neither one was Bey.

"Good. Thank you, doctor. How much time do we have, Nicholas?"

"Ten minutes, Your Excellency. Are you sure you wouldn't rather...?"

"No. I told you. I want to do this personally."

"As you wish, Ambassador."

Beth opened her eyes. A face loomed over her, swaying in and out of focus.

"How're you feeling, Justice?"

An off-comer. Not Bey. Older. Self-satisfied. Familiar. The Commonwealth Ambassador. And he was smiling.

"Beth? Can you hear us?"

A new voice. Known. Disliked. Undersecretary Maitland, standing next to the Ambassador – and he, too, was smiling.

She wanted to spit, but didn't have the energy. Nor could she sit up; her body wouldn't cooperate. She subsided back onto... something too comfortable to be a proper bed. Off-comer tech? And the ceiling behind the ambassador was organic, repulsive. Where was she?

The Ambassador held up an avuncular hand. "No, please don't try to get up, dear lady. You're in no fit condition to move. You're lucky to be alive."

Was this the embassy? She tried to speak, but only a whisper came out. "I have to get to the Assembly."

The Ambassador shook his head. "I'm sorry, Justice, but you're not going anywhere for a while. You need to rest."

"You have no right to keep me here!" This time, the words were louder, fueled by anger. "I have information vital for national security. Any attempt to restrain me will be construed as an act of war."

"It's all right, Justice. It's over. You've been unconscious for two days. The coup failed."

"It failed?"

"Yes, it failed. Jimawn's dead. Just relax and concentrate on getting better. I came here to give you this... Cherayn, the award!"

A young man appeared at the ambassador's side, handed him a strange piece of jewelry; a multi-colored pearl, outsized and twisted into a fantastical shape. "This is a token of our appreciation, Justice. You'll be the first Noya to be recognized as a full citizen of the Commonwealth. There have been misunderstandings between us in the past, but we want everyone to see what two free peoples can achieve when they cooperate willingly for the common good. This award will symbolize a new dawn in relations between Noyan and the Commonwealth. You may be a Justice of the Family Court, but thanks to you, the Gallaskians have been defeated, and Noyan is forever safe within the bosom of the Commonwealth. Together, we... Yes, Justice?"

"Within the Commonwealth...?" She'd never felt so old or so useless.

"Of course, you won't know. The Assembly passed a Motion of Incorporation. Noyan's a Commonwealth Dependency now."

"A depen..."

"That's right. Now, you won't officially get this award until the ceremony, but I thought–"

"Go impregnate yourself!"

The Ambassador blinked, shocked into silence. Maitland stepped smoothly into the void. "I'm sorry, Your Excellency. I'm afraid Justice Beth doesn't like us very much."

"So it seems." All the warmth was gone from the Ambassador's voice. That, at least, was something to be grateful for. "But it doesn't really matter what she likes, does it? I'll leave you to explain the facts of life to her, shall I?"

"By all means, Your Excellency."

The Ambassador moved out of her line of sight. Maitland watched him go, then sat down on the bed. Sadly, still not within spitting distance.

"I'm sorry, Justice. I would have spared you that, if I could."

"Why?"

It was strange to be pitied by someone she detested.

"I'm not one to triumph over a defeated enemy. You've lost. I see no reason to make this any harder for you than it needs to be. It was my duty to oppose you, as I'm sure you felt it was yours to oppose us. I bear you no ill-will. You're true to your principles, however misguided. I respect that, even if I disagree with you. Even if it makes you dangerous. But enough of the past. How are you feeling?"

"Pregnant."

"I'm not surprised. You were lucky to survive." He turned to the young man, still hovering attentively nearby. "Mino, the pain killer."

The lackey nodded, and placed something insectile against her wrist. She flinched, feeling it crawl to a vein. And then relaxed, as a pleasant warmth spread through her arm.

Maitland stood up. "Well, goodbye Justice. No hard feelings, eh? Come on, Mino. Time to go."

Beth's eyes were starting to close. She tried to speak, but only a whisper emerged. "B...B.... Bey?"

"Hotep? Don't worry about him, Justice. He's going to be a hero. He fits the bill. Very useful, a Massowic hero. Isn't that right, Mino?"

"Absolutely, Undersecretary."

"And he thoroughly deserves it, too. After all, we didn't know a thing about the coup until he warned us, did we?"

"Not a thing, Undersecretary."

"No indeed. How incredibly lucky for us that our assets just happened to be in the right places at the right time. Anyone would think someone planned it that way."

"Oh, surely not, Undersecretary..."

"Goodbye, Justice Beth. Sleep tight. You can rest assured that your young friend will get all the credit he deserves, and then some. He's very useful that way. Just like dear old Ambassador Ashef. Goodnight, Justice. And goodbye."

They were still chuckling as they left the room. It was the last thing she was aware of before she slipped back into unconsciousness.

CHAPTER 48

It is my hope that I have afforded my readers a different perspective on the Noyim. They are not the story-book monsters of popular imagination. Many are honorable people of high (if misguided) principle. I can honestly say I am proud to have played a small part in bringing Noyan into the Commonwealth. For me, it is a matter of everlasting regret that my closest native friends did not live to see that day.

– From: My Time on Noyan, Memories of a Youthful Exile, *The Rt. Hon. Beynan Hotep na Massowic*

The cremation was a dignified affair. The Marshtop settlers had refused a State Funeral: such things were off-comer intrusions, alien to Noyan tradition. Nor were any media welcome. It was a private Marshtop ceremony, with only a few outsiders permitted, and just one 'off-comer'. Bey felt the honor keenly, even in the midst of his sorrow.

Ruth lit the pyre. Beth's mother had chosen not to do so. She was nearby, leaning on Miriam's shoulder and weeping silently. He turned back to the fire, eyes pricking.

The flames were small at first, hesitant. They guttered and seemed to go out, and then came flickering back into life. Then, suddenly, they were everywhere, roaring out from the deep interior where they fed on oil-soaked wood. Great gouts of flame poured out and lapped around the white-shrouded body. Smoke rose, grey and black, high into the air, carried on tall pillars of fire.

Ruth retreated, walking past him without acknowledgment or the least sign of recognition. He tried not to take it personally. Her expression was blank, distant. She probably didn't even know he was there.

He turned his gaze back to the fire. Somewhere within that mass of flame, Beth's remains were being consumed. He'd expected to be horrified by the desecration of the body. But now that it came to it, the practice hardly seemed barbaric at all. Except for the smell: there was no disguising the stench of burning flesh, not even with scented wood.

The crowd leaked away in ones and twos until finally only a handful of observers remained. Even Beth's mother had gone, helped away by a small circle of friends. That was some relief. He'd dreaded having to talk to her. It was always worst for those left behind.

Miriam was still there. Waiting for him. Trying to catch his eye. He headed over to where Ruth stood gazing stolidly at the pyre. She didn't look up.

"I'm sorry, Ruth. They did everything they could. She just wasn't strong enough."

He waited for a reply, but none came. The silence stretched awkwardly, punctuated by the crackling of the flames.

"Is there anything I can do? Do you need a place to live while they're rebuilding your house? You can have my house. It's empty now."

And finally, she looked up. But not with gratitude. "Your house? Never. Beth was right. We should have rejected everything about you, including bi-tech. Go away, off-comer. You're not wanted here."

"It's not my fault, Ruth. Your Assembly voted for the Motion of Incorporation. You can't blame me."

"Can't I?"

The words were still uncompromising, but at least her

tone was less hostile. It wasn't exactly reconciliation, but it was something.

"What'll you do now?"

"Fight on. What else is there to do? We still have the Assembly. And the Family Court. For now. We've lost, but that doesn't mean we can't keep on fighting. Just like Beth would have."

"You didn't lose, Ruth. You had a choice, the Autarchy or the Commonwealth. You picked the right one. And at least you'll have decent medicine, proper modern technology now. People will live longer, healthier, more comfortable lives. You wouldn't have got any of that with the Autarchy. Jimawn couldn't have cared less about the Noyim. You'd have been just another—"

"Enough, Hotep. We're done." She stalked off to the far side of the pyre. He didn't follow. He'd tried his best, but there came a point where you just had to accept defeat.

And Miriam was still waiting. He couldn't put it off any longer.

"Hello, Bey."

"Hello, Miriam."

"It's been a long week."

"Yes. Yes, I suppose it has."

Had it really only been a week? So much had changed in such a short time.

"How are you, Bey? Really?"

"I'm all right. I was lucky. A few bruises, a black eye. Not like…. I did my best to save her, Miriam. I really did. She wouldn't have made it off that roof without me. I did everything I could. It just wasn't enough."

"I know you did, Bey. I'm proud of you. We all are."

"That's good to know. It means a lot to me… Only… Um, I don't know how to say this, but…"

"You're leaving."

"Yes. You knew?"

"Ruth told me. It was on the 3-V. The ambassador gave you some kind of award?"

"The Order of Merit. Yes. They wanted to give it to Beth, too. Posthumously. But her mother refused."

"Do you think Beth would have accepted it?"

"Not in a million years."

He smiled in fond memory. She smiled back. "I'll come with you, if you want."

His cheeks reddened. Taking to Ruth had been difficult; this was so much worse.

"I wish you could, Miriam. I really do. But it just wouldn't work. You wouldn't be happy away from Marshtop. And my family…"

"Your family?"

"Yes… my family." Was she really this naïve? Or was she deliberately making this awkward? "It's a Commonwealth thing. My family wouldn't approve. And families really matter to us."

"And they don't to us?"

"No. I didn't mean that. It's just… They matter differently. I'm not a free agent, Miriam. I have to do what the head of my family says."

Within reason. But she didn't need to know that. Besides, Grandfather Massowic definitely saw it that way.

"So, don't leave. Stay here. With me."

Miriam's tone was less inviting than her words. She'd finally understood. That was good. Uncomfortable, but good.

"I'm sorry, Miriam. I can't. And look, I'm sorry, but the autocopter's waiting…"

"You'd better go, then."

"Yes. I wish things were different, but…"

He let the words trail off. She was already on her way back to the village. He watched her go, wishing he could call to her, tell her to come with him. But it was no good. He had to let her go. He could hardly bring her home to Grandfather. She'd never do as the mother of his children.

Besides, he had other choices now. He was young, handsome and a hero. He'd been given a second chance.

He'd be mad to throw it away for the sake of a native girl.

The autocopter was barely a five-minute walk away, discreetly tucked away behind a small stand of trees. It was there for one purpose only: to wait for him. A week ago, he'd been a fugitive running for his life. Now, nothing was too good for him. Only last night he'd been seated at Ashef's right hand at dinner. Everywhere he went, he was the darling of the hour: the man who'd brought about Jimawn's defeat. And he could hardly remember a thing about it. No wonder he kept having to pinch himself to be sure he wasn't dreaming.

Undersecretary Maitland – the same man who'd brutalized him in an embassy cell – was waiting for him in the autocopter. He waved Bey to a seat, gave the order to depart, and asked how he was feeling.

"Okay, I guess. It's strange. I never thought I'd end up caring so much about a Justice of the Family Court..."

"No, indeed. But then, she was an admirable person in many ways. We owe her a great debt. Without her, Jimawn's coup would have succeeded. It was a shame she had to die."

They were already in the air. Below them, the delta was spread out like a map: a branching green highway between the desert and the sea. Would he miss the desert, when he was back in the green lushness of Homeworld? Maybe. He'd certainly never forget it.

They chatted inconsequentially, passing the time during the short flight; Maitland doing his diplomatic best to show a polite interest, wanting to know how long it had been since Bey was last on Homeworld, and what he was looking forward to most – and hoping that Bey didn't harbor any hard feelings...

"You mean about the time you...?"

"I mean just that."

"No. No hard feelings. Not about you, anyway. I've plenty of hard feelings about the people who tried to kill me."

"Yes. I can't say I blame you."

"What'll happen to them?"

"That depends. It's up to the Commission. Some of them will be disciplined, of course..."

"Disciplined? For attempted murder? For treason?"

"It's not as simple as that, Beynan."

"It's totally fucking simple. You should have seen what they did to Ruth's house. The bastards tried to kill me!"

"I know it looks that way. But really, it was more of a mistake than a conspiracy."

"Of course it was a fucking conspiracy. Jodan said—"

"Yes, yes. And Regulator Hyrom was a good man – heroic, even. But don't you think he was... shall we say, a little obsessional?"

"Well..."

"Don't get me wrong: we need people like him. Without Hyrom, none of us would have known about the breach in the embargo until it was too late. But that doesn't mean he was right about everything. There was no cover up. Just miscommunication. No one took Hyrom seriously. Everyone thought he was delusional. He had quite a reputation with his colleagues, you know. He was so very... intense."

"He was right!"

"Yes, he was. And we won't forget it. He'll get a posthumous award in the next round, and there'll be a pension for his family. We owe Hyrom a great deal. The Autarchy came very close to gaining a major strategic advantage. If they'd managed to get their hands on bi-tech of that level..."

"Can you be sure they didn't? Jimawn could have shipped any number of buds off-planet, before he was caught."

"He could. But he didn't. Imperial subjects don't cooperate like free citizens of the Commonwealth, Bey. They compete. Not for wealth, or not *just* for wealth – for status. Jimawn was risking everything to earn a title. He couldn't afford to let anyone else have access. He had to keep his prize here, under his personal control, for fear of one of his rivals taking the credit for himself."

"But you can't be certain he—"

"Yes, I can. We have access to... information... from within the Gallaskian Mission."

"Spies, you mean."

"I didn't say that."

"No. I did."

Poor Jodan. He'd been so certain Hozefa was rotten. But the likes of Maitland would hardly protect a traitor. On the other hand... "The embargo's not just about the Gallaskians, though, is it? Jodan was worried about Noyan, too. That it'd go the way of Nephrate."

"And he was right to worry. But that won't happen now. Not with Noyan part of the Commonwealth. The mistake we made with Nephrate was sharing too much technology with them when they were still independent. It's different here. We're in control. And I'm afraid the Office of Regulation can be overly conservative on these matters. The reality is we can safely modernize far more rapidly than they'll ever admit."

"I suppose."

It wasn't worth arguing over. Nephrate was Jo's obsession, not his. And the autocopter was about to land. It wouldn't be long now, and he'd be on his way home.

They were still some distance from the city. Native regulations prevented the ship's boat from landing in populated areas. No doubt that would change, now that Ashef was Governor General. But not yet. One thing at a time.

"You know, Nicholas..." It was nice to be in a position to call Maitland by his first name. "There's one thing I still don't get. None of this would have happened if Sanja hadn't been murdered, and we still don't know who did it."

"Isn't it obvious? Jimawn. Or someone working for him."

"No. I don't think so. He said not, and I believed him. He had no reason to lie. He didn't think we were going to live long enough to tell anyone."

Maitland shrugged. "Interesting – but a lot of violent people worked for him. Maybe one of them overstepped their orders? Or Sanja caught them doing something Jimawn wouldn't have liked, and they killed him to keep him quiet."

"I suppose… But if it hadn't happened… If someone hadn't killed Sanja. Or if Beth hadn't insisted on investigating… Jimawn would have won, wouldn't he?"

"It's possible."

"No, it's more than possible. Jimawn would have won. And Noyan would have joined the Autarchy, not the Commonwealth. It's amazing how things worked out. It couldn't have gone better if we'd planned it. We were so bloody lucky."

"Indeed. And now, I think we're safely down, so…" Maitland picked up Bey's bag and escorted him to the door. It was only a small bag. There wasn't much he wanted to take with him, except memories. And many of those were best left behind.

The ship's boat was only a short walk away. Its glistening amber bulk towered over them. Bey turned and took the bag. The two of them shook hands.

"Goodbye, Nicholas."

"Goodbye, Beynan. The Governor General sends his regards to your grandfather, when you see him."

"Of course."

He walked down the steps, and turned for a final goodbye – but the door was already closed, the autocopter leaping into the air. He watched it dwindle to a small green speck, and then climbed the ramp into the ship's boat.

The main cabin was virtually empty. Its single occupant, a young woman, was standing by the viewport, her back to him. If her face was anything like her figure… Time to see what this hero business was good for.

"Hello. I'm..."

He stopped, nonplussed. The woman's entire face was disfigured by a mesh of branching green lines. She was in the middle of a muto-virus transformation, and it was every bit as disconcerting as people said. Why was she putting herself through something so extreme? There was no sign of injury beneath the bizarre coloration. But then, there shouldn't be by now; not if the virus was already this advanced. There was no knowing what she looked like before. Except that he couldn't help feeling that...

"I'm sorry. Have we met?"

She looked him up and down. Slowly.

"I don't think so."

He blushed. He hadn't meant to sound so crass. This whole encounter was turning into one big embarrassment. And he wasn't really interested anymore. Not with her looking like that. But he had to salvage some kind of dignity from this encounter. They were going to be shipmates. The journey would be a lot more comfortable if she thought of him as a hero, not an oaf.

"No, really, I'm sure we must have. My name's Beynan Hotep. Perhaps I can get you a drink?"

"No, thank you. I already have one."

He stared at her empty hands. "Really? Where?"

"Here."

Bey turned. A man was heading towards them, his face masked by an identical tracery of viral green. He was holding two drinks in his left hand. His right was...

"Fuck! What happened to your hand?"

Bey flushed deep, mortified red. What was he? Five? It was one thing to think it, another to say it out loud. But really... The man's hand was solid green from wrist to fingertips, and half the size it should be. A regrow, and a fresh one, too. "I'm so sorry. I didn't mean to..."

"This?" The man held up the baby-sized hand. "It was nothing. The coup..."

The coup. Of course. And that explained why these

two needed muto-virus. They must have been injured in the fighting. No wonder the woman wasn't interested in him; she already had a hero all of her own. He took a step backwards, keen to extricate himself.

"The coup. Right. I'm so sorry. I was just startled. I didn't mean to cause offence."

"None taken. It's a bit of a shock, when you first see it."

Bey stopped retreating. This was getting ridiculous. That voice. He knew that voice...

"Look. I'm sorry, but either I'm having a really bad attack of déjà vu, or I've met both of you before..."

The woman shook her head. "I don't thi–"

"Of course, you have. I'm Naja Habada, and this is my assistant, Mirri. We met at Sanja Gwahnal's eighteenth birthday party. I'm amazed you remember us at all. There must have been hundreds of people there."

"Right. Yes. Of course. That explains it. The only thing I remember about that night is just how horribly drunk I was."

"Wasn't everyone?"

"Probably. Poor Sanja. I miss him, you know. I don't care if his parents were traitors. He was only a kid. He didn't deserve to die like that."

"No. Nobody does. Such a waste. He was a very intelligent young man. Far brighter than his parents."

"I suppose so. You knew him well?"

"I wouldn't say that. I only met him a few times. We had... business dealings."

"Anything legal?"

Habada laughed obligingly, and handed his assistant her drink. "Oh, absolutely. Everything strictly in line with embassy requirements. And Sanja was always very serious about business, wasn't he, Mirri?"

"Absolutely. Very challenging to deal with."

"Yes. Observant, too. Never forgot a face. And very hard to pin down."

The woman coughed. Her drink had gone down the wrong way. Either that, or she and Habada were enjoying a private joke at his expense. Yes, there was definitely something off about the man's expression; hard as it was to read anything behind that vivid green mesh.

"Really? Well, maybe I'll see you around." He stalked off to the back of the cabin, and stayed there for the rest of the brief journey into space.

There was a welcome banquet waiting for him in the starship's viewing room; the finest Homeworld wines, and better food than he'd tasted since Grandfather kicked him out. He was delighted, not least by the fact that his fellow new arrivals were virtually ignored. Obviously Habada was a much lower grade of hero than himself. Confidence restored, he relaxed and wallowed in the attention while the ship's single enormous wing slowly unfurled outside.

He returned there daily as long as they were in system, watching Noyan shrink until it became just another white dot, indistinguishable from the stars that shone unblinking all around. And he made sure to be there at the exact moment when the Mothership reached its transfer point, folded its giant wing, and twisted out of alignment with the universe.

The event itself was the usual non-experience. Nothing happened, nothing changed. Except the stars. One moment he was waiting impatiently, the next he was half a galaxy away. The wing unfurled once more, tacking against the light of a different star and bringing him safely home again.

The change in the deeps brought a new sense of perspective. He'd suffered a great deal on Noyan. He'd endured pain and terror and loss; but now it was over, and he could look back and see that somewhere along the line he'd finally grown up. It was time for him to put his wild youth behind him. He would accept his responsibilities as a Massowic, settle down, marry, have children – maybe even go into politics. There should be plenty of opportunities in that line for an ex-hero. He could barely wait to get home.

Grandfather was going to be pleased.

AFTERWORD:

This book has been a long time in the making. When I began it, I was the same age as Bey, and working as a youth worker in London's East End; now I'm the same age as Beth, a computer consultant, and I live in Massachusetts. I have rewritten New Dawn Fades many times over the years, and set it aside for as long as a decade before picking it up again to try to make it what I always wanted it to be.

If you enjoyed it, please write a review on Amazon. It really is the best/only way for Indie writers to gain any traction. To all those who have reviewed my earlier books, and to those who will (hopefully) do so for this one: THANK YOU!

A lot has changed since I began this book. Lab-grown meat, pure speculation when I began, is now a reality. Even the language itself has changed. The word 'choice' has narrowed, and carries a far more political edge than it once did. The 'Choosing' ceremony was the 'Choice' ceremony until almost the final draft – a wording I still far prefer, as I can think of no better way of expressing one of the central tenets of the Noyan world view – that moral obligation can only ever derive from choices we make. Sadly, I felt I had no choice (ha!) but to change it, for fear that some readers would interpret this book as a commentary on abortion, which it most decidedly is not (though the Noyim, give their moral framework, must of course be against it, except where no choice [that word again...] is involved in conception).

There are various individuals to whom I owe a debt of thanks: Tom Taylor, for a conversation long ago about why trees don't have windows – a conversation that led to bi-tech; Jim and Marina, for a Bolton Science Fiction Group meeting in the Old Three Crowns, which led to a combination of their names (together with some poetic license) giving me Moyem Jimawn; Gary Taylor, for reading a (much) earlier draft of this novel, and whose interest in reading it again pushed me into finishing it – I have, therefore, dedicated the book to him; and Graeme Hurry for beta-reading once again (and for suggesting the Glossary). I must also thank Keith Marsland, who read and commented on early drafts of the novel when we were both much, much younger than we are today.

And last, but by no means least, I owe the most thanks of all to my wife and editor Elise McMahon, for years of patiently listening to me talking about this story, and for helping me to make it a better book.

GLOSSARY:

Assembly, The:
a. The governing body of Noyan, with elected representatives from across the planet.
b. Local institutions with full, direct participatory democracy and a universal franchise.

Autarchy of Gallask, The:
The Autarchy are the Commonwealth's main rivals. They are an openly imperial power, ruled by an Autarch and espousing self-sufficiency. They are less technologically advanced than the Commonwealth, and less powerful. The Autarchy has an interest in absorbing Noyan – if only to prevent it from joining the Commonwealth.

Auxiliary Court, The:
Subsidiary to, but separate from, the Family Court, the Auxiliary Court is responsible for policing criminal law – that is statutory laws created by the Assembly. They have no direct responsibility for murder, which is a breach of Custom and comes under the Family Court. They provide auxiliary manpower/resources to the Family Court as needed.

Bi-tech:
The advanced biological technology used by the Commonwealth.

Casab:
A native tree cultivated for its fruit.

Casabey:
A local liqueur derived from the fruit of the casab tree. It tastes rather like honeysuckle smells.

Choice of Life, The:
See the Choosing Ceremony

Choice of Death, The:
See the Choosing Ceremony

Choosing Ceremony, The:
A Noyan coming of age ceremony that takes place at age 20. Advocates speak on behalf on the Choice of Life and the Choice of Death. In the vast majority of cases, the event is a celebration of the bond between parent and child. If, however, the child chooses death, the parents must choose between assisted suicide, or sterilization and becoming an outcast.

Commonwealth, The:
A technologically sophisticated power with colonial ambitions, the Commonwealth comprises many worlds, and is growing rapidly. Notionally democratic, it is in fact an oligarchy with power centralized in a few old families on Homeworld, where the Commonwealth originated. It uses biological technology, but restricts what it makes available on less advanced planets for fear of damaging their economies/societies, and as a means of maintaining control.

Custom:
The immutable laws of Noyan – above mere civil or criminal law, because Custom cannot be changed by the Assembly. Custom is what gives the Assembly and the Family Court their authority, and is intimately linked to the Choosing ceremony.

Embargo, The:
A varying set of restrictions of the level of bi-tech that can be sold on a technologically backwards world.

Family Court, The:
The premiere institution on Noyan. The Family Court administers the Choosing ceremony. For historical reasons (deriving from parents killing their children in order to avoid the Choice of Death), they are also responsible for investigating murder and other crimes that are breaches of Custom, and not mere statutory law.

Homeworld:
The primary world in the Commonwealth, and center of political power. Homeworlders are a privileged caste within the Commonwealth, especially those from the powerful families who comprise what is effectively an oligarchy under a more democratic veneer.

League of Free Noyim, The:
A militant traditionalist group that is the real reason for New Beginning's existence. Every settler is a member of the League, though some are more active than others. The League engages in sabotage, primarily against bi-tech targets, and has many supporters outside New Beginning.

Militia, The:
The Family Court can call on Noyan citizens to serve temporarily in the militia – a kind of informal extension of the Auxiliary Court – when additional manpower or specialized knowledge is required. The militia has no structure or organization, and there are limits to the length of time any individual can be called upon to serve.

Movement for Tradition and Continuity, The:
Supposedly a non-violent traditionalist group run out of New Beginning. In reality, a fake organization used by the League of Free Noyim for propaganda purposes, and as cover for their illegal activities.

Nephrate:
The first world to which the Commonwealth introduced bi-tech. The result was social and economic devastation for a society that was not ready for such a sudden, radical change. The example of Nephrate is the primary driver behind the embargo on selling advanced bi-tech on technologically backwards worlds.

New Beginning:
A traditionalist settlement and home of the League of Free Noyim.

Noyan:
An independent world with limited technology and a singular culture revolving around the Choosing Ceremony. Noyan has only one major city – the capital, Spate. Most of the population lives in settlements. Noyan has a distinct culture deriving from its origins as a Nullist colony, and the institutions it holds in highest regard – the Choosing ceremony, and the Family Court that administers it – are widely despised by outsiders.

Nullism:
A radically anti-natalist philosophy/religion. The founders of Noyan were Nullists. The Noyim are heavily influenced by Nullist philosophy, but descend from apostates who chose to have children, and created the Choosing ceremony to resolve the contradiction between their Nullist moral outlook and the desire to have children.

Off-comers:
A widely used (and often pejorative) Noyan term for non-natives (i.e. people who have *come* from *off*-world). Applies to both Commonwealth and Gallaskian citizens.

Office of Regulation, The:
The Office of Regulation polices the embargo on
sophisticated bi-tech, and has extensive extra-territorial
jurisdiction. Each local planetary office is headed by a
commissioner, and run by regulators, assisted by various
ranks of bi-technician.

Spate:
The primary (and only) city on Noyan, and seat of its
government. Named after the river Spate that flows
through the city.

Traditionalists:
Also known (pejoratively) as 'trads'. Noyim who are
resistant to outside influence, and fiercely defensive of
traditional Noyan culture, especially the Choosing
ceremony and the Family Court. A broad movement that
ranges from opposition to bi-tech to hatred of all
'off-comers'. Most traditionalists operate though the
political sphere, but some engage in terrorism, especially
acts of sabotage against off-comer interests.

ABOUT THE AUTHOR

Kevin Rattan has worked as a computer consultant and trainer, a script writer, a youth worker in London's East End, and had so many different jobs in television production (cameraman, extra, autocue operator, script reader, subtitler...) that he can't even remember all of them.